Jilted by a Cad

Book 1 of the Jilted Brides Trilogy

CHERYL HOLT

Praise for *New York Times* Bestselling Author
CHERYL HOLT

"Best storyteller of the year . . ."
Romantic Times Magazine

"A master writer . . ."
Fallen Angel Reviews

"The Queen of Erotic Romance . . ."
Book Cover Reviews

"Cheryl Holt is magnificent . . ."
Reader to Reader Reviews

"From cover to cover, I was spellbound. Truly outstanding . . ."
Romance Junkies

"A classic love story with hot, fiery passion dripping from every page. There's nothing better than curling up with a great book and this one totally qualifies."
Fresh Fiction

"This is a masterpiece of storytelling. A sensual delight scattered with rose petals that are divinely arousing. Oh my, yes indeedy!"
Reader to Reader Reviews

Praise for Cheryl Holt's "Lord Trent" trilogy

"A true guilty pleasure!"
Novels Alive TV

"LOVE'S PROMISE can't take the number one spot as my favorite by Ms. Holt—that belongs to her book NICHOLAS—but it's currently running a close second."
Manic Readers

"The book was brilliant . . . can't wait for Book #2."
Harlie's Book Reviews

"I guarantee you won't want to put this one down. Holt's fast-paced dialogue, paired with the emotional turmoil, will keep you turning the pages all the way to the end."
Susana's Parlour

". . . A great love story populated with many flawed characters. Highly recommend it."
Bookworm 2 Bookworm Reviews

BOOKS BY CHERYL HOLT

ISBN: 978-1-64370-969-7 (Print version)

Cover Design Angela Waters
Interior format, Dayna Linton, Day Agency

Jilted by a Cad

PROLOGUE

"WHAT TIME IS IT now?"

Josephine Bates, simply called Jo by her acquaintances, whispered the question to her half-sister and lone sibling, Maud.

"Almost one-thirty," Maud whispered in reply. "Something must have happened to delay him."

"He'll be here any second," Jo loyally insisted.

"Yes, I'm certain he will be," Maud halfheartedly agreed.

They shifted uncomfortably, jumping as the vicar cleared his throat. They were seated in the front pew at the church, so he was able to glare down at them with stunning effect. He checked his timepiece, and he wasn't discreet about it. Then he cast an exasperated scowl at his wife. She tiptoed over to Jo and leaned down so they could speak quietly.

"Miss Bates," she said, "my husband has another wedding to perform. The bride and groom are waiting."

Jo and Maud didn't have to peek over their shoulders to realize that fact.

The church door kept opening, and they would whip around to see who had entered, being positive Jo's fiancé, Mr. Cartwright, would march in. He'd be laughing and full of apologies as to why he'd been late for the most important appointment of his life.

But it had never been Mr. Cartwright. Couples were lined up to wed after Jo, and they were accompanied by their friends and families. Jo was the only person with no entourage. Her only guest and witness was to be Maud. Mr. Cartwright wasn't bringing anyone either.

The members of the nuptial party behind them were occupying several rows and impatient for Jo to get out of the way so they could start their own joyous event. Their glowers cut into her back.

When Mr. Cartwright had scheduled the ceremony, the vicar had firmly explained that it would be *wedding* day at the small chapel. Every half hour, he would officiate with a new bride and groom. He offered a quick service for those who didn't have a pile of money to waste on frivolities or who couldn't abide the enormous fuss and bother of a big celebration.

Jo was definitely part of that group. She craved a fast conclusion where she could shuck off the past and become a bride. She was eighteen, and with her pretty looks, sunny demeanor, and acceptable dowry, it was an opportunity she'd always expected to occur. Yet she hadn't expected it to occur quite so soon.

Mr. Cartwright had burst into their world like a comet streaking across the sky. With very little effort, he'd swept Jo off her feet. Her head was still spinning over how swiftly it had all coalesced.

She was about to have her own home, was about to escape Maud's snits and rages. It was so thrilling to be marrying, to have found a spirited, amiable husband like Mr. Cartwright. She couldn't believe she'd been so lucky.

"I'm sorry to have been an impediment," Jo said to the vicar's wife. "Please tell your husband to proceed with the next ceremony. My betrothed, Mr. Cartwright, should be here shortly. If your husband is amenable, perhaps he can squeeze us in afterward."

"Yes, that will work." The vicar's wife frowned at Maud, then at Jo. "Should we send someone to check on Mr. Cartwright? He's over an hour late."

Jo would have declared that he'd appear at any moment, but before she could defend him, Maud butted in. "Maybe we should send someone, Jo. I'm worried he might have suffered an accident."

At the prospect, Jo's pulse raced. "He hasn't had an accident, Maud. Don't jinx us. There has to be a perfectly good reason for his failure to arrive."

The vicar's wife didn't seem to think so. "I can have my son, Tim, ask after him. We'll all be relieved to receive some answers."

Jo wanted to remain steadfast, wanted to argue that Mr. Cartwright hardly needed to supply any answers, but Maud silenced her with a dour grimace.

He rented a room at a men's boarding house. Maud provided the address to Tim. He nodded and rushed off.

Maud and Jo moved to the rear pew so the newcomers could have the front. They sat through the ceremony, then the next one, and the next one too. Jo's spirits had flagged to their lowest ebb. People passing in and out cast curious glances at her, having heard her groom hadn't shown up.

She slunk down, wishing she were invisible. Who treated a bride as Mr. Cartwright was treating her? Who treated any woman—bride or not—so shabbily?

Yes, Mr. Cartwright was always late. He joked about it, and initially, she'd been irked by his sloppy manners. But then, after she'd learned how jolly and carefree he could be, she'd set aside her aggravation. He wasn't like other men, and she was glad he wasn't.

She'd grown up at her father's estate in the country. Her mother had perished when she was a baby, and Jo's father had been a detached parent who'd mostly stayed in London. She'd been raised by servants, with Maud as her sole companion. Maud was five years older than Jo, and she was stoic, petty, and vain. She barked and criticized, so having her as a companion was like having no one at all.

Jo had lived a modest, simple existence, and she hadn't had any experience with wooing or romance. The chief male to whom she could compare Mr. Cartwright was her deceased father. He'd been grouchy and unhappy, so Mr. Cartwright was a breath of fresh air who'd brought excitement into her dreary world.

He didn't *love* her. They hadn't known each other long enough for strong feelings to develop, but he certainly possessed a tender regard. He wouldn't leave her in the lurch. Still though, it had been two hours.

The weight of the day pressed down on her, and it was incredibly difficult to maintain her calm façade.

"I have to step outside," she mumbled to Maud, and she hurried away without pausing to discover if Maud followed.

She walked out, and she tarried, studying the busy street. They were in London, at a chapel to which she and Maud had no connection. She'd have liked to be married at her local church, but she'd let Mr. Cartwright convince her that London was better.

He'd been anxious to proceed immediately with a Special License, then he planned to whisk her away to Manchester so he could introduce Jo to his sister. It was easiest to depart from London. She'd agreed to his every suggestion, and why wouldn't she have?

She was thoroughly smitten, and he was such a delightful fellow. Even Maud liked him—when she didn't like anyone. But now, with Jo standing by herself—her hair curled and braided and her bouquet wilting—she was beginning to panic.

What did she really know about Mr. Cartwright? She'd had no parent to make inquiries or furnish advice. There was only Maud, and Maud—her guardian—was as eager to be shed of Jo as Jo was to flee their tedious home. When Mr. Cartwright had proposed, Maud hadn't hesitated to consent.

The church door opened, and Maud sidled out.

"Has he jilted me, Maud?" she asked.

"I refuse to speculate."

"If he doesn't come, I'll die. I'll just die!"

"Nobody's dying." Maud's tone was very stern.

"Where is he then?"

"It's his habit to be tardy."

"It's been over two hours!"

Jo burst into tears. She couldn't help it. The stress of the prior few weeks had finally caught up with her. With Mr. Cartwright's speedy courtship and his insistence on a quick wedding, she'd barely had time to pack her belongings and say her goodbyes.

One minute, she'd been a young lady living with her spinster sister in the house Maud had inherited from her grandmother. Then the next, she'd been engaged and racing toward her new life as a bride. It was too much to take in.

Maud pulled out a kerchief and stuffed it in Jo's palm.

"Don't cry," Maud scolded. "You always look horrid when you do. What if he strolled up this very second and your face was all red and mottled?"

Jo chuckled miserably. "Dear Maud, you never cease to put me in my place."

"Someone has to. Otherwise, you'd be quite out of control."

"Yes, that's me—a wild, unrestrained girl."

A hysterical laugh bubbled up, and she swallowed it down. There was no more boring, reserved person in the kingdom than Josephine Bates. To consider herself as ever being *out of control* was hilarious.

Down the block, the vicar's son, Tim, was returning, and they stiffened. He was alone, Mr. Cartwright not with him. Maud actually clasped Jo's hand and squeezed her fingers.

"Miss Bates?" Tim said as he ran up. "I checked on Mr. Cartwright for you."

"Yes. What have you learned?"

His cheeks flushed as if he was embarrassed. "I'm sorry, Miss Bates, but Mr. Cartwright left town this morning. At dawn."

Jo cocked her head as if he'd spoken in a foreign language she didn't understand. "Left . . . for where?"

"Apparently, he was off to Scotland for some hunting."

Maud sucked in a sharp breath, and Jo weaved side to side, scarcely able to keep her balance. She couldn't have heard correctly.

"You're sure?" Jo asked.

"Very sure." Tim withdrew a letter from his coat and offered it to Jo. "The proprietor of the boarding house made me give you this."

Jo gaped at it as if it were a venomous snake. She was afraid to reach for it, but ultimately, she grabbed it and read it slowly as Maud tried to peek over her shoulder.

"What does he say?" Maud asked.

"It's a bill for Mr. Cartwright's lodging," Jo murmured. "He didn't pay what he owes, and the proprietor is demanding we pay for him."

"You're joking!"

"No."

Maud yanked the letter away and scanned to the bottom to the amount that had accrued. "Well, I never!" she huffed. "What gall! What insolence! How dare he?"

Jo couldn't decide if Maud was referring to Mr. Cartwright or the proprietor.

There was an awkward silence, then Jo said to Tim, "By any chance, was there a message for me from Mr. Cartwright?"

"No, Miss Bates. He simply packed his bag and departed. He...ah...claimed he'd had enough of London and the people here."

"I see..."

"I told the proprietor about your wedding."

"And...?" Maud asked when Jo couldn't.

"Mr. Cartwright never mentioned any wedding," Tim responded, "and the proprietor had no idea he was betrothed. He'd been...ah...keeping company with an actress the entire time he was staying at the man's house."

"What?" Maud gasped.

"I thought you should know," Tim muttered.

Jo's knees gave out, and she collapsed down onto the step.

Behind her, Maud was whispering to Tim. She slipped him a coin, telling him to talk to his mother, to apprise the vicar that Jo's name could be scratched from his schedule. But Jo couldn't focus on them.

She could only ponder handsome, cheerful Mr. Cartwright who was supposed to rescue her, who was supposed to provide the contented future she'd dreamed of having.

"What now?" she wailed to the gray sky.

It had been cool and cloudy all day, and it was starting to sprinkle. The drops plopped on the sidewalk, on her shoulders and bonnet too. The rain was cold and uncomfortable, but she didn't feel it. She didn't feel anything at all.

Two years later . . .

5 June, 1815

From: Mr. Richard Slater
Estate Agent to the Earl of Benton
Benton Manor
To: Miss Maud Bates

Miss Bates,

As I'm sure you remember, a decade ago, you were intimately acquainted with his lordship, Neville Prescott, Earl of Benton. You ultimately presented him with a daughter, Daisy Prescott. These past nine years, she has resided at the Benton estate where she has been generously supported and educated by the Prescott family.

Due to changing circumstances, it will no longer be possible for the Earl to support or house your daughter. New arrangements must be made for her care and upkeep, and I'm afraid the burden must now fall on your shoulders. I ask that you contact me at your earliest convenience so we may discuss the appropriate situation for her. I'm certain you understand that time is of the essence. You must have made preparations for her removal from Benton by 15 July at the very latest.

I await your reply.

Most sincerely,

Richard Slater,
for the Earl of Benton

CHAPTER

1

Jo walked down the pretty lane, enjoying the summer day. The sky was so blue, the woods so green. It was a perfect morning to have snuck away from home, to be out on her own. She was glad she'd seized the chance to have an adventure.

She spent too much time on her own and—with Maud's wedding approaching—her sister was in London, shopping for her trousseau, so the house was even quieter than usual.

Jo was bored and lonely, so her current task had arisen just when she needed it the most. It gave her an excuse to fritter away several hours that otherwise would have been wasted by watching the minutes tick by on the clock.

Maud had received the strangest letter from the Earl of Benton's estate agent, a Mr. Richard Slater. Since Maud was busy in town, Jo opened all the mail, even the correspondence addressed to Maud. Mr. Slater's message had made no sense, and she'd had to read it over and over before the import became clear.

He seemed to believe—when Maud had been a decade younger—she'd engaged in salacious conduct with the Earl that had resulted in the birth of a child named Daisy. The notion was so preposterous that Jo chuckled whenever she considered it.

Maud was the fussiest, grumpiest, vainest female in the kingdom. She would never have succumbed to passion.

She and Jo had the same father, but different mothers. Their father, Harold, had been a gentleman, and Maud's mother—his first wife—had been a baron's daughter. Jo's mother had been their father's second wife. She'd been the fetching, sweet nanny hired to tend Maud after her own mother had died.

Because of it, Maud viewed herself as being grand, interesting, and very much above Jo in class and station. She lorded herself over Jo, constantly referring to the disparity in their antecedents and reminding Jo of their separate places in the world.

After his horrid marriage to Maud's mother, their widowed father hadn't been able to resist Jo's mother. His fixation had been disturbing and scandalous, and it still shocked the conscience of many of their neighbors.

Maud definitely never forgot about it, and Jo should have been offended by Maud's condescension, but she was twenty now, and she was used to Maud's irksome ways.

Her sister would never change, and Jo thought Maud was quite ridiculous. When—precisely—would straitlaced, finicky Maud have found the opportunity to participate in a wicked fling with Lord Benton? How and where would she have perpetrated it?

Maud was twenty-five, five years older than Jo, and they had always lived at Bates Manor, the lovely mansion on the large estate that had belonged to the Bates family for generations. Then, after their father had perished and they'd had to sell to pay his debts, they'd moved to the small house outside Telford that Maud had inherited from her grandmother.

There was nothing odd about their childhood or adolescence. They'd been raised as typical British girls by their very typical British father. Maud was pious, prim, and moralistic, and Jo was positive Mr. Slater had contacted the wrong Maud Bates by mistake. Yet there was that year when Maud had been sixteen, and she'd gone abroad to France on a school trip.

With Mr. Slater's troubling missive to Maud, Jo couldn't deny being curious about that trip. Maud hadn't written Jo a single letter while she was away, and when she'd returned, she hadn't brought any souvenirs. Jo had barely been eleven, and she'd been hideously disappointed.

Should Jo be questioning that entire event? Could it be? Could Maud have birthed a bastard child fathered by Lord Benton when she was sixteen?

No! It simply wasn't possible . . .

As far as Jo was aware, they'd never met the Earl of Benton and weren't acquainted with the Prescott family. And Maud wasn't an attractive female. She was blond and blue-eyed, but chubby and fleshy, and there was a hardness in her expression that made her appear cruel. It put people on edge.

If an earl had been bent on seduction, Maud was the very last woman such an exalted nobleman would have selected.

Jo intended to speak with Mr. Slater, apprise him of his error, and urge him to locate the correct Maud Bates so the poor girl, Daisy, could have a beneficial conclusion. Then she'd hurry back to Benton village and take the public coach to Telford. It was only ten miles, and the summer sun was setting very late. She'd be home in plenty of time to have a quiet supper with just the servants for company.

Finally, she arrived at the gate to the estate, and a man was approaching from the other direction. He was older than she was, probably thirty or so. He waved a greeting, and she waved too.

She dawdled as he neared, but she should have kept on. After all, she was on a deserted stretch of road. Since she'd left Benton village, she hadn't stumbled on another soul. But he seemed friendly, and she perceived no menace.

He was incredibly handsome—tall, broad in the shoulder, thin at the waist—with black hair and striking blue eyes. He had a firm stride and erect bearing that had her wondering if he'd ever been a soldier. He looked the sort who would be proficient at barking orders and having them obeyed.

While she wasn't concerned for her safety, she caught herself bracing nonetheless. Ever since the pathetic afternoon when Holden Cartwright had jilted her at the altar, she'd been wary of handsome men.

Mr. Cartwright had proved she had no aptitude for judging a person's character. She was as naïve as the flightiest debutante and effortlessly swayed by outlandish comments that couldn't be true.

She'd gotten past that terrible episode, had forgiven herself for her stupidity. She'd forgiven Maud too, even though it had been difficult to absolve her sister. Maud was Jo's guardian, and a few days before the wedding, she'd signed over Jo's dowry to Mr. Cartwright. He'd absconded with it and had vanished without a trace.

They'd been gullible fools who'd seen no reason to be suspicious, so they'd been easy prey for such a dodgy fiend. Who could have imagined such duplicitous cads existed? Not Jo and Maud, that was for certain.

Jo had accepted her fate as a penniless spinster, that she'd have to live with her unlikable sister forever. The situation would be even more untenable when Maud married her betrothed, Thompson Townsend, in September.

Jo couldn't abide Mr. Townsend. He teased Jo and whispered risqué remarks—as if he and Jo shared a secret. Her circumstances had always been trying, but with Mr. Townsend about to move in, they would become quite horrid. But with her dowry squandered, there would be no escape.

She'd adjusted her thinking and lowered her expectations, but she *hadn't* shed her distrust of handsome men—and she never would.

"Are you headed to the manor?" the man asked.

"How did you know?"

"It could be that I'm possessed of uncanny mental abilities or it might also be that you're standing under the *Benton* sign."

She laughed. "You're very clever."

"It's what everyone says about me." He gestured up the lane. "May I walk with you? Allow me to brighten your stroll."

"Yes, of course. I'm sure you'll brighten it."

"People say that about me too."

"What? That you brighten strolls?"

"Strolls and other . . . things."

There was a profusion of innuendo in the boast that she didn't like. "Are you flirting with me?"

He grinned. "Maybe."

"We haven't even been introduced which makes you appear very fast."

"Or very friendly."

She scoffed. "I'll stick with *very fast*."

"May I hope *friendly* will soon follow?"

"It depends on whether you mind your manners."

"I shall be the epitome of decorum."

"I'll be the judge of that." Her prim tone was evidence that she spent entirely too much time around her sister.

Like a trained gallant, he offered his arm. She hesitated, then took it.

What could it hurt? It was hardly a crime to walk with a manly man on a sunny day. It wouldn't kill her. Anymore though, she was just so accursedly cautious.

Gradually, she realized she was enjoying herself. Since her debacle with Mr. Cartwright, she rarely socialized. In Telford, it wasn't as if there had been a line of swains waiting to grab his spot. Because of her mother—who was viewed as a voracious hussy who'd snagged the king of the castle for her own—Jo was suspected of inheriting the same base tendencies.

Men kept their distance—except for Mr. Cartwright who'd been from London and hadn't been apprised of her dubious antecedents.

She'd forgotten how pleasant a gentleman's company could be. Though it sounded odd, there was a peculiar charge in the air, as if the universe had engineered the encounter and approved of their meeting.

"Are you employed at the estate?" she asked.

He paused forever before answering. "Yes, you could say I'm employed there."

"It was awfully difficult for you to admit it."

"I was debating my response. I'm not positive what I do should be called *work*."

"Your comment has ignited my curiosity. What is your position?"

"You wouldn't believe me if I told you."

"I might."

"I doubt it."

He gazed down at her, his expression warm and full of mischief. For a quick instant, they seemed frozen in place, as if they were locked together in an arresting way. She didn't care for the sensation at all, and she yanked away and focused on the lane where the manor was visible through the trees.

"Why are *you* at Benton?" he asked. "Will you tell me straight out or shall I guess?"

"I'd force you to guess, but I'm afraid I'd be alarmed by your replies. I peg you as the type who likes to make a girl blush."

"You'd *peg* correctly, but I'll guess your purpose anyway."

"I wish you wouldn't."

His keen attention was unnerving. He was acting as if he found her pretty and fascinating, and no one had ever stared at her like that but for her dastardly ex-fiancé.

She knew she was very pretty. She had two eyes in her head and could see herself in a mirror. Her mother had been a great beauty, and Jo resembled her exactly: auburn hair, big blue eyes, rosy cheeks, pert nose.

Standing just five-feet-five inches in her shoes, she was thin but curvaceous, and her shapely figure caused men to steal second glances when she passed by. Yet she didn't want a man to think she was fetching. She didn't want him to behave in a flirtatious fashion. She was too much of a dunce to assess male regard with a clear lens.

He was studying her outfit, and his appreciation was so blatant that she had to tamp down a spurt of vanity.

She never had any money, but Maud did, and she spent it on clothes. When she tired of an item, she let Jo have her castoffs. Over the years, Jo had become adept at tailoring. She could take anything Maud gave her and turn it into a delightful piece. She had a knack for style and color, and she liked simple designs, but the simplicity left her looking extremely glamorous.

"You must be here to have tea with Lady Benton," he said.

She sputtered with amusement. "Do I appear to be the sort of female who would pop in to have tea with a countess?"

"Yes, you absolutely do."

"My goodness. You're practically spouting poetry."

"I guarantee it's very unusual for me, but you have that effect."

"I'm flattered."

"The lavender fabric of your gown matches your eyes perfectly. Is it from Paris?"

"No."

"You're sure?"

"Yes, I'm very sure." She scowled. "If I was here to see the Countess, wouldn't I have ridden up in a grand coach-and-four with outriders hanging from every corner?"

"Perhaps you like to flout convention."

"I can categorically state, sir, that I have never once flouted a convention."

"How dreary your life must be."

"It can be terribly dreary," she facetiously said, "but I try to muddle through."

"You poor thing."

"You still haven't told me your position at Benton."

"Nor have you told me the purpose for your visit."

"I'm not certain of my purpose."

"Ah . . . a woman of mystery."

"Yes, *mystery* is my middle name."

She wasn't about to confide her intent. She had to speak with the estate agent, Mr. Slater, had to inform him that he'd contacted the wrong Maud Bates, but she would inquire about the girl, Daisy, too.

Mr. Slater had warned that the Earl was ending his financial support. What would happen to her? Would she be sent away? To what future?

"Are you acquainted with the Earl of Benton?" she asked him.

"Oh, yes, I know him exceedingly well."

"What's he like?"

"He's quite an ogre."

She missed her step, and he leapt to steady her.

"How is he an ogre?"

"He's bossy and dictatorial, and he thinks he's very special. He never listens, and he demands to have his own way at all costs."

"Wouldn't that describe all aristocrats?"

"He's worse than most of them."

"You don't seem to like him very much."

"Sometimes, I like him just fine, but more often than not, I can't abide him."

"So the two of you are close?"

"We are."

"Would you say he can be cruel?"

"When cruelty is required? Yes—much as I hate to admit it."

He was grinning, his eyes alight with mischief again, and she scoffed with aggravation.

"You probably don't even know Lord Benton. You're probably the gardener—or not even that. You've likely never even been inside the manor."

"I'll never confess the truth."

She couldn't decide what to believe. He was definitely full of himself, but he wasn't a common laborer. His speech and mannerisms proved him to be from the upper classes. His clothes gave him away too. He was wearing casual attire—blue jacket, tan trousers, black boots—but they were sewn from expensive fabric, and they fit him like a glove. He had the money for a skilled tailor.

"What is your connection to the Prescotts?" he asked.

"Is that the Earl's family?"

"Yes."

"I've only heard of one of them. Neville Prescott? Isn't he the Earl?"

After another lengthy hesitation, he said, "Yes, that's him."

"As I have entrusted the remainder of my stroll to you, might I have the honor of knowing *your* name?"

"How about if you call me Peyton?"

She was startled by the request. "Is that your Christian name?"

"Yes."

"That's dreadfully bold of you, and I can't imagine why we should be on familiar terms. You must have an ulterior motive. What is it?"

"Considering the kind of life I live, I don't have many reasons to stand on form."

"The kind of *life* you live? What does that mean? Do you travel with a pack of wolves? Are you a performer in the circus? What?"

"No, I simply can't predict what might transpire from one day to the next."

"Why are you in such constant peril?"

"I'm a sailor—in the Royal Navy."

"I suspected you were in the military—or that you had been in the past."

He raised a brow. "I can't determine if your keen appraisal should make me happy or wary. I like to assume I'm an enigma. Am I actually very transparent?"

"Yes, but then, it wasn't hard to deduce your vocation. You have the demeanor of a fellow who likes to shout commands and have them obeyed."

"You are a shrewd judge of character."

Not really . . . "Are you home on furlough?"

"Yes, and now that you're aware of my dangerous profession, you understand why I refuse to miss out on a friendship. I asked that you call me Peyton, and I'm afraid I have to insist."

"That's quite a mouthful."

"I don't like to beat around the bush, especially when I meet a pretty girl."

The compliment was like a warning bell, and her pulse fluttered with alarm.

"It's occurred to me," she said, "that you are very brash."

"Yes, I am incredibly brash."

"So you'd be much too forward for me. It's not in the cards for us to be friends."

"You can't be sure of that." He switched subjects. "What is your name?"

"It's Miss Bates to you."

"Won't you give me more information than that?"

"No."

He smirked and crushed a fist over his heart. "You wound me, Miss Bates."

"I couldn't possibly have."

"What is your Christian name?"

Why not tell him? What could it hurt? "If you must know—"

"I must."

"It's Josephine. Josephine Bates."

He studied her so meticulously that she might have fidgeted if she was the type of female to fidget.

"You're so small and slight," he said. "I feel compelled to point out that *Josephine* is too much name for you."

"It's the only one I have."

"If it were up to me, I'd shorten it and call you Jo. Jo would suit you much better."

"I won't fan the flames of your vanity and state that everyone calls me Jo."

"Then on the day when I'm allowed more liberties, I shall call you Jo too."

"I doubt that day will ever arrive, so you will have a very long wait."

"Oh, I wouldn't count on it." He sounded cocky and confident. "Who can guess what might happen in the future?"

"Who indeed?"

They walked out of the trees, and they halted for a moment so she could absorb the breathtaking vista. The property was glorious, and her initial thought was that the Prescotts were much richer and grander than she'd realized.

The manor looked like a modern castle. It was several stories high, constructed from a russet brick. There were hundreds of windows, spires, and turrets on the corners. An impressive driveway meandered to the imposing front doors. It was surrounded by park land, with acres of manicured gardens and a placid lake behind.

Sheep grazed in a meadow, and horses frolicked in a pasture. It was bucolic, like a painting that depicted rural England on a perfect summer afternoon.

"Well, isn't that just lovely," she murmured.

He wrinkled up his nose. "It's a bit ostentatious for my tastes."

"Don't be churlish. It's lovely. Admit it."

"I suppose *some* people might think it's lovely"—he flashed a dour glare at Jo—"but the rooms are cold in winter, and the chimneys don't draw smoke as they should. It takes too many servants to run it, and it drains money like a sieve."

She tsked with irritation. "I'm convinced you've never even been inside."

He chuckled. "I'll never tell."

"You're such a dreary complainer. Does any topic make you happy?"

"I'm always happy when I'm chatting with a pretty girl. Other than that, no, there's not much that makes me happy."

"Stop flirting. I don't like it."

"You don't like flirting?"

"No, and stop complaining. I don't like that either."

"Your wish is my command, my lady." He gave a mocking bow.

"It is not. I'm positive you've never obeyed a woman in your life."

"Probably not."

He winked at her. He winked! And she yanked away and started toward the manor. He accompanied her to the front doors.

"It was delightful to meet you, Miss Bates," he told her.

"I'd say the same, but I haven't decided if it was delightful or not."

"You're charmed by me. Don't deny it."

"I'm *something* all right, but it's not charmed."

"You never did tell me why you've come."

"No, I didn't."

"You're not here to have tea with the Countess."

"No, I'm not. I don't know her."

He leaned nearer and whispered, "You're fortunate you don't."

"Honestly! You are horrid."

"I can be."

"Go away." She shooed him off with her hand. "I have an appointment, and since I have no idea who you are, I don't want the butler to peek out and find you with me. If you're a notorious character, I'd be so embarrassed."

"I am notorious."

"I'm certain you are."

He grinned wickedly. "Who is your appointment with?"

"That's none of your business, and it's excessively impertinent of you to inquire."

"Seriously, Miss Bates. Who is it with? I'll give you my opinion of the person."

"There's no reason to seek your opinion. I wouldn't believe you, and I like to make my own assessments."

"You wound me again, Miss Bates."

"I pray none of the blows have been fatal."

"What if they have been? After we part, I may languish and waste away."

"I'll offer up a prayer for you at church."

Their banter dwindled, and they tarried, the quiet settling. As she studied him more closely, he looked tired and weary, as if he was carrying heavy burdens, and she suffered a spurt of guilt. Perhaps she should have been kinder, but then, he was a rogue who needed to be kept in his place.

"Good luck with your appointment," he said. "I hope it goes well."

"So do I."

"Will you visit us in the future? Should I expect you? It would elevate my mood if I thought you might return."

"No, I don't think I'll ever be back."

"What a pity," he mused. "Will you call me Peyton? Just once?"

"No. Why would I?"

"I'm simply eager to discover if I can coerce you into it."

He was precisely the sort who could coerce a female in numerous ways that didn't bear considering. She was lonely and much too isolated, and she was already wishing she could see him again. Would she never learn?

"Goodbye," she said.

"Goodbye. Thank you for enlivening my day."

"Have I enlivened it?" she asked.

"Definitely."

He spun and sauntered away, and she watched him until he vanished around the side of the house. She wondered if he would use the servant's entrance, but he hadn't seemed like a servant. She couldn't figure out what he *seemed* like, and it dawned on her that she felt a bit sad at his departure. The afternoon was no longer quite so vivid or fun.

She'd assumed he'd glance back at her before he disappeared from view, but he didn't, and she shook her head at her foolishness. Then she went to the door and banged the knocker.

CHAPTER

2

"Are you sure?"

"Yes, Miss Bates, I'm very sure. I can't explain it more clearly."

Jo stared at Mr. Slater. They were in his office at the rear of the manor. He was seated at his desk, and she was sitting in the chair across.

He was thirty or so, with blond hair and pleasing features, but he had severe blue eyes that made him appear very angry. He didn't seem the type who smiled very often.

"I'm not trying to be difficult," she said, "and I'm not usually so slow to grasp a concept. I'm just so shocked."

"I understand."

"We had no idea."

"Well, that's not precisely true."

"What do you mean?" Jo asked.

"Your sister, Maud, certainly knew, and your father arranged for Daisy to be brought here. It was hardly a family secret."

"My father arranged it?"

"Yes, he personally delivered Daisy to Benton after she was born. It was either that or put her in an orphanage, and neither he nor the Earl wanted that. Those places are dreadful, and she likely wouldn't have survived for long."

Jo couldn't believe it. She'd always thought her father had been fond of her, that he'd liked her much more than he'd liked Maud. Maud's fussy quirks had irked and humored them in equal measure.

Now Jo was questioning her memory of their relationship. She felt as if Maud and her father had been on one side of a fence and Jo had been on the other side, without her ever realizing she'd been excluded from their tight circle. With Maud's disgrace exposed, what else might have been concealed?

Maud had had an affair with the Earl of Benton when she was sixteen. There had been no school trip *abroad*. She'd gone to a facility for unwed mothers to hide her condition. Then she'd returned home and had carried on as if it had never happened. She'd given her baby to the Prescotts and had never looked back.

Who could be so callous? Who could be so coldhearted?

Yes, the world was rigid and inflexible, and women were condemned for the smallest lapse of conduct. A female couldn't birth a baby with no husband to slip a ring on her finger. There were laws against it. There were community standards. There were church rules.

Jo's father had been a respected gentleman, so it was ludicrous to suppose Maud could have publically pranced about with Daisy as if no scandal had transpired.

But still . . .

A spurt of fury raced through Jo. Maud constantly acted as if she were Jo's strict, unbending mother. Jo couldn't count the times she'd been lectured for the least little infraction, when in fact, she'd been a perfect child, a perfect daughter, a perfect sister. It was galling to learn that Maud had such an illicit incident in her past, but Jo calmed her temper.

Outrage was pointless, and she had to focus on her current predicament. How should she proceed?

"When I wrote your sister," Mr. Slater said, "it never occurred to me that someone else would open the letter."

"She's not home at the moment. She's in London shopping for her wedding trousseau."

"Oh, dear. What a tangle that will pose!"

"You're a master of understatement, Mr. Slater." She laughed miserably. "I've been answering her correspondence, and I came to Benton to inform you that you must have contacted the wrong Maud Bates."

"There's no doubt it's her. We send her annual reports. We always have."

"Really?"

"Yes. I can't guess if she reads them or not, but we've continued according to the agreement we reached with your father."

Jo studied the floor, her mind awhirl with concerns and problems. The wisdom of Solomon was required to solve this riddle. She was only twenty, and she didn't view herself as being overly clever. She didn't want this burden thrust on her shoulders, but who was available to deal with it?

There was just her, Jo, having to devise a good ending for her niece, Daisy. Her immediate opinion was that she'd like to take Daisy with her to Telford, but their house didn't belong to Jo. Maud had inherited it from her grandmother. As Maud relentlessly mentioned, Jo lived there because Maud let her live there.

If Jo had had any other option, she'd have left. It had been the main reason she'd latched on to Mr. Cartwright so fast. He'd offered her an escape. She was in no position to order Maud to behave appropriately toward Daisy. Nor could she traipse in the front door with Daisy, not without garnering Maud's permission first. It simply wasn't possible.

"You've demanded that Maud remove Daisy in the next month," Jo said.

"Yes, by July fifteenth."

"May I ask why?"

"Circumstances have changed at Benton."

"I'd like to bring Daisy home with me, but I'm worried about my sister's reaction—especially with her about to marry."

"When is the wedding?"

"September."

"I don't imagine she'd have confessed this fiasco to her betrothed."

"I'm sure not," Jo said. "I need some time to ponder this. I have to talk to my sister about it."

"You certainly can, but you have a month to get it resolved."

"What if I can't persuade her?"

"We'll probably place Daisy in a convent. We'll tender a donation on her behalf, so she can remain there until she comes of age. It would be better than an orphanage."

A convent? An orphanage?

Jo rippled with alarm.

"I'm confused, Mr. Slater. Why can't Daisy stay on? She's been at Benton for most of a decade. Is she a troublemaker? Is she cruel or petty? What's produced this new attitude with regard to her?"

"She's a sweet girl, Miss Bates. People like her very much."

"Then . . . why?"

He scowled at her, his gaze irked and condemning—as if the current difficulty was all her fault.

"May I be frank, Miss Bates?"

"I hope you will be."

"Daisy's presence has been a great humiliation to the Earl's wife."

"Oh. I hadn't thought about her."

"I was positive you hadn't." Ire flashed in Mr. Slater's eyes, but he tamped it down. "Lord Benton has two of his other children here as well."

"Other . . . ah . . . illicit children?"

Jo couldn't figure out the correct terminology, and she stumbled over the words. She hated to be rude or judgmental, but the conversation had abruptly descended into the most risqué in which she'd ever participated.

"Yes, *other* of his illicit children," Mr. Slater said. "The Countess has been shamed each and every minute that they have tarried at the estate."

"Of course she has been," Jo murmured.

"She's suffered terribly, and it's time for all of them to go."

Jo blew out a heavy breath. "May I meet Daisy? Would that be allowed?"

"She's not home today. She's had a growth spurt, so she and her governess are in London, buying her some clothes." He must have expected Jo to argue about it, for he hurriedly added, "She can have all of it when she leaves. We're not misers; we won't send her off looking like a pauper."

"That's kind of you."

"She'll be back tomorrow afternoon if you'd like to stop by then. I'll get you properly introduced."

"It's a bit of a journey, but I'll try to return."

"If you could take her with you tomorrow, that would be wonderful. We could have her packed and ready."

"I won't have arranged a spot for her by then," she wanly replied. She felt awash with dismay. "I'll . . . ah . . . have to travel to London to speak with my sister. I'll have to discuss this with her."

"Just so you work out a solution by July fifteenth."

"I will."

He stood, indicating the appointment was over. "Thank you for coming."

"Thank you for having me."

"I wish it had been for a happier reason."

"Believe me, so do I. Might I see Lord Benton before I depart? If I conferred with him, would you suppose—"

Mr. Slater cut her off. "I'm handling the situation for him. He doesn't care to be bothered over it. He's done more than enough over the years."

"He definitely has," Jo retorted as she realized the remark would sound impertinent.

"Anyway, he's not here today either."

"All right. Thank you again."

Jo went to the door and stepped into the hall. The footman who had escorted her to Mr. Slater's office was waiting to guide her out. He gestured for her to follow him, and she trudged along, barely noticing the grandiose surroundings as they meandered down gilded halls to the foyer.

As they arrived, a second footman delivered her shawl and bonnet. She was putting them on when she heard him whisper that *the Earl* was back and in his library. The news caused both men to raise their brows and share an indiscreet glance she shouldn't have witnessed.

She'd never been an assertive person, but she would love to talk to Lord Benton. She would thank him for his lengthy support of Daisy, but she was also annoyingly curious about him. She was dying to catch a glimpse of the cad who had seduced Maud.

"You mentioned that the Earl is back," she said.

"Yes, Miss Bates, he is."

"So I haven't missed him after all. Mr. Slater told me I could have had an audience, but he was away from the house. Might I speak with him? If he agrees, it will save me from having to make another trip to Benton. It's quite a distance for me."

The two men shrugged at each other, then her escort said, "I'll check as to whether he can fit you in."

"Marvelous. I'm very grateful."

He was only gone a minute, and he was smiling. "He's free, Miss Bates. If you'll come with me?"

He marched off, and she rushed after him, but she couldn't help nervously peeking over her shoulder, being panicked that Mr. Slater might show up to challenge her. But luck was with her, and he didn't appear.

The footman entered the library and announced, "Miss Bates, my lord."

Jo entered too, finding herself in a dramatic, imposing room. Three of the walls were lined with bookshelves and stuffed with books that rose all the way to the ceiling. The fourth wall was all windows that looked out at the park. There was a large desk in front of the windows and a man in the chair behind it.

To her stunned surprise, it was the cheeky fellow, Peyton, who'd walked her to the manor. Before she could stop herself, she blurted out, "You're Neville Prescott? You deceitful rat! You told me your name was Peyton!"

"It is Peyton. Peyton Prescott, and I'm delighted you asked to see me. You've brightened up what was otherwise a very dreary afternoon."

"I'm sure you spew a similar comment to every young lady you encounter."

"Are you a drinker, Miss Bates?" was his reply. "I'm betting you're not."

"Of course I'm not," she churlishly scoffed.

He waved to the footman. "Bring us some tea."

The footman left, and Peyton/Neville motioned for her to approach. She nearly spun and huffed out in a snit. With his unsavory past revealed by Mr. Slater, it was no wonder he used a fake name. It was probably a subterfuge he regularly employed.

In the end though, she didn't stomp out. Her curiosity hadn't been assuaged, and she went over and sat in the chair across.

"You look just as fetching as you did when we were outside," he said.

"Don't flirt, Lord Benton. I've already warned you that I don't like it."

"You seem put out with me. Why? We're barely acquainted, and I could swear we had a pleasant chat out on the lane."

"Why would you lie about your identity? It's not funny."

"I'm not Neville, Miss Bates. Neville was my brother, and he's deceased."

"Really?" she snidely asked.

He snorted out a laugh. "Yes, really. I think I would know if my brother is dead or not."

She inhaled a deep breath and regrouped. "I'm sorry. I finished my appointment, and it was . . . difficult. I'm in a terrible mood, and I'm taking it out on you."

"Yes, you are, but you're forgiven."

"Thank you."

"Will you tell me who you met with? I hope no one was awful to you. I wouldn't want to hear that you were mistreated during your visit."

"I wasn't mistreated. It was merely a distasteful discussion, and I'm still reeling from it."

"If that's the case, I insist you tell me about it."

"It was your estate agent. Mr. Slater?"

"Ah . . . dear Richard." He was amused by the notion. "He's my brother-in-law. His sister, Barbara, was married to my brother. He can be pompous and pretentious. Was he rude to you? If so, I'll speak to him."

"He wasn't rude. He simply imparted depressing information."

"Why was it depressing?"

She studied him, trying to determine if he was aware of the disaster.

Mr. Slater had claimed to be in charge of the situation, that the *Earl* had directed him to deal with it. To which earl was he referring? How long had Neville Prescott been deceased? How long had Peyton Prescott been earl?

If Neville had ordered Daisy to be evicted, then Peyton Prescott might not necessarily realize a tempest was brewing. But if Peyton Prescott had ordered Daisy to be sent away, then Jo didn't like him at all.

Yet she couldn't insult or enrage him. She'd like to win his assistance—or at least his commiseration and sympathy. Perhaps even his advice. He was older than she was, and he might have wise counsel to offer.

"It has to do with Daisy," she said.

"Who is Daisy?"

"She's my niece, and I guess—technically—she's your niece too."

"No, I have two nieces, Alice and Nancy."

So . . . maybe he doesn't realize.

"How are you at learning awkward news, my lord Benton?"

"I'm very good at it, and I still wish you'd call me Peyton. I've only been Lord Benton for a few months, and while I have very broad shoulders, it's an odd and heavy yoke to bear."

"I wouldn't feel comfortable calling you Peyton—especially now that I've discovered your true identity. I'll stick with Lord Benton, if you don't mind."

"I mind very much. How about if we settle on Commander Prescott?"

"Is that your rank in the navy?"

"Yes."

He'd befuddled her. She couldn't decide what was appropriate, and she skipped over the debate about it and pressed ahead. "You don't appear to know that you have a niece named Daisy."

"I told you my nieces are Alice and Nancy."

"They're your brother Neville's daughters?"

"Yes, with Barbara."

"Apparently, your brother had . . . ah . . . some other children as well."

"What do you mean by *other* children?" He scowled, then comprehension donned, and his cheeks flushed. "Oh! *Other* children."

"Am I the first to apprise you?"

"Yes. I hadn't heard a whiff about it."

"Neither had I, and I'm overwhelmed."

"Were you notified of how many *others* there might be?"

"No. I believe Mr. Slater said *several*."

"Several! My goodness. It sounds as if he and I are due for a blunt conversation."

Jo, herself, yearned to avoid the current one. She had no desire to confer about Neville Prescott's amorous proclivities.

"Could we...ah...focus on Daisy for now?" she asked.

"Certainly."

"I don't possess any details about the others, and I'm not too keen to delve into their problems. I have enough of my own with Daisy."

"I understand."

The footman knocked and brought in their tea, so Jo was provided a respite as the tray was laid out and the cups arranged. Lord Benton shooed the footman out, then shocked her by offering to pour before she had a chance to offer herself.

Once he finished and handed her her cup, he sat behind the desk again. He placed his own cup on the desktop and shoved it to the side, giving every indication that he'd rather have had a stronger libation but was too polite to drink liquor in front of her.

"What about Daisy?" he asked.

"She's living here at the estate."

"Here? Honestly, Miss Bates, you are simply full of surprises."

"She's nine, and your family has supported her all these years, but that support is ending, and Mr. Slater is demanding my family take charge of her."

"Has he explained why?"

"It's been a humiliation for your sister-in-law, having your brother's other children around and underfoot."

"I can imagine. She's in a perpetual snit."

Jo remembered his cryptic comment out on the lane where he'd insisted the Countess wasn't very likeable.

"Mr. Slater has announced a deadline of July fifteenth for Daisy's removal. It's why I was eager to speak with you."

He grinned a wicked grin she felt clear down to her toes.

"I figured it was because you couldn't bear to depart without seeing me one more time."

"Out on the lane, I had no idea who you were. When I begged for an audience with the *Earl*, I was expecting to talk to your brother. My being in your library had naught to do with you."

"Drat it! I was hoping I'd enticed you beyond your limit."

She rolled her eyes with exasperation. "Would you please stop blathering about how marvelous you are so we can get back to the topic at hand?"

"What was it again?"

"Our mutual niece, Daisy. I guess she's Daisy Prescott. I don't know if your brother gave her his name or not."

"I suppose I ought to find out."

"Yes, and would you allow me a request?"

"I can't guarantee I'll grant it, but you're welcome to raise it."

"I'd like to have Daisy come home with me, but there are significant issues that might prevent that conclusion."

"What issues?"

"Could I simply not say? Could you take my word for it that it's complicated?"

"No," he curtly responded. "What are the issues? Let's lay them out on the table so I have all the facts."

"I've only learned what Mr. Slater shared with me a few minutes ago."

"And that was . . . ?"

"My sister, Maud, was seduced by your brother when she was sixteen."

He looked genuinely stricken. "I'm very sorry."

"She birthed Daisy at an unwed mother's home, then Daisy was brought to Benton by my father. She's always lived here, and your brother supported her."

"You're slaying me with your revelations, Miss Bates."

"You claimed you wanted to hear about my issues."

"Maybe I don't really. Maybe they're so hideous they'll be the death of me."

She chuckled. "I doubt that."

He stood and went to the sideboard, and he returned with an empty tea cup and a bottle of what was probably brandy. He filled his cup and gulped the liquor in one swallow, then he plopped down in his seat.

"All right," he said, "I'm sufficiently fortified. Go on."

"Maud is older than I am."

He frowned. "How old are you? You can't be more than nine or ten."

"I'm twenty, and she is twenty-five. While my father appears to have known about Daisy, *I* never knew."

"If your sister was sixteen when it happened, then you were what? Eleven?"

"Yes, and I never had an inkling about any of it. Maud has been in London for weeks, and while she's away, I've been opening all the mail. Mr. Slater wrote about Daisy, and I assumed he must have contacted the wrong Maud Bates. It's why I came today. I intended to apprise Mr. Slater that he was mistaken."

"But he wasn't?"

"No." She sighed, feeling yet again that it was all too much, and there could be no benefit to her getting involved. "I have to talk to my sister, Lord Benton. She's in London."

He studied her, and his gaze grew sympathetic. "It will be difficult for you."

"Very difficult. We don't have the best relationship, and she's about to marry."

"Oh, no."

"Oh, yes, and I'm sure she'd never have confided the situation to her betrothed. He's rather a pompous fellow."

"You're in an appalling bind."

"Yes. I'm excited to discover that I have a niece. Maud and I have a very small family, with no other siblings or even any cousins worth mentioning."

He snorted with amusement. "In light of my own hoard of kin, I wouldn't deem that a bad thing."

"Yes, but I don't have the funds to support Daisy. I live with my sister, and actually she's my half-sister. She owns our home, and she has an income—where I do not. I can't bring Daisy there unless Maud agrees, and if she doesn't—and I'm positive she won't—I couldn't move elsewhere and rear Daisy by myself."

"I see."

"So I was wondering—if I can't arrange for her by the fifteenth—could she remain here for a bit while I continue to work on it?" He didn't answer, and she added, "I will fuss with it constantly, Lord Benton, until I arrive at a resolution. I swear it."

"I don't question your drive or veracity, Miss Bates, but I need to speak with Mr. Slater about this. I can't make promises and throw out guarantees until I'm certain of the road I'm traveling."

He poured himself another glass of liquor, and he drank it down. Then he stood, indicating their appointment was over. She stood too, and she hated that it was time to leave. Her crossing paths with him had been an exotic experience, and she didn't suppose she'd have an opportunity to be with him in the future.

"Have you met Daisy?" he asked.

"No."

"Shall we locate her? We'll track down her whereabouts, and we'll introduce ourselves."

"I'd love to, but Mr. Slater advises me that she's in London for the day. She's outgrown her clothes, and her governess is buying her new."

"You've astonished me again, Miss Bates, with your recitation of facts of which I'm blindly unaware. As you've bluntly cited, I have other nieces—and perhaps nephews too. I employ a governess, and I'm paying for children's clothes. I'm so glad you trekked to Benton. If you hadn't, I might never have been exposed to half of what occurs in this accursed place."

"I'm sure that's not true."

"Trust me, if ever there was an outsider in this world, it's me. I'm as much of a stranger here as you are. I don't have a single friend in residence, and I definitely claim no allies. Evidently, I don't even have a servant who will give me candid information."

It was a shocking speech that he shouldn't have voiced in her presence, but she was delighted that he had. It made her feel closer to him. It made her feel that he liked her and valued her opinion.

"Daisy and her governess won't be back until tomorrow afternoon," she said, "and I can't afford to tarry until then."

"You should stay at the manor. It's just until tomorrow, and this oversized mansion has dozens of bedchambers. I have no doubt we can find a bed for you to sleep in."

"I didn't bring a bag. I presumed I would have a quick conference with Mr. Slater, then depart. I didn't plan for an extended visit, and I would never be so rude as to impose."

"It wouldn't be an *extended* visit. It would be for the one night—so you can meet your niece."

"I couldn't," she repeated.

"Where do you live? Not in Benton village, I don't think. You're much too pretty and unusual to hail from such a dreary spot."

"I can't deal with such ribald flattery, Lord Benton. Please stop showering me with it."

"I can't stop. Where you're concerned, the compliments just burst out of me. I can't control myself."

"Don't have me fearing that you're as wicked as your brother."

"I'm probably much worse."

"We should hope not, and if you might be, you shouldn't brag about it."

He ignored the scolding she'd tried to impart and kept pestering her. "Where is your home? You haven't told me."

"It's on the other side of Telford."

"Not far then. What's the distance? Ten miles or so?"

"A bit more than that."

"It seems patently ridiculous for you to travel all that way only to turn around in the morning to travel back."

"I don't mind. I'm rather excited about seeing Daisy."

"Is anyone waiting for you? Your sister is in London which signifies you have no doting parent who's anxious over your absence."

"No, there's no one to fret but a few servants, and if I failed to arrive, they'd barely notice." She glanced down at the floor, mortified to have confessed such a terrible reality.

"Then it's settled," he said.

"What's settled?"

He didn't respond, but swept from behind the desk and marched to the door. He called for a footman, and the one who'd previously escorted her rushed down the hall.

"Yes, my lord?"

"Miss Bates has decided to spend the night."

"Lord Benton!" she complained. "I have not."

He ignored her again, and she was beginning to realize it was his customary habit. He told others to jump, and they simply asked, *how high?*

"Have the housekeeper prepare a room for her," he said to the footman, "and I'll need a man from the stables to ride to Telford for me. Right away."

"Yes, my lord."

The footman hurried off, and Lord Benton came back and sat down. She was still standing, and she felt as if she was a student at school and about to be reprimanded by the headmistress. She slid down too.

"I can't stay," she protested, "and I don't want to stay."

"Why not?"

"It's . . . it's just odd, that's all."

"Out on the lane, Miss Bates, did I—or did I not—explain that I like to seize the day?"

"Yes, you did."

"I've been at Benton for three tedious weeks, when I've hardly ever been here since I was seven. I'm bored to death, and I would like your company. I'm determined to have it."

"I believe you're a bachelor, sir. You can't assume it's appropriate for me to remain."

"I have dozens of servants, and all of my brother's in-laws live in the manor—including his mother-in-law. If you're afraid for your virtue—"

"I'm not!" she huffed.

"—you don't have to worry. I wouldn't dare misbehave with her being present. She's quite vicious, and I'm scared of her. You're safe with me."

"I'm glad to learn that you're scared of someone, but you're being a bully."

He scowled as if he'd never heard of the word. "A bully? How?"

"You're pressuring me horridly."

"Well, you should succumb to my demand. In your interactions with me, it's much easier to accommodate my whims. It's impossible to thwart me."

"That's likely the truest comment you've ever uttered."

He leaned forward, his elbows on the desk. His gaze was warm, his eyes very blue. She felt as if she was drowning in them, and she couldn't look away.

"Josephine—Jo—spend the night," he murmured. "I insist."

His voice was low and seductive, reeling her in, but she had to resist his magnetic pull. "I shouldn't, and I can't. I'm sorry."

"How did you travel from Telford earlier this afternoon? When I stumbled on you, you were walking to the manor. You didn't have a carriage."

"No, I took the public coach."

"I suppose that's how you plan to get home."

"Yes."

"Now that we've met, you have to know I won't permit it. You'll force me to have one of my own carriages harnessed. Then I'll be honor-bound to send it back to fetch you in the morning. Will you really put me to all that trouble?"

"I'm perfectly capable of utilizing a public conveyance."

"And *I* am not the sort of gentleman to let you traipse off across the countryside alone. Why didn't your maid come with you?"

"I don't have a maid, and anyway, I'm an adult. I make my own decisions and arrange my own schedule."

At the admission, she blushed furiously. While seated in his ostentatious library, it seemed a personal failing to not have a maid. After their father's death, they'd been reduced to a barebones staff. Maud's sole extravagance was a lady's maid, but she would never share her with Jo. Nor would Jo request the woman's assistance.

"But you have a few servants?" he asked.

"Yes, but I'm used to being on my own."

"I am absolutely devastated to hear it."

She chuckled. "Why would you be?"

"No female as pretty as you should ever have to take care of herself."

Apparently, it was more of a gallant speech than he'd intended. He was blushing too, and he tried to pretend nonchalance. He shoved the inkpot and a jar of quills at her.

"Write a note to your housekeeper," he said. "Tell her that Lord Benton has invited you to stay the night. While in the past, I've been the very humble Commander Prescott, these days, I'm incredibly grand. Surely she can find no fault or impropriety."

"If she found fault, her only act would be to tattle to my sister."

"What is there to tattle about? You're to be the special guest of Lord Benton. What complaint could she raise?"

"You'd be surprised."

"You lead a dreadful life, don't you?"

"It's all right."

She told the lie with a straight face. She wasn't about to describe her strained relationship with Maud, how their mothers had been from the opposite ends of the social classes, how Jo was a pariah because of it. She wasn't about to describe how Maud treated her.

If she started to talk, she might spew such a torrent of angry words that she'd ignite the entire world. She swallowed them all down.

"Lord Benton, don't push this on me," she begged.

"It will be fine, Jo. You shouldn't fret so much."

"I'll feel so out of place."

"I'm predicting you'll fit in perfectly. I'm not concerned about it, and you shouldn't be either."

Boots sounded out in the hall, and a man entered.

"You needed a rider, my lord?" he asked.

"Yes. I've badgered Miss Bates into tarrying overnight, but she wasn't expecting to remain. You'll ride to her residence outside Telford and transport a message about it to her housekeeper."

"I'll be happy to, my lord."

"You're to have the woman pack a bag for Miss Bates, then you'll bring it back with you."

"I will."

Lord Benton had a wicked gleam in his eye. He realized how he was coercing her, and he reveled in it. He retrieved two pieces of paper from a drawer and laid them in front of her.

"Explain the situation to your housekeeper," he advised, "then jot some directions for my man so he knows where you live."

She glowered at him, her exasperation clear, and they engaged in a brief war of wills she could never win. She wasn't a fighter. She was polite and gentle and could never see the reason for strong emotion to be voiced. From all her years of tiptoeing around volatile Maud, she'd learned that potent sentiment was pointless and only led to more discord.

Ultimately, she shook her head to indicate her aggravation. In response, he simply grinned his devil's grin, and she stood and dipped the quill in the ink and penned the letter and the directions. After she finished, he snatched them away and gave them to the man from the stables.

"Inform her housekeeper," Lord Benton instructed, "that she'll be at Benton tomorrow for sure, but if circumstances warrant, she might be here a day or two beyond that."

"Lord Benton!" Jo objected.

"What if Daisy's journey is delayed?" he asked Jo, then he continued speaking to the other man. "If Miss Bates doesn't return right away, they shouldn't worry. We'll deliver her there safe and sound after her business with us is concluded."

"I will tell her, my lord," the man said, and he left.

If he had an opinion about the odd exchange between Jo and Lord Benton, it was concealed. She and the Earl were frozen in their spots, listening as his strides faded down the hall.

Once it was silent again, Lord Benton said, "That wasn't so bad, was it?"

"It was pretty bad."

He laughed. "You'll get over it."

"I might not."

"You're made of stern stuff, Jo Bates. You can survive whatever I throw at you."

"I hope so. You're like a hurricane. If I'm not careful, I'll be blown away in the tempests you stir."

"It's possible."

"That's what I'm afraid of."

"You stay where you are. I'll locate my housekeeper so she can settle you in. Don't move a muscle until she comes for you."

Then he was gone, and she exhaled a heavy breath. For a woman who refused to socialize with a handsome rogue, she'd certainly jumped into the soup pot.

She was spending the night? As the special guest of Lord Benton himself? How had that transpired exactly? She couldn't quite figure it out.

She was dizzy and disoriented, as if she'd been swept into a quagmire from which there could be no escape. She sunk down in her chair, terrified to discover what would happen next.

CHAPTER

3

"HELLO, RICHARD. FANCY MEETING you here."

Peyton had the pleasure of seeing Richard jump.

After he'd gotten Miss Bates squared away with the housekeeper, he'd marched to the estate agent's office at the rear of the manor, and he'd made himself comfortable. He was sitting at Richard's desk, the ledgers spread in front of him.

He didn't have much of a head for numbers. They bored him silly, so he hadn't looked at them, but he liked Richard to believe he'd been pouring over the columns. He needed to have an outside appraisal completed, and he thought he'd show them to his First Officer and friend, Evan Boyle.

Evan lived and breathed mathematics which was a fascination Peyton had never understood or shared.

If Evan announced himself too lazy to assist, Peyton now had a slew of bankers, accountants, and lawyers who could do it instead. In the meantime, he liked to have Richard squirming. On a dozen occasions, he'd asked to review the ledgers, and Richard always had excuses as to why it wasn't convenient. His reticence left Peyton extremely wary.

Barbara was Neville's widow, and Richard was her twin brother. They were thick as thieves and so closely attuned that they finished each other's sentences. They would share a glance across the dining table, and an entire conversation was held in their minds.

Peyton wasn't exactly clear on when Richard had assumed the role of estate agent or who had decided it was a good idea. Peyton didn't countenance the notion of employing relatives. If matters soured or if the person proved inept, it was so bloody difficult to fire them.

He also wasn't convinced that Richard should manage such a large venture. The Benton assets were vast and widespread, and Richard's father and older brother, Roger, were gamblers. They'd bankrupted the Slater family, and their recklessness had ultimately caused them to lose their own property.

The father was deceased, but Roger wallowed in reduced circumstances in London where he continued to squander funds he didn't have. Peyton couldn't guess if Richard was cut from the same cloth, but in case he had similar tendencies, Peyton didn't suppose he ought to take any chances.

From what Peyton could discern, the property was flowing along in a stable condition. The house was fully staffed. The fields had crops growing. The animal herds appeared healthy. The trees in the orchards were laden with fruit.

Yet he wasn't a farmer, had never wanted to be a farmer, and didn't know much about farming, so he could be wrong. He sensed an undercurrent of crisis at Benton, but he couldn't deduce the source. Was it due to Richard's handling of the finances?

Peyton would have to be a dunce not to realize that part of the problem was Barbara disliking him. She was incensed that she'd birthed no sons, so Peyton had inherited when Neville died. He was home and suddenly in charge when, evidently, Neville had rarely bothered with Benton.

Barbara and her twin brother had had free rein for years, and Peyton was mostly a stranger to them, so it seemed as if an unwanted guest had swooped in and seized what was theirs.

Neville had bequeathed everything to Peyton. He'd even been designated as guardian of Barbara's two daughters, Alice and Nancy. Barbara was furious about the conclusion Neville had engineered, especially the guardianship of her daughters, but he suspected she was even more enraged by the fact that Peyton had control over all the money.

Neville hadn't left Barbara a penny. He'd simply advised Peyton to support her in the *style* to which she was accustomed. She couldn't buy a new bonnet without seeking his permission first.

"May I help you, Peyton?" Richard asked.

"You've been too busy to show me the ledgers, so I popped in to study them on my own."

"May I explain any of the entries to you?"

"No, but I might invite a friend of mine out to study them too. Or perhaps I'll take them to London and leave them with the accountant I've hired."

"An . . . accountant? How interesting. Are you finding fault? The man we use has always been competent."

"I'm sure he has been, but I'll be bringing in some of my own people."

Richard nodded obsequiously. "Are you implying that you'll be getting rid of *me*? I consider Benton my home, and I'd hate to hear that you were unsatisfied with my service."

"Should I be?"

"No." He smiled nervously. "You must proceed as you deem best. I'm certain we'll all adapt."

"I'm certain we will too."

Peyton was deliberately being an ass. He'd commandeered Richard's desk, in Richard's office. Richard was standing and fidgeting, obviously wishing Peyton hadn't stopped by, wishing he could tell Peyton to move, but he couldn't. The office and every item in it belonged to Peyton now.

If he wanted to sit at the desk, he could, and Richard didn't dare complain.

"Have a seat." Peyton gestured to the chair across. "We have to discuss a complicated subject."

Richard hesitated, nearly voiced a protest, then sank down. "What is it?"

"An issue has arisen, and I have some questions about it."

"About the ledgers?"

"No, not about the ledgers." Richard looked relieved until Peyton added, "Not yet anyway."

"They're in excellent shape."

"I hope so."

Peyton was almost thirty, and Richard was the same age, but Peyton seemed a hundred years older. He'd lived a life most men only read about in books. He'd sailed the globe, had been to China and India and Australia. He'd chased pirates in the Caribbean and had fought upstart Americans on their coast. He'd drunk wine and chased doxies in the most notorious port towns. He'd explored the Earth's wildest places with Britain's finest sailors.

He'd been wounded over and over, decorated for bravery a dozen times. When he donned his dress uniform, the coat was adorned with so many medals that it was embarrassing to wear it out in public.

He'd joined the navy at sixteen, immediately after he'd graduated from school. Since then, he'd thrived on excitement, adventure, and danger. In contrast, Richard had attended university, then had come to Benton to stay with his sister after their father went bankrupt. That was the extent of his life experience.

He was steady and boring, a tad grumpy, loyal to his sister, and very set in his ways. They were so different it was hard to believe they were members of the same species.

"I had an intriguing visitor this afternoon," Peyton said. "You met with her just before I did. Josephine Bates?"

"Oh." Richard's expression was completely blank. If he had an opinion about pretty, fascinating Josephine, it was carefully concealed. "I wasn't aware she'd bothered you. I told her not to."

"It was no bother. I chatted with her out on the road when she initially arrived."

"I didn't realize that."

"You wouldn't have. I was happy to confer with her after she finished her appointment with you."

"I see."

"Tell me about Daisy Prescott." Peyton scowled. "Is her surname Prescott? I guess I should know."

"Yes, it's Prescott."

"I'm informed that she's lived at Benton for most of a decade."

"Yes."

Richard wasn't inclined to offer any details, and Peyton was irked that he'd have to pry them out.

"Where is her lodging?" he asked.

"In a cottage—at the edge of the estate, out toward the London road."

"I gather there is more than one child there with her?"

"Yes. Another son and daughter."

"And they are . . . ?"

"Bobby and Jane."

"Neville is father to all three?"

"Yes."

"So he has three bastards."

"Actually, he has nine—that I've learned of."

Peyton sputtered with astonishment. "Nine!"

"Yes."

"Where are the other six?"

"With their maternal kin. Daisy, Bobby, and Jane didn't have that option for . . . ah . . . various reasons, so we sheltered them here. Your brother insisted."

"Were you planning to tell me about them?"

"I don't think so," Richard bluntly admitted.

"Why not? Have you ever considered that I might like to be apprised?"

"It's a difficult situation, Peyton. I wasn't sure how to broach the topic."

"You're sending Daisy away," he said. "Are Bobby and Jane going too?"

"I'm expecting to find an arrangement for them, yes."

"And if you can't locate a suitable spot?"

Richard shrugged. "I'll cross that bridge when I come to it."

"Meaning what?"

"Meaning I'll cross that bridge when it appears in front of me."

Peyton was flummoxed by the entire imbroglio.

He and Neville had been born five years apart, but their childhoods couldn't have been more different.

Neville had been the precious heir their father needed so desperately. He'd been spoiled and worshipped and adored, particularly by their father who'd acted as if Neville could do no wrong. With his golden blond hair and handsome looks, he'd been viewed as an angel, a faultless boy who was incapable of sin or mischief, a precocious little darling who was perfect.

Peyton, on the other hand, had been treated like an orphan, like a waif dragged in off the street. His earliest memories were of vicious whippings. At age seven, he'd been exiled to a military boarding school, and he'd never been allowed home for summer or holidays.

Upon graduating, he'd enlisted in the Royal Navy, and after that, there'd never been a question about his returning to Benton or receiving support. He hadn't been urged to attend university or pick a safer, saner career.

It wasn't until Peyton was fourteen that he'd heard whispers from a classmate that his father *wasn't* his father. Peyton had black hair and blue, blue eyes, and with his muscular physique and six feet of height, he hadn't resembled the Benton men in even the slightest way. Supposedly, Peyton's mother had had an affair, so Peyton was a cuckoo in the Benton nest.

His mother—whom he'd barely known—had been deceased by then, so he hadn't been able to dig out the truth, but it certainly clarified many things. Now that Neville was dead and Peyton was earl, it was humorous to recall that old scandal.

But Peyton simply couldn't wrap his mind around Neville being such a philandering rogue. It didn't match his recollections of Neville at all. What sort of cad sired nine bastards?

"Why are you evicting Daisy?" he asked. "She must feel Benton is her home. Why yank it away from her?"

Richard gaped at Peyton as if he was the thickest man ever. "Why?"

"Yes. She hasn't caused any problems. What's changed?"

"Your brother died, Peyton."

"I'm aware of that fact. I'm here in his place, aren't I?"

"Can't you work out the dilemma on your own? Must I explain it to you?"

"I guess you must."

"My sister can't abide their being in residence another second."

"Oh. I hadn't thought about her opinion."

"I'm not surprised." Color marred Richard's cheeks. "Your brother demanded those children live at Benton—right under my sister's nose. Barbara and I vehemently fought with him over it, but he wouldn't listen."

"Why was he so adamant? Was he close to them? Did he dote on them?"

"No. As far as I'm aware, he never saw them. He merely liked to humiliate my sister. He loathed her and enjoyed tormenting her."

"Really? I hardly knew Neville, but from what I remember, I'd never have pegged him as being overly cruel."

"Well, he was very cruel. Why, Daisy was born the same month as Alice! Can you imagine my sister's shame?"

"No, I can't."

"Neville is deceased, and Benton Manor is my sister's home—unless you plan to kick her out of it."

"No, I don't plan that."

"She's suffered enough, and she's anxious for his by-blows to depart. I beg you not to be spiteful about it—as your brother was spiteful."

"I'm not a spiteful person, Richard."

"We can only hope."

Peyton breathed out a heavy sigh. He didn't care about Benton—his father had drummed out any fondness—and these types of familial quagmires were exactly the reason he was so aggravated over the inheritance.

He simply wanted to head back to sea. He wanted his crew to unfurl the sails so they'd crack in the wind. He wanted to stand at the bow of his ship while the sea spray splashed his hair and clothes.

What he *didn't* want was to fuss with Barbara and Richard. They deemed him an interloper, and they were correct. He was. If he'd been more honorable, he'd have signed over the entire estate to them. He couldn't give them the title, but he could give them everything else.

Why didn't he?

The pathetic fact was that he garnered enormous satisfaction from becoming earl so unexpectedly. He groused and complained about it, but secretly, he was sure his awful father was rolling in his grave. Wasn't that a pretty picture to ponder?

"You've ordered Miss Bates to remove Daisy by July fifteenth," he said, "but she might have some difficulty accomplishing it by then."

"Yes, she was very candid about it."

"If she can't make arrangements by then, she's asked if Daisy could stay on for a bit. What would you think about that?"

"I *think* her sister, Maud Bates, has had ten years to come up with a better idea. We've constantly pressed her about it, but she's refused to take any responsibility."

"How old was she when Neville seduced her?"

"I believe she was sixteen."

"And Neville was what? Twenty-five or so?"

"Yes."

"She was practically a girl when it happened, and Neville was an adult. Can any of it have been her fault? Must she accept any responsibility?"

"Probably not for the affair, but has she any duty now? It's a decade later, and she's the child's mother. Can any obligation be attached to her? Ever? Oughtn't it to be?"

"I understand."

"Do you?" Richard snidely inquired. "Do you really?"

"I'm staggering through this debacle, Richard. If I let Miss Bates have more time, what would your opinion be?"

"My opinion would be that you shouldn't allow it."

Richard was so livid that he was trembling. Clearly, this was an issue that had vexed the Slaters for an extended period, and they'd been determined to resolve it with no interference from Peyton.

As to himself, he couldn't choose the best course. Despite what he selected, someone would wind up hurt or angry. Normally, he felt that thorny matters settled themselves without much intervention. Circumstances or attitudes changed, and in his experience, it was silly to overreact.

If he inserted himself in the predicament, would he only make it worse?

"I haven't reached a decision," he said. "I told her I have to consult with you, then reflect on a conclusion."

"What shall I tell my sister? You've been here a few weeks, and on a daily basis, you ignore the estate and how we carry on. You all but brag about how you don't care. Will this be what finally sparks your interest? Will you push yourself into the middle of it when, so far, you've avoided all other subjects?"

Peyton might have argued the point—and chided Richard for his insult—but Richard's assessment was spot on, and Peyton valued frank speaking.

"We're all finding our way around each other, Richard. Would you rather I had blustered in and evicted all of you?"

"It wouldn't have surprised me," Richard baldly admitted, "and you haven't answered my question. What shall I tell my sister? Will you keep your brother's bastards here? Will your first substantial act be one that crushes her? Will you insist that she continue to be shamed by your family?"

Peyton spun away and gazed out the window at the park. He wished he could see the ocean from Benton. If he could, maybe he wouldn't hate the place quite so much. The sea was where he belonged. A sailing ship was his true home. Not this land-locked estate where people were so cantankerous and unhappy.

He noticed someone walking down a path, and he focused in, gradually recognizing it to be Jo Bates. On observing her, the most pleasant wave of contentment swept through him. It was always delightful to watch a young lady stroll in a flower garden, but there was something extra about her that tantalized him.

It was more than her being very pretty. Her auburn hair was a stunning color he'd never witnessed on another female, and her blue eyes were an odd hue. She was wearing a lavender gown, so they appeared more violet than blue. They were the sort of eyes that made a fellow look twice, that held him rapt when he should have pulled away.

She was only twenty, but she exuded a calm and mature demeanor so she seemed much older than that. She was funny and self-deprecating, and after they'd chatted in his library, he'd learned that she was a damsel in distress too. What gentleman wouldn't be eager to save a damsel in distress? He certainly couldn't resist that type of challenge.

"I'll contemplate all of this," he said, "and I'll let you know my views—once I figure out what they are."

Richard inhaled a deep breath and tucked away his fit of pique, but he couldn't completely conceal his sarcasm. "I can't wait to hear what you devise."

"I guess Daisy is in London today."

"She is."

"I want to meet her tomorrow. I'll want to meet Bobby and Jane too."

"To what end?"

"Well, they're not dogs or chickens, Richard. They're children—my dead brother's children. I'd like to garner a sense of who they are."

"Fine. Have it your way."

"And I've invited Miss Bates to spend the night so she can meet Daisy too. It was ridiculous for her to travel home, then have to turn around and travel right back."

Richard was aghast. "You invited her to stay?"

"Yes."

"But . . . but . . . why?"

"I told you, Richard: to meet her niece."

Richard sputtered with offense. "Will you expect my mother and sister to dine with her this evening?"

"She's not a wild animal. I'm sure she has sufficient manners to sit at the table with all of you. I doubt she'll eat with her fingers. I'm positive she'll have been taught how to use a spoon and a fork."

Richard shook his head with disgust. "You pretend to understand this mess, but you really don't."

"I understand enough."

"Can you even try to consider my sister's feelings?"

"I can *try*. That's all I promise."

Peyton was weary of bickering. He stood, so Richard had to rise too. Just to disconcert the other man, he scooped up the account ledgers and left with them. If Richard had an opinion about Peyton's absconding with them, he didn't dare voice it.

Peyton grinned and kept on to his bedchamber. He'd drop the ledgers there, then he'd hurry out to the park. If he was lucky, the very charming Miss Bates might entertain him all afternoon.

"He what?"

"He invited Josephine Bates to spend the night."

Barbara glared at her brother, Richard, and she wanted to shake him. Or perhaps shout and demand he take control, but with Peyton having arrived at Benton, Richard couldn't manage their affairs any more competently than she could.

From the moment of Neville's death, when he'd been mortally felled by a lung infection, she'd been enraged. Neville had been annoyingly healthy, had bragged about never being sick. How could Fate have laid him low?

She and her husband hadn't gotten on at all. They were two different people, with different habits, tastes, and dreams. *And* Neville had been a philandering dog.

For her part, she hadn't meekly ignored his peccadilloes. They'd constantly battled over his tendencies, and the more she'd protested, the more blatant his conduct had become. He hadn't cared about any of the illegitimate children he'd sired, but he'd enjoyed throwing them in Barbara's face. He'd enjoyed humiliating her.

It had been a twelve-year slog of recrimination and nastiness, and it had been almost a relief when he'd passed away. That is until his Will was read and she'd discovered he would continue to plague her from the grave.

She'd met Peyton on precisely one occasion, that being on the morning of her wedding to Neville. He'd put in an appearance at the ceremony as his brother's best man, but a day later, he'd snuck away and they hadn't seen him again. Not until six months after Neville had been buried, when Peyton had finally staggered home to assume his rightful place.

None of them knew what to think of him. He carried on as if he were an alien being who'd been dropped into a world where he didn't understand the customs or language.

He was aloof and detached, clearly demonstrating that he didn't like any of them and didn't consider himself to be a member of the family. He didn't join them for meals or any other events. He preferred to waste pointless hours walking in the woods and talking to the tenants and neighbors.

Barbara and her brother tiptoed around him, terrified they might unwittingly antagonize him, and Barbara simply wished he'd slink back to the navy and sail off into the sunset.

Richard had once asked him if he intended to resign his commission and return to Benton for good, and he'd claimed he had no desire to retire and probably wouldn't. *Probably?* What kind of answer was that? Where he was concerned, how were they supposed to make plans?

Because of how she and Neville had bickered, he'd rarely tarried at Benton, so she and Richard had had free rein to run things however they liked. They wanted their free rein again, but it could only happen if Peyton left. She hadn't been informed as to the length of his furlough, but it couldn't end soon enough.

"Why would he have Miss Bates stay the night?" she asked her brother.

They were in the front parlor, huddled on a sofa, their heads pressed close, so they could whisper their secrets.

"Who can guess?" he said. "The man is a complete mystery to me."

"He didn't seek my permission."

"Well, he wouldn't, would he?"

"Are we to entertain her? Are we to have her down for tea? How about for supper?"

"I'm not certain about tea, but you should expect her for supper."

Barbara grumbled with frustration. Her initial impulse was to brawl and win any skirmish. She was countess at the estate, and she'd been in charge ever since she'd married Neville at eighteen.

She should have marched out and located Peyton. She should have apprised him that Barbara still had rights in the manor, first among them being the authority to decide who was welcome in it and who wasn't. But she would never have that conversation with him.

Neville hadn't liked or trusted Richard, so he'd bequeathed everything to his brother, even total power over her daughters, Alice and Nancy. Barbara hadn't received a single farthing, so she was fully dependent on Peyton for the least little expenditure.

If she angered him, he could evict her, take her daughters, and leave her a penniless widow, begging for shelter from her acquaintances in London.

Although she hadn't broached the subject, she thought he should marry her. Why not? It was the perfect solution to her problem. He hated Benton, and it was obvious he was desperate to escape. If they wed, he could flit off to the navy he loved so much, and *she* could resume the life she'd always lived.

He was about to turn thirty, and so far, he'd avoided the matrimonial noose, but he was an earl now, so he couldn't remain a bachelor. He *had* to wed. He couldn't delay, and if he didn't pick Barbara, he'd pick someone else. He'd bring in another female and give her Barbara's home.

She was only thirty as well, and she was much too young to be the dowager countess. She'd kill any woman who lined up to become Peyton's wife, and she'd already devised numerous dirty tricks she could play on any candidate stupid enough to contemplate it.

"Does Miss Bates even have clothes for supper?" she asked.

"He sent a rider to fetch some of her belongings."

"Isn't that sweet?" Barbara sarcastically crooned. "Have you met her?"

"I told you I had."

"And . . . ?"

"She's pretty and charming, but a bit bewildered by the situation with Daisy."

"She had no idea her sister was such a whore?"

"No. She'd never heard a word about the scandal."

"I want Daisy gone!" Barbara seethed. "It doesn't matter how Miss Bates bats her lashes at Peyton. This must be resolved once and for all!"

Neville's three bastards were departing Benton by July fifteenth. Barbara was finished with tolerating her husband's insults, and she didn't care about Peyton's opinion. If the children's families refused to take them, then she would place them in an orphanage—and her conscience would be clear.

"You'll be shed of them by the fifteenth," Richard said. "I guarantee it. Don't worry."

"I do worry, Richard. How can I not?"

"Peyton won't be at Benton forever."

"Let's hope he's not. I can't bear much more of this upheaval."

"He can promise whatever he likes to Miss Bates, but the minute he heads back to the navy, Daisy will vanish."

"Swear it to me."

"I don't need to swear. Have I ever failed you?"

"No."

"Then I won't fail you now."

CHAPTER

4

PEYTON BOUNDED DOWN THE stairs to the foyer. The ledger book was stashed in his bedchamber, and he'd grabbed a jacket so he looked more presentable. He was eager to catch up with Miss Bates out in the park.

He couldn't figure out why she fascinated him, but with his having spent three tedious weeks at Benton, she was a fresh face and a distraction from his having to deal with Barbara and Richard.

With each passing day, he was more unsettled by his position. It seemed wrong that Benton had been bestowed on him. He should chuck the whole bloody thing and return to the navy, but that would mean abandoning the property to Barbara and Richard.

A crueler person would kick them out, but he wasn't an ogre. Benton was their home, and *he* was the interloper.

He'd like to hire a new estate agent, one he'd chosen and who would be loyal to Peyton rather than Barbara, but he couldn't imagine firing Richard. Not without it causing a huge uproar.

Ooh, but he detested all the budding dilemmas! Life was so much simpler when he was at sea. It was just waves and water and weather. He had to get back there.

He was about to proceed down the hall when Barbara stepped out of the front parlor.

"Peyton, there you are," she gushed. "Richard and I were just talking about you."

"The notion makes me shudder. What sin have I committed now?"

"Nothing, silly. Don't be so testy."

He kept walking, but she tagged along, matching him stride for stride. With how he was hurrying, she was practically running. He forced himself to slow down so it didn't appear as if he was trying to escape—which he definitely was.

"Richard advises me we're to have a guest for supper," she said.

"Yes, Miss Bates will join you. I was sure you wouldn't mind."

His stern tone warned her to give the appropriate reply, and she obliged him.

"Any guest you invite is fine with me. It's your house after all."

He snorted with grim amusement. His ownership galled her, and she'd never been able to conceal her exasperation at the predicament Neville had created.

"It's nice to hear you've finally realized the house is mine," he said.

"Of course I have. Ah . . . ah . . . Richard mentioned he'd discussed Neville's other *children* with you. Please tell me you won't be difficult about their leaving."

"I haven't decided what I think of your plan. I've only just learned about the children, and I'm still coming to grips with the news."

"This situation has been an open wound for me for years. I'm very weary at having had to constantly abide it."

He pulled up short. "I understand, Barbara. I truly do."

"Your brother wasn't the easiest husband."

"So I'm told, and believe me, there's a reason I never visited Benton. You don't have to convince me how horrid it can be here."

Actually, Neville hadn't spurred Peyton to stay away from Benton. He'd barely known his brother, and they'd had no significant issues. The rancor had been caused by their father.

When Peyton had first been sent away to school, he'd been very lonely. The other students would depart for holidays, but he'd remain behind.

Initially, it had hurt very much, but his friend, Evan Boyle, had toughened him, had helped him to develop a hard shell. A professor had been incredibly kind too, had filled Peyton's hours with busy tasks so he didn't focus on how he was being shunned by his parents.

Gradually, he'd stopped missing Benton. It had begun to feel as if he'd never resided at Benton Manor, as if he'd never had a brother named Neville. He'd grown up so detached from all of it that he might have been hatched from an egg.

"May we discuss this in the future?" she asked. "I would never nag at you, but I would like to lay out my position more clearly—in case Richard hasn't."

"Richard was very clear."

"I'm glad."

She flashed a nervous smile, and he might have laughed if it hadn't been so tragic.

She was a beautiful woman, but in an icy, aloof manner. There was a brittle edge to her so she always appeared about to fly into a rage.

She had Richard's blond hair and blue eyes, and his same facial features, but not his bodily type. Richard was thin and lithe, but she had gotten chubby from the rich diet at Benton. While a few extra pounds could make a female seem very voluptuous, it hadn't worked with her. She merely looked as if she'd stretched the seams on her gown as far as they could go.

From the moment he'd arrived, she'd been hinting that she'd like a closer relationship with him. No doubt she and her brother had devised a scheme where she would charm Peyton, then suggest a marriage between them.

In a normal world, he'd have agreed that it was the perfect solution, but he didn't live in a normal world. He was a commander in the navy who'd inherited an earldom and estate he'd never wanted, and he would never exacerbate his problems by marrying his brother's churlish, unlikable widow.

Besides which, he'd been seriously flirting with Evan's sister, Amelia, and he'd been blatant enough about his interest that they would be expecting a proposal.

Amelia was pretty, fun, and very independent, so she'd be an excellent wife for a seafaring man such as himself who was absent from England for long stretches of time. He'd persuaded himself that marriage to her wouldn't be the worst idea, and he *was* almost thirty, so it wouldn't kill him to wed.

Of course that was then, and this was now. She might have been a good choice in the past, but with his being an *earl*, she was quite a bit below him— if he was concerned about that sort of thing. He'd never previously been, but his elevation to the title was messing with his head. He was ceaselessly considering issues he'd once deemed absurd.

Barbara had taken his arm and was holding tight. She always cleverly forced him to socialize, and if he wasn't careful, he'd wind up spending the rest of the afternoon with her.

"Will you excuse me?" he said. "I have an appointment."

"I'm sorry. I didn't realize I was delaying you."

"It's all right."

"You'll join us for supper, won't you? You can't leave us to entertain Miss Bates on our own."

He rarely dined with the Slater family. He'd quickly discovered that it was an unpleasant and awkward experience. "I can't guarantee I will, but I'll let the butler know what I decide. I wouldn't be too sure of Miss Bates either. After what she's learned about your plans for her niece, she might not be anymore keen to eat with you than you are to eat with her. Maybe she'd rather have a tray sent up to her room."

At the snide comment, Barbara bristled. "The little tart better not act that way."

"Now, now, don't be a snob. And don't call her names. I like her."

He whipped away and hurried off, and he lengthened his strides, so she couldn't keep up. He rushed out a rear door and crossed the verandah, and he stood at the balustrade searching the park. Jo was on a bench out by the lake, and an odd wave of emotion swept over him. He dawdled briefly, desperate to figure out what it was.

As he recognized it to be extreme delight, he was a tad startled. Yes, he was bored and lonely, but Josephine Bates could never divert him in any fashion that mattered.

He skipped down the stairs, and there was a definite spring in his step. She noticed him approaching, and she smiled.

"Hello, Lord Benton," she said. "I was wondering if I'd bump into you again before I left."

"Why wouldn't you? These days, I'm a rich, indolent aristocrat. I have nothing to do."

"Well, sit yourself down and do *nothing* with me. It's such a lovely afternoon, and you should tarry for a few minutes to enjoy it."

She patted the spot next to her on the bench, and he sidled over and plopped down. She'd removed her bonnet, and she scooped it up to make space for him.

"I took off my bonnet so the sun could shine on my face," she said. "Are you shocked?"

"You'll find, Miss Bates, that there is not much that shocks me."

"I agree that you're quite stout of heart."

"I've been in the navy since I was sixteen. I've engaged in more *living* than most men could manage in a hundred lifetimes."

"How old are you? Eighty? Ninety?"

"About to turn thirty, you minx."

"You elderly codger, you."

"Did the housekeeper get you settled?"

"Yes, and everyone has been very kind. She even assigned a maid to help me which seems silly when I don't have a brush or an extra gown to change into. I feel like a princess in a fairytale."

"I'm glad the servants are spoiling you, and you'll have your belongings very soon—unless you provided bad directions to my man and he's lost."

"I was very precise, so if he's waylaid, it's not my fault. It will mean he can't read."

"Hm, I hadn't thought of that. When I gave him your note, his literacy—

or lack thereof—never occurred to me. He might end up wandering the rural roads for decades."

"I'd hate to be responsible for any adversity he might suffer."

They were quiet for a bit, the scenery soothing. Butterflies drifted by, and birds cawed in the trees. The grass was so green, and the foliage smelled marvelous. It left him nostalgic for things he couldn't describe.

"I envy you," she said.

"Really? Why?"

"Because you're in the navy, so you've been able to have adventures. Have you seen many interesting sights? Even if you haven't, lie to me and tell me you have. I want to envision you having a grand and exciting life."

"I don't have to lie. I've visited many exotic locations: China, India, Arabia. I've sailed the globe. I've even floated down the Nile on a barge."

"You haven't!"

"I have."

"You men are so lucky. You can just pick up and *go* while we women have to sit by the hearth and mend socks."

"A fate worse than death I'm sure."

"I'm so jealous."

"You should be jealous. It's been very fun."

"I've never been anywhere. Have you any notion of how fortunate you are?"

"Yes, I constantly realize it."

He hadn't joined the navy to travel the world though. At the time, it hadn't crossed his mind at all. It had been a more mundane decision.

He'd enlisted after nine years in a military boarding school. All of his teachers had been sailors or soldiers, and every summer, he'd worked on sailing ships, learning how to handle the ropes, how to gauge the wind, how to plot a course and arrive at a destination.

On graduating, he'd never imagined any other option than to become a sailor. Why would he have craved another option? And he still felt the same way.

Yet as he stared at the manor, it was from a vantage point he'd rarely observed prior, and it produced a wistful tug of *home* that rattled him.

He'd wasted his days trekking the length and breadth of the estate, investigating all of its nooks and crannies. He'd met the tenants and neighbors, had studied the woods and the deserted lanes.

It had been in the Prescott family for three centuries. It was steeped in British history, with all the famous and infamous historical characters staying in it. Ghosts walked the halls.

The entire place was his, the mansion, the barns, the fields, the pastures. The money was his too, the servants, the animals, carriages, and equipment. The stunning amount of riches given to him—simply because his brother had died—was almost obscene. It seemed sinful for one person to possess so much, but it was his now. For good or ill.

"I have a question for you," he said. "Or perhaps it's a warning."

"What is it?"

"Barbara, my brother's widow, always serves an ostentatious supper. The pomp she displays can be embarrassing."

"And . . . ?"

"I told her you might join her, but I'm not certain you should. She's the biggest snob ever, and I don't believe you'd like her. She'd probably be very rude to you too. If you'd rather, you can skip the dining room and have a tray in your bedchamber, but I'll leave it up to you."

"Lord Benton, you've denigrated your sister-in-law on several occasions, but you shouldn't be so frank with me."

"Why not? If I share a secret, it's not as if you'll run out and sell it to the newspapers."

"No, I never would, but you hardly know me. I can't bear to hear that you don't like your relatives. It makes me sad, and if you have such a need to reveal your dislike, I wish you'd find someone who is a more appropriate confidante."

"There's no one else here, Miss Bates, and you're a good listener."

"You're correct. I am."

"You'll have to put up with me while I vent my petty objections."

"Why don't you like her?" she asked.

"I won't list the reasons, but you'll likely meet her before you depart. You'll see what I mean. What did you think of her brother, Mr. Slater?"

"He was . . . cool and detached."

He grinned. "You don't have to be so polite. What did you really think?"

"He was cool and detached," she repeated, her tone scolding. "Don't pester me about him. You'll never goad me into a disparaging comment."

"Are you always this kind?"

"I try to be."

"How admirable. As to myself, I generally try to be brutally candid."

"Then candor might be your ruin someday. It's frequently unwise to speak what's on your mind."

"Maybe, but it shortens the path through any discord. I like to cut to the heart of a matter. I don't beat around the bush."

"How is that tactic working for you?"

"Not very well. Barbara and her brother don't like me anymore than I like them."

"Why is that? Have you been horrid to them?"

"No, it's because I had the gall to inherit. They've been managing on their own, and I've barged in and seized control. They view me as an interloper."

"Are you?"

"Yes, definitely."

The admission had her laughing, and he smiled, liking the sound of her voice.

His world was one of ships and men and lengthy voyages away from England. When he spent time with females, it was with crude doxies in port towns, so he enjoyed being home and flirting with beautiful women who understood English and all the customs he took for granted.

He was astonished that he'd divulged so much to her. Yes, he trusted her and she'd never blab his secrets, but he wasn't talkative. It was so odd for him to babble on, but when he was in her presence, he was disconcerted as a green boy with his first girl.

Evidently, he was desperate to impress her, and he couldn't shut up.

He yearned to tarry with her all evening, yearned to chat and loaf and learn every detail there was to know about her, so his fascination had reached an absurd level. He couldn't figure out why. Perhaps the dreary weeks at Benton were driving him insane.

"I never expected to inherit Benton," he confessed, "and Barbara and Richard weren't expecting I would either."

"It can't have been that much of a surprise. You're the sole male offspring after your brother, and he never sired a son."

"Well, as you and I have recently discovered," Peyton caustically pointed out, "he sired *sons*, but not with his lawful wife, so maybe we shouldn't mention them."

"Yes, I suppose we shouldn't. The world's a strange place, isn't it? He had all those children, but *you* are the only one who counted."

"I can't decide if I've been insulted or if you're simply stating the facts."

She cast a sly glance that didn't tell him anything. "I would never insult you."

He smirked with derision, but still, he relished the chance to catalog his complaints. "All of this is so complicated."

"How?"

"I love the navy, and I loathe it here."

"You poor baby," she sarcastically chided. "You've been showered with a title and an estate and a fortune. How dreadful your life is."

"I realize I seem ungrateful."

"Yes, you do."

"In my own defense, I was never welcomed at Benton as a boy, so it's never felt like *home* to me. My boarding school was home."

She scowled. "Why weren't you welcome?"

"My father didn't like me. He has to be rolling in his grave now that his precious earldom is mine. If he wasn't already dead, the prospect would kill him. I'm taking some solace from that."

"What an awful comment! Don't you dare take solace from it."

"All right, just for you, I'll try not to."

"I'd appreciate it. I should locate the nearest church so I can offer up a prayer for your immortal soul. I'm very worried about it."

"How about if you skip the worries about my immortal soul and focus on the very mortal man?"

"Yes, we've been discussing how difficult your life is."

"Barbara and Richard don't want me here, and I don't want to be here."

"So go back to the navy and let them have it."

"I don't think I should. I'm not certain they're good stewards."

"Then hire some competent managers and bring them in instead."

"You make it sound so easy."

"I'd give ten pounds to have half your problems. You're wealthy and important. You hold a respected position in the military, and as part of your job, you travel the globe. Your family is prominent and esteemed. Stop whining. You annoy me."

"I don't mean to, but please explain this to me: How does a fellow fire his relatives? Especially when the property seems to be theirs rather than mine."

"That is a tough situation."

"I'm constantly besieged by internal debates about what's fair—and what's not. I have to take charge while ruffling as few feathers as possible."

"Can you?"

"I doubt it. I'm predicting every feather in my path will be ruffled."

"And you like to bluster about like a bull in a china shop."

"Yes, I've been known to bluster. It's not in my nature to be calm or quiet."

"I've noticed that about you." She shook her head and chuckled. "How can I convince you to cease confiding in me? It's so inappropriate for you to tell me your troubles."

"I can't be silent. In the past three weeks, you're the first person I've encountered who's too polite to stomp off when I wax on about how I'm vexed to the bone."

"Should I be less polite? Would that work?"

"Yes. If you're weary of hearing my list of grievances, you should be extremely rude."

She snorted with amusement. "I'm never rude. I never acquired that skill. My sister, Maud, is the one who's pompous and irritating. I'm the complete opposite."

"I've sensed that about you. Will it be hard to speak with her about Daisy?"

"Very hard, and I've been sitting here, trying to envision our conversation. I find it quite unimaginable, and I'm sure she'll shoot the messenger."

"You'll be fine."

He reached out and patted her hand. It was a simple gesture of support, but it rocked him in ways he hadn't intended. He felt shocked by it, felt electrified by it. If he was suddenly informed she was a sorceress and she'd bewitched him, he wouldn't have been surprised.

He had to pull himself away and leave her alone. He couldn't loiter in the garden and hang on her every word. He was behaving like an idiot, like a smitten swain, which was deranged.

"I have an idea," he said.

"What is it?"

"You shouldn't have supper with the family."

"They won't gobble me up—if that's what's bothering you. They could never intimidate me."

"I'd hate to have them be awful to you though."

"You should join us too. We can be a united bulwark to push back against their snobbery."

"I never eat with them."

"Never?"

"No, so what if you and I have a private supper in my room?"

She studied him strangely, as if the request was too bizarre to fathom, and he had to admit he was stunned to have voiced it. A bachelor didn't invite a young lady to his bedchamber for any reason. It wasn't allowed.

"You and I?" Her alarm was obvious. "Have a *private* supper?"

"Yes."

"No!" she firmly stated. "You and I will never share any private moments. You shouldn't presume that we might."

"I apologize if I offended you."

"I'm not offended. I'm merely making my position clear. I may be a guest in your home, and I may not have a chaperone to watch over me, but I'm not easy prey. You shouldn't assume I am."

"Easy prey!" he huffed. "Give me more credit than that. I simply wanted to dine with you. I thought it would be enjoyable."

"It might have been, but your suggestion has reignited my fear that you are much more like your brother than you would ever acknowledge."

"I'm nothing like him."

"Let's hope not."

She stood, crushing him with the realization that he'd chased her away. He wasn't usually such a bungler.

"Don't be angry," he said.

"I'm not angry. You're a bit more *man* than I can handle. I can't deal with a sophisticated fellow like you, and I learned the hard way that I have to be careful."

"It's just supper."

"Maybe or maybe not." She stared down at him, looking very shrewd and very wise for a girl who was only twenty. "I believe I will have a tray sent to my room, but I will eat by myself. Now then, if you'll excuse me? I should check if your rider has returned with my bag."

"I'm sorry to have upset you."

"I never permit handsome gentlemen to upset me," she claimed, "but I am always wary."

He raised a brow. "You think I'm handsome?"

"You know you are. Don't be vain about it."

She started off, and he called after her, "I'll see you tomorrow."

"Why?"

"We'll go together to meet Daisy. Don't forget that I'm not acquainted with her either."

She nodded. "I suppose we can go together—so long as you mind your manners."

"When have I not?"

She scoffed with disgust. "You're impossible."

She walked on, and he dawdled until she vanished into the manor. With her departure, it dawned on him that he was very morose. Gad, did he . . . he . . . *miss* her?

The notion didn't bear contemplating.

He rose and went to the stables to saddle a horse. He'd spend the remainder of the afternoon galloping down rural lanes. By nightfall, any poignant emotion she'd generated would have evaporated, and he'd be restored to his usual condition.

At least he expected he would be, but as he pondered the next day and how he'd be with her for several hours, he caught himself grinning from ear to ear.

CHAPTER

5

Jo PEEKED OUT THE window of her carriage, and she sighted Daisy's house. It was a fine dwelling, two stories high and painted white with green shutters. There were flowerboxes under the windows and a stone walk leading to the front door.

It was the sort of place where a successful farmer or perhaps a retired local merchant might have resided, so they didn't have Daisy living in squalor which was a relief.

Lord Benton was leaned against the gate, his horse tied to the fence, and Jo couldn't decide if she was thrilled or irked to see him.

After their encounter in the garden the prior afternoon, she hadn't spoken to him again. He'd flirted outrageously, and she couldn't deny that he fascinated her. No doubt he believed she'd been flirting in return, and she probably had been. But when he'd suggested she share a private supper, she'd recognized her folly quickly enough.

She'd hurried to her room and had stayed there for the remainder of the evening.

She'd assumed he would travel to Daisy's house with her, but a maid had told her she'd be riding alone, so she'd figured he wasn't coming after all. Yet here he was, smiling and looking wonderful, as if he'd been impatiently watching for her to arrive.

As the carriage rattled to a halt, he marched over and opened the door himself, taking her hand and guiding her down.

"Good afternoon, Miss Bates," he said.

"Good afternoon, Lord Benton."

"That mode of address sounds so exhausting to me. Would you call me Commander Prescott instead?"

"No."

"Why must you always be so difficult?"

"I can't help it, my lord. I like to torment you."

"I bet you weren't expecting me."

"No, I wasn't. I'd quite given up on you."

"I wouldn't miss this for anything."

"Have you been inside?"

"No."

"Shall we go in together?" she asked.

"Yes, let's do."

He escorted her through the gate, and as he banged the knocker, he glanced at her and asked, "Are you nervous?"

"Not nervous precisely. Mostly excited I suppose."

"I sent word that we would visit."

"I'm glad you thought of it."

He knocked a second time, and a housemaid ushered them into a cozy parlor. A young woman about Jo's age stood to greet them. She was pretty, blond and blue-eyed, tidy in her appearance and professional in her bearing. There was a tea tray on a table, so they'd be welcomed with refreshments.

They sat on the sofa, and the woman sat in the chair across from them.

"Lord Benton, Miss Bates," she said, "thank you so much for coming. I'm Daisy's governess, Winifred Watson."

"Hello to you, Miss Watson," Lord Benton replied. Jo merely nodded.

"I had Daisy wait in her bedchamber," Miss Watson said, "until we've had a few minutes to confer amongst ourselves."

"I don't mean to be rude," Jo said, "but I don't wish to chat for long. I'm so eager to meet her."

"Of course you are," Miss Watson agreed. "I'll be very brief."

Lord Benton said, "I was told I have another niece and a nephew lodged with you as well. May I meet them too?"

"Yes, Bobby and Jane are here," Miss Watson said. "They're all upstairs, and I've ordered them to be quiet, although I doubt they'll manage it. We're located at the end of a deserted lane, so we don't get many guests."

There was an awkward pause where numerous comments went unvoiced. The identity of the children would be bandied in the neighborhood, and they'd be viewed disdainfully by many.

It was sad that people were so judgmental, but as her own mother's situation had proved, rural sensibilities were easily offended. But why should Neville Prescott's children be shunned? *They* hadn't committed any sins. If there was shame to be leveled, it ought to begin with the late earl.

"Before I bring them down," Miss Watson continued, "I wanted to explain that this has been a very trying experience for them."

"Are they aware they might be departing?" Lord Benton asked.

"Yes, I've kept them fully apprised. There's no reason to shield them from reality."

"What a refreshing attitude," he said.

Miss Watson stared at Lord Benton, and her gaze was pleading. "I realize I have no right to interfere, Lord Benton, but I urge you to be kind to them. Actually, I'll *beg* you to be kind—if that will help."

"You don't have to beg, Miss Watson. I don't intend to be cruel, but you must understand—until Miss Bates arrived yesterday—I had no idea that these three children even existed. I'm finding my way through the whole maze, and I haven't decided how any of this should resolve."

"The three of them have always resided here," Miss Watson said, "and they're a family. They're half-siblings after all, and they're quite distressed at the notion of being separated."

"How old are they?" Jo asked.

"Jane is eleven, and Bobby is twelve."

"And Daisy is nine," Jo put in.

"My brother was a busy man," Lord Benton sarcastically muttered, and Jo cast a scolding glare in his direction.

"Don't be vulgar, Lord Benton," she warned. "Miss Watson has just been introduced to you. You'll give her the wrong impression, and she'll think you're crude."

His cheeks flushed with chagrin. "I apologize, Miss Watson."

"Apology accepted, my lord. I teach children for a living. I'm not faint of heart."

"That's good to know."

He smiled a charming smile that Jo was annoyed to see but was glad to have witnessed. She'd assumed the smiles he bestowed were for her alone, that he deemed her to be special and favored, but apparently, he smiled at every female the same way. In her dealings with him, she shouldn't ever forget it.

"If you kick them out, Lord Benton—" Miss Watson started, but he cut her off.

"No one will be *kicked* out, Miss Watson. We'll choose a viable conclusion for all concerned. I'll be speaking to Mr. Slater about it."

"Will you?" Miss Watson's eyes flashed with temper. "Well, then, I hope you make your opinion very clear. He has a bit of a problem with his hearing."

"What's the matter with his hearing?" Lord Benton asked.

"He doesn't like to listen," Miss Watson said.

"Oh." Lord Benton snorted with amusement. "I've noticed the same issue myself, so you're a very astute judge of character."

Jo butted in. "May I meet Daisy now? I really can't bear further delay."

"Yes, I'll fetch her," Miss Watson said.

"Has she been told about her mother and how she came to Benton?" Jo inquired. "Has she been told that Neville Prescott is her father?"

"Yes, Miss Bates, she's been told. I've ensured there are no secrets in this house. There may be plenty of secrets over at the manor, but not here."

Miss Watson went to the foyer and summoned Daisy. As they waited, Jo glanced at Lord Benton.

"Let's bring Daisy down by herself," she said. "The three of them together might prove a handful."

"That's fine," he agreed.

Shortly, Daisy's footsteps echoed on the stairs, and they rose to greet her. She entered the room, and Jo got her first glimpse of her niece.

She was pretty as a picture, blond and blue-eyed, thin and lithe. Her hair was braided down her back in a single braid, and it hung to her waist. She was wearing a blue dress, with a white pinafore over top, and the blue of the dress enhanced the blue of her eyes. She looked fresh-scrubbed and well-tended.

It was obvious she was Maud's daughter. There were many similarities, but it was as if all of Maud's defects had been wiped away. The flaws were gone and only the very sweetest parts remained.

Fleetingly, Jo wondered if it was Neville Prescott's aristocratic blood that had vanquished Maud's lesser traits. Whatever had rendered such a lovely combination, Jo was delighted.

"My, my, aren't you beautiful?" she murmured as her opening salvo. She was so ecstatic she couldn't hold in her words.

"Daisy," Miss Watson said, "this is Lord Benton, and he's brought your Aunt Bates."

"Hello, Lord Benton," Daisy said. "Hello, my Aunt Bates."

She executed a perfect curtsy to Lord Benton, and she didn't appear nervous at all. She seemed confident and merry, and she wasn't shy or modest, wasn't sullen or morose as Maud was apt to be. Again, Jo wondered if Neville's traits were leading the charge or if Miss Watson had instilled a huge dose of poise and optimism.

The adults sat down, but Daisy dawdled by Miss Watson's chair. She studied them, and they studied her.

No one could figure out how to begin, and Jo broke the awkward silence, telling Daisy, "You should call me Aunt Jo. I think *Aunt Bates* sounds as if I'm a hundred years old."

Daisy grinned. "I will call you Aunt Jo. I'd like that."

Lord Benton asked, "Would you call me Commander Prescott?"

At the request, Daisy was horrified, and she peeked at Miss Watson for guidance. Miss Watson shook her head, and Daisy said, "I don't believe I ought, Lord Benton. Miss Watson wouldn't like it."

"Your aunt won't call me Commander Prescott either." He sighed dramatically. "Is there one female on this blasted estate who will obey me?"

"No," the three females retorted in unison, and they all laughed which cut through the tension.

"I didn't know about you until yesterday," Lord Benton told Daisy.

"Yes, I heard. Miss Watson explained everything."

"Do you like it here? Have you been happy?"

"I've been very happy, Lord Benton." She paused, and Miss Watson made a slight gesture, urging her on. "I would like to say that I hope you'll be kind to my brother and sister, Bobby and Jane. I don't care so much what is arranged for me, but I worry about them. They've been very anxious. Especially Jane. She's a worrier."

"We'll find a good ending for everyone," he graciously responded, and Daisy relaxed, clearly receiving great comfort from his comment.

Jo peered over at Miss Watson, then Lord Benton. "Would the two of you mind if Daisy and I take a walk? I'd like to spend some time alone with her."

"It's fine with me," Miss Watson said. "How about you, Lord Benton?"

"Yes, and while you're gone, Miss Bates, I'll chat with Bobby and Jane. Why don't we meet up in an hour? We can ride to the manor together."

She wanted to refuse, wanted to declare that she would tarry much longer than that and she would return to the manor by herself. But she wouldn't argue with him in front of the others, and it was several miles of winding country roads back to the manor. She wasn't sure she could locate it on her own.

Anyway, she could visit Daisy in the future. This didn't have to be the only occasion.

"Yes, an hour should be plenty," Jo said.

Miss Watson smiled at Daisy. "Why don't you show your aunt all your favorite spots? You'll give her some idea of how your life is structured."

"Might I show her my bedchamber too before she leaves?"

"Of course," Miss Watson said.

Jo added, "I'd like that very much."

Jo stood and approached her niece, and a very dear sense of connection flitted between them. It seemed as if they'd always known each other, as if they'd never been strangers a single moment.

"Let's go, shall we?' Jo said. "We'll stroll as slowly as we can while you tell me every important detail I should discover about you. I'd like to become a Daisy expert."

"First off," Daisy said, "I'm very smart. Aren't I smart, Miss Watson?"

"You are the smartest girl in the world, Daisy." Miss Watson chuckled. "You're very humble too."

"I am not humble," Daisy protested.

"That was a joke, Daisy," Miss Watson said. "Now go with your aunt, so Bobby and Jane can be introduced to their uncle."

"Goodbye, Lord Benton." Daisy curtsied again.

"I'll be here when you get back," he said.

Jo flashed a look to inform him that she was overwhelmed and glad he'd attended the appointment with her. He flashed a look too, informing her that he felt the same.

Then she clasped her niece's hand, linked their fingers, and they walked outside.

DAISY GAZED UP AT her Aunt Jo, and she couldn't stop staring.

Her aunt was young and beautiful and very, very kind. Kindness practically oozed out of her. For the past three years, Miss Watson had been their governess, and Daisy often pretended that Miss Watson was actually her mother. She hadn't thought she would ever like a woman more than Miss Watson, but her Aunt Jo was perfect. Miss Watson had been replaced in her affections.

Their hour had passed much too quickly, and they were on the way back to the cottage. Daisy had showed her the woods and their barn where they had a milk cow and chickens. They'd loafed by the stream where Bobby liked to fish.

Miss Watson had let them have a dog, and after significant debate, they'd named it Rex. He was trotting behind them, and he appeared as enchanted by her aunt as Daisy was.

Daisy was very worried about Rex. Once they all left and the cottage was shut down, what would happen to him? He'd be forlorn without them, and she was desperate to bring him with her. She was hoping it might be allowed, but with the future so uncertain, she didn't dare mention the problem.

"We have a few minutes remaining," Aunt Jo said. "Shall we sit?"

"I'd like that."

There was an old rock wall bordering the lane. They waded through the grass and plopped down. The forest was very quiet, and Aunt Jo smiled as she studied the surroundings.

"It's pretty here," she murmured.

"Very pretty."

"You told Lord Benton that you've been happy." Her aunt frowned. "Have you been? Or were you merely being polite?"

"I've been happy."

"What do you think about having to depart?"

"I'll miss Bobby and Jane."

"Have you any idea where they're headed?"

"Jane has an uncle in Cornwall, but Bobby doesn't have anyone. Mr. Slater has written to Jane's uncle to request that the man take them both. I guess he has a huge farm, so it might work. Miss Watson has written too, but he hasn't answered."

"If he never replies, has there been any gossip as to what Mr. Slater has planned?"

"No, but . . ."

Her voice trailed off. She liked her aunt so much, and she was afraid to offer a comment that would make her aunt *not* like Daisy in return.

"But what?" her Aunt Jo asked.

"I don't know if I should repeat a grownup conversation. I probably shouldn't."

"You can tell me. We shouldn't ever have secrets."

"Mr. Slater can be . . . difficult. That's what Miss Watson says about him. He visits us occasionally, and they argue. We hear them."

"I'm sorry that you have. You children should be spared any adult bickering."

"Last time, she called him a heartless monster."

"My goodness. I'm surprised she still has a job."

"It's ending when we leave Benton." Daisy wrinkled up her nose. "I don't like quarreling."

"Neither do I."

"I'm afraid for Bobby and Jane. If Jane's uncle won't take them, Mr. Slater warned Miss Watson they'll be sent to an orphanage."

"I'm sure he didn't mean it."

"If I eventually come to live with you, could they come too? And how about Rex? Could he come?"

"No, Daisy. If I can make arrangements, it will have to be just for you. I couldn't assist them. I'd like to, but I can't. I'll have enough of a problem getting you settled."

"I understand," Daisy mumbled.

She'd been a burden all her life, and she was aware of her lowly place in the world, but just once, she'd like to be somewhere where people were glad to have her. It didn't seem like too much to ask, but maybe it was.

"Did you know your father very well?" Aunt Jo inquired.

"No. He didn't stop by very often."

"But when he did stop by, what was your opinion of him?"

"He was very handsome and funny. He told jokes, and he always slipped a penny into my pocket. I have all of them in a jar. I've never spent any of them." She blushed, her cheeks heating. "I like having them. I like looking at them."

"Of course you do. They're from your father."

"I don't have very much from him, but I have those."

"Has Miss Watson shared much information about your mother?"

"A bit, but she's never had much information."

"You shouldn't have any illusions about the sort of person she is."

"Miss Watson said much the same. I haven't gotten my hopes up."

"Your mother is a hard woman, and she's never been very happy. I'll speak with her about your living with us, but I'm certain she'll be very opposed."

"What would happen to me then?"

"Don't worry about it yet. The adults are working on a resolution."

"What if you can't figure it out?"

"We'll cross that bridge when we have to."

"I wouldn't be scared of an orphanage—if I could be there with Jane and Bobby. If I can't be with you, I'd like to stay with them. I hate for us to be split apart."

"Oh, Daisy . . ." Her aunt sighed. "You're very brave."

"I'm trying to be."

"I've just met Lord Benton, and he's very kind. If I can't devise a path on my own, I'm positive he'll help me."

Daisy forced a smile, determined to never upset her aunt, but Lord Benton was a Prescott, and Daisy had been raised at Benton.

For years, she'd listened to the servants gossiping about her exalted relatives, and she had her father's conduct toward her as a measure of what would likely occur. She didn't expect her uncle to behave any better than her father had.

Aristocrats were busy. Earls were busy. Men were busy. She'd heard it constantly. They didn't have the time or energy to fuss over one little girl.

"I'm going to London tomorrow," Aunt Jo said.

"Why?"

"Your mother is there, and I have to talk to her about you. She's engaged to be married, and her wedding is in September. She's shopping for her trousseau."

Daisy's spirits sank. If her mother was about to marry, she wouldn't be concerned about a daughter she'd abandoned a decade earlier.

"Who is her betrothed?" she asked.

"Mr. Thompson Townsend."

"Is he persnickety? From his name, it sounds as if he might be."

Jo chuckled. "Yes, he's very persnickety. You've pegged his character exactly."

"Would you imagine my mother has told him about me?"

"I doubt it very much, and I won't lie to you. Her marriage is definitely an issue for us. It's why I have to talk to her."

"If it was your decision, I could live with you?"

"Yes. If it were up to me, I'd take you with me today."

It was the nicest thing anyone had ever said to her. "I wish I could go with you today too."

"In the meantime, I'll write to keep you posted as to where I am and what I'm doing. But only if you promise to write back."

"I will write back."

"And I'll visit you as soon as I can—if Miss Watson won't mind."

"She won't mind. She's the best person in the world—besides you."

Daisy couldn't stop herself. She threw herself against her aunt and hugged her as tightly as she could. Her aunt hugged her too, her grip so firm that Daisy could barely breathe.

"I'm glad you're my aunt," she whispered.

"So am I." Her aunt kissed the top of her head, then eased away. "After I've spoken to your mother, I'll let you know what she says."

"Will you always tell me the truth? Please? It's so frustrating to fret and not be sure. Even if she doesn't want me, don't fib about it. Just tell me straight out."

"I will. I swear." Her aunt stood, and she pulled Daisy to her feet too. "Now then, we should get back. We're running late, and Lord Benton is probably pacing."

"I hate that you have to leave."

"I hate it too, but I'll see you again before you can blink."

"I can't wait."

"WHAT A TANGLE."

"I agree."

Jo was in the carriage with Lord Benton and on her way to the manor. He'd tied his horse to the rear and had climbed in with her.

When she'd returned to the cottage, he'd been out front with Bobby and Jane. They'd all been introduced, and Bobby and Jane were as charming as Daisy. They'd been polite and interesting, but there had been an obvious current of dismay that permeated their every word.

It had to be terrifying to be so young, to have their fates being determined by adults who weren't necessarily concerned about them.

"What is your opinion of Bobby and Jane?" she asked Lord Benton.

"I liked them very much, but when I was chatting with them, all I could contemplate was my brother and his being such an irresponsible ass. What was he thinking, having so many affairs? And to sire so many illicit children! Is it any wonder my sister-in-law is outraged?"

"No, I can't blame her for being upset, and I'm impressed that she tolerated it for so long. If I'd been his wife, I never would have."

"I'm at a loss, Jo. About all of it—but mostly about my brother. We were hardly acquainted. I was sent off to boarding school when I was seven, and I rarely came home after that."

"So you had no idea?"

"No, and I'm stunned. When we were boys, my father treated him like a saint."

His anguish evident, he leaned into the window and gazed out at the passing trees.

"What now?" she inquired after a bit. "What should be done?"

"I haven't a clue." He glanced over at her. "I'm wretched. How about you?"

"I can hardly claim to be marvelous."

"I like Daisy. She seems very sweet."

"She was. She is."

"You have to talk to your sister. What will she say?"

"It will be so rude and shocking that I could never repeat any of it to you."

"It can't possibly be as bad as my having to confer with Barbara."

"She's your brother's widow? The Countess?"

"Yes, and she won't be any more rational than your sister. I can't decide which of us has the more difficult task."

"Perhaps it's a draw."

"Perhaps."

They were sitting side by side on the seat, and he reached over and laid a hand atop hers. It was a kind gesture of solace and support, and she should have pulled away, but she didn't. She was extremely overwhelmed, out of her element, and in desperate need of a friend.

"I'd better go to London tomorrow," she said. "I have to get this resolved. I shouldn't delay."

"I'm off to town myself. We'll go together."

"I probably shouldn't," she was compelled to protest.

"If you don't come with me, how will you travel? On the public coach again?"

"Well, yes."

He scoffed. "Don't be ridiculous. You know I won't permit it."

"You're not my father. Nor am I one of your sailors. You're not allowed to command me."

"We're both headed to town on the same day. It's silly to use separate vehicles."

"You've already been much too gracious, and I've imposed on you horridly. If you're not careful, I'll start to assume you're wonderful."

"I can be—when I feel like it." He peered over at her, his expression exasperated and firm. "We'll take my coach. Don't argue about it. You can't win."

"No, I don't suppose I can."

She blew out a heavy breath.

She was being lured into his life in ways she shouldn't be. She was like a fish on a hook, and he was reeling her in with great skill. She shouldn't let him, but she couldn't resist.

Despite her past, despite her history with Mr. Cartwright, she was quickly forgetting every painful lesson that had been imparted.

What would be the point of being trapped in a carriage with Lord Benton? What would be the point of flirting and growing more fond? He was so far above her in rank and station that he was like an angel in Heaven who'd swooped down to tempt her with what she couldn't have.

Warning bells were chiming, but just that moment—when his hand was still casually lying on hers—she couldn't think of a reason they shouldn't be cordial.

Apparently, she would travel to London with him, and if she could save the coach fare, wasn't that prudent? Or was she simply making excuses?

But what could it hurt? In the coming weeks, she might need to write him and seek his advice. She'd need to prevail on him on Daisy's behalf. There could only be a benefit to a closer connection. At least . . . that's what she was telling herself.

Where a handsome man was concerned, she always acted like a fool.

Once they arrived at the manor, she'd rush up to her room, and she'd stay there until it was time to depart. She would pass the nocturnal hours, reviewing every appalling fact she'd discovered about men and their motives. When morning dawned, she would be fortified with moral tenacity.

What could go wrong?

It was all for Daisy. Wasn't it? To ensure her safety and security? To protect her? For her niece, the one she'd just met but whom she liked so very, very much, it was clear she might do anything.

CHAPTER

——◆——

6

"You'll stay with me at Benton House, of course."

"I will not."

"You will."

Peyton glared at Jo, and his expression was very firm. He'd already figured out —in dealing with her—he could wear her down simply by being obstinate. She didn't like to quarrel, and she was exhaustingly nice, so it was easy to get his way.

They'd finally arrived in London, and he wasn't about to let her slink off. Once she left to be with her sister, he didn't imagine he'd ever see her again. There wasn't any reason too, and he wouldn't begin inventing reasons.

But it would be lovely to spend one last evening with her. What could it hurt?

They were at his town house, and the afternoon had waned. It was too late for her to traipse across the city in search of her sister. Nor was he keen on having her do that.

"What is your plan, Jo?" he asked her.

"I'll find Maud and talk to her."

"She's at the Claremont Hotel?"

"Yes."

"What if you quarrel? I don't imagine the rest of the night would be too pleasant."

"No, probably not."

"You'd be trapped with her. Or what if she's not there and they won't allow you into her room? London is incredibly expensive. Have you any money to purchase your own lodging?"

"You know I haven't, but I'll figure it out."

"No. You'll remain here. We'll have a quiet supper, and you can visit her in the morning. I'm afraid I have to insist."

They were in the front foyer, and the butler—Mr. Newman—was hovering off to the side. Newman was forty or so, short, slender, and dapper, with graying hair, a trimmed mustache, and a placid demeanor. Peyton motioned to him.

"Take her bag upstairs, Newman."

"Very good, my lord." Newman gestured to a footman, and the boy grabbed her portmanteau and started off.

She scowled and stepped nearer, and their proximity was thrilling. The air seemed charged with energy, as if sparks were shooting between them. He'd never felt anything like it.

"Could I speak with you for a minute?" she murmured. "Alone?"

"Certainly."

He escorted her into the receiving parlor, and Newman followed, no doubt eager to eavesdrop so he could repeat every word down in the kitchen.

"Pour me a brandy, Newman," Peyton said. "How about you, Jo? Would you like a glass of wine?"

"No, thank you."

"Just the brandy, Newman, then leave us."

Newman complied and after he'd disappeared, she whispered, "What are you doing?"

"I'm merely being a gracious host."

"Really?" Her skepticism could have knocked him over.

"Yes, really. What other reason could there be?"

"What reason indeed?"

"You're a young lady who's without a chaperone, and I'm trying to be gallant and offer you assistance."

"*You* are trying to be gallant?"

"It's not entirely outside the realm of possibilities."

She scoffed with disgust. "You're bullying me again, and I wish you'd stop."

"I like bullying you. When you're angry, your eyes flash with temper. You become even prettier than normal."

"Desist!" she scolded. "I won't have you flirting."

"I can't help it."

"You're behaving so strangely, and it's annoying."

"How am I acting strangely?"

"What exactly are you hoping to accomplish with me? Explain yourself."

"I told you, Jo. It will be dark soon, so it's ridiculous for you to wander off. We'll have supper, and you'll have a good night's sleep. Then you can set out in the morning. You'll be more relaxed and in a better condition to cope with her."

She studied him, her shrewd assessment digging deep, and he had to work hard not to fidget.

"Oh, I understand now," she ultimately said. "You're bored and lonely, and you can't bear the prospect of being by yourself in this drafty mansion. I get it. You need me to keep you company."

He waved away her astute insight. "If that were true, I'm much too manly to ever admit it."

"You don't have to admit it. I can practically read your mind, so you can't hide your emotions from me."

"Am I that transparent? What a horrifying notion."

"Why do I know so much about you? There's not a single secret I can't unravel."

"I have no idea why you'd believe that."

He could guess though. It was all wrapped up in their physical attraction.

It burned hot as the sun. She was a maiden though, so she wouldn't note the odd forces pulling them together. He wasn't about to enlighten her either.

"Our peculiar connection," she said, "makes me think I like you more than I should."

He chuckled. "You should like me."

"No, I shouldn't."

"Look," he grumbled, "I've simply enjoyed our acquaintance, and I don't want it to end quite yet. Is that so terrible? Let me aid you a bit more. I don't have many chances to be generous."

"You can always be generous. You don't have to wait for special chances."

"Stay, Jo. Just for the night. It's foolish not to."

He could almost see the wheels spinning in her head as she devised excuses to refuse. Her every thought was visible to him, so evidently, he could read her mind too. They were that attuned.

He whipped away and walked to the window. He drew back the drape and pointed outside. "Dusk has fallen, Miss Bates. Are you really prepared to meander around London?"

Her shoulders slumped. "All right, you win."

"Why fight me? It's futile."

"Once I'm gone for good, and you no longer have me to torment, how will you entertain yourself?"

"I'll probably start picking on the footmen."

"Those poor boys," she muttered.

He laughed, and to his stunned surprise, he nearly leaned down and kissed her. It seemed so natural that he would, and he only stopped himself at the last second.

"Settle yourself in your bedchamber," he said, "then meet me down here in an hour."

"To do what?"

"To eat, you silly goose. We'll use the small dining room. Not the formal one. If we were in there, our voices would echo off the ceiling."

"Whatever you choose is fine with me."

"I'll have a dozen footmen standing guard, so your virtue is safe."

She snorted. "I don't require a dozen. One or two will suffice."

She had a satchel of clothes, packed by her housekeeper, and he wondered if she had a gown she could wear to the theater. If so, he'd escort her out on the town to show her off. On observing her, every other man would be green with envy.

Yet he doubted she had a suitable outfit, and Evan's sister, Amelia, regularly attended the theater. With Peyton having displayed such an interest in her, her expectations had been raised—Evan's too—so it wasn't wise to strut about in public with a beautiful girl on his arm.

Even if he didn't bump into Evan or Amelia, gossip would filter back to them.

He could be a vain ass, but he wouldn't flaunt his worst tendencies in front of his best friend and his best friend's sister.

"I'll see you in an hour," he said.

"I will be very prompt."

"Is there anything particular you'd like to have for supper? Or anything you detest and I should instruct my cook to avoid?"

"I like everything."

She sauntered out, and he couldn't take his eyes off her.

Briefly, he tried to figure out his purpose, but there was no need to figure it out. He was smitten as a green boy, and the sooner she left the better. But first, he'd have this final night with her. He'd have her all to himself for an entire meal. Afterward, if he was lucky, perhaps he could convince her to sit and chat by the fire.

It was a mundane activity he'd rarely enjoyed in his life. For ludicrous and very sentimental reasons, he wanted to enjoy it with her. He would thoroughly immerse himself in her delightful presence, and when she departed in the morning, he'd have had his fill of her. Wouldn't he have?

He couldn't bear to answer that question, so he poured himself another brandy. Maybe if he had several glasses before she came down, he would quit behaving like such an idiot.

"WILL THIS ENCOUNTER BE awkward?"

"Why would it be awkward? We're never awkward together. Don't be ridiculous."

Jo stared caustically at Lord Benton, and he casually stared back. As she'd requested, there were two footmen by the sideboard, so it wasn't as if she was a maiden about to surrender her innocence by sneaking off with a cad.

Still though, she was confused as to her motives. He'd pressured her, and she'd let him. It wasn't that she was a meek or submissive person. She could be adamant when obstinacy was necessary.

It was just that he was much more determined than she was, and his demands made perfect sense. The trip in his carriage had saved her money. The invitation to spend the night had saved her even more. And he'd been absolutely correct that it was dangerous to traipse off across London in the dark.

Why bicker over any of it?

She recognized what was happening though. He'd bossed her so she'd tarry a bit longer. For all his pomp and wealth, he was very lonely. She was lonely too. How could it hurt to flirt for one evening?

She'd told herself to keep her distance, but why should she? She would build a store of memories, and when she was back in the country by herself, she'd fondly recollect his every enticing word.

"I had them prepare a buffet," he said. "I thought we could serve ourselves."

"That's fine."

She was seated at the table, and he jumped up and went over to where the food was waiting for them in covered pans. He snooped under the lids.

"They've delivered enough to feed an army," he said.

"It smells delicious."

"There's sliced beef and ham, vegetables, bread, and it appears there's some sort of potato pie, as well as puddings and a soup. What is your pleasure?"

"Dish up a plate for me. I'll be happy with what you select."

"Ooh, I like you when you're so docile. We didn't have to argue about a single item."

"Don't get used to it."

"I won't."

He grinned, sending a swarm of butterflies winging through her tummy, and she was so flustered she had to glance away.

He filled two plates, one for her and one for him. The footmen scurried about, pouring wine and making them more comfortable.

"It looks wonderful." She peered over at a footman. "When you go down to the kitchen, tell the cook it's all marvelous, and we're delighted."

"I will, Miss Bates."

Lord Benton shooed them out, and suddenly, she was sequestered with him. She nearly rushed to the door and called them back, but it would have been juvenile conduct that would have provided the servants with a week's worth of gossip.

Instead, she picked up her fork and was about to begin when she realized Lord Benton was studying her intently.

"What?" she asked. "Why are you staring?"

"You're very gracious, aren't you? And very kind?"

At hearing his flattering remark, she blushed furiously. "I try to be."

"It never crosses my mind to thank the cook."

"It should."

"Yes, I suppose you're right. My father claimed the servants were doing what they were paid to do, so why compliment them?"

"That's a rather harsh position. Servants are human beings—in case you hadn't noticed."

"I've noticed. I'm not a complete dunce."

"Everyone likes a little praise occasionally."

"I'll remember that."

He dug into his food with great relish, and she struggled to ignore him and enjoy her own food, but the privacy of their situation had her a tad unnerved.

When she'd been engaged to Mr. Cartwright, she'd often socialized with him, but Maud had always been present, and he'd been a perfect gentleman. He'd never coaxed her into mischief, had never led her into a dark corner.

He had managed to kiss her a few times when Maud stepped out of the room, but his advances had been quick and cordial with no sense of illicit plotting. So she was constantly startled by Lord Benton, by the way he held his fork, by the way he tipped his wine glass, by the way he cut into a slice of beef.

"You're not eating," he said.

"I find all of this to be extremely strange."

"Why?"

"I'm never alone with a man like this."

"I'm sure you'll survive. Would you like me to summon a housemaid? She could stand behind your chair and play the part of the glowering nanny."

"No, I don't need a nanny."

"I'll behave. I swear." He pointed to her plate. "Now eat. If you just sit there while I'm gobbling every morsel in sight, I'll feel like a glutton."

She chuckled, then dug in too. He made their interactions seem especially normal. Had he always been so imperturbable or was it a trick he'd learned in the navy? She imagined he was adept at getting his sailors to acclimate and pitch in.

"May I ask you a question?" she inquired.

"Yes. I won't promise to answer, but you can ask."

"Why didn't you spend much time at Benton when you were a child?"

"My father didn't like me."

"I'm sorry to hear that. Were you a scalawag? Is that why? Were you incorrigible?"

He scowled. "I was only seven when I was sent to school. I wasn't old enough to be a troublemaker yet."

"You were so young! Your mother didn't mind?"

"My father was an ogre. He demanded I go, and she would never have stood up to him."

"Was it hard to be away from home at such an early age?"

"It was initially. My father refused to allow me to visit on holidays."

"Lord Benton! Your story is stirring an enormous wave of pity."

"Is it? I'll keep on then. Maybe you'll like me more because of it."

"I like you fine now, but please continue with your history."

"In the beginning, I was very homesick."

"Of course you were. You were seven!"

"Yes, but I was befriended by my chum, Evan Boyle. He's still with me to this day—he's First Officer on my ship—and I had a teacher who was kind. I got by."

"No wonder you're so lonely. You never had anyone to care about you."

"I'm much too masculine to be lonely."

"If you say so," she muttered. "How did you end up in the navy? Did you always want to be a sailor?"

"My boarding school was a military academy. In the summers, we were out on the water and taught to navigate."

"It must have been fun for you."

"Yes, it was very fun. It was a terrific life for a boy."

"So you joined the navy when you graduated. You didn't attend university?"

"No, I enlisted right away."

"Since then, you've had one adventure after the next."

"It's rarely been boring, I admit it."

"Then your brother died, and you became the earl."

"As I believe I've mentioned, it's a fact that I'm certain has my father rolling in his grave."

She tsked with exasperation. "You are horrid. You shouldn't speak ill of the dead. Were you never informed?"

"No. I was reared by a bunch of grizzled old soldiers. We didn't focus much on manners or decorum."

"You liar. You know how to act like a gentleman."

"I can—when I'm in the mood."

"With you having inherited, will you remain in the navy? Or will you resign and return to Benton to take charge?"

"I haven't decided. It's a conundrum that vexes me."

"Were you aware that the servants are betting over it?"

"I should find out what odds they're offering. Perhaps I can win a few pounds."

"You will *not* siphon money from your staff, Lord Benton. It wouldn't be fair."

"You ride such a moral high horse."

"Someone should."

"I like it when it's you. It saves me the bother."

"You haven't answered my question," she said. "Will you remain in the navy?"

"I constantly debate, but I can't reach a conclusion. If I trudge to Benton, I'll have to figure out what to do with my sister-in-law and her family. Benton is their home, but I can't bear the notion of living there with them. Yet I'd feel too guilty to kick them out."

"Ah . . . you have a conscience after all."

"Yes, I have a conscience. I just don't let it nag at me very often."

He stood and filled their plates again. He refilled their wine too, and it occurred to her that it was very delicious and she'd already had two glasses. She had to slow down and be careful, but when he was being so interesting and chatty, she had no desire to slow down.

"What about you?" he asked. "Tell me your entire life's story."

"My past is so dull that you'd fall asleep in the middle of it."

"I doubt it. I deem you to be quite fascinating."

"I have no idea why you would."

"Honestly, Jo Bates, you are incredibly captivating. Hasn't any man ever told you so? Don't claim I'm the first fellow to notice. I'll never believe you."

She was always unnerved when a handsome man used words like *fascinating* and *captivating*. Mr. Cartwright had mesmerized her with flowery compliments, but she was wiser now. A bit of flattery wouldn't kill her, and she was too smart to take it seriously.

"I had a beau once," she said.

"What happened to him?"

She calmly and blithely replied, "He changed his mind."

"Well, he's an idiot. I officially declare it."

"I agree with you, and it was his loss."

"Absolutely."

He lifted his glass, and she lifted hers, and they toasted his pronouncement.

For a moment, she worried he might press her for details, but he didn't. He forged on to other topics.

"Who was your father?" he asked.

"A gentleman farmer."

"Wealthy though, wasn't he? The evidence is clear from how you dress and carry yourself."

"I suppose he was rich, but he died deeply in debt. We had to sell our property and move to a small house that my sister inherited from her grandmother. We were lucky to have it."

He frowned. "I hate to hear tales of woe like that."

"It was a grueling experience."

"How old were you when he passed away?"

"Thirteen."

"And your mother?"

"Gone too—when I was a baby."

"What's your sister's name? Maud?"

"Yes."

"Any other siblings?"

"No."

"But she's difficult."

"Did I tell you that?"

"Yes—or maybe I gleaned it from some of your comments."

"I should be more circumspect."

"Don't you dare," he said. "I've commanded you to spill all, remember? You can't hold back any information."

"You've learned about my deceased father and my grouchy sister and how we're living in reduced conditions. That's the sum total of my existence."

"Who was your mother? Who was her family?"

"I hope you won't faint, but my mother was Maud's nanny."

He blanched, then laughed. "My goodness, how shocking."

"Yes, it was very shocking."

"Were the neighbors scandalized?"

"Definitely. She was viewed as a seductive, up-jumped tart, and it's the main reason my sister and I don't get along. Her mother was very grand, and my mother wasn't, and she never lets me forget it."

"Your mother must have been extremely beautiful to have enticed your father."

"People insisted she'd cast a magic spell on him. Either that or my father had lost his mind."

"Was she beautiful? Am I correct?"

"Yes, she was."

"Your auburn hair and blue eyes"—he pointed to them—"they came from her?"

"Yes."

"I understand why your father couldn't resist."

She loathed being the focus of attention and having to talk about her family. She never liked having to justify her mother's marriage.

The simple fact was that a rich man had grown besotted with her, and she'd latched on to the security he'd offered to provide. What woman wouldn't have latched on?

Jo stood and dished them each a piece of apple pie. They finished their desserts, then declared themselves stuffed. She'd intended to thank him and escape to her bedchamber, but before she could, he was leading her to a parlor down the hall. It was small and cozy, and a cheery fire burned in the fireplace. There were two chairs positioned in front of it.

"Shall we sit?" he suggested.

"Haven't you had enough of me?"

"Not yet."

She sighed. "I probably shouldn't, Lord Benton."

"Don't be a nuisance, and don't aggravate me. Sit down."

"All right, all right," she groused.

She plopped down, as he puttered about, pouring himself a brandy and another glass of wine for her. Then he settled into the other chair, and they stared at the flames. A companionable silence blossomed. It was so effortless to be with him. It was pleasant and addicting.

"What is your plan for Daisy, Bobby, and Jane?" she asked after a bit. "Have you reached any decisions?"

"I have to have a serious conversation with Richard and Barbara, but I'm so keen to avoid a fight with them. I'll likely procrastinate as long as possible."

"Mr. Slater wants them gone by July fifteenth."

"I can certainly counter that edict, and there's no rush, is there? The three of them have lived at Benton for most of a decade. If we require a few more weeks or months to make arrangements, there's no harm done."

"I don't trust Mr. Slater though. Daisy told me he's awful to their governess, Miss Watson. I guess he yells at her, and the children hear him."

"I'll put a stop to that." He scowled over at her. "What is your opinion? If their maternal relatives could take them away from Benton, wouldn't that be better? Their cottage—conveniently located in the middle of nowhere—seemed rather lonely to me. In the Benton area, they'll always be notorious as Neville's by-blows. What if they could reside where their ancestry wasn't a ball and chain?"

"It depends on the situation the maternal kin can supply. I'd hate to have their circumstances deteriorate."

"No, I wouldn't allow that."

"Would you consider letting them stay on at Benton? What if no one can devise an alternative? What then?"

"The problem is that I understand Barbara's position." The comment wasn't really an answer. "Their presence has been incredibly galling to her, so I need to ponder her view and contend with it."

"Of course you should."

He wasn't inclined to discuss it further, and he grabbed a book off a shelf. He handed it to her. "Would you read some poetry to me?"

"Poetry? That sounds positively domestic, Lord Benton."

"Well, I'm feeling quite domestic, and just for tonight, would you call me Peyton?"

She gazed at him, thinking how much she liked him, how much she was enjoying herself. It was insane to dig a deeper hole for herself, but why not? "How about if we agree on Commander Prescott for now?"

"I'll take what I can get from you."

They frittered away the next two hours chatting and reading to each other. It was all very dear, very special. She caught herself wondering why they had to part in the morning, and the fact that she would engage in such a flight of fancy was alarming.

Peyton Prescott was from a different world and on a trajectory that would propel him to the highest circles in the land. She had no place in that world, and she was being ridiculous.

"I should go up," she finally said.

"Must you?"

"I have a big day tomorrow, and I should sleep as much as I can."

"Will you and your sister quarrel?"

"I'm certain of it."

"I'm sorry for how my family's issues have impacted you."

"My family is involved in it too, and my sister and I always have discord. My relationship with her has never been easy."

He shifted in his seat to study her, and his fond expression was frightening. She could have tarried forever, basking in his glow.

"I'm glad we spent this evening together," he said.

"So am I."

"You were so afraid it would be horrid, but admit it. It was very fun."

"Yes, it was."

"It saddens me to suppose our connection will be brief," he told her. "Would you like to keep in touch? Could we correspond? What would you think of that?"

She chuckled at the absurdity of the notion. "Are you actually the type of man who would sit down and write a letter?"

"Not usually, but for you, I might make an exception."

Her imagination scrolled through a dozen thrilling scenarios where they were friends, where they penned letters and shared confidences and sent each other little gifts. It was such an exciting prospect, but she simply couldn't participate.

If they had any enduring contact, she would attach too much meaning to it. She would mope and pine away and fall in love. She was a romantic ninny, and she would never tamp down her expectation that he was about to arrive and declare himself. She'd drive herself mad with unreciprocated anticipation.

"We shouldn't correspond," she said.

"Are you sure?"

"Yes, I'm sure. It's not a good idea."

"I disagree. I never have bad ideas."

She laughed. "Never?"

"No, and I would always be interested to hear how you're getting on."

"There are never any changes in my life, so you wouldn't need a letter to find that out."

She realized he was in no hurry, and if she didn't terminate the encounter, she might never escape. She stood, so he had to stand too. A thousand unvoiced remarks swirled between them.

"I won't say goodbye tonight," he said.

"No, it's not goodbye. Not quite yet."

"We'll have breakfast."

"I'd like that."

"How about at nine o'clock?"

"Nine will be perfect."

They hovered, neither able to walk out. Then he dipped down and kissed her. She'd like to insist she was surprised, but that would be a lie.

After all, she wasn't a complete innocent. She'd previously been betrothed, and she recognized budding desire in a male.

It was a sweet embrace, just a quick brush of his lips to her own. As he pulled away, she smiled and said, "You shouldn't have done that."

"I couldn't resist."

She tried to make light of the situation. "Are you claiming I'm irresistible?"

"Definitely, and I want to do it again."

He bent down and captured her lips once more, but the second embrace was nothing like the first. His arm slid around her waist so their torsos were pressed tight all the way down. Her breasts were crushed to his chest, their feet and thighs tangled together.

He kissed her deeply, passionately. He kissed her as if she were the last woman on Earth and he were the last man and they were the last two people who would ever kiss. Ever. His tongue was in her mouth, his hands in her hair. His busy fingers roamed over her shoulders and back, learning her shape.

It was delightful and dangerous and very, very wicked. She joined in with a great deal of relish, and while she comprehended that she shouldn't have, she couldn't seem to force herself to care.

She couldn't guess how long they continued, but it was long enough that the fire dwindled and the temperature grew cold. Gradually, they drew apart. She peered up at him, vowing to never forget how grand he looked at that moment.

"Come to my room," he fervently requested. "Say yes."

He overwhelmed her so thoroughly that she nearly consented before she somehow mustered the fortitude to decline. "I never could. I can't believe you asked."

"I hate for the evening to end like this. Come with me."

"No," she firmly responded. "Never."

"It would be marvelous."

"In some other universe perhaps, but not in this one." She stepped away, instantly regretting the loss of his bodily heat. "Goodnight. I'll see you in the morning."

He reached for her, and she jumped back. If he touched her again, she might not be so adamant in her refusal. She whirled away and ran for the stairs.

He murmured her name—desperately, ardently—begging her to stop, but she ignored him and kept on.

CHAPTER

——•◆•——

7

Jo was across the street from the Claremont Hotel. It was where Maud always stayed when she came to town, but Jo had never stayed with her. Maud would never have thought to bring her along.

Maud had a small trust fund from her grandmother, so she had a bit of money. She spent it on herself and never shared any of it with Jo. Jo tried not to be jealous—her sister was who she was—but on occasion, it was difficult to accept their disparate situations.

The hotel was close to Maud's favorite dressmaker, and she was in a clothing frenzy, desperate to have her trousseau completed before the wedding. She'd made a deposit in order to get the seamstresses sewing, but the remainder of her bill would be paid after the ceremony was over and her dowry had been released to Mr. Townsend.

At least Maud was hoping Mr. Townsend would pay the bill. Jo doubted Maud had ever discussed it with him, just as she wondered if any of the shopkeepers realized Maud's ploy. She was charging to her account like an aristocrat.

Jo fretted about problems Maud never paused to consider. They had no father to guide them in their fiscal decisions which had proved disastrous in their dealings with Mr. Cartwright. She didn't like Maud's betrothed, Mr. Townsend, but she had no one with whom to share her qualms. Not Maud, that was for sure.

By Mr. Townsend's meager standard, Maud was a great heiress. He was a fifth son with no prospects, and his oldest brother, Charles, was Maud's lawyer. Charles had introduced them and had pushed the match.

Maud—with her house in the country, trust fund, dowry, and elevated bloodline—was actually quite a catch. That is if a person ignored her temper and rages.

Jo might have felt sorry for Mr. Townsend and his not being apprised of Maud's true nature, but he was a dodgy character. He and Maud deserved each other.

There was a break in the traffic, and to her surprise, he emerged from the hotel where he'd probably been visiting Maud. With his trim physique and dapper suit, he looked successful and fashionable, but he was neither, and Jo was in no mood to chat with him.

In light of the marvelous, dangerous evening she'd passed with Lord Benton, she was in a conflicted state, her emotions a tad pummeled.

They were to have had breakfast together, but she'd risen early, packed her bag, and tiptoed out without a word. Lest he worry, she'd penned a thank you note and had placed it on her bed. The tone had been cordial, but cool, providing no hint of her overwhelmed condition.

She was absurdly attached to him, but their stunning attraction couldn't lead anywhere. She kept recollecting how he'd begged her to sneak up to his room, and the memory left her weak in the knees.

When her marriage to Mr. Cartwright had approached, she'd had a blunt talk about marital obligation with their widowed cook. The woman had explained what it entailed, and while Jo didn't grasp all the particulars, she had a fairly good understanding of what was expected.

If she'd accompanied Lord Benton to his bedchamber, was that the sort of behavior he'd intended? Would they have removed their clothes and climbed under the blankets to touch each other in intimate ways?

Her imagination was on fire, her patience exhausted, her disposition weary, and she couldn't bear to spar with Thompson Townsend.

She shifted out of sight, the crowd milling around her so she was shielded from view, but the woman next to her suddenly shouted, "Thompson! It's me!"

She was brash and flashy, as if she might be an actress or singer. Her blond hair was intricately curled, and she was wearing a bright red gown that was cut very low in the front. An elaborate bonnet was perched on her head, and exotic feathers trailed behind.

He recognized her voice, and he smiled and waved, then hurried across the street, darting past carriages and proceeding directly toward the woman. He rushed up to her and kissed her on the mouth—right out in the open where anyone could observe them.

"Was she there?" the woman asked him.

"Yes. We had breakfast, and I gave her a little gift, so I've done my duty for the day."

"Thank the Lord."

"Let's get going."

They turned, arm in arm, and there was no chance to avoid them. In two quick steps, they nearly ran into her.

Mr. Townsend blanched, and it was obvious he was engaged in mischief. His cheeks flushed with embarrassment, but he swiftly regrouped.

"Josephine! Why are you in London?" he asked. "I'm ... ah ... astonished to see you here."

"I had to speak with my sister. There was an issue at home."

"Nothing horrid I hope."

"No. I just wasn't sure how she'd want me to handle it."

She glared at him, and when he awkwardly pretended not to notice, his companion blustered forward.

"I am Miss Smith. Miss Prudence Smith. Everyone calls me Pru."

"Hello, Miss Smith," Jo murmured.

"I'm an old ... *friend* of Mr. Townsend's." Jo didn't reply. She simply continued to glare at him, and Miss Smith said to Jo, "And you are ... ?"

Her sharp question jolted Mr. Townsend out of his stupor. "Pru, this is

Maud's sister, Josephine. Jo Bates. I've told you about her."

"Yes, you have." Miss Smith scathingly assessed Jo. "She's quite a bit prettier than you described her to be."

"Yes, she's always been pretty." Mr. Townsend was practically stammering. "Jo? This is Miss Smith."

"I heard her, Mr. Townsend," Jo said.

"Well, good." He tipped his hat to Jo. "Enjoy your trip to London."

"I will."

"If we could . . . ah . . . keep this encounter between you and me, I'd be ever so grateful."

"Don't worry, Mr. Townsend, I would never be brave enough to tell Maud about any of your acquaintances."

He hesitated, as if he'd defend his conduct, but he thought better of it. He and Miss Smith sauntered off, and Jo exhaled a heavy breath. Clearly, Miss Smith was much more than a friend, and if Mr. Townsend had illicit tendencies, Jo wouldn't be surprised. She'd never liked him, and she liked him even less now.

Was Miss Smith his mistress? Would he support her with Maud's dowry? Was that his plan?

Her mind raced as she tried to determine what her response should be. Should she mention the incident to Maud? Or should she stay out of it? Husbands usually had secrets from their wives. Why should Maud's marriage be any different?

With Jo having so recently learned about Neville Prescott's many peccadilloes, she was extremely disheartened. Were there any honorable men left in the world?

On the spur of the moment, she couldn't decide the best course. She wasn't a liar, and if she remained silent, she would be committing a lie by omission. If Jo were about to be a bride, would she be eager to hear this sort of damning information?

How about Maud? Would she believe a story like this? Probably not, so what was the point of veracity?

Besides, Daisy had to be the main topic of conversation. Mr. Townsend and his possible amour were immaterial to Jo's current task.

She entered the hotel and announced herself at the front desk. Shortly, she was escorted to her sister's room. The building was very grand, and the rental rates very high, so Maud was spending a fortune she didn't have, but appearances mattered to her sister.

Her suite was as grand as the foyer, like a small apartment, with posh furnishings and expensive rugs and drapes. There was a desk by the window, and Maud was seated at it and writing a letter.

"Jo! You're the very last person I expected to see in London," her sister said after the servant had departed.

"I had to talk to you."

"I'll be home in a few days. It couldn't wait until then?"

"No."

"For pity's sake. You're always in such a dither."

"Am I? It doesn't seem that way to me. I generally picture myself as being very calm."

"Trust me, you constantly act as if the sky is about to fall."

"It has fallen on us occasionally, Maud. Perhaps I'm wise to fret. Perhaps you should fret a tad more."

It was mid-morning, and her sister was up and dressed. There were food remnants on a table by the hearth. Jo had fled Benton House without eating, and she was starving. She walked over and sat down. There was still tea in the pot and muffins in a basket. She helped herself as Maud went into the bed-chamber to primp in the mirror.

"As I arrived," Jo called through the door, "I bumped into Mr. Townsend."

"Yes, I asked him to come by. I was hoping we could visit his tailor to check on his wedding suit, but he was busy."

Jo nearly choked on her muffin. "Was he?"

"He's an important man," Maud testily said. "He can't waste time on frivolous activities."

"I'm sure not. He was with a Miss Prudence Smith." There was a lengthy pause, and Jo added, "Have you been introduced to her?"

"No. Why would I have? He's very popular here in town, and he has many friends."

"I didn't like her. She seemed a bit vulgar to me."

"Your opinion about his companions is irrelevant."

That was as far as Jo dared to go with any disclosures about Mr. Townsend. Maud could assess the remark however she wished.

Jo went into the bedchamber too, and she balanced her hips on the edge of the mattress. Maud ignored her and sifted in her jewelry box, slipping a bracelet on her wrist, slipping it off, trying on another.

Jo studied her, struggling to discern hints of Daisy, but Maud's features were hard and brittle while Daisy's were sweet and happy. It was difficult to find any resemblance.

"What is it?" Maud eventually asked. "What's brought you all this way? If you'd drag yourself to the city, it must be hideous."

She spun on her stool so she was facing Jo, and Jo couldn't bear to begin. For the moment, none of the scandal was real, but the minute the words were voiced aloud, there could be no taking them back, and their lives would never be the same.

"You received a letter the other day," she said. "You'd told me to deal with all the correspondence, so I opened it without wondering if I should."

"And . . . ?"

"It was from Mr. Slater at Benton Manor."

Panic flashed in Maud's eyes, but it was hastily concealed. She gazed at Jo dispassionately, her demeanor bored.

"Should I know who he is?" Maud asked.

"Don't feign confusion, Maud. I traveled to Benton to speak with him, so I've learned all the gory details. You don't have a secret from me anymore."

"You traveled to Benton? You little mouse. I can't believe you mustered the courage."

Jo sighed, recognizing the discussion would be just as horrid as she'd imagined. "Would you like me to tell you why he contacted you?"

"Since I have no idea who he is, I can categorically state that I don't care."

"I met Daisy."

"Who is Daisy?" Maud had the temerity to inquire.

"Maud! Stop it!"

"Stop what?"

They engaged in a staring match, and while Maud was bigger and older and in charge of their money, Jo always held the moral high ground in their quarrels. She possessed a decency and integrity that Maud could never equal.

Maud's cheeks flushed, and she yanked off her bracelet and threw it on the dressing table. "Fine. You met Daisy. I won't pretend to be unaware of who she is."

"Thank you."

"What did Slater want?"

"Neville Prescott has died."

"The bastard's finally dead?" Maud crudely spat, "Good riddance."

Jo was desperate to pry out the particulars of Maud's affair with Neville. Did he force himself on her? Or had she been willingly seduced? Had she naively expected he'd marry her afterward? Had she hoped she'd become his countess—without her realizing he already had a countess in place?

But Jo doubted her sister would freely provide any information.

Instead, she said, "His death has altered things for the Prescott family—and for you."

"What things?"

"Daisy's shelter at Benton is ending. With Neville Prescott no longer present to protect her, his widow is demanding she leave."

"Why bother me with this?"

"Mr. Slater is working to find a new home for her. He's asked if we could bring her to live with us at Telford."

"No!" Maud vehemently huffed. "Absolutely not. I won't have it."

"If we won't take her, he'll send her to an orphanage."

"Why would that concern me?"

"Maud! Shame on you. I won't listen to that kind of cruel comment."

"Jo, this really isn't any of your business. It's a Prescott problem, and I suggest you butt out."

"Not my business! She's my only niece—unless there are others you've been hiding from me too."

"Others! What a ghastly remark. How dare you impugn me!"

"If you intend to act in a ghastly manner, then ghastly remarks are required."

"I won't be scolded by you," Maud fumed.

"Yes, you will. I had no idea Daisy existed. Now that I've learned about her, can you actually suppose I'll permit you to abandon her?"

"It's not up to you."

"She's not a stray kitten you can toss by the side of the road. For years, you've avoided your responsibility to her, but your neglect has caught up with you. She's your daughter!"

"No, she's not. Not by any standard that matters."

"How can you say that?"

"Father let the Prescotts have her, and they promised to support her forever. They swore they would. We have a written agreement!"

"Well, it appears they will decline to honor it."

"We'd planned to put her out for adoption, and they insisted we shouldn't, so we delivered her to them instead. It was *their* choice. At this late date, they have an incredible amount of gall to renege."

"Their situation has changed."

"Only because Neville's dear widow is complaining. Why would I care about that?"

Maud uttered the words *dear widow* with significant venom, and her tone piqued Jo's curiosity. Evidently, her suspicions were correct: Maud had expected to be Countess of Benton. Could it be one of the reasons she was so bitter?

"Aren't you worried about Daisy at all?" Jo asked.

"No."

"If she winds up in an orphanage, you'll feel no guilt?"

"Maybe a bit. Those facilities are terrible. I wouldn't wish one on any child."

"She's your own flesh and blood!"

Maud scowled. "You're very confused, Jo."

"*I* am confused? Over what fact?"

"A decade ago, when I was little more than a girl, I had a baby I didn't want and couldn't raise. I gave her to her father's family, and I went on with my life."

"I realize that."

"I'm about to marry, Josephine!"

"I understand that you are."

"What would Mr. Townsend think if I suddenly showed up with a bastard daughter?"

"Perhaps you and Mr. Townsend need to have a long, frank talk."

"I'd rather pluck my eyes out than tell him about her."

"I can tell him for you," Jo brashly stated. "I don't mind."

Maud blanched with alarm. "You'll tell him over my dead body."

"How will you keep this secret from him? He'll be your husband. What if he finds out about it and discovers you tricked him? What then?"

"Mr. Townsend will never find out, and if he does, I'll know who tattled. I'd kill you for it, Jo. I truly would. You shouldn't push me on this."

Jo scoffed with exasperation. "Don't be melodramatic, and don't threaten me. You're being ridiculous."

"I'm not being ridiculous. Just betray me, and see what happens."

"I don't plan to *betray* you. We have to assist her. How can I persuade you that it's our duty?"

"It's not our duty," Maud infuriatingly replied. "She's a stranger to us."

"Stop saying that." Jo threw up her hands. "She's your daughter and my niece. I can't desert her. I won't. You can't force me to."

"Can't I? Who supports you, Jo? Who feeds you, clothes you, and shelters you? Who is letting you remain with me after I'm wed? It's *me*, remember? It's your sister, Maud Bates, who's about to be Mrs. Thompson Townsend. You will not wreck this for me!"

It was the cudgel that allowed Maud to lord herself over Jo. The house they resided in belonged to Maud. All their money belonged to Maud. Their father hadn't left a farthing to Jo, thanks to Maud's scheming when he'd suffered through his last illness.

Jo had been a girl, and Maud had convinced him to name her as Jo's guardian. She'd insisted she would watch over Jo, and their father—with his deteriorating mental acuity—had believed her.

Jo's dowry had been funded when she was first born, but no other financial arrangements had been instituted after that. When her father died, none of their assets had been put into a trust for her, so nothing had been protected from creditors.

If was another sin to lay at Maud's feet. If money had been stashed away in a trust, they'd still have all of it. As with Jo's dowry, Maud had implemented numerous fiscal decisions that were reckless and foolish, and because of it, Jo was at her sister's mercy.

She had to live by Maud's rules or she had to depart. The trouble was that she'd never had anywhere to go.

Jo prayed for patience. "I'm not trying to *wreck* your marriage, Maud."

"It certainly sounds like it. I'd be mad to welcome that child when I'm about to have a new husband."

"I'm just anxious to aid her. Is that too much to ask?"

"Yes, Jo, it's too much."

Jo hadn't made an inch of headway, but how could she have imagined a different ending? Still though, she couldn't back down. Daisy's future hung in the balance.

"We could pretend she's one of my mother's relatives," Jo said.

"No."

"We could claim she's a distant cousin of mine who was orphaned."

"No!" Maud repeated more firmly. "I would never risk it."

"We can't ignore her."

"Yes, we can. Haven't you been listening? I gave her away, and it was the right option for me. I won't reconsider."

"What would you suggest then? If she perishes from lung fever in an orphanage, are you fine with that conclusion?"

"If she succumbed to a fatal malady, it would be a tragedy, but how could I prevent it?"

"Let me bring her home, Maud. Please!"

"You can bring her anywhere you like, Jo. You can play the role of savior and work a miracle. As soon as you walk out of this room, you can race to Benton and fetch her. Just don't show up on my stoop, hoping for sanctuary. I won't provide it."

Jo's spirits flagged. They glared at each other, and Jo nearly called Maud's bluff. What if she conveyed Daisy to Telford despite Maud's demand that she not? Would Maud really bar the door? Would she kick them out on the road? Could she behave that despicably to her only daughter and only sister?

She'd always been horrid to Jo, and Jo often felt her function in life was to be Maud's moral compass, to nudge her sister so she wasn't quite so selfish. Had they finally arrived at the spot where it was impossible to guide her into better conduct? What then?

"If you would meet her, Maud." Jo was begging. She couldn't help it. "She's pretty and sweet. It would soften your attitude toward her. I'm positive it would."

"It wouldn't, Jo. I'm sorry, but it wouldn't."

"She's so cute. She's blond and blue-eyed like you. She's educated and funny and—"

Maud cut her off. "That's enough! I won't have you badgering me."

"Maud!"

Her sister spun around so she was facing the mirror, and she started fussing with her hair as if she hadn't a care in the world.

"Will that be all, Jo?" she blandly asked. "Was there anything else you needed to discuss? If not, you should head home. If you delay much longer, you'll miss the last coach."

Jo could have raged and quarreled, but in light of Maud's intransience, what was the point?

She'd known her sister forever, and over the years, she'd figured out how to coerce her. She hadn't succeeded on this occasion, but she hadn't expected to.

There would be plenty of opportunities to whittle away at her stern opinion. Lord Benton had promised to rein in Mr. Slater, had promised to wipe away the July fifteenth deadline, so no immediate resolution was required. It meant she had time to plot a strategy that would change Maud's mind—and she *would* change it.

Of that fact, she had no doubt.

She whipped away and left without a goodbye.

MAUD FROZE AS Jo stomped out. Once the door closed, she breathed a sigh of relief.

Her hands were shaking, and she rushed to the sitting room where there was a brandy decanter. She poured herself a tall glass and swallowed it down, then she went to the window and stared outside.

She wished she could see her sister leaving the hotel to be sure she was gone, but her suite looked out on an alley. The front entrance wasn't visible, so she was denied the satisfaction of furtively watching.

She'd met Neville Prescott when she was sixteen. A school classmate had invited her to London for the Christmas holidays, and the girl's mother had been a lazy chaperone. They'd had few restrictions on their choice of activities or companions.

Her first night out on the town, he'd been at a party hosted by some friends. She'd been a naïve girl from a village in the country while he'd been a dashing, sophisticated man who was almost a decade older. She'd been bowled over by him, and she hadn't stood a chance of resisting his advances.

They'd spent a wild month, engaged in what she'd thought was a clandestine love affair. When she'd returned to school in January, she'd been ruined, but she'd been *in love*. She'd believed he was a bachelor who would propose, and they'd live happily ever after.

It was only after weeks of writing poignant, unanswered letters that she discovered he was already married.

There had been no concealing her condition from the headmistress. Her father had been summoned, her shame revealed, but to her surprise, he'd been quite grand about the entire debacle.

He had devised the false story about an academic trip to France. *He* had found the facility where she'd given birth. *He* had dealt with the Prescott family and had made it clear they would have to be responsible for the child.

Through it all, Maud had been numb. She'd viewed her pregnancy as a sort of morbid illness she'd barely survived. She'd expelled the growth from her body, then it had been whisked away and delivered to the Prescotts.

She'd seldom reflected on any of it ever again. She was adept at ignoring unpleasantness, and the calamity had been the greatest unpleasantness of all.

Mr. Slater was in charge of the girl's care and maintenance. How dare he break his word! How dare Jo chastise Maud over the issue!

Maud snorted out a laugh that sounded a tad deranged. Jo was kind and decent, possessed of all the honest traits Maud lacked. She would yearn to bring the child to Maud's home, but it would never happen.

At a very aged twenty-five years, Maud had begun to suspect she would remain a spinster. She recognized that she was no beauty. Nor was she the most agreeable person. Yet she had a trust fund, a house, and a dowry, so she'd never understood why no man had stepped forward.

Her lawyer, Charles Townsend, was the one who'd arranged her future. He'd realized she was a hidden gem, and he'd suggested she might like to meet his younger brother, Thompson, with an eye toward matrimony. When Mr. Townsend had proposed, she'd accepted immediately.

He was a bit rough around the edges, but mostly, he was handsome and charming, and she couldn't have done better for herself. Well, she might have done *better* if her father had still been alive and rich and able to contract a suitable match.

But that era was behind her. On her lawyer's advice, she was marrying Mr. Townsend in September, and she would never jeopardize her chance to become his bride. She was certain that news of a bastard daughter would be a death blow to her happiness.

Jo might worry about an urchin being wrenched from Benton and sent to an orphanage, but it was Jo's habit to worry. It wasn't Maud's.

Maud didn't regret and she didn't feel guilty, and she had some errands to finish. She'd start by visiting the tailor who was sewing Mr. Townsend's wedding suit. It would be a very busy day.

CHAPTER

8

"Have you decided?"

"No."

"You should."

Peyton frowned at Evan Boyle and inquired, "Why? Am I in a hurry?"

"I think you are."

Peyton had completed his business in the city, and he was back at Benton. Evan had ridden in shortly after he'd arrived, so his friend was available to provide the entertainment he desperately required.

He'd loafed for two weeks at his town house, and after all those days away, he'd thought he might have a more positive attitude about his return to the estate. But he didn't. There were too many awful memories, and he couldn't set them aside as he ought.

He was bored to death and wondering why he would ever retire from the navy. If he resigned his commission, it would mean an end to his wayfaring. He'd have to declare himself a farmer, then lock himself in at Benton Manor where he would watch the crops grow.

At the notion, he shuddered.

"What is wrong with you?" Evan asked. "Are you feverish?"

"No, I was just contemplating how dreary it would be to retire here."

"Oh, do be silent. I swear, you complain more than any man I've ever met."

"Well, it would be dreary."

"Then hire a good manager and reside in London. You can amuse yourself at balls and parties, and you'll travel to Benton in the autumn for the hunting and to check your agent's figures to ensure he isn't cheating you too badly."

"Speaking of figures, I need you to look at the ledgers."

"Am I to be your unpaid accountant?"

"Yes."

"What's the matter?" Evan oozed sarcasm. "Don't you trust your brother-in-law, Mr. Slater?"

"I have no idea if I should trust him or not. That's the problem."

Evan smirked. "I never liked him. He's pompous and dodgy."

"So am I. So are you."

They were in a cozy parlor, sitting by the hearth and drinking brandy. It was a cool, rainy afternoon, and they were being extravagant by having the servants light a roaring fire. It was one of the privileges of rank that he enjoyed.

He'd spent much of his life in unpleasant weather—cold, wet, wind, ice—and it was lovely to be warm simply because he felt like wasting some logs.

Evan was Peyton's same age, and they were similar enough in appearance—black hair, blue eyes, tall height—that they could have been brothers. Evan was a much better person though. He was stable and loyal and devoted to his mother and sister. Peyton had grown up as a sort of orphan they'd adopted, and he possessed few of Evan's stellar traits.

As a boy, Evan had socialized with Richard Slater, but Peyton hadn't been acquainted with Richard or Barbara. He'd been introduced to them at Neville's wedding which was the only *family* event he'd attended during the years he hadn't been welcome at Benton. He'd never understood why Neville had invited him to be his best man.

Basically, they'd been strangers, but curiosity had lured Peyton home, and he'd forced himself to oblige his brother who probably hadn't deserved any courtesy.

Richard and Barbara were strangers too, and they were all tiptoeing around, trying not to rock any boats. He wished he could wave a magic wand and make them vanish. If he wasn't constantly compelled to consider what they wanted—and what was fair—he might be able to more quickly resolve his own issues.

The butler entered, but Peyton didn't know him. He preferred Mr. Newman who was at the house in town.

"We've received the afternoon post," he said to Peyton. "There was a letter for you."

He handed it over, then hovered in the corner where he could eavesdrop and report their comments to Barbara. Peyton shooed him out, and he was definitely slow in departing.

"Cheeky bastard," Evan muttered once he was gone.

"They're all Barbara's people. She brought them from the Slater property when it was sold."

"I bumped into her brother, Roger, in town the other day. He was a sorry sight, addled with whiskey at my club. It was embarrassing. The footmen had to escort him out and put him in a cab."

"Their father's recklessness cost them dearly. It was difficult for all of them."

"I'm not certain about *all* of them." Evan snickered maliciously. "Richard, Barbara, and their mother seem to have landed on their feet. They lost their own home, and they appear to have taken over yours."

"Don't remind me."

"You still haven't answered my question."

"What was it again?"

"Are you coming back to active duty with me? You're a bloody earl now, so you can dawdle in England forever if you like, but I am a commoner, and I can't remain on eternal holiday. I have to return to work. If you're not ready, I'll have to go without you."

"You'd accept an assignment to another ship and sail off without me?"

"I'm in the *navy*, Peyton. I can't tell my superiors to sod off merely because I'm waiting on you to fix your life. I don't have a choice."

While Evan had been rambling on, Peyton opened the letter the butler had delivered and was delighted to find it was from Jo Bates. On observing her signature, he suffered such a thrill that he was mortified by his reaction.

He snorted with disgust, and Evan said, "Are you laughing? At what? As far as I can see, nothing is funny."

"No, I'm just . . . ah . . . appalled with myself."

"Well, you are an appalling fellow, but what has you finally noticing it?"

Peyton didn't dare mention Jo. Evan most likely assumed Peyton was about to propose to his sister, Amelia. She was fetching and vivacious, and they got along famously. He hadn't ever been overly keen on being a husband, but age thirty was swiftly approaching, so it was time to bite the bullet. He'd persuaded himself she would be an excellent wife.

But that was before he'd ascended to the title. Did Evan understand that fact? Should Peyton have to spell it out? Amelia wasn't the best candidate anymore, and he probably ought to admit it. Yet as with so much else that was vexing him, he couldn't bear to stir that pot. It would wreck his relationship with Evan, and he couldn't hurt his old friend in such a dastardly way.

He peeked down at Jo's letter, not surprised to discover that her sister was refusing to let Daisy live with them. Jo promised to devise a solution and begged that he not allow Richard to take action on July fifteenth. As opposed to all the other problems plaguing him, it was easy to grant her request.

He read her note over and over, then he folded it and stuck it in his coat.

Since the night he'd kissed her so ferociously at the town house, he hadn't seen her again. It had never occurred to him that she'd sneak out without a goodbye. That last morning, when she didn't arrive for breakfast, he'd sent a maid to check on her. When the woman conveyed the news that Jo had fled, he'd been yanked to his senses.

He had no business flirting with her, particularly in light of his brother's conduct toward her sister. He'd mostly forgotten about her, but she'd slithered back. Her letter put the whole subject of Daisy, Bobby, and Jane front and center.

"Do I detect feminine handwriting?" Evan slyly pried.

"Yes."

"Anyone I know?"

"No, you don't know her."

He sighed and gazed out the window. He'd like to visit her, but it was impossible. He had to be careful about exhibiting any heightened interest in a female. It had been important before, but with him being an earl, it was doubly important. Evan's sister was a clear example of the trouble he could instigate when he glanced in the wrong direction.

"You won't believe the situation I've stumbled on here," he said.

"Yes, I will. Tell me."

He tapped the pocket where Jo's letter was hiding. "It's what I was just contacted about. Would you be shocked to hear that Neville was a rutting dog?"

"Aren't most men if given the chance?"

Peyton scoffed with derision. "I suppose, but Neville was the consummate champion."

"What do you mean?"

"He sired nine bastard children—that I'm aware of."

"No!"

"Yes. There may be more trotting around the kingdom, but if so, I haven't been apprised."

"Gad. I'm . . . stunned."

"Let me *stun* you further. Three of them are living at Benton."

"What?"

Peyton explained about the lonely cottage at the edge of the estate, about Daisy, Bobby, and Jane, about Neville bringing them to Benton for the express purpose of tormenting Barbara.

"She and Richard are demanding I evict them," Peyton said. "Neville's not present to block any removal, so they're clamoring for a resolution."

"Will you cede to their demand? Will you send the children away?"

"I must admit to being torn. Wouldn't it be better—for the children—if they left? Wouldn't they be happier somewhere else?"

"It depends on where that *somewhere* is."

"Richard is trying to convince maternal relatives to take them."

"Has he had any luck?"

"No. The letter I just received? It's from one of the aunts. She's made no progress."

"You realize, don't you, that you've voiced the perfect reason to get your butt back to the navy? Who would want to deal with this quagmire? No matter what route you select, people will be furious. Especially your in-laws. If you don't side with them, you'll stir a hornet's nest that will never end."

"Exactly," Peyton agreed.

"I'd dump it all in Richard's capable hands. *He* can be the ogre."

"I'm definitely considering it."

Except that Peyton kept thinking about Jo Bates. What if he failed to intervene and Richard behaved horridly toward Daisy? Jo would never forgive him, and even though he was determined to never see her again, he couldn't bear to disappoint her.

Yet he couldn't confess it to Evan. Not when Evan's sister, Amelia, was all but sitting in the spot between them and begging Peyton to notice her.

"Is it still raining?" Evan inquired.

"Yes."

"I'm bored. Let's play cards. We can gamble, and you can permit me to win some money off you."

"We're not gambling. You cheat, remember?"

"Not always."

"Ha! I know you too well."

"No, we should gamble. If you win, you'll simply empty my wallet. If *I* win, you'll bid Benton *adieu*, come back to the navy, and we'll sail out of England on the quickest tide we can find."

"Don't tempt me."

"Who's tempting you? I'm exhausted by your dithering. You can't make up your mind, so I will force you to."

Peyton stared out the window at the gray, soggy afternoon.

Why not head to the navy? It was the only place he'd ever been content. It was the only place he'd ever truly belonged. The slow days at Benton dripped by like a kind of medieval torture, and he couldn't abide much more of it.

In every other facet of his life, he blustered forward without second guessing his every step. He could hardly captain a navy ship any other way. It was just over issues at Benton where he was frozen and unable to pick a path.

His equivocation was ridiculous and exasperating, but he didn't feel that Fate should have tossed the estate in his lap, so the problems didn't seem as if they should be *his* dilemmas to solve. Obligation was gradually creeping in, and he couldn't escape its weighty pull.

He wished Jo Bates could see him when he was in such a pitiful condition. She'd have a few pithy words to share about his wretched inability to decide.

Evan yanked him out of his miserable reverie.

"Amelia sends her regards."

"How is she?"

"She's grand. If it ever quits raining, how about if we ride to town? We can stop by and chat with her."

Peyton tamped down a reaction. Any misconceptions Evan and Amelia Boyle had about his intentions were his own blasted fault. How was he to repair the false perception he'd generated?

"Yes, we should do that," Peyton said, rather than argue or offer a comment he'd regret later. "Now ring for the butler, and we'll have him dig up a deck of cards. I hope your purse is full—so I can empty it."

"I'm off to town."

"For how long?"

"I don't know."

Richard peered over at Peyton and kept his expression carefully blank. It was the best news he could have received.

When Peyton had initially come home on furlough, he'd spent three tedious weeks at Benton where he'd snooped and eavesdropped and made a nuisance of himself. Then he'd traveled to London and had spent two weeks there.

His recent visit had only lasted for a day. His friend, Mr. Boyle, had arrived, and they'd been trapped in the house by rain. They were masculine, dynamic men, and they'd prowled about like lions locked in a cage.

The weather had cleared, and they were leaving for the city again, their horses saddled and out in the drive. He and Peyton were standing in the foyer, and Mr. Boyle was down with the horses, so he and Peyton were alone.

"Mr. Boyle looked through the ledger books," Peyton said.

"I realize they're your books, Peyton, and you may use them as you see fit, but must you parade them outside the family?"

"It appeared to him as if we're broke. Are we?"

"I suppose *broke* is a relative term."

"How relative?"

"Your brother was a gambler and wastrel, Peyton. You knew that."

"No, actually, I didn't."

Richard shrugged. He'd loathed Neville, with his licentious affairs and wild routines. Richard's deceased father and his own brother, Roger, had carried on just as flagrantly. His family had lost everything due to their reckless habits. If Barbara hadn't married Neville before calamity had struck, they'd all be living in a small flat with Roger in London.

Richard had no patience or sympathy for negligence. He most especially couldn't abide how Neville had disgraced himself with his doxies, how he'd repeatedly shamed Barbara. But no one had been able to stop him from engaging in any offensive act that tickled his fancy.

They'd been at his mercy, and now, Peyton had inherited, so they would be subject to his whims and impulses. He had deliberately separated himself from them, so it had been difficult to ascertain what sort of person he really was. Was he cunning like a fox? Or was he simply too dimwitted to delve into complex details? It was a frustrating question that Richard couldn't answer.

For the most part, he would tread cautiously around Peyton, would bow to his authority and let him have his way, but he wouldn't budge on matters involving his mother or sister. He would do whatever was necessary to protect them.

"Your brother wasn't concerned about our finances," Richard said.

"Is any aristocrat? I've always heard they're very stupid about money."

With Peyton being an earl, the remark seemed like a bog that could suck Richard in, so he bit down on his opinion.

"We have debts," he said instead.

"Are they enough to bankrupt us?"

"Time will tell I guess."

"I'm taking the ledgers to London. I'll have my accountants there double-check the numbers."

Richard continued to mask his discomfort. "As you wish."

"Depending on how they view it, we may have to make some changes."

"What changes? Am I about to be terminated from my post?"

"No. I'm merely getting some outside advice, then we'll see what happens."

"In my own defense, I can categorically declare that I constantly counseled your brother to behave better. I shouldn't be blamed for any problems. They're systemic and deeply ingrained in how the Prescott family has always done things."

"Then perhaps the Prescott family needs to develop some new strategies."

Peyton's demeanor was very bland, but Richard accepted the comment as a threat.

He and Barbara ran the estate together. She had control of the manor, and he had control of the exterior property. They were happy with that arrangement and didn't want it to be altered. If Peyton fired Richard and brought in his own people, he and Barbara would lose their position of power.

"There are many processes we could implement," Richard said. "I'm eager to upgrade and modernize."

"So jot down a list. I'll look at it."

"I will. Thank you. Will you be returning to Benton?"

"I'm not certain. I have to firm up my status with the navy."

"Will you be heading out to sea?"

"Maybe."

"When will you decide?"

"Soon."

Peyton was so accursedly vague that Richard yearned to shake him. He couldn't figure out if Peyton was a man who ceaselessly vacillated or if he'd settled on a path but declined to share it with Richard and Barbara. If so, it was a shrewd scheme. It kept them at a heightened level of anxiety.

"My sister is curious about the household accounts," he said, "and she's wondering if you'll provide her with an allowance."

"Make a list about that too. Inform me as to what she thinks would be fair."

"Will you be staying at Benton House? Could I contact you there?"

"I suppose."

"And if you shore up your plans about the navy, I'd appreciate it if you'd apprise us as quickly as you can."

Peyton grinned. "Why? Are you keen to be rid of me?"

"Your brother's death has wreaked havoc for my sister. Surely you don't begrudge her for seeking some answers from you."

"No, I don't begrudge her on any topic, but any request for funds will have to wait until I have a clearer understanding of our situation. If we're out of money, then the amount she desires will have to be slashed."

It was the closest Richard had gotten to a solid reply since Peyton had first arrived at Benton, and it incensed him.

"Might I remind you, Peyton, that my sister is your brother's widow, and she is still Countess of Benton. She can hardly be expected to live like a pauper."

"If we're broke—as you seem to be implying—then her standards will have to be lowered a bit."

Richard actually thought he might jump into an unwinnable quarrel, but Mr. Boyle bounded up the stairs.

"Let's go, Peyton," he said. "Time's wasting."

"I'll be right there." Peyton waved Boyle away. "One last thing, Richard."

"What is it?"

"About Neville's children . . ."

"You mean his lawful daughters, Alice and Nancy?" Richard knew he referred to the others out in the cottage, but he asked the question just to be spiteful.

Peyton sighed with aggravation. "No, I don't mean them. I mean Bobby, Jane, and Daisy."

"What about them?"

"You gave them a deadline to vacate the premises by July fifteenth, but you are *not* to enforce it."

"Why not?"

"Because I'm not a cruel man, and I won't kick three children out on the road."

"What if we don't hear from their maternal relatives? Is it your intention for them to remain forever?"

"No."

Richard was so irate that he started to tremble. "Well, then, what do you intend?"

"I haven't a clue." Peyton's equivocation was typical and maddening. "I'll notify you once I've pondered a resolution. But *don't* enforce that deadline. Their kin require more of an opportunity to work matters out. If they exhaust every possibility, but still can't help us, we'll talk about it then."

"Fine." Richard was terrified to say more lest it would be a remark he'd very much regret.

"If the manor burns down, write to me in London," Peyton said. "Otherwise, carry on as you have been. For now, there are no changes on the horizon, and I don't need any reports."

"When will we see you again?" Richard was determined to pry out a concrete response.

"Maybe never?"

Peyton chuckled, then strutted out. Richard stood in the foyer, wishing he had the temerity to march out after him and pick a fight.

Peyton was so rude and dismissive, his dislike of Benton and his Slater in-laws too hideous to be born. Why was he so flippant? Why keep them on edge and off guard?

It was likely a ploy to rattle them, to leave them nervous and agitated. At least he suspected it was. The more infuriating notion was that Peyton wasn't conniving at all. Perhaps he was simply a lazy dolt who refused to focus on any issue.

Through the open door, he watched Peyton and Mr. Boyle ride down the lane. They were laughing and chatting, acting as if Benton and its problems were of no consequence whatsoever.

As they were disappearing into the trees, Barbara strolled up.

"What are you staring at?" she asked.

"Peyton and Mr. Boyle just left."

"Good."

It was an indiscreet comment, voiced aloud with a footman dawdling a few feet away, but they didn't have to worry about him. The servants were all Slater servants, saved from destitution when their father, then brother, Roger, had gone bankrupt. Barbara had brought them to Benton, and they were loyal to *her*. Not Peyton Prescott.

"They're off to London," Richard said.

"He just got back though," she complained, "and he's departed again. I can't decide if I should be relieved or not."

"It's always a benefit to have him out of our hair."

"You're correct," she agreed. "Is he returning to the navy? Did you discuss it?"

"No, but listen to this."

"What?"

He glanced at the footman. They were Slater servants, but still, there were some topics that had to be a secret.

"We should confer in the parlor."

They went into the room and shut the door.

"What is it?" she said. "If you couldn't mention it out in the foyer, it must be bad."

"Before he walked out, he raised the subject of Daisy, Bobby, and Jane. He forbade me to implement the eviction deadline on July fifteenth."

She gasped with affront. "They're to stay on? For how long?"

"I pressed him on that very issue, but you're aware of what he's like. He never tells me what he's really thinking."

"Am I to suffer their presence forever? How much shame will the Prescott family be allowed to inflict on me?"

There was a lamp beside her on a decorative table, and she batted at it and sent it crashing to the floor. The footman heard the noise, and he raced over and peeked in.

"Are you all right, Mr. Slater?" he asked.

"We're fine," Richard insisted, and he shooed the man out. Once they were alone again, he murmured, "I don't care what Peyton said. We'll stick to the original plan and deadline."

"It's next week. What if he finds out that we ignored his edict? What then?"

"He's completely detached from estate affairs. I'm betting those children will never cross his mind in the future."

"But what if they do? What if he inquires about them someday?"

"We'll lie and claim their maternal kin took them as we'd demanded."

She considered the ruse, then nodded. "Yes, I suppose that would work."

"They will not remain past the fifteenth, Barbara."

"Swear it to me."

"I swear. They'll go, and they'll never be back to plague us."

CHAPTER

9

Jo WALKED UP THE deserted lane to Daisy's cottage. There was a carriage parked out front, but she didn't have the energy to worry about who else might be present.

Her mission was dire, and she couldn't guess how it would resolve, but if Lord Benton had been standing there, she'd have punched him in the nose.

During their abbreviated association, she'd assumed they were friends. He'd promised he wouldn't let Mr. Slater implement his July fifteenth deadline, and she'd believed him which only proved she was a gullible fool. Would she ever learn?

She arrived at the gate, and as she opened it, Mr. Slater emerged from the house. She had questions to ask him and answers that needed to be supplied, but mostly, she needed to fetch her niece away from the horrid Prescott family. Who would leave a child in the care of such despicable people?

"Hello, Mr. Slater," she said as he approached.

"Miss Bates, isn't it? I assume you've come to fetch Daisy?"

"Yes."

"Thank you for being prompt."

"I didn't have much choice, did I? What aunt could sit idly by while her niece is sent to an orphanage?"

"I'm in no mood for insults, Miss Bates. I hope we can converse like two civilized adults as we accomplish this change of custody."

"I'm a very *civilized* person, Mr. Slater, so if there's discord between us, you will have been the cause."

"It's unfortunate that matters have descended to such a low point. Please remember that we supported Daisy for most of a decade."

"Don't act as if you were being charitable. We both know the former earl used her as a prop to enrage your sister."

"I won't deny it, but now, my sister is due a bit of consideration for how she's suffered. After significant reflection, Lord Benton agreed with me."

"I demand to speak to him," she said.

Mr. Slater frowned. "Haven't you heard? Lord Benton has gone back to the navy. He sailed last Wednesday."

The news wounded her. Peyton was gone? He'd left without a goodbye? She hadn't been informed!

The frantic thoughts flitted by, and she forced herself to recollect that she had no claims on his affection. It was ridiculous to suppose she would have been notified. Still though, it was a crushing blow.

"When will he return to England?" she asked.

"It could be years. He was posted to the Caribbean in the past, and apparently, he's once again been assigned to patrol those waters."

"I should like to write to him. May I have his address?"

"No, you may not have it. Can you actually imagine he'd like you pestering him about this?"

"It's irrelevant to me if he'd *like* it or not. There are several comments I would like to share with him."

Mr. Slater ignored her paltry protest and gestured to the cottage. "Your niece has packed her bag, and her governess, Miss Watson, has some money for you to ease your way in the beginning."

"How very generous you are, Mr. Slater!" Jo couldn't tamp down her sarcasm.

"Lord Benton mentioned this in his letter to you, but I'd like to repeat it. You should never contact us in the future for any reason. Our commitment to Daisy is finished."

"Yes, yes, I understand."

She swept by him, her fury so intense that it could have lit him on fire.

As she reached the door, he called to her. "I'm sorry it had to end like this, Miss Bates."

Jo glared at him over her shoulder. "No, you're not, Mr. Slater. Don't pretend."

"I'm not sorry to see these children depart Benton, but I never like to quarrel. I hope—eventually—you'll realize this was for the best."

"Yes, you've been a veritable saint, and I'm sure it will all work out perfectly. I'm delighted that your conscience is clear."

Jo whipped away, but she sensed him hovering behind her, eager to offer further justifications, but she wouldn't listen. Lord Benton had curtly spelled out his decision in the letter she'd received, and it had been more than enough.

She hadn't breathed a word of the situation to Maud who was in London again, so she and Daisy would head home and wait for Maud to return. What would happen then was scary to contemplate.

Jo prayed—after the deed was done—that she could persuade Maud to be rational, but she wasn't optimistic. She was out of ideas, running on luck, and juggling impossible options. She would behave as was morally appropriate, and she would fuss with the consequences later.

She knocked, and Miss Watson answered.

"Miss Bates!" She looked very woebegone. "Mr. Slater told us to expect you."

He was next to his carriage, and she flashed a caustic glower at him, then she grabbed Jo's arm and yanked her inside. She shut the door with a determined click.

"What an ass," Miss Watson muttered.

"I enthusiastically concur."

Miss Watson led her to the front parlor, and they sat across from each other. There was a tea tray on the table between them, and Miss Watson poured them a cup.

"I'm so glad you showed up today," she said. "If you hadn't, I can't predict how Mr. Slater might have dealt with Daisy. I truly fear he would have tossed her out on the road to fend for herself."

"I came as soon as Lord Benton's letter arrived."

She'd been shocked by the tone and contents. During their brief acquaintance, he'd seemed so kind and cordial. Why had he become such an ogre?

Of course aristocrats were a different breed of animal. They banded together. They protected their own interests, and Neville Prescott's bastards were a stain on the family's reputation. Obviously, he planned to wipe the slate clean.

"Where is Daisy?" she asked.

"She's upstairs with Bobby and Jane. They're saying goodbye."

"It must be so difficult for all of you."

"I can't begin to tell you, Miss Bates."

"When are Bobby and Jane leaving?"

"Tomorrow morning. It's why I'm relieved you're here now. I'd have been terrified to go without Daisy being settled."

"Have you heard from Jane's uncle in Cornwall?"

"No, he never replied."

"Then what's occurring? They can't be headed for an orphanage."

"No, I'm simply traveling with them to Cornwall so I can speak to him face to face. I will throw myself on his mercy and beg him to take them in."

"What if he can't or won't?"

Miss Watson chuckled miserably. "I refuse to focus on that prospect. I'll scour the area to see if Jane has other kin nearby. After that . . . ah . . . I guess I'll return to London and search for a job."

It appeared Miss Watson was making slapdash decisions just as Jo was. Jo wanted to urge caution and inquire as to whether she'd fully pondered her mission. But Jo—with her hasty choice to bring Daisy home—was in no condition to lecture anyone.

"Will you have an address, Miss Watson?" Jo asked. "I'd like to keep in touch with you. I'll worry about you, and I'm sure Daisy will fret about Bobby and Jane."

"I have a cousin where you'll always be able to contact me, but don't concern yourself over my situation. I have a bit of money saved, so I won't starve on the streets."

"That's good to know."

Miss Watson bristled and furiously stated, "They're siblings, Miss Bates. How can Lord Benton separate them like this? How can Mr. Slater? I realize the Countess has issues with them, but is the answer to evict them and divide them forever? Those two men have no heart at all, and the Countess is worse than both of them put together."

"You'll get no argument from me, and I must admit to being very surprised by Lord Benton. I pleaded with him to halt this, and he promised he would."

"Well, we've learned the value of a Prescott promise, haven't we?"

"Too true, Miss Watson. Too true."

"I'll jot down my cousin's address, but I'm hoping I won't end up there. If I can convince Jane's uncle to let her and Bobby stay with him, I'll try to wrangle a post as their governess."

"It would be wonderful if you could."

"I'll keep you apprised as to where I am."

Miss Watson went to a desk in the corner and wrote down the pertinent information. She brought it over to Jo, and Jo stuck it in her reticule.

"I hate to rush Daisy," Jo said, "but we have to catch the afternoon coach."

"I understand." Miss Watson walked over to the stairs and called to Daisy.

Momentarily, several pairs of feet tromped down. When the three children trudged in, they were a meager trio. Daisy and Bobby looked stoic and resigned, but Jane was very emotional and had been crying.

Jo stood. "Hello, Daisy."

"Hello, Aunt Jo."

"I'm sorry to meet again under these painful circumstances."

"It's not your fault." Daisy sounded very mature, very grown up.

"I'm sorry to make you hurry, but the coach to Telford will stop in the village soon. We can't tarry."

"I'm just glad you're here. If you hadn't arrived, I'd have been very afraid."

Jo couldn't abide the grief that permeated the room. She hugged Daisy tight.

"It will be all right," Jo said, not meaning it.

"Do you really think so?"

"Yes."

Miss Watson gave Jo an envelop that contained the funds Mr. Slater had claimed he'd provide.

"This should help you through a few rough patches," Miss Watson said.

"It will definitely come in handy," Jo responded, and she turned to Daisy. "We have to go. I need you to say your final farewell."

The three children hesitated, then stepped into a circle, their arms around each other. They whispered comments, nodded, and whispered some more.

"Bobby, you have to take care of Rex," Daisy murmured.

He replied, "I will."

"Don't leave him behind."

Poor Jane cried harder, and Daisy dried her cheeks and soothed her. "Hush now. I can't bear for you to be so sad."

"Jane, you must calm yourself," Bobby said, the man of the group, "or you'll have me blubbering too. I can't be all sentimental. I'm not a girl."

His remark had them chuckling, but despondently, then Daisy said, "We have to always write letters. The second you're in Cornwall, you have to let me know."

"I have an address for Miss Watson," Jo told them.

"We'll never forget each other," Daisy added. "Never! You're my sister and my brother, and we'll see each other again before too much time has passed."

"Yes, we will," Bobby agreed, but Jane was too overwhelmed to speak.

Jo was about to burst into tears herself. The entire encounter was hideous.

Daisy's portmanteau was by the sofa, and she picked it up and came over to Jo.

"I'm ready, Aunt Jo," she said.

"We'll be fine, Daisy—you and I together. Don't you worry."

"I'm not worried." Daisy spun to Miss Watson. "Goodbye, Miss Watson."

"Goodbye, Daisy."

"Thank you for everything."

"You're welcome."

Daisy threw herself against Miss Watson, and as they hugged each other, Jo was at her limit. Tears dripped down her cheeks, and she swiped them away.

"Goodbye, Bobby," Jo said. "Goodbye, Jane. Be strong. Be tough. You'll get through this."

"I'm certain we will," Bobby concurred, but Jane was still incapable of a retort.

Miss Watson went to the door and pulled it open. Jo and Daisy walked over to her.

"I'm so relieved you came," Miss Watson said to Jo.

"I couldn't do anything else, could I?"

"No, I guess you couldn't."

Jo reached out and squeezed Miss Watson's hand. Then Jo and Daisy exited, and Miss Watson closed the door, saving them the repugnant spectacle of further weeping in the driveway.

The dog, Rex, was sitting there, and he seemed to realize a tragedy was in progress. Daisy knelt down and buried her face in his soft coat. For a lengthy interval, she held onto him, then she drew away and stood. He sensed her misery, and he whined in commiseration.

Jo hovered with Daisy for a minute, feeling shocked and disoriented, then Daisy asked, "Will I ever see Bobby or Jane again?"

Jo should have lied, but she was too distraught. "I have no idea if you will, Daisy. I truly don't know."

"How was London?"

Jo stared at Maud and tried to act nonchalant.

"London was the same as always," Maud said. "Noisy, filthy, crowded. I hope Mr. Townsend doesn't expect me to travel there very often."

"Don't be silly." Jo forced a smile. "You'd love it if you had reasons to stay in town on a regular basis."

"You constantly assume you're aware of my preferences, Jo, but you aren't."

Maud had just arrived, her bags still in the front foyer. They only had one footman, and he was running errands and would have to carry them up to her bedchamber once he was back. Maud would never do it herself, and Jo wasn't inclined to pitch in.

Besides, she couldn't let Maud go upstairs yet. They had too many important matters to hash out.

"I'm starving," Maud said. "Is there anything to eat?"

"Of course, but could we chat first?"

"No. I'm hungry."

Maud huffed into the dining room where there was a tea pot and scones on the table from Jo having a snack earlier with Daisy. They'd been hunkered down for four days, bracing for the moment Maud strolled in.

That *moment* was finally upon them, and Jo felt as if she was out of her body and watching some other foolish woman ruin her life.

Maud sat and poured herself a cup of tea while Jo slathered butter and jam on a scone. She shoved it across to her sister, observing as Maud dug into her food.

"I have to talk to you," Jo mentioned after a bit.

"So you said. What is it this time? You're practically trembling with nerves."

"I have to confess an action I took without your permission. You won't like it, but it was an emergency, and I'm not sorry. We simply have to decide how to proceed."

Maud smacked down her teacup with a sharp *crack!* "What have you done? Tell me quickly—before I get angry."

"It's about Daisy," Jo bluntly stated.

Maud blanched, then leaned toward Jo and hissed, "You would speak that girl's name aloud in my home? What is wrong with you?"

Jo ignored Maud's spurt of temper and pressed on. "She had to leave Benton by the fifteenth. I've been trying to find a spot for her, but I couldn't."

"Why would you suppose I'd be interested in this?"

"I thought I had received a reprieve from Lord Benton—that is Peyton Prescott who is the new earl."

"I don't care if he's the bloody king of England," Maud crudely spat. "I told you to forget about this."

"I didn't listen. He promised to wave the deadline until I could arrange a solution, but he changed his mind. A few days ago, he wrote to apprise me that I had to fetch her or she'd be sent to an orphanage."

"And . . . ?"

"I traveled to Benton, and I brought her to Telford."

A dangerous silence festered, and Maud cocked her head as if Jo had babbled in a foreign language she didn't understand.

"You what?"

"I brought her here."

"She's here now? In my home?"

"Yes, and it's my home too. I want her to live with us, and I demand to have a say."

"Not in your wildest dreams is any of this house yours."

"You may have inherited it from your grandmother, but all the furnishings are from father's estate. It should give me some rights."

Maud laughed in an eerie way that raised the hair on Jo's neck, then she pushed herself to her feet and pointed a condemning finger at Jo.

"Get out."

"No."

"Get! Out!"

"No. Don't be ridiculous."

"I won't provide shelter to you another second!"

"Calm down this instant," Jo scolded, "or the servants will hear you shouting."

"I haven't begun to shout at you."

Jo stood and, projecting a feigned serenity, went to the foyer and called, "Daisy, would you come down please? My sister has arrived, and I'd like to introduce you."

She and Daisy had rehearsed this scene a dozen times. Jo had been very candid with Daisy, and Daisy wasn't expecting any miracles. She appeared on the landing, then marched down. She was very stoic, very brave, and as she neared, Jo led her to the dining room. Maud was still next to her chair.

"Maud, this is my cousin's daughter." Jo uttered the lie with a straight face. They'd already told it to the servants, and it had been accepted without a blink of curiosity. "I mentioned her to you. She was recently orphaned, and I've invited her to stay with us."

"How dare you!" was Maud's reply.

She didn't acknowledge Daisy, but stormed out and tromped up the stairs as Jo and Daisy huddled together, staring up and wondering what to do. Suddenly, Maud started throwing clothes over the banister.

Jo's portmanteau soon followed, then Daisy's, and they jumped out of the way to keep from being hit by the heavy bags as they crashed to the floor.

"Wait here," she whispered to Daisy. "I'll talk to her."

Daisy looked as if she'd like to respond, then thought better of it. She flashed a wan smile at Jo. Jo smiled too, then headed up the stairs.

Maud was in Jo's bedchamber, and as Jo entered, her sister was holding Jo's cloak and bonnet. Maud shoved them at her, but when Jo refused to take them, Maud tossed them over the rail too.

Jo continued to watch, stunned, as Maud hastily searched the room. She grabbed some of Jo's personal items—a brush and a picture of Jo's mother—and she walked over and hurled them down to the floor too. Then she whipped away and raced down to the foyer.

She stuffed what she could into the two portmanteaux. Once they were packed full, she carried them over to the door and pitched them outside.

Jo and Daisy gaped at the spectacle—Jo from the landing and Daisy from the dining room. Daisy peered up at her, her expression grim and tragic.

Maud didn't provide an opening for discussion. She pounded back up the stairs and advanced on Jo in a menacing manner that had her cringing. She seized Jo by the arm, dragged her to the stairs, and started down.

"I warned you about this," Maud seethed.

"Maud, stop it!"

Jo pried at Maud's fingers, but she couldn't escape. Maud was taller and bigger and angrier than Jo, and she couldn't halt their descent. Their housemaids had heard the commotion, and they dawdled in the corner, gawking in shock. They looked as if they yearned to intervene, but were too afraid.

Maud kept on out the door and into the drive. Jo struggled to maintain her dignity, but with her sister behaving like a lunatic, it was incredibly difficult.

"For heaven's sake, Maud!" Jo chided as Maud released her. "Are you happy now? Do you feel better?"

Maud glared with what could only be described as a great deal of hatred. "You are no longer welcome in my home. You are no longer welcome in Telford. Take your urchin and go. Don't make me tell you twice."

"Don't be absurd," Jo protested. "You can't kick me out."

"If you don't depart—at once!—I'll call for the law and claim you stole jewelry from me. I'll have you prosecuted, and you'll be transported to the penal colonies as a felon. What will happen to your precious Daisy then?"

Jo scoffed. "You would never have me arrested."

"Wouldn't I? Then I'll visit the vicar and inform him that I've learned you were consorting with a boy in London, and you've disgraced yourself. I'll insist I evicted you because of it. There's not a person in the neighborhood who will condemn me. Not with your mother's history."

"Maud, would you relax? There's no need for all this drama."

"Isn't there?"

"I've fixed everything," Jo attempted to explain. "The servants believe she's my cousin's daughter."

"I warned you," Maud said as she had in the house. "I will be married to Mr. Townsend in September, and I will not allow you to jeopardize that event."

"Let me take her back to Benton." Jo tried to sound reasonable, even though she was certain Lord Benton and Mr. Slater would never permit it.

"No!"

"How about if I inquire in the village? Perhaps there's a family who would be willing to have her."

"No!" Maud repeated more vehemently. "Her presence is a danger to me."

"She's poses no danger!"

"You have five minutes to get off my property, then I will look out the window. If you are still standing in my driveway, I will summon the law."

"Maud!"

"I've always hated you, Josephine. Always."

At the terrible admission, Jo gasped. "You don't mean that."

"Yes, I do. You—with your lowborn mother—are so far beneath me. Father and I often discussed how we could be shed of you."

Jo ignored the wound Maud had inflicted. "He loved my mother."

"No, he lusted after her—like the rutting dog all men are—and I have suffered egregiously due to his blunder, but I won't suffer in the future. You're not wanted here, Miss Bates."

"I'm your sister, Maud. I'm your *only* sister in the entire world. How can you hurt me like this?"

"It's easy, Josephine." Maud laughed her eerie laugh. "When father was dying, I was obligated by his final wish that I serve as your guardian, but those days are over. Your actions have guaranteed that my obligation to you—and him—has ended."

"But where will I go? How will I support myself?"

"It's none of my concern."

"Isn't that convenient for you? *You* are the one who gave my dowry to Mr. Cartwright so I have no money of my own."

"It wasn't my fault!" Maud fumed. "If he tricked anyone, he tricked *me*. I was simply trying to help you wed which is what you were so desperate to have occur. Don't rewrite your memory of the incident."

"You let him steal from me, and now, *you* are stealing all of what father left us. It's not *all* yours. Half of it is mine."

"What a child you are, Jo. Father could have bequeathed items or funds to you, but he didn't because he didn't care about you!"

"After all these years—where I've been your only friend!—I've never wavered in my affection. You're my sister, and this is how you repay me? You toss me out? Shame on you, Maud!"

"Sticks and stones, Jo. Sticks and stones. You brought that girl home in spite of my specific order that you not. You've proved that I can't trust you. Ever! Now go. I'll be watching the clock, and I swear—if you are here in five minutes—I will call for the law as I've threatened. Don't force my hand."

Maud whirled away and stormed inside. Daisy had been observing from the stoop, the two maids nervously hovering behind her. Maud grabbed Daisy and pushed her out, then she slammed the door and spun the key in the lock.

Daisy came over to Jo, and they tarried, staring at the house, as Maud went from room to room, yanking the drapes closed so she wouldn't have to peer out at Jo loitering in the driveway.

Jo had never been more incensed. She marched up to the door and began to knock, and she continued knocking until her knuckles were bruised from rapping on the wood. Ultimately, a maid opened it just a crack, her body blocking any attempt to enter—unless Jo felt like wrestling which she didn't.

"You need to leave, Miss Josephine," she whispered. "Please? Miss Maud sent the other maid out the back to fetch the magistrate. I truly believe she intends to have you arrested."

"I see," Jo murmured.

"Perhaps you could talk to her in a few days—after she's calmed down."

She shut the door and the key was spun again.

Jo turned to Daisy, and a thousand comments were unspoken between them. It was late in the afternoon, and soon it would be evening.

Maud's vicious words rang in her ears, her genuine opinion of Jo voiced aloud once and for all. Clearly, Maud had tamped down an enormous amount of loathing, and Jo had suffered her sister's mistreatment for much too long.

She peeked into her portmanteau, relieved to note that Maud had stuffed in her reticule. The money Mr. Slater had provided was in it, unspent and unused. It wasn't a lot, but they wouldn't starve.

"Let's get out of here," she said. "If we don't, she'll devise other ways to humiliate me, and I'm too furious to dawdle."

"Maybe we should wait though. People say things when they're angry that they don't mean. She might change her mind after a bit."

Jo remembered all the years she'd been denigrated and maligned by Maud, all the years she'd been scoffed at and ridiculed. Maud was cruel and awful, and Jo had had enough.

"She won't change her mind," Jo said, "and even if I thought she might, I would never force you to live with such a horrid person."

"She didn't seem to like me at all."

"Well, she's *never* liked me, and I'm weary of her disdain. We should find some help before it's dark."

They picked up their bags and walked away.

CHAPTER

10

"Happy birthday, Lord Benton!"

"Happy birthday, Commander Prescott!"

Peyton's guests raised their glasses in a toast, and as they cheered him, he rolled his eyes in exasperation. He'd never been keen on being the center of attention, and it had always seemed silly to him to be lauded for having a birthday. It wasn't as if he'd caused it to happen. He'd simply been born.

Another year had slid by, and he was thirty. It sounded very old, much older than twenty-nine.

"Speech, speech," Evan called merely to needle him.

He wasn't certain why he'd agreed to host the party, or to host it at the town house, just as he couldn't figure out why he was loafing in London. Now that he was an earl, his superior officers were showing him incredible deference. They kept telling him to take all the time he required to get matters squared away at Benton.

The navy, apparently, would still be there if and when he decided to return to it.

Their lenience was allowing him to be idle and was preventing him from moving forward. Tendrils from Benton were worming their way into his mind, and he was starting to recognize that a pride of ownership was sneaking in. Previously, he hadn't thought he was concerned about any of it, but had he been wrong?

An independent accountant had reviewed the estate ledgers, and the fiscal situation was as dire as Richard had explained. Peyton would catch himself devising plans he could implement, and he loved a challenge. If he was really a Prescott—and according to rumor, he probably *wasn't*—the property had been in the family for three centuries. There was history there, *his* history. Maybe. Shouldn't he build on what his ancestors had created?

When he'd notice how he was obsessing, he'd shove away any sense of connection. He'd never cared about Benton. It was a bedrock principle shaping his life. Was he ready to change that attitude?

"You must have a comment," Evan goaded. "It's not every day you turn thirty *and* become an earl. For example, has your good fortune bestowed any wisdom?"

"No," Peyton said, "but thank you all for coming."

"Do you feel older?" Evan asked.

"Yes, definitely."

"Do you feel smarter?"

"No, definitely not."

People laughed and toasted him again.

Evan's sister, Amelia, was hovering by Peyton's side as if she belonged there. The party had been her idea. If it had been left to Peyton, he'd have been drinking at his favorite club.

But Evan had nagged about how Amelia had been eager to arrange it, how it would make her happy, and Peyton hadn't had the heart to refuse. She would deem the event as a sort of trial run where she could prove to him that she was prepared to assume the duties of wife and countess.

By consenting to the party, Peyton was encouraging her, but he never could hurt her feelings, and he couldn't deduce how to gently apprise her that he might not wed her after all. Despite what reason he might supply, she'd be gravely insulted. She'd believe it was because of his ascension to the title—that she'd once been the perfect candidate but wasn't now—and he'd never convince her otherwise.

She had Evan's same black hair and blue eyes, and she was twenty-two, thin and petite, very pretty, smart, educated, and vivacious. And she was very independent. If she had an absentee husband such as Peyton who sailed around the world for lengthy stretches of time, she would have no difficulty managing on her own.

Her husband wouldn't have to worry about her. She'd be fine, but did he want a bride who'd be fine without him? Wasn't he more conventional than that? Wouldn't he rather have a wife who desperately needed him to be the *man* of the house?

Who could guess? Marriage was a mystery, and matrimony could end up being a blessing or a trap. No fellow could ever be sure of how it would unravel.

"I'm starving," he murmured to her. "Will supper ever be served?"

"Your butler, Mr. Newman, informs me he'll seat us in half an hour."

"I may waste away by then."

"I will hold you up so you don't collapse."

She grinned up at him, appearing impish and merry, and he grinned too. It was impossible not to like her, and he liked her very much, but if he didn't watch himself, he'd be marching to the altar with her very soon. He wouldn't be able to avoid it.

She'd arranged a sit-down meal for twenty, then she'd invited another hundred or so to stop by later for dancing and cards. It was all very formal, very fancy, his guests dressed to impress, their jewels dazzling.

It was a crowd of the rich and glamorous, so the conversation seemed more fascinating. A small voice in his head whispered like a warning, *This is your life now.*

It wasn't necessarily a bad notion. Was it?

"When are you going back to the navy, Peyton?" Amelia asked.

"I don't know."

"My brother claims you're being a big baby about it, and you can't make a decision on any topic."

Peyton snorted. "Well, it's easy for him to be firm on a topic. It's a bit trickier for me."

"I wish you'd be happier about all these changes that have been thrust on you."

"I'm happy enough."

"No, you're not. You're scowling at everyone."

"I didn't realize I was, so I'll force myself to look more pleasant. Since you worked so hard on this party, I can't have people thinking I'm miserable."

"It was no bother. In fact, I enjoyed it. I'm delighted that you gave me the chance to pamper you."

"Am I being pampered? Is that what's happening?"

"We're all here to remind you of how splendid you are. That sounds like pampering to me."

"I suppose."

He was searching each of her comments for veiled meaning, and he hated to be so wary. He *liked* her, and she was a terrific person, but anymore, he was suspicious of every remark from a female.

Was she auditioning her organizational skills? With her quip about his not returning to the navy, was she trying to ascertain when he might be available for a major occasion? Their wedding perhaps?

He smirked with aggravation. There were no hidden depths with her. They were friends. They'd always been friends. She wasn't angling for him to place a ring on her finger. She was simply chatting.

"There's a new theatrical play opening tomorrow night," she said. "I'm dying to see it."

"Let me guess why you're telling me: You'd like me to escort you."

"My, my, but you are so insightful."

Apparently, it was beyond him to rebuff her as he ought. "I haven't been to the theater in ages. I would be glad to escort you."

She slipped her arm into his and nestled herself closer so her body was crushed to his all the way down. She was very shapely, and fleetingly, he wondered what it would be like to fornicate with her.

When he recognized where his thoughts had strayed, his cheeks heated.

Was he actually considering her in a carnal fashion? Was he forgetting that she'd been like a little sister to him?

What the hell? he mused. Why not marry her? It would put an end to all these ghastly encounters where he constantly conveyed the wrong sentiment.

"What time shall we leave for the theater?" he asked.

"The curtain is at eight, so how about if you pick me up at seven?"

"Will you be home before then?"

"Yes, I'll be home all day."

"I'll stop by a bit early. I'd like to talk to you about something."

She froze, but didn't inquire as to what the subject would be. Then she cast a glance at her brother, and they shared a silent message. A man didn't *stop by* for no reason. A man stopped by to propose.

Was that what he intended? Why not? As he'd told himself over and over, it wouldn't kill him to be a husband, and she would be an excellent wife.

Mr. Newman approached, and he noticed how she was snuggled so tightly to Peyton's side. He frowned, then wiped his expression clean.

"May I speak with you, Lord Benton?"

Amelia chuckled. "He called you *Lord Benton,* rather than *Commander Prescott*, and the Earth didn't spin off its axis."

"He won't use any moniker but Benton," Peyton complained. "I insisted on Commander Prescott, but he wouldn't heed me."

"You poor thing," Amelia mocked. "You're rich and important, but no one will do as you bid them. How will you ever survive?"

"What is it, Newman?" he asked. "And don't pay any attention to Miss Boyle. She likes to be a nuisance."

Amelia popped in with, "May I help you instead, Newman? It's his lordship's birthday, and he shouldn't have to fuss with any issue."

Newman was flummoxed and not anxious to disappoint Amelia which was a good sign. If the butler liked her, any marriage would begin on a smooth note.

"I apologize, Miss Boyle," Newman said, "but it has to be Lord Benton. Alone."

"Ooh," Amelia teased, "that sounds serious. You'd better see what he wants."

"I'll be right back."

He followed Newman out to the foyer, and the man halted and explained, "I didn't feel I should mention this in front of Miss Boyle."

"I hope it's nothing horrid."

"No. It's just that you have a visitor."

"Well, I have many, many visitors tonight. The house is open to what must be half of London."

"I'm certain this . . . ah . . . person wasn't invited by Miss Boyle."

"Who is it?"

Newman leaned in, and when he whispered the name, Peyton could have fainted from shock.

"She's here now?"

"Yes. In the kitchen."

"You didn't need to hide her."

"With Miss Boyle appearing to be your *special* guest this evening, I deemed it best. If you'll come with me?"

"JOSEPHINE BATES! WHAT ON earth are you doing in my kitchen?"

Jo whipped around, trying not to be incensed as Peyton Prescott rushed toward her. He was dressed in formal attire, and there was a large party in progress.

On her trudging by the mansion, on observing the windows all lit and the wealthy, attractive people strolling in, she'd brazenly strolled in too. Mr. Newman had immediately intercepted her though, and he'd hustled her away.

She was in the servant's hall, sitting at their table. Footmen and maids scurried by, carrying trays of food and champagne. Even though the staff was very busy, she'd been courteously treated, supplied with tea and cakes, but her temper was on a slow boil.

She understood that Mr. Newman had a responsibility to manage the residence, but she wasn't a doxy who had stumbled in by mistake. During the prior occasion when she'd arrived with Lord Benton, she'd stayed in a bedchamber on the upper floors. She'd eaten supper with him in the small dining room.

She'd refused to make a scene, so she'd bitten her tongue, but she was furious at Mr. Newman for acting as if she was shameful and disgraced.

Lord Benton walked up and clasped hold of her hands. "Tell me why you're in London. I must admit to being stunned and thrilled."

"I think the more pertinent question is: Why are *you* here?"

He scowled. "Ah...this is my home? Why wouldn't I be here?"

He bent down and kissed her on the cheek, and she leapt away. Two maids were passing by, and they witnessed the inappropriate contact. Gossip would spread like wildfire that the Earl was kissing a stranger in the kitchen.

He studied her, and his scowl deepened. "Are you angry with me? You can't be angry. It's my birthday. Let's go upstairs so I can introduce you."

"No, thank you, Lord Benton." She cast a scathing glare at Mr. Newman. "Your butler decided I wasn't fit to mingle with your lofty friends, and I couldn't impose."

Mr. Newman had the grace to look abashed. "I'm sorry, Miss Bates, but I thought...ah...I simply thought you'd be more comfortable if...if...."

"Yes, I'm very comfortable, Mr. Newman."

"Don't worry about any of that now." Lord Benton peered over at Newman. "She and I have to talk. Where is a good spot?"

"The housekeeper and I have an office down the hall. I'll show you."

Newman led the way, she and the Earl behind him. He gestured for them to enter the room, then he attempted to enter too, but Lord Benton prevented him.

"Give us a moment, Newman." Lord Benton smiled at Jo. "Have you eaten? Are you hungry?"

"I'm not hungry," she replied, and she never liked to seem churlish, so she added, "While I was waiting for you, your servants were very kind. I've already been fed."

He said to Newman, "I'll return to the party when I'm finished with her."

"I must remind you, my lord, that supper will be served in about twenty minutes."

"They can start without me."

"I doubt anyone would want that. The celebration is in *your* honor."

"I'll try to hurry."

The Earl shut the door in Newman's face, then he spun to Jo, and he was grinning his devil's grin. His warm gaze washed over her as if he'd missed her every second. Obviously, the man was mad as a hatter.

"This is the nicest surprise," he said. "I can't tell you how many times I nearly rode to Telford to find you."

"Yes, I'm sure you were pining away."

"You still haven't told me why you're in London. And why are you wandering the streets after dark? I realize you like to strut about on your own, but I'll be alarmed if you're alone."

There was a decanter of wine on the desk, and he poured himself a glass. He was babbling on as if all was fine between them, as if he hadn't evicted her niece.

Jo had been in London for a fortnight, having come to the city after exhausting every avenue of assistance in Telford. As Maud had threatened, she'd disseminated wicked stories about Jo, and neighbors had eagerly swallowed Maud's lies.

Jo had had enough of their cruelty and spite. She'd taken her money and Daisy and left, and she would never look back. She hadn't seen her sister again and likely never would. Her final memory of Maud would be as she'd screamed her vicious comments in the driveway.

Jo kept that image front and center so she'd never forget. It was fueling quite a torrent of rage. She'd lost everything, and Lord Benton was so oblivious that he was hosting a huge party. But it was his birthday. Why wouldn't he make merry?

Had he the slightest clue of the catastrophes he'd orchestrated?

"Would you like a glass too?" he asked, and he dipped the wine decanter in her direction.

"Yes, actually, I would."

It would occupy her hands so she didn't wrap them around his beastly neck.

"I remember that you like to drink wine," he said. "We certainly enjoyed our share that lovely night when we were last together."

"It seems a lifetime ago."

"Why did you sneak off the next morning, you scamp? I was loafing in the dining room, expecting you to join me for breakfast, but you never arrived. Eventually, I sent a maid to locate you, and she found your note." He clutched a mocking fist over his chest. "It broke my heart."

"Yes, it's clear you've been wasting away."

He leaned on the desk, his hips balanced on the edge, and he scrutinized her intensely.

"You're so angry with me," he murmured. "Why are you upset? I could have sworn we parted as friends."

"Some *friend* you are."

"Whoa!" he groused. "What's that supposed to mean?"

"As if you didn't know."

"I don't know! What's wrong? What sin have I committed?"

"Will you really stand before me and pretend to be innocent?"

"Jo, I'm not pretending. I have no idea why you're so livid. I demand you apprise me at once."

"By any chance, do you recall that I have a niece?"

"Yes, Daisy. What about her?"

"Then you must also recall that I had a deadline of July fifteenth to remove her from your property."

"Yes, but we waved it, so what's the problem? Are you having trouble with Richard Slater because if you are—"

Jo held up a hand, stopping him. "You promised I could have more time."

"Yes, you can have as much as you like. It doesn't matter to me if Daisy tarries for a bit. I'm positive you'll work out a good solution."

"When did you last visit Benton Manor?"

"It's been a few weeks."

"So you haven't checked on conditions?"

"No, why? Has the manor burned to the ground?" He laughed as if such a calamity would be funny. "I told Richard to write me if it happened, but I haven't heard from him, so I'm assuming it's not that."

There was a chair behind her, and she slid down, her knees shaky, as if she might collapse. She gulped down her wine and placed the glass on the floor.

She'd rented a room in a women's boarding house. It was clean, safe, and quiet, and the price was reasonable. She was searching for a job, but so far, she'd had no luck.

With the money from Mr. Slater, she'd be all right for several months—if she was frugal—but then what?

She would never return to Telford, would never beg Maud for shelter or help. Her sister could wallow away the years with her horrid Mr. Townsend. Jo was delighted to be shed of both of them, but she was in a pickle.

An upscale salon that served the richest ladies had been anxious to hire a seamstress, and she'd just interviewed for the position. She was adept at sewing, but also at shaping and redesigning the clothes Maud used to give her. She'd thought she would be an asset to a business like that.

But numerous other women had shown up for the interview too. It had been such a lengthy line of candidates that it had taken forever for the proprietress to speak with her. While the woman had liked Jo's outfit very much—a lavender dress with cream colored lace on the color and cuffs—she'd been bluntly candid that Jo was too chic and stylish to be the girl she sought.

She'd doubted Jo would stay at her post, and despite how fervidly Jo had argued, the woman wouldn't change her opinion.

It had been a depressing blow, and as she'd staggered home, she'd realized Benton House was in the area. She'd decided to see if the residence was shuttered, and if it wasn't, she'd planned to ask the servants if they had an address for Commander Prescott so she could contact him.

Mr. Slater had claimed he was at sea, and like a gullible ninny, she'd accepted the story without question. She couldn't quite wrap her mind around the astonishment of learning that he hadn't sailed off after all.

While she'd been panicked and afraid and struggling to forge a path for herself and her niece, he'd been carrying on as he always had. He'd been celebrating his birthday.

She must have looked particularly dejected because he laid a palm on her shoulder and inquired, "Jo, what is it?"

"Mr. Slater told me you'd gone back to the navy."

"He what? What an ass. That's not true, and he's aware it's not. I may return to the navy. In fact, I probably will, but nothing is definite."

"He said—before you departed—you instructed him to enforce the deadline."

He frowned, at first not comprehending. "Do you mean the July fifteenth deadline? The one where Daisy and the others had to be out?"

"Yes, I mean *that* deadline."

"I didn't tell him that, Jo. I never would have."

She gazed up at him, and her heavy burdens caught up with her. Tears dripped down her cheeks, and she swiped them away. He pulled up a chair and sat in front of her so they were very close, their feet and legs tangled together.

"I believed him," she miserably admitted. "Why wouldn't I have?"

"We haven't been friends all that long, but I'd like to suppose you know me better than that. I would never be that cruel."

"I received a letter from you."

"What did it say?"

"I had to fetch her from Benton by the fifteenth. If I didn't, you'd directed Mr. Slater to send her to an orphanage."

Lord Benton froze, seeming chilled by the news, and he shook his head with disgust. "I didn't write you a letter, Jo. I specifically ordered Richard to give you as much time as you required. It was my last command to him as I walked out the door to leave for London."

"Well, then, either he feels no need to obey you or he is deaf."

"Where is Daisy? Is she still at Benton?"

"No, Lord Benton! Pay attention. I had to fetch her away from there. Bobby and Jane had to go too. Their governess, Miss Watson, traveled with them to Cornwall."

"Why?"

"She hopes to meet with Jane's uncle and beg him to have mercy on them."

He appeared stunned. "Richard evicted them?"

"Yes."

"And where is Daisy?"

"She's waiting for me at our boarding house. I've rented a room there."

"A boarding house! You have to be joking."

"When I left Benton with her, I took her to the home I used to share with my sister."

"The one you *used* to share?"

"My sister was extremely irate, and she kicked us out on the road."

His shoulders drooped, his dismay obvious. "Oh, I'm so sorry to hear it."

"So we came to London, and I've been trying to find a job."

"A job!" he huffed as if it had never occurred to him that a woman might have to work.

"Mr. Slater provided some money to tide us over, so for now, our situation isn't dire. But if I don't land a position soon, I can't predict what will happen." Her tears had become a veritable flood. She couldn't hold them in. She'd been so frightened, and she was terrified about the future. "I desperately need some help, Lord Benton, and I have nowhere to turn."

"Yes, you do. *I* will help you, Jo."

He dragged her off her chair and nestled her on his lap, and she rested against his chest and had a cathartic cry. It was wonderful to be able to lean on him, to let him carry her burdens just for a bit.

He'd insisted he wasn't responsible for Mr. Slater evicting Daisy, Bobby, and Jane, but Jo was too weary to figure out if she believed him. For the moment, she would accept his statements as true, but later, when she was stronger, she would assess his veracity more carefully. Ultimately, she might decide he was lying, but she wouldn't part from him again without garnering some serious promises of support.

Daisy was his niece. Daisy was his deceased brother's daughter, and Jo expected him to behave appropriately toward her.

She had no idea how long she wept, but she continued until there were no tears remaining, and she felt hollowed out.

"We'll retrieve Daisy from the boarding house," he said. "Immediately."

"I've been gone for hours. She's probably worried sick."

"The two of you will stay here with me while we devise a plan to keep you safe. I'll ensure that Richard never interferes."

Jo wanted to decline his offer, wanted to say *absolutely not,* that she didn't trust him, but she had to think of Daisy, so she couldn't be proud or vain. "I guess we can stay with you, but you have to swear you'll always be honest with me."

"I shouldn't have to swear, Jo. You should know I will always be honest."

"The past few weeks haven't won you any gold medals."

"My first act, after I get you and Daisy settled, will be to ride to the country and have a talk with Richard."

"Good. I hope you'll be very vicious with him, for he has certainly been vicious to me and mine."

Their banter dwindled, and she drew away and straightened herself. They were very close, so close, and he dipped in and kissed her, just a quick brush of his mouth to her own. She should have deflected it, but her spirits were at their lowest ebb, and it was precisely the balm she needed.

"Let's locate the housekeeper," he said, "and I'll have her prepare a bedchamber for you. Then we'll have Newman order my carriage."

"What about your party?"

"Don't concern yourself over it. Your dilemma is more important."

Before they could stand to depart, the door opened, and a very pretty young lady peeked inside.

"There you are, you sly devil!" she said.

She started to laugh, but swiftly swallowed it down as she noted the intimate way Jo and Lord Benton were snuggled together on the chair.

"Oh, hello, Amelia." His cheeks flushed with chagrin, and he gestured to Jo. "This is . . . ah . . . my friend, Josephine Bates."

The woman's cheeks flushed too. "Supper is ready, and . . . well . . . Newman is in a dither. We can't go in without you."

"I've had an issue arise," he said. "I won't be joining you for supper."

The woman, Amelia, looked stricken, and Jo hastily stated, "Lord Benton, you don't have to fuss with me. You should entertain your guests."

"My *guests* are all adults. They can eat without me."

"No, no, I insist," she hurriedly told him. "I can find Mr. Newman, and I'll fetch Daisy on my own. It's your birthday. You should enjoy yourself."

She slid off his lap, but he was holding her hand. Amelia saw that he was, and Jo was incredibly embarrassed.

Who was Amelia? Was she a sweetheart? Gad, might she be his betrothed? She was definitely scowling as if he belonged to her, as if she'd like to scratch Jo's eyes out.

Jo yanked away and rushed out without further comment. If he was about to *explain* himself to Amelia or if the pair of them was about to quarrel, Jo refused to listen.

She marched down the hall, stopping a footman to ask after Mr. Newman so she could have a carriage arranged. She'd pick up Daisy, then come right back. It appeared Miss Amelia might have a huge problem with that situation, but Jo couldn't worry about it.

For once, she could only worry about herself.

CHAPTER

11

"I THINK YOU SHOULD join me."

"I wouldn't lower myself."

Amelia frowned at Evan, wishing she could encourage him with a smile. They were in their carriage outside Benton House. It was early afternoon, and she had charged him with one of the more difficult tasks he'd ever assume.

He had to talk to Peyton for her.

The prior evening, when she'd hosted his birthday party, was to have been the perfect event. It should have settled their nagging question with regard to Peyton: Would he propose or not?

But the entire occasion had collapsed into a debacle.

Evan had been Peyton's best friend since they were eight, and they were closer than brothers. They'd learned to sail together, had enlisted in the navy together, had served together ever since. Evan was his First Officer and had stood by him through thick and thin.

Peyton had been like an abandoned orphan, so the Boyles had furnished the family his own family had refused to supply. He'd been welcomed by them for holidays, school breaks, and navy furloughs. They resided in London with their widowed mother, Lydia. She had felt sorry for Peyton, and she'd doted on him. He'd become a regular fixture in their lives.

Amelia was eight years younger than he and Evan were, and she'd played the part of little sister to Peyton. That is until he'd come home when she was eighteen, and she'd been all grown up.

From that moment on, there had been a special chemistry between them, and the Boyles had believed it would blossom into love and marriage. Peyton had never given them a reason to suppose he wouldn't wed her, so Amelia had never bothered with courting anyone else.

There had been no need. She figured she'd found her husband.

Yet when Neville had died and Peyton had inherited the title, it had caused frantic discussions around the Boyle dining room table. Was he too grand now to have Amelia as his bride? Would he pick a girl who had a loftier status?

Even then, even recognizing how his path had veered off from theirs, they hadn't wavered in their conviction that he'd proceed. They'd been so certain of him. He might be an earl, but it wouldn't alter who he was deep down.

The previous night, he'd elevated her expectations to the very highest level. He'd agreed to escort her to the theater, and he'd asked if he could stop by early to raise an important topic. No woman in the kingdom could fail to grasp the implication of a request like that.

He'd been planning to propose. Why wouldn't she have thought so?

At least it had seemed to be his intent—until it had been time to lead his guests into supper. He'd vanished, and Amelia had gone in search of him. A footman had directed her to the butler's office behind the kitchen, and she'd walked in on Peyton who—if he was about to betroth himself—had clearly been misbehaving.

Nothing had been the same since.

"Who was she again?" Evan inquired.

"Josephine Bates."

"I've never heard of her."

"Are you sure, Evan? He never mentioned her? Tell me the truth. I realize you have a relationship with him that doesn't include me. Has there been a secret you couldn't share?"

"No! I'm as stunned by this as you are."

"I'm not mistaken about what I witnessed. She was sitting on his lap, and it appeared as if they'd been kissing."

"If he was sweet on someone besides you, he would have told me."

"Are you positive? Any admission of that sort would indicate he'd changed his mind about me."

"Can I pose a scenario that might hurt your feelings?"

"Do you mean hurt them more than they already have been?" She chuckled miserably. "Go on. What is it?"

"She might be a...ah...doxy, a passing fancy. Men have dalliances, Amelia."

"I'm aware of that fact."

"Peyton is no different or nobler than the next fellow. He might simply be enjoying a fling before he's engaged. If that's his scheme, his association with her has naught to do with you."

She scoffed. "Naught to do with me!"

"He wouldn't have confided it to me either. Not with the two of you being...well...so fondly attached."

"You should have seen how he was looking at her. She wasn't a dalliance, Evan, and she wasn't a doxy. She was beautiful and elegant and quite fascinating. *He* was absolutely captivated."

"Are you imagining she's an aristocrat's daughter? Is that it? Are you afraid he's chosen a more appropriate candidate?"

"It will kill me if he has."

"If he's about to spurn you, why would he ask to stop by this evening?"

"Maybe I misconstrued about a proposal, and instead, he would deliver the news that it was over for us."

"And then what? After he broke your heart, you'd trot off to the theater together?"

"I can't predict what might have happened, Evan. All I can state with any certainty is that he was sequestered in an isolated room with a female on his lap, and it wasn't *me*."

She moaned with dismay and rested her head on the side of the carriage, her eyes closed, her frustration acute. She hated to place Evan in the middle of such a quagmire. Any discord that arose would end up severing his bond with Peyton.

He and Amelia had a very small family. It was basically him, their mother, and her. They had a few scattered cousins and that was it. Their father had been in the navy too, and he'd perished at sea when Evan and Amelia were young. The tragedy had created a tight link between them, and he was extremely devoted to her and their mother.

He felt very protective of them, and it was a burden he'd assumed as a boy when they'd received the dreadful report about their father. The naval officer who'd conveyed the grim tidings had quietly murmured to Evan, *You're the man of the family now.*

Those words had become the bedrock of how he carried on. His world revolved around her and their mother and how he could keep them safe and happy.

He was the most loyal person on Earth while Peyton wasn't loyal at all. They'd remained friends because Evan worked at it and deemed it important. If the situation had been left up to Peyton, their connection would have swiftly dwindled.

His father's cruel treatment had hardened him, but Evan had managed to chip away at his shell. He understood what Peyton was like. If Peyton crushed Amelia's expectations, how would they continue on in a cordial way? It didn't seem possible.

"I refuse to believe there's mischief occurring," he said.

"You're so naively faithful, Evan. You always have been. It's what I cherish most about you."

"I won't listen to more of your suspicions. I'll talk to him as if nothing is wrong."

"You're very brave."

"Or very foolish." He snorted with disgust, then he urged, "Come in with me."

"Don't be daft. What if Josephine Bates is there? What if he admits he isn't visiting me tonight? You know what it would signify. Are you prepared for it? For *I* am definitely not prepared."

"There has to be an explanation. I'll pester him until I learn what it is."

"Good luck."

He reached over and squeezed her hand, and she smiled wanly.

"Will you wait for me?" he asked.

"Are you joking? I wouldn't want him to glance out as I'm loitering in his driveway like a lovesick girl."

"But you *are* a lovesick girl."

"I won't have him pitying me, and if he's tossing me over, after all these years of my being so accommodating, I'd like to be apprised right away so I can move on."

"Honestly, it sounds as if you've already given up on him, but you shouldn't surrender so easily. Don't you think he's worth fighting for? Don't you think *you* are worth having? Shouldn't we remind him that you are?"

She sighed with resignation.

She was much smarter than her brother. She had a woman's pragmatism, and she saw matters as they truly were rather than how she wished they would be.

After she'd stumbled on Peyton with Josephine Bates, she'd dragged him back to the supper, but every minute of the meal and the socializing afterward had been incredibly awkward.

He'd kept sneaking off to have severe conversations with Mr. Newman. He'd ignored his guests, had declined to dance or play cards. Eventually, he'd disappeared for over an hour with no clarification as to why. Amelia had been so embarrassed that they'd called for their carriage and departed.

Had he ever returned to the party? If so, had he noticed her absence? She was terrified he might not have.

"Go inside, dear brother," she said. "Speak to your friend. Find out what's happening with him."

"He might not tell me."

"You'll pry it out of him. I have no doubt, and maybe you'll cross paths with the enchanting Josephine Bates too. We'll chat again after you have."

"Are you heading home?"

"Yes. I'll be there in a bit. Please don't delay. I'm starting to recognize that I've waited quite long enough for Peyton Prescott. My patience may have finally been exhausted."

Evan blew out a heavy breath and climbed out of the carriage. He motioned to the driver, and Amelia rolled away, being intent that Peyton never presume she'd been pondering him for a single second.

EVAN WAS SITTING IN Peyton's front parlor when the most beautiful woman he'd ever seen strolled into the room. With auburn hair and big blue eyes, she was the kind of female who caused a man to gape and behave like an idiot.

She was wearing a simple gown, a lavender print with cream-colored lace on the neck and cuffs, but from the way it hung on her slender frame, it looked exceedingly elegant, as if it had been sewn by the finest dressmaker in Paris.

He had a sinking feeling that he'd bumped into the alluring, elusive Josephine Bates. No wonder Amelia had been so devastated. If Evan had witnessed this vixen nestled on Peyton's lap, he'd have been devastated too.

"Oh, hello," she said as he stood to greet her. "I didn't realize we had a guest."

"Hello." He struggled to be cordial, even as he was raging on the inside. "Let me introduce myself. I'm Evan Boyle. I'm a friend of the Earl's."

"Mr. Boyle! He's spoken of you so often."

Her comment indicated a lengthy acquaintance of which he was unaware, and he forced a smile. "I've known him since we were boys, so I have no secrets from him. I hope he hasn't shared any shocking details."

"Heaven's no. It's all been good."

She approached, and he watched her carefully, deciding she was graceful and polished, and he speculated as to whether Amelia hadn't been correct. Was this an aristocrat's daughter? Her demeanor painted her as someone from the upper echelons of society.

But she said, "I'm Miss Bates. Josephine Bates." So . . . not an aristocrat's daughter after all. "I'm a friend of the Earl's too."

"Pardon me for being blunt, but I thought I knew all his friends."

"I'm new. We only met the past month or so."

"How nice for you."

He kept his expression blank, not eager to provide a hint of his distress. She was very much at home in the parlor. Gad, were she and Peyton living in sin? Had matters progressed so far? If so, how could Evan not have guessed?

Mr. Newman poked his nose into the room. "Lord Benton will see you, Mr. Boyle, but he's moving slowly today."

"What a sluggard he's become." Evan tried to make the remark sound funny, but it fell flat.

Miss Bates loyally explained, "He was up very late."

The observation contained an incredible amount of innuendo, and to Evan, it was like a jab with a sharp stick. "Yes, it was quite a party. I'm sure he was *up* until dawn."

Newman gestured to the foyer. "He'd like you to come upstairs—if you wouldn't mind."

"No, I don't mind."

Evan was glad he and Peyton would confer in private. Evidently, they had numerous tricky issues to discuss, and he couldn't bear to have Miss Bates hear any of them. He couldn't continue to ignore the problem with Amelia. Nor could Peyton continue to prevaricate and delay.

With Miss Bates arriving on the scene, they were beyond the spot where they could pretend naught had changed.

"It was lovely to meet you, Mr. Boyle," Miss Bates said.

"And you as well, Miss Bates."

"I talked to the Earl a few minutes ago, and he was a tad grouchy. Don't let him bite your head off."

"He wouldn't dare."

She flashed a dazzling smile that caught him off guard. He didn't want to like her, didn't want to be fascinated, but she was irresistibly appealing, and he had no weapons to employ that would prevent him from being charmed.

Newman left, and Evan followed him up to Peyton's bedchamber. He was loafing in his sitting room, dressed—thank goodness—and having breakfast at a small table by the window. He waved Evan in and pointed to the chair across.

"Have you eaten?" Peyton asked by way of an opening. "Shall I order a plate for you?"

"As it is after one o'clock, I can admit to having eaten twice already."

"Where were you last night? I was called away for awhile, and when I came back, you and Amelia had departed."

"It was late, and she was exhausted, so I took her home."

He studied Peyton, anxious to glean an inkling of his mood, but he couldn't deduce a single clue. Peyton was shoveling down food as if he were about to march to the gallows and it was his final meal.

Did he understand how rude he'd been to Amelia? Did he care?

"Miss Bates introduced herself downstairs," Evan said. "She's stunning."

"Isn't she just?"

Evan paused so Peyton could fill in the gap with some information about her, but he was maddeningly silent. Evan had to nudge him along.

"She tells me she's been friends with you for a month or so."

Peyton considered, then nodded. "Yes, I suppose that's about right."

"You never mentioned her."

"It didn't seem important."

"Is it important now?" There was another lengthy pause, then Evan asked, "Is she staying with you?"

"Only until I can make other arrangements for her."

"Since she's *Miss* Bates, she's obviously unmarried, and you're a bachelor. Isn't it a tad improper?"

"Yes, it's all very improper."

"Aren't you concerned for her reputation? Or maybe for yours?"

Peyton scowled. "First off, *no*, I'm not concerned about that sort of thing—as you're well aware. And second, who is there to complain?"

"She must not have any male kin to watch out for her best interests."

"No, she doesn't."

"Perhaps *I* should watch out for them and protect her from you."

"Don't be ridiculous. She's fine with me."

"Is she?"

Evan's tone was very sharp, but then, his disgust was very great. At times,

Peyton could be an ill-mannered cur, and he wouldn't even realize that he was behaving badly.

It was just a simple fact that he was very vain, and he was never worried about what other people thought. He'd also been raised in a military boarding school where the social graces were never the most essential skill to be learned.

He noticed Evan's pique, and he put down his fork.

"You're in a snit. Why? What have I done?"

Could he really be so oblivious?

"I won't tiptoe around you," Evan said. "I'll blurt it out."

"Please do. I can't abide guessing games, and I won't play them."

"I visited you because Amelia is upset and puzzled."

"Why?"

"She walked in on you and Miss Bates down in the kitchen."

"Yes, it was all rather awkward."

"It seemed to her as if Miss Bates might be . . . ah . . . *special* to you."

"I like her very much," Peyton blandly stated.

"How long are you planning on her being here?"

"I have no idea."

"Will it be a few days? A week? A month? What?"

"She'll be here until I can find somewhere for her to go. For the moment, that's all I can tell you."

Evan's temper was flaring, and he tried to cool down, but with Peyton being so flippant, it was impossible.

"Who is she to you?" Evan demanded. "How close is she? Have you obtained a mistress without confiding in me?"

"Gad, no."

Peyton scoffed at the notion, but his cheeks reddened, providing ample evidence that he was lying.

"You agreed to escort Amelia to the theater tonight," Evan reminded him.

"Oh, I'd forgotten. I won't be able to escort her. Will you see her this afternoon? Can you inform her for me? Or should I send a note?"

"Why can't you take her?"

"Well, Jo has arrived, and I'm busy fussing with her."

"So it's *Jo,* is it? Not Miss Bates? Not Josephine?"

Peyton breathed out a heavy sigh. "You're dancing to a pertinent point, Evan. What is it? Let's get it out on the table."

"You told my sister you'd stop by early, that you had an important topic to address. We both know what the topic was to be, so don't pretend to be confused."

Peyton stared at Evan for an eternity that was excruciating. Ultimately, he said, "I'm not confused, and I probably won't be stopping by to ask her any questions."

"Today? Or ever?"

Peyton eased back in his chair, and he debated his response. He'd want to avoid a quarrel, but in light of the ledge where they were suddenly perched, a fight couldn't be avoided.

Mr. Newman was hovering, ready to assist if needed, but eavesdropping too. Peyton gestured to him. "Would you give us a minute, Newman? Step out and shut the door behind you."

Newman hesitated, curiosity practically oozing out of him, but he couldn't decline to obey. He sidled out, and once they were alone, a dangerous silence descended.

There was a decanter of brandy over by the fireplace. Peyton grabbed it and brought it over. He poured some into his tea cup, and he used an empty water glass to pour some for Evan. He pushed the glass to Evan, but Evan didn't reach for it.

Depending on the next words that came out of Peyton's mouth, this might be the last time they spoke, so it might also be the last time they shared a drink. But Evan was so incensed that if he'd tried to swallow any of the liquor, he'd most likely have choked on it.

"We should have had this discussion ages ago," Peyton said.

"You've been sniffing around my sister for four years. When would we have had it?"

"I won't feign indignation over your accusation. I recognize that I haven't always acted appropriately toward her."

"Acted *appropriately*?" Evan sneered. "She never allowed any other boys to court her—because of you. She sat in my mother's parlor, waiting for you to propose."

"She shouldn't have," Peyton bluntly huffed.

At the horrid comment, Evan gasped with affront. "I hope you didn't mean that the way it sounded."

"No, no," Peyton hurriedly insisted. "I possess the highest regard for Amelia."

"Yes, your *high* regard will certainly keep her warm on cold winter nights."

"I'm too damaged, Evan. You realize that I am. My childhood has left me broken, and there are empty parts that will never be filled. Why would you want your sister to wind up with me? I'd be an awful husband."

"She was counting on you!"

"I should have told you sooner."

Evan snorted with derision. "Has it occurred to you that she doesn't mind your damaged parts? Has it occurred to you that she's in love with you and she'll take you just as you are?"

"You're being absurd. She's not in love with me. We're very fond of each other, but we shouldn't read more into this than there has ever been."

"Prick," Evan spat.

"Yes, I suppose I am."

"Is this because of Miss Bates?"

"Not because of her precisely. She simply yanked me to my senses."

"Where had your *senses* gone?" Evan caustically asked. "I wasn't aware they were missing."

"With my turning thirty, I've been wondering if I should marry, but with my ascending to the title, I've recently endured so many changes."

Evan nearly lunged over the table and pummeled his old friend. The remark had him that enraged.

"Don't you dare claim you're too bloody good for Amelia now. If you try it, I'll beat you to a pulp."

"I'm not claiming that. I merely think I should consider my options."

"What is it you're considering? Could it be that Miss Bates has arrived, and you've noticed there are other pretty fish in the matrimonial sea?"

"It's not that."

"What is it then? You've been pondering Amelia for *four* years!"

"I know, I know, but it's not as if I have a father to guide me in this. It's a monumental decision, and I'm on my own and floating free. It's difficult."

"You poor thing! Your life is so hard."

"There's no need for sarcasm. I'm attempting to explain myself so you'll comprehend my reasoning."

"Oh, I comprehend it all right. While you're *considering,* will Amelia's name ever pop into your head? Or must I notify her that it's over between you? Should I tell her to move on?"

Peyton paused, and an eternity passed at a snail's pace. They both understood—once Peyton replied—it would wreck what they'd had. Once he cut Amelia loose, once the words were uttered out into the universe, there could be no going back.

Peyton's shoulders slumped with what looked like genuine regret. "No, Evan, Amelia will not be who I'm contemplating. I'm sorry."

"You're sorry!" Evan fumed. "Is it so you can lift Miss Bates's skirt without feeling guilty? Is that it?"

"I won't dignify that comment with a response."

"Of course you won't, you bastard."

Evan glanced down at his lap, and he stared at his hands, desperate to figure out how to finish the hideous encounter.

They'd walked out onto their hazardous ledge, and Peyton had shoved him over. Evan was falling down and down, and it would be a very rough landing. When he hit bottom, he would be completely destroyed, and if he wasn't, his sister certainly would be.

A flicker of fury ignited in his belly, and he fanned it, being delighted to let it grow into an inferno.

He thought of all the years he'd been kind to Peyton, that he'd been Peyton's staunchest chum. He thought of all the cozy evenings spent at the Boyle's house where Peyton had been one of them, like a brother to Evan, like a second son to Evan's mother.

Mostly, Evan thought of his sister and how she'd thrown away her other chances, being positive that Peyton would come up to snuff in the end.

Part of it was her own fault because she possessed much of their mother's gentle nature, but a bigger part of it was Evan's fault because he'd wanted Peyton to be Amelia's husband. He'd imagined them bouncing through the decades, happy and friends forever, with Peyton accepting the greatest gift Evan could ever bestow, that being his dear sister.

And now, a beautiful girl—Miss Bates—had slinked in and ruined his plans. He yearned to hate her for usurping Amelia's spot, but she couldn't be blamed. She'd simply forced Peyton to realize there were better nuptial choices, and none of them were Amelia.

No, Evan could never hate Miss Bates. He viewed himself as a knight in shining armor, a protector and defender of women.

It was clear she was all alone in the world, with no male relatives to guard her from a cur like Peyton. Evan wished he had a connection to her, so *he* could step in, so *he* could shield her from whatever damage Peyton would ultimately inflict.

"Prick!" he muttered again.

He swiped his arm across the table, sending all the cups, glasses, and plates crashing to the floor. Much of the expensive glassware shattered.

"Dammit, Evan!" Peyton leapt away so the teapot didn't spill hot water in his lap. "Look at the mess you've made!"

Evan jumped up too, and he wondered if they might brawl. They never had. Not even when they were boys.

"Don't ever stop by our home again," Evan said.

"You're being ridiculous."

"No. Don't stop by. Don't contact my sister."

"I can't agree to that. After all we've meant to each other, I should talk to her about this in person."

"After all we've *meant* to each other? If you would treat her like this, how can I believe she's been special to you in even the slightest way?"

"I have no idea what else to say, except that I'd like to visit her later this afternoon so we can resolve this face to face."

Evan worried the top of his head might blow off. "Are you mad? You actually imagine she'd listen as you explained yourself? And you don't even have an explanation! You're just being a pompous ass!"

"I won't let it conclude like this. Not with you or with her."

"Fuck you."

Evan had shouted the crude epithet, and Mr. Newman peeked in. "Is everything all right, gentlemen?"

They ignored him, and Evan kept his deadly gaze locked on Peyton. "If you ever knock on my mother's door, if you ever speak to my sister, I will kill you. I swear it."

"Evan!" Peyton scolded.

"You think I'm joking, but I'm not."

"You need to get control of your temper. We'll discuss this when you're not quite so angry."

"We will *never* discuss this in the future, and I hope you're happy with your precious Miss Bates. Good luck to both of you."

Evan whipped away and stormed out. Mr. Newman was in the doorway, and he staggered back or Evan would have run him over. He marched down the hall and down the stairs, and his mind was awhirl with how miserable the coming weeks and months would be.

He knew Peyton, and Peyton knew him. Peyton would expect Evan to calm down and forgive him, that they would revert to the cordial relationship they'd previously enjoyed. But Peyton had forgotten the most important fact about Evan: Evan loved his sister and his mother, and he would do anything for them.

Amelia was twenty-two and about to turn twenty-three. She was very old to not have wed, and Peyton's actions would likely guarantee she would never marry, that she would live out her life as a spinster. What brother could excuse such a ghastly development?

He'd reached the foyer when Miss Bates emerged from the parlor.

"What's wrong, Mr. Boyle?" she asked. "I thought I heard you quarreling with Lord Benton. Please tell me you weren't."

Evan halted and studied her. She was young and pretty, and she appeared to be very vulnerable, a female in trouble who required a strong man to lean on.

Evan could absolutely understand why a cad like Peyton might be swept away, but whatever his ploy, it could never be to her benefit.

Peyton would take what he craved from her, and she wouldn't be able to resist giving him what he requested. Where would she be when he was finished with her?

Evan went over to her, and he brazenly clasped hold of her hands.

"Miss Bates," he said, "promise me you'll be careful."

She frowned. "Of course I will be. I'm always careful."

"It's just that I've been acquainted with Lord Benton for a very long time, and I doubt he has your best interests at heart."

"I disagree. He's been kindness personified, and I'm very grateful to him."

Evan could have told her about Peyton and his dalliances, about his lack of regard or loyalty for others. He could have enlightened her as to Peyton's childhood, how facets were missing from his character. Peyton didn't view the world as others did, and he never felt guilty about any act he perpetrated.

But what would be the point of any declaration? She hadn't been harmed by Peyton yet, so she'd never believe Evan.

"Be careful," he warned her again, "and be assured, if you ever need a friend, you can find me and I will help you. You needn't rely on Lord Benton."

"Well . . . ah . . . thank you, Mr. Boyle." His strident comment had her unsettled. "I'll remember your offer of assistance, and I'm honored by it. I haven't ever had much compassion bestowed on me, and I appreciate it."

"I'll worry about you."

"You shouldn't. I'm fine."

"Goodbye, and watch out."

He left, and he didn't glance back.

CHAPTER

12

"I'm glad we're here."

"So am I."

"How long will we be allowed to stay?"

Jo smiled at Daisy and said, "I don't know."

"I didn't like that boarding house."

"I didn't either."

Daisy sighed. "I wish we could live here forever. I wish we never had to leave."

They were in the bedroom that had been provided to Daisy. She had climbed under the covers, and Jo was sitting in a chair next to the bed and tucking her in for the night. It had been a wild few weeks for both of them, and Daisy was fading fast.

The prior evening, Jo had stopped by Benton House almost by accident. She'd simply hoped to ask the servants for Lord Benton's contact information in the navy. Instead, she'd stumbled on the Earl himself. He'd claimed to not have been part of Richard Slater's scheme to evict Daisy, and in the end, she'd decided to believe him.

It was interesting how swiftly a rich man could fix a problem. With the snap of his fingers, the nod of his head, she'd been plucked from peril and delivered to a safe haven.

Life was extremely easy in the fancy residence, and she was being lured into a false sense of security. She was barely acquainted with Peyton Prescott, yet she'd cast her lot with him. Misery and poverty were intriguing companions. They could push a woman to make choices she probably oughtn't to make.

She was unmarried and on her own, with no family or friends to advise her, and Lord Benton was a bachelor, so she had no business being in his home. But he'd offered, and she'd accepted. She was so grateful that she might do anything to keep him happy which was a very dangerous attitude.

"I like Commander Prescott," Daisy said.

"We should address him as Lord Benton."

"He told me he liked *Commander Prescott*. He asked me to call him that."

"Then you should."

"Or should I use *Uncle Prescott*? Or maybe *Uncle Peyton*?"

Jo had no idea what was most appropriate. Would Lord Benton like to be ceaselessly reminded that he was Daisy's uncle? In most people's opinion, she was the bastard child of the dead earl. Who would want it dredged up with every reference?

"You should stick with Commander Prescott for now," Jo said. "Once we know him better, we can figure out if it should be different."

"Can I tell you a secret?"

"Certainly."

"He's nicer than my father."

"In what way?"

"When he talks to me, he looks right at me, and he really listens."

"Your father didn't listen?"

"No, but then, I hardly ever saw him." She lowered her voice to a whisper. "He didn't like us very much."

Jo's response was diplomatic. "It's difficult to predict what a man like that is thinking. Were you sad when he died?"

Daisy carefully considered the question. "I wouldn't describe it as sad. I was more . . . worried I guess. We were afraid about what would happen to us. Mr. Slater was so mean. It was scary."

"It hasn't gotten any easier."

"You're wrong, Aunt Jo." Daisy grinned. "Everything has improved. I'm with you, aren't I? We're together?"

"Yes, that's been the best ending we could have had."

"I've decided you're my favorite aunt."

"Very funny. I'm your *only* aunt, you scamp. Now go to sleep."

Jo tugged the blankets under her chin, and she yawned, already drifting off as she drowsily mumbled, "Will you be here in the morning?"

"Yes, I'll always be with you—wherever we are. You shouldn't fret about it."

"I won't, especially not when we're with Commander Prescott. He wouldn't allow anyone to hurt us."

"I'm sure he wouldn't."

Jo blew out the candle, and she dawdled, watching Daisy as her eyes fluttered shut, as her respirations slowed.

The previous night, she'd coerced a very grumpy Mr. Newman into furnishing a carriage. She'd hurried across the city to fetch Daisy and their meager pile of possessions. When she'd arrived at Benton House, she'd been hustled in a rear door and whisked up to the bedchambers that had been opened for them.

The party had still been in full swing downstairs, but Jo hadn't been irked to be hidden from the posh guests. She hadn't been concerned about any issue but the fact that she and Daisy were safe.

She couldn't imagine how long sanctuary would be provided, but Lord Benton wouldn't toss two desperate females out on the road, particularly when one of them was a little girl *and* his niece besides. He'd promised to assist them, and she had resolved to let him.

She simply needed to be helpful and accommodating so he never regretted his invitation. Mostly, she had to dodge any encounters with Mr. Slater or his sister. If Jo kept out of their way, she was positive she'd be fine.

She was as fatigued as Daisy. She'd had a very lonely day where she'd been apprehensive every second. She'd had a quick hello with Lord Benton in the morning when she'd been walking down a hall, and he'd come toward her from the other direction.

He'd seemed pleased to see her, and he'd inquired about the servants and if they were being attentive, and of course, people had been wonderfully obliging. Then he'd disappeared.

Mr. Boyle had stopped by in the afternoon, and apparently, he and the Earl had had a terrible fight. Jo hadn't heard any gossip from the servants as to what it had been about, but they constantly peeked at her when they thought she wouldn't notice.

Had the quarrel been about *her*? Was Mr. Boyle angry about Jo's presence? She definitely hoped she hadn't been the cause. She refused to stir any trouble.

After Mr. Boyle had stormed out, Lord Benton had departed too, having fled before she realized he had. She had no idea where he'd gone or when he might be back, and she was determined that the following day not be as distressing as the first had been. They had to confer about her situation. And what if Mr. Slater showed up when he was away? What then?

She tiptoed out, and as she closed the door, Lord Benton was down the hall and frowning at her, as if she'd kept him waiting too long. Butterflies swarmed in her tummy. When he stared at her like that, it was impossible to pretend she wasn't thrilled.

He didn't speak but extended his hand to her. She hesitated, aware that she should gesture to the stairs so they could descend to the front parlor, but he had such a firm, steely manner of looking at a person. She couldn't disobey.

She went over and clasped hold. He stepped into her bedchamber, bringing her with him. Before she could comment, he'd shut and locked the door, then he swooped in and stole a kiss.

"Oh!" was all she could manage.

It was obvious he was happy to have dared an advance, and she certainly hadn't prevented it, so why not try it again? He wrapped an arm around her and drew her to him so their bodies were pressed together all the way down.

He kissed her thoroughly, until she was quite bowled over. All of it left her dizzy and disoriented. She knew the rules: He shouldn't be in her room. She shouldn't be sequestered with him. They shouldn't be kissing.

What was he thinking? What was *she* thinking?

Gradually, he pulled away, and she couldn't determine if she was relieved or disappointed.

"I missed you," he said, "and I'm glad you're back in my life."

"You could have fooled me. You've barely glanced at me since I arrived."

"I was busy, *and* I was deliberately avoiding you."

"Why invite me to stay, then avoid me? You're being ridiculous."

"You leave me all jumbled on the inside. You make me question my choices."

"*I* do that?" Jo asked. "I must be a sorceress."

"Yes, that's what you are: a sorceress. I'm feeling completely bewitched."

"Your condition isn't my fault. I can't cast a single magic spell."

There was a cozy fire burning in the grate, two chairs positioned in front of it and a table with a decanter of wine in between. He led her toward the chairs and the wine, but just when she assumed they'd sit down, he turned them toward her bed instead.

He flopped onto the mattress and tugged her down with him. If she hadn't already been prone, she might have collapsed from shock.

"What are you doing?" she fumed.

"I'm exhausted."

"We're not lying down. There are two perfectly fine chairs by the fire. Let's move over to them. Better yet, we should go down to the parlor and have our wine there."

"No."

She struggled to scoot away, but he draped an arm across her waist and a thigh across her legs. Their proximity produced many exhilarating sensations, but she was alarmed too. He was eager to push her into acts he had no business contemplating.

"Release me," she protested. "At once."

"No," he said again. "I want to relax with you like this."

"Well, *I* don't want to relax with you. You're scaring me."

"I'm not scaring you. Don't be absurd."

"What if the servants catch us? No one would blink an eye about you, but I'd never recover."

"I sent everyone to bed. No servants are wandering the halls."

He rolled onto his back, so she was sprawled on his chest, her ear resting over his heart so she could hear it beating. It was the most delicious moment of her life, and her mind was awhirl, chastising her for being a reckless ninny, but her torso was happy right where it was. She exhaled a heavy breath and tried to relax as he'd commanded.

"I'll remain here for a few minutes," she said, "but if you attempt any mischief, I will slap your face and stomp out."

He chuckled. "You will not."

"I might. Am I safe in your home or not? I presumed I was, but if you suppose I will misbehave to repay you for your kindness, you're deranged."

"You're being silly. I don't expect any compensation from you. In my view, I owe *you* quite a lot—due to Richard's shabby treatment of Daisy."

"I'm delighted you concur."

"And yes, you're safe with me. Don't insult me by suggesting you might not be."

"Since we're on my bed together, it doesn't feel very safe. Apparently, I have no moral fortitude."

"Perhaps, deep down, you're a strumpet. Perhaps you've been dying for an adventure like this."

"Only a man of dubious character would think so."

They were quiet for a bit. He studied the ceiling as she catalogued details: the heat of his skin, the hardness of his masculine frame, the smell of the soap emanating from his clothes. She would never forget what it was like to be so close to him.

"I missed you," he mentioned again. "I missed you all day."

"You keep saying that, but in light of your lengthy absence, I can't imagine why I'd believe you. Where have you been? It was so awkward to be here without you. The servants were peeking and whispering. The speculation swirling in the kitchen has to be humiliating."

"I don't care about the servants' opinions. I don't pay them to *like* me. I pay them to serve me."

"That's a hideous attitude to have, and I *do* care about other's opinions—even the servants, especially the servants. I court everyone's esteem. You should try it some time."

"They were peeking and whispering, but were they attentive?"

"Very attentive, and you still haven't told me where you were. I was hoping we would chat about my predicament."

"My friend, Mr. Boyle, stopped by this afternoon."

"I know. I met him."

"We had a vicious quarrel."

"I thought I heard shouting. Why were you quarreling? Can you tell me?"

He shifted them so they were facing each other. He scrutinized her, as he debated how much to reveal, and ultimately, he waved away any candor.

"It was nothing. Evan gets on his ethical high-horse and lectures me when he shouldn't. It's annoying, and it upset me. I went riding."

"All day and into the evening? Until it was dark outside?"

"Yes. I reined in at pubs and coaching inns and drank myself into a stupor."

"That news frightens me. I've been worried sick, and I wasn't even aware that you were being negligent. Now I'm aflutter with anxiety."

"You were worried sick? Really? I don't ever recall anyone worrying about me."

"Why not?"

"It's a long story."

"Well, *I* shall make up for all that lack of worrying. I promise to fret constantly."

Her comment had him smiling, and he dipped in and kissed her again. As he pulled away, they both sighed with pleasure.

"I didn't want to inflict myself on you when I was so grouchy," he said, "so I stayed away until I'd calmed."

"You're not grouchy now?"

"No."

"Good. I can't bear to deal with people when they're in a temper. Is your quarrel with Mr. Boyle over?"

"No."

She should have dropped the subject. After all, she was determined to never be a bother, but she was afraid her presence had precipitated the fight.

"Tell me the truth," she said. "Were you arguing about me?"

He dithered, then finally claimed, "Not about *you* precisely."

"What was it then?"

"If I admit to horrid conduct, will you hate me?"

"I've never hated anyone, and I don't intend to start with you. Nor will I accept that you were horrid to him. Confess your offense, and I shall decide if punishment is warranted."

"You're as honorable as Mr. Boyle. You'll side with him."

"I'll *try* to judge you impartially." Her tone oozed sarcasm.

"Heaven's no. Don't be my judge. I'd rather have you as my partner in crime."

"I would never conspire with you. Just confide in me. What did you do to your friend? Let's see if we can fix it."

"We can't fix it. Or at least I can't. It's what I figured out while I was riding and drinking. All those rural roads cleared my mind."

He didn't offer more than that, but she wasn't about to permit him to remain silent.

"What's wrong?" she pressed. "You can't hold it in. Not when I'm so concerned over what part I might have unwittingly played in it."

He blew out a heavy breath. "Remember the woman who interrupted us last night?"

"Yes, she was very shocked. Is she your betrothed? I've been panicked that she might have been."

"No, she's not my betrothed."

"Look me straight in the eye and swear it—and don't lie. Tomorrow, I'll ask the servants if you're engaged, so I'll find out for sure."

"I'm not engaged. I probably should have been, but I'm not."

"Your remark calls for a thorough clarification, and don't you dare decline to provide it."

"Jo, my life is such a mess."

"I believe I've previously mentioned that I have no sympathy for you and how *hard* your life is. Stop feeling sorry for yourself. It's infuriating."

He laughed. "You're so good for me. You keep my feet on the ground."

"Someone should. From my vantage point, you're always quite absurd."

"I don't mean to be, and I realize my situation seems grand, and it is now. Mostly. But when I was a boy, it was very rough." He paused, then quietly added, "Very rough indeed."

"How was it rough?"

"My father didn't like me. He was very stern and cruel, and there were rumors about my mother and how she might have had a . . . well . . . we'll just leave it at that. He was anxious to be shed of me, and he sent me away to school when I was seven."

"You were a child!" she huffed with indignation.

"Yes, and I lived like an orphan there. I was never allowed home on holidays. I was never welcome at Benton."

She scowled. "That's the most repugnant story ever. Your father must have been an ogre."

"He was, and he thought my brother, Neville, was perfect. He didn't need to have another son."

"Neville was perfect?" She scoffed. "Neville—with the nine illegitimate children? *That* Neville was perfect?"

"My father doted on him."

"Not only was your father an ogre, he was an idiot too. It must have been awful for you, Peyton," she murmured, not hesitating to use his Christian name.

"It was, but Mr. Boyle—Evan—befriended me at school, and I grew up as if I were his brother or maybe a fond cousin. The Boyles kept it from being awful. As the years went by, I rarely pondered Benton. I viewed the Boyles as my family."

"I would have too, but how does the young lady from last night fit into all of this?"

"She's Evan's sister, Amelia."

"Oh."

"We've always liked each other, and most people assumed we would marry."

She frowned. "Who are *most* people?"

"Amelia, of course. Evan and his mother. I suppose our acquaintances too."

"What about you? Were you expecting to wed her?"

"I frequently considered it, but I could never proceed. And with the title having been bestowed on me, I'm in more of a quandary than ever. I can't decide the best path."

It took her a moment to comprehend his implication. "You think she's beneath you now? Is that it? For if so, I must tell you it's a disgusting opinion to hold of a female you like very much."

"It's not that. She's wonderful, but I'm questioning every aspect of my life. I've constantly walked up to the edge of asking her, then I'd back away. I've finally put her out of her misery."

"You won't ask her after all?"

"No."

"What was the determining factor?"

"You."

"Me!"

"Yes, when you showed up in my kitchen, it became clear."

"You don't mean that. You *can't* mean that. You hardly know me, and I can't be the reason you would toss her over."

"I was so excited to bump into you, and it forced me to recognize I'd never felt that way about her. She's been like a pesky little sister to me. It's why I could never forge ahead. I couldn't picture her as my wife."

"How long has she been waiting for you to propose?"

"Four years or so?"

"Four years!"

Jo was aggrieved on Miss Boyle's behalf. Jo, herself, had nearly married Mr. Cartwright, but it had been after a whirlwind courtship. Even though her romance had blossomed very fast, she'd been devastated when it had ended. What if it had continued for four years? She couldn't imagine the pain that conclusion would render.

"Amelia is why Evan and I were fighting," he said. "He and I have been dancing around this situation for ages, and it erupted this afternoon."

"How did you leave it with him?"

"I wanted to speak to her—to apologize—but he told me if I knocked on their door, he'd kill me."

"Was he serious?"

"Probably."

"Will he ever calm down? Maybe in a few weeks or months, he'll feel differently."

"His father died at sea when he was a boy, so he's protective of his mother and sister. He dotes on them."

"Good for him."

"He could never forgive a person who hurt Amelia."

Jo's spirits sank. She'd planned to never be a bother, but she'd only been in residence for twenty-four hours, and she was already causing chaos.

"Should Daisy and I depart in the morning?" she asked.

"No!" he firmly stated. "You're not going anywhere until I've had a chance to make arrangements for you."

"I can't be responsible for ruining your relationship with Mr. and Miss Boyle."

"You didn't ruin anything," he insisted, but it certainly sounded as if she had.

She slid away from him, and she sat up, her hips balanced on the edge of the mattress, her feet on the floor. He was stretched out behind her, and he laid a palm on her back.

"You agreed to be my judge," he said. "I've behaved badly, haven't I?"

"Yes. You led her on for years, and you spurned her when you shouldn't have. There's no other possible verdict."

"I can't marry her though."

"It's what you claim now, but you should ponder a bit more so you're sure."

"I've had an eternity to decide. It's what Evan couldn't bear to hear. It's why we were quarreling."

She stood and moved away from the bed. When he was touching her, it was so difficult to concentrate.

"I want to share an incident from my past," she said. "I never talk about it."

He sat up too. "What is it?"

"Your predicament with Miss Boyle is very distressing to me."

"It shouldn't be. You've never even met her. It's my problem and none of yours in even the slightest way."

"Yes, but when I was eighteen, I was jilted at the altar by my fiancé."

He gasped. "What?"

"I was in the church, waiting for him, and he never arrived."

"What happened to him? Were you able to find out?"

"Yes, actually, and it's so embarrassing. Maud was my guardian, and before the ceremony, she had signed my dowry over to him. He absconded with it."

"What is his name?"

"Holden Cartwright."

"Did you search for him?"

"No. We were informed that he'd fled to Scotland, and we didn't have the money to chase after him. Anyway, I'm positive—if I had found him—my dowry would have been squandered."

"I wish I'd known you then. I'd have located him for you. First, I'd have beaten him to a pulp, then I'd have had him arrested for theft and breach of promise."

"It would have liked that." She grinned. "Especially the beat-him-to-a-pulp part. I'd have liked that very much."

"Aren't you worried that he's out there cheating other potential brides?"

"I hope not, but he's very charming, so he definitely could be."

His sympathy wafted toward her. "I'm sorry, Jo."

"I'm over it," she lied, "but this story about Miss Boyle is agonizing to me. I hate for any woman to be rejected by a man."

"It's agonizing for me too. I detest that I've hurt her, but in my own defense, I was only ever very cordial with her. I never blatantly encouraged her."

"Your view is irrelevant. *She* assumed you would propose. That's all that matters. No one cares what the male thinks about it."

"I suppose," he grumbled.

"You need to fix this with them."

"I will—after more time has passed. I'll make overtures to approach her face to face."

"I'm glad. In the interim, you and I must be very cautious. I can't have rumors circulating that *I* was the cause of your break from Miss Boyle."

"Who would believe that?"

Was he really that thick? "Everyone would believe it, you dolt. The servants are probably already speculating, and if that's the conversation in the kitchen, it will spread down the street fast enough."

She went to the door and fumbled with the key in the lock. She peeked into the hall, relieved to see it was empty. She motioned for him to depart.

"We can't meet like this in the future," she told him.

"Yes, we can."

"It's not up to you. I won't shame myself with you, and I won't have gossip disseminated that you and I are romantically involved. The news would crush Miss Boyle, and I won't be implicated in your folly."

"My relationship with you won't lead us to perdition." From the hot look in his eye, it was obvious he didn't mean it.

Men were so different from women. He could profess all sorts of honorable intentions, but in the heat of the moment, he'd ignore them. And *she* was too naïve and lonely to resist him.

"You're an earl," she said, "and if Miss Boyle—whom you've known all your life—is suddenly unsuitable, then I am certainly in the same boat. Since I could never be your countess, there's no spot I can occupy."

"I'm very fond of you though."

"Of course you are, and I am very fond of you too, but we'll leave it at that. Don't sneak in here again."

"I can't swear that I won't."

"I'm putting my foot down. You're a man, so you can't be expected to act appropriately, but *I* am a female, and I don't have that luxury. I have to behave or I'm doomed." She gestured to the hall. "Please go. This is getting awkward."

He dithered forever, studying her. No doubt he presumed he could coerce her into changing her mind, and she figured he was correct. He probably could, so she had to erect some barriers and keep them firmly in place.

"Goodnight, Lord Benton," she said.

At her mode of address, he snorted with amusement. "When you were on the bed with me, you called me Peyton."

"It was temporary insanity."

"My dilemma with Amelia doesn't have anything to do with you."

"Don't be absurd. It has everything to do with me, and we're not discussing it again. Goodnight."

Evidently, she appeared obstinate and adamant because he pushed himself to his feet and came over to her. He hovered, gazing down at her, his regard warm and affectionate. She yearned to reach out and wrap her arms around his waist, but she didn't.

"You're quite a lioness, aren't you?" he murmured. "If you feel strongly about an issue, you're an absolute warrior."

She chuckled at the very idea. "I'm not tough—not by any stretch of the imagination. This is simply a topic that haunts me."

He bent down and tried to steal a final kiss, but she was wiser now. She turned her head so he brushed her cheek instead.

They stood, frozen, wondering what a proper comment would be, but there didn't seem to be one. He smirked and strolled out.

She closed the door and spun the key in the lock.

CHAPTER

13

"Peyton! How...ah...nice to have you back."

"Is it *nice*? When we both know you don't mean it, is that the word you should choose?"

Richard stared at Peyton, and his first inclination was to hurl a snide retort, but he managed to control himself. Peyton Prescott was Earl of Benton, was Richard's boss, was Barbara's landlord and trustee, was guardian to Alice and Nancy, and there was naught to be gained by taunting him.

"What brings you to the country?" he said instead. "We hadn't heard from you, so we weren't certain if you'd sailed off with the navy or if you were gamboling in town."

Peyton flashed a wily smile. "Yes, that's me. All I do is gambol."

"It was your birthday. There was a rumor that you hosted a party at Benton House to celebrate."

"Why would there have been a rumor about it? Are the servants reporting my activities to you? Should I be concerned about spies?"

Richard frowned. "No, they're not spying. Someone mentioned it, that's all. I don't remember who. If it was a servant, several of them are cousins and siblings. Between the town house and the manor, it would have simply been family gossip."

"I suppose that's an explanation."

Richard forced his own smile. "Happy birthday! You turned thirty. That's a big milestone, isn't it?"

"I didn't find it particularly big—or interesting. If it were up to me, I'd just as soon still be twenty-nine."

They were in the dining room, and Peyton was eating a late breakfast. Footmen scurried about, determined to wait on him hand and foot—and that he be pleased with their efforts.

He'd ridden in without warning, and a maid had rushed to locate Richard to apprise him. He'd raced around, whispering orders and sending the staff creeping about to check that conditions were perfect.

Peyton hadn't bothered to rise when Richard entered. Richard was standing, hovering like a sycophant. He wasn't sure if he'd be welcome to sit too, and he suspected Peyton understood the moment was awkward, and he enjoyed harassing Richard very much.

Apparently, Peyton's belly was full, for he pushed his plate away and leaned back in his chair. He studied Richard, his impertinent gaze roaming up and down Richard's torso, then he gestured to the chair across, and Richard slunk down.

"Let's chat, Richard. We have some issues to discuss."

The footmen were all ears, deliciously eager to eavesdrop, and Richard asked, "Would you rather retire to my office? We'd have some privacy there."

"I don't require privacy for what I'm about to tell you, and I don't care if the footmen listen. They likely already know what happened anyway." Peyton glanced at them. "Didn't your sister convey all of them to Benton after your father went bankrupt?"

"Well . . . ah . . . most of them."

"So the Prescott servants lost their jobs, some—I might add—whose families had worked here for generations."

"I wouldn't put it that way," Richard said.

"How would you put it?"

"Barbara was the new countess, and she had to establish her household. Every bride does. It's not unusual. She needed people who would grasp how she liked to run things."

"Yes, I'm positive the Slater servants were much more competent and obliging than the Prescott ones."

"Your brother never had any complaints."

"He's dead though, so we can hardly ask him, can we?"

Richard blew out a heavy breath and prayed for patience. "What's wrong? You seem vexed with me. Have I angered you? If so, I wish you'd toss it out in the open so we can address it like adults. I hate all this innuendo and spite. It doesn't get us anywhere."

"No, it doesn't, but I like how it discomforts you. I'm a rude ass, and you're a pompous ass, and I love seeing you so unnerved." He poured himself some tea, drank down the contents, then changed the subject. "How are Neville's bastard children? Have you found homes for them or are they still in the cottage?"

"Their maternal relatives came forward, and they've all left."

"Have they?"

Peyton scrutinized Richard as if he were vermin, as if he were a clot of dung Peyton might wipe off his boot. His focus was so potent and so intense that Richard squirmed in his seat.

"Before you dig a hole for yourself, Richard," Peyton said, "I should probably inform you that I have become friendly with Josephine Bates."

"Oh."

Outside, it was a gray, cloudy morning, the weather so inclement that Richard couldn't fathom why Peyton would ride from London. It was definitely a day to be caught in a deluge out on the road. A burst of lightning streaked across the sky, and a crack of thunder boomed so loudly that it rattled the glassware. Everyone jumped except Peyton.

"Remember the last time I was here, Richard?" Peyton asked. "You and I chatted in the foyer."

"Yes, I remember."

"Good. So we don't have to pretend we never talked. Do you recall my instructions? They would have been my final words as I walked out the door."

Richard's cheeks heated with embarrassment. Who could have guessed that Miss Bates would cross paths with Peyton? And so soon too!

Richard thought he'd tricked her. She'd demanded to speak with Peyton, and Richard had lied and claimed he'd sailed away to the Caribbean. She'd accepted Richard's statement without argument. How should he proceed through the debacle?

There was no viable route but to brazen it out.

"Yes, I recall your final instructions," Richard said.

"I specially told you *not* to enforce the July fifteenth deadline, but it appears you enforced it immediately." Peyton drummed his fingers on the table. "I'm at a loss, Richard. We have a problem with you recognizing my authority over you."

"I have no problem. It's my duty to carry out your orders."

"If that's how you view it, then why would you flagrantly disobey me?"

"I disagreed with your decision, and I felt it was important to countermand it. Surely I must have some leeway to manage things."

"I understand you need leeway, but *you* need to understand—if you were one of my sailors—I'd have you flogged, then I'd lock you in the brig for a few weeks so you could contemplate your choices. Let's review, Richard. Who is in charge? You or me?"

"You."

It was the only suitable answer, but it didn't seem as if Peyton should be in charge. The property seemed to belong to Richard and Barbara. Neville had never cared about Benton and had preferred to revel in town with dissolute companions.

He'd handed the estate's reins to Richard, and Richard had eagerly assumed control. He'd run the place for most of a decade, and it was infuriating to have Peyton bumble in and seize power.

What did he know about Benton? He'd never visited, had never corresponded with Neville or feigned any affection for his brother. Since he'd arrived on furlough, he'd been distant and aloof and bored. What gave him the right to interfere? What gave him the right to chastise or chart the course? He wasn't worried about Benton and was too disconnected to learn any details.

Yet Richard didn't dare mention any of that.

"How should I respond to this fiasco?" Peyton pressed. "I'm curious as to your opinion."

"I swore to my sister that I would rid her of those children, and I kept my promise."

"They were my nieces and my nephew. They have my deceased brother's blood flowing in their veins."

"With all due respect, Peyton, they are your deceased brother's *bastards*. They're a disgrace to your family."

"Are they? I suppose it depends on whose morals we apply."

"And they are a permanent stain on my sister's marriage to your brother. Certainly, we can agree on that much."

"Yes, I can agree with that part of your assessment, but I'd like to set all that aside for a moment."

"Fine, set it aside."

"How can I ever trust you in the future?"

"I'm an excellent administrator," Richard fumed.

"Are you? That's debatable. Aren't you the fellow who advised me we're nearly bankrupt?"

"Yes, we are!" Richard's voice and temper were rising. He couldn't tamp them down. "But it's because of your brother! We were never able to contain his profligate habits. I tried to curb his extravagance—I constantly tried!—but talking to him was like talking to a wall!"

The footmen shifted uneasily, suddenly wishing they'd been kicked out before the conversation had started. Peyton deemed it amusing to have them hear the quarrel, but Richard wouldn't allow them to loiter and gawk.

Richard gestured to them. "All of you, get out, and close the door behind you."

Peyton didn't contradict the command, but as the last boy passed by, he said, "Find the Countess, would you? Tell her I must speak with her at once, and she can't refuse to attend me."

"I will, my lord," the boy muttered, and he hurried off to locate Barbara. As their strides faded, Richard asked, "Why do you need Barbara?"

"We'll discuss it when she arrives."

"I won't permit you to confer with her without my being present. I won't have you browbeating her."

"I don't mind if you listen in while I browbeat her. Now where were we?" He poured himself more tea, and he looked very calm, as if he wasn't disturbed in the least by their heated bickering. "Oh, yes, we were dissecting your blatant disregard of a direct order from me."

"Those children couldn't remain. They were a humiliation to my sister!"

"Yes, they were, but the issue we're pondering is between you and me. It doesn't involve her."

"Everything at this estate involves her."

"Not this. For you see, Richard, I'd really, *really* like to return to the navy."

"So go! What's stopping you? It's obvious you hate it here."

"If I sailed away, and I was away for months or years, how could I leave you at your post?"

"Your brother was satisfied with my service."

"Was he?" Peyton snidely said. "Again, he's dead, so we can't pry an answer out of him."

"Ask anyone at Benton. They'll tell you I've been good at my job."

They'd delved to the crux of the dilemma, and he didn't have much of a defense. Peyton had told him to be lenient to the three children, and Richard had ignored him.

"How did Miss Bates track you down?" Richard inquired—when he probably shouldn't have. "Why would she feel free to poke her nose into this situation?"

"Does it matter?"

"She has some nerve, accosting you."

"Only you would think so."

"I sent those children away because my sister begged me to, and I won't apologize for it."

"I'm not seeking an apology from you."

"Then what is it you want?"

"I'm trying to figure out how we should muddle forward."

"I am your agent. If you don't like the procedures I've implemented, then I guess you ought to terminate me."

"All right, you're fired."

Richard gasped with offense. He'd offered himself on the chopping block as any competent manager would when faced with his boss's displeasure. He'd confessed his sins and given reasons for them. Peyton—if he'd been a rational, sane employer—should have jumped to insist there was no need for theatrics or drastic measures.

Instead, Richard had dangled bait, and Peyton had swallowed it whole.

"I'm . . . I'm . . . fired?" Richard sputtered.

"I suppose *fired* is a tad harsh. We'll say we're making arrangements for your departure—and the sooner the better."

"But . . . but . . . my sister is here. My mother is here. I live with them. Benton is our home now. You can't just chase me away."

"I can't? You're confused, Richard. Who is your boss? Who owns Benton? Who is earl? The reply to each of those questions is *Peyton Prescott.*"

They engaged in a staring match Richard could never win, and tears flooded his eyes. They were tears of fury, not of sadness, but they were tears nonetheless. He was so overcome that he wondered if he might break down and bawl like a baby.

"Prick," he spat before he could bite down the horrid word.

Peyton laughed. "That's the second time in two days I've had that moniker flung at me. Perhaps I should wear it with my other medals."

Barbara took that moment to rush in. Instantly, she recognized something was terribly wrong.

"What's happened?" she demanded.

"I've been fired," Richard told her.

"By who? By him?" She pointed a condemnatory finger at Peyton.

"Yes."

"Absolutely not!" she huffed. "I won't allow it."

Peyton merely tsked with exasperation, and he glared at Richard. "You and I just established the name of the true owner at Benton. I'll leave it to you to explain it to her."

Barbara forced a smile. "Can we discuss this?"

"No." Peyton stood and threw his napkin on the table. "Your brother tells me that the estate is almost bankrupt."

She cast a scathing glance at Richard. Early on, they'd agreed that they would provide no information to Peyton unless he dug it out of them with a shovel.

"We have some minor financial problems," she claimed. "It's not serious."

"Nice try, Countess, but I've had accountants scouring the books, and it's much worse than either of you would ever have admitted."

"How would you know?" Barbara unwisely scolded. She never liked to be chastised. "You rode in for your first visit a few weeks ago. You're in no position to strut about and hurl accusations."

"I won't waste my breath arguing with you." Peyton looked very fierce, very determined. "I will be sending a team of investigators to complete an inventory and property examination. While I wait for reports from them, funds for running the house will be severely curtailed, and the pair of you will no longer have access to any of the bank accounts. I suggest you start cutting back."

Richard leapt to his feet. "Now see here, Peyton!"

"No, you need to *see,* Richard. You shouldn't have crossed me, but you chose to, so now, you have to pay the price. I won't toss your sister out on the road—as you did to those children—but I'll give *you* a month to make plans for yourself."

"What sort of plans?"

"One month from today, you'll have to be living elsewhere. I'll be locking the estate office so you won't be permitted to use it."

"You can't stop me from doing my job! I'll . . . I'll smash a window and climb in."

"Don't be absurd, and don't be difficult. You had to have known I'd find out about your shenanigans. You had to have known what the result would be if you were caught."

Richard sank down in his seat. The actual fact was that he'd never imagined Peyton would discover Richard's scheme. Who would have notified him? And if someone had, why would he have cared? Those children had been a pain in the ass for years, and Richard had relieved the family of their unwanted presence. Why quibble?

Barbara frowned at Peyton. "What have you found out? What are you talking about?"

"Your brother can explain that too. The major issue for you is that I'll be opening the Dower House. You and your daughters will have to have moved there by the time your brother departs in a month."

"Move! To the Dower House? I won't!"

"Fine, then. You can depart with your brother. Your daughters will remain at Benton without you though. They're my wards, and you can't flit off with them."

Barbara blanched, then reined in her temper and her attitude. "I realize you're angry with us, and I truly apologize for any misunderstanding. I'm stunned to learn you're unhappy with Richard. Perhaps we could have him step out so you and I can confer in private."

"I have no desire to confer with you on any subject, and you couldn't change my mind anyway."

"Please let me try."

"No. I'll be in town and staying at Benton House. My investigators will show up tomorrow—unless the weather prevents them from traveling. I've already spoken to the housekeeper to have rooms organized for them."

"What tasks will occupy you in town?" Barbara sounded almost hopeful.

"I'll be meeting with my bankers and lawyers. Once I've gathered all the pertinent information, I'll be back, and we'll discuss your situation further. In the interim, you will prepare to move. You have thirty days."

He walked out, and Barbara peeked out the door and watched him vanish down the hall.

"Well . . . I never!" she muttered after he'd disappeared. She came to the table and sat down next to Richard. "This is a disaster. What should we do?"

"There's nothing we can do," Richard said. "As he so ungraciously apprised me, *he* is boss, owner, and earl, and we are out in the cold."

"I will never surrender Benton to him!" Barbara vowed. "Where would I go? He can't suppose we'll cram ourselves into an apartment in town with our dear brother, Roger."

"You say that as if Roger would welcome you and Mother. I doubt he would. Mother, especially."

"Why is Peyton so irate?"

"He arrived in a snit. Apparently, he heard that I evicted Neville's bastards—after he told me I shouldn't."

At the comment, Barbara was so livid that Richard wondered if the top of her head might simply blow off.

"What did he expect?" she raged. "Was his intent to continue shaming me as his brother always had?"

"I can't guess what he expected. He's a madman. The trouble was caused by Miss Bates, Daisy's aunt? She tracked him down somehow and tattled about how we kicked them out."

"Miss Bates! That little tart! How dare she!"

"She seemed the type who'd be accursedly loyal, and she's very pretty. Peyton obviously enjoyed acting as her champion."

"We'll just have to get even with her, won't we? We're so far above her in station. She has to comprehend that there are consequences when a common person like her crosses people like us. What retribution could we extract that would harm her the most?"

"I have no idea."

"Don't worry, Richard. I'm certain I can devise an appropriate penalty."

JO WAS STANDING ON a sidewalk with Daisy. They'd been shopping, and they were tired and eager to return to Benton House. She was anxious to hail a cab so they could ride back. It wasn't that much of a distance, but the sky was threatening, thunder rumbling, and it looked as if it was about to pour.

Peyton—no, Lord Benton; she couldn't think of him in a more familiar manner—had risen early and trotted off to parts unknown. Mr. Newman had mentioned he'd be out for hours which had meant she and Daisy were on their own again. It might have been awkward, as their first day had been, but Jo had pushed the notion aside.

She wasn't a child who needed a nanny, wasn't a debutante who sought constant amusement. She was used to being alone, and she could definitely entertain herself. Lord Benton was a busy, important man, and he didn't have to loaf with her to ensure she was happy.

To her surprise and delight, he'd left her some pin money. When Maud had tossed them out, they'd trudged away with what had been stuffed in their two bags, and it had been a pile of haphazard choices, so much of what they required was missing.

If she'd been prouder or shyer, she might have refused the money or have been too bashful to spend it. Most of what she'd purchased had been for Daisy anyway, and Daisy was his niece. There was nothing wrong with him buying her clothes.

As to Jo, she had a complete and beautiful wardrobe in Telford—if Maud hadn't donated it to the church basket by now.

She'd like to have all those garments. Dare she ask Lord Benton to help her retrieve them? If she could once again dress like the young lady she'd been raised to be, she wouldn't feel like such a charity case.

Thunder rumbled again, and Daisy jumped and snuggled close. "I hate storms."

"Will we find a cab before any raindrops fall?" Jo asked. "Shall we bet on it?"

"Betting is a sin, Aunt Jo. Our vicar at Benton regularly sermonized about it."

"The vicar in your tiny, rural church preached about wagering?"

"Bobby said he wasn't really concerned about wagering. He just despised my father for his bad habits. I guess my father liked to gamble."

"I can't believe any vicar would be that brave. A preacher shouldn't bite the hand that feeds him. What if your father had found out he was being denigrated from his own pulpit? The parson probably would have lost his job."

Daisy scoffed. "My father wouldn't have heard any scolding. He never went to church."

"If he'd strolled through the front door, he'd have been struck by lightning."

"Aunt Jo!"

"Well, he would have been. I won't lie about it."

She couldn't persuade any cabs to stop. With the weather so inclement, everyone was hurrying off the streets, so the vehicles were all full.

When Jo had announced she was going out, Mr. Newman had begged her to take a carriage—and a maid too—but she was determined to not be a nuisance, so she'd declined them. Yet with the clouds so dark, she was kicking herself.

Why was she so stubborn? Newman had offered what he would have supplied to any guest, and as a raindrop plopped on her nose, she resolved to be less obstinate in the future.

"Let's walk around the corner to the next block," she said. "Perhaps we'll have more luck there."

"If we get drenched, I'm claiming it's your fault."

"I shall deflect the accusation. I'm the adult in this pathetic duo. If anyone asks why we were so negligent, I shall state that *you,* the child, convinced me to traipse off without coach or parasol."

"You would not."

"I might."

They started off, and as they passed a shop, the door opened, and to her great astonishment, Maud hastened out so briskly that they nearly ran into each other. There was an awkward pause, where they couldn't figure out the correct greeting. Jo wasn't about to pretend all was fine or that she was glad to see her sister.

She wasn't. If it had been her choice, she would have continued on, but Maud was intent on chatting.

"Jo." Maud nodded. "I heard you had left Telford."

"Yes, not that it's any of your business."

Maud peeked at Daisy, but didn't acknowledge her. For a moment, it looked as if Daisy might say something, and Jo laid a palm on her shoulder, a subtle request to be silent.

"Why are you in London?" Maud inquired.

"That's not any of your business either."

Maud bristled. "Why must you always be so difficult?"

"Why must *you* be?"

Jo supposed a bigger person, a better person, would have leapt in to mend their rift, but she'd exhausted herself, working to placate Maud who was miserable and discontented and who had revealed herself to be exceedingly cruel too. Jo couldn't fix any of her sister's problems, and she'd given up trying.

She glanced down at her niece. "We should go, Daisy."

Maud huffed with indignation. "I'm not done speaking to you, Josephine."

"Well, *I* am done listening."

"From your attitude, it's evident you blame me for your recent problems."

"I don't blame you. Actually, I never think about you at all."

A gig clattered by on the other side of the street, and Jo might not have paid any attention to it, but a clap of thunder roared, and the horse shied. They all peered over at the commotion.

There were two passengers in the vehicle, a man and a woman snuggled together on the seat, and the woman was giggling.

"Maud," Jo said, "there's your betrothed, Mr. Townsend. Who is he with? Why, it's his special friend, Miss Smith. I told you about her, didn't I? It's interesting how frequently they socialize, don't you agree? Have you met her?"

Panic crossed Maud's face, but it was quickly masked. The gig raced on by, and Maud yanked her gaze away and focused it on Jo.

"I have no idea what you mean," Maud staunchly insisted. "Mr. Townsend isn't even in the city today."

"Suit yourself, Maud. I don't care if he's a cheating dog. You're the one who has to live with him after the wedding. Not me."

Maud's expression became bleak and desolate. She appeared much older than twenty-five, the stark lines carved by years of spite and temper clearly visible.

In the past, she'd had Jo in the house to advise and commiserate. With her tossing Jo out, there were consequences. Maud didn't have any real friends, no relatives worth claiming, and Mr. Townsend rarely visited. Her existence was probably very empty, very quiet without Jo, but Jo couldn't repair that situation for her.

"We should go," Jo said to Daisy again.

"Goodbye, Mother." It was the only time Daisy had ever talked to Maud.

Maud was taken aback by the sound of Daisy's voice. She gaped at Daisy, then frowned and shook her head.

"You have me confused with someone else, little girl. I'm no one's mother, and I'm certainly not yours."

It was a malicious comment, but Daisy handled it well. She didn't respond with a snide rebuke or—worse yet—burst into tears. Maud didn't deserve any tears, and they'd both previously concurred that she didn't.

"Miss Bates!" a man suddenly called.

She and Maud both whirled to see which one of them was being summoned. It was Jo, and a footman from Benton House was waving to her.

"Mr. Newman sent me to find you," he explained as he rushed up. "He was afraid you'd be caught in the rain."

"It was kind of him to worry about us."

"The carriage is around the corner. The driver found a spot to wait. Can you come?"

"Yes, we're finished here. We're finished forever."

She and Daisy hurried after him, and she could feel Maud staring, dripping with curiosity. Obviously, Jo had landed on her feet, and it had to irk Maud unbearably to discover that Jo wasn't imperiled.

"Jo!" Maud ultimately shouted.

Jo ordered herself not to stop, but she couldn't help it.

"What?"

"Where are you staying?"

"With an acquaintance," she said, being as enigmatic as possible as she kept on.

"But what if I need to contact you? How would I?"

Jo didn't reply. Let Maud fume. Let Maud wonder.

Lightning flashed, and huge raindrops began to pelt them. The carriage wasn't far, and the footman lifted them in, then climbed into the box. The driver cracked the whip, and in a matter of seconds, they rolled away.

They passed the place where they'd encountered Maud, and Jo peeked out the curtain. Her sister was still there, looking lost and forlorn, as if she couldn't decide on a direction.

Jo released the curtain, and she put her arm around Daisy and pulled her near. They were warm and dry and on their way to Benton House. If she was lucky, Lord Benton might be there when they arrived.

Life wasn't perfect but—considering how it all might have gone—it was very, very close.

CHAPTER

14

PEYTON HEARD A CREAK on the floorboards, and the noise had him glancing around the dark foyer. He'd been riding all day, the lengthy hours only interrupted by his contentious visit to Benton.

He was cold, wet, weary, and incredibly glad to be in London.

It was raining like mad outside, and he'd constantly paused, figuring he should find a barn and stop for the night, but Benton House had beckoned like a safe haven. He couldn't deny that thoughts of Jo, waiting impatiently for him to arrive, had spurred him to continue through the deluge.

Daisy was lurking in the shadows, dressed in her nightgown and ready for bed. She was being quiet as a mouse, watching him stagger in and clearly wondering if she should make her presence known or if she should remain hidden.

"Why are you still awake, you scamp?"

"The thunder scared me."

"I'm not surprised. It's bad out there."

She studied his sodden coat and boots. "You must have been out in it a long time."

"Yes, I went to Benton. I just got home."

She lifted her hand to show him she was holding an apple.

"I was hungry," she said, "so I snuck into the kitchen and helped myself. Is that all right? Should I put it back?"

"No, you shouldn't put it back. You may eat any morsel of food in this house, and you don't need to ask permission."

She smiled tentatively. "I was hoping you'd think that. Aunt Jo is afraid we'll become a nuisance, and I'd hate for you to suppose we were a bother."

"Well, you've only been here for two days, and in such a short period, you couldn't aggravate me. Maybe after you've been here a few weeks, I'll decide you're a pest."

He'd been joking, but she appeared stricken, so apparently, he had to practice the skills required when talking to a young girl.

"I'm never a pest," she vehemently stated. "I promise."

"I was teasing, Daisy. You couldn't be a pest if you tried. Nor could your Aunt Jo. I'm happy to have you."

"Are you sure? We've been worried you didn't really want to invite us to stay with you."

"There's one thing you should know about me."

"What's that?"

"I never do anything I don't wish to do."

"Is that because you're an earl now?"

"No, it's not that. I've always liked to have my own way. If I hadn't wanted you to be here with me, I wouldn't have suggested it."

"If we start to irritate you, will you tell me? I couldn't bear to learn that you were angry with us and I didn't realize it."

"You couldn't possibly make me angry."

She was very pretty, and she looked just like Neville: blond and blue-eyed, with agreeable features and a thin frame. She seemed nicer than Neville though, so she'd inherited his bodily features but not his personality.

According to Josephine, Daisy's mother, Maud, was dreadful too, so Daisy hadn't inherited her attributes either. Perhaps her sweet nature was from a throw-back generation, and he suspected the traits were deeply buried in Maud's side of the family. In the Prescott bloodline, Peyton couldn't recall a single kind relative.

"It's icy down here," he said. "You should get to bed."

"I'm afraid of the storm."

He waved away her concern. "Ah, storm's are for sissies, and you're not a sissy."

She grinned. "No, I'm not."

"Would you like me to walk you up to your room?"

"Would you?" She frowned. "Unless you're too busy. I can go on my own."

"I don't mind."

"You're dripping all over the floor. Mr. Newman won't like that."

"We could just not admit it was me."

At the notion, she was aghast. "What if he thought it was *me*?"

"Then I'd have to confess."

He held out his hand to her, and she gazed at it warily, but in the end, she grabbed on.

"You're freezing!" she scolded as she felt his skin against her own. "If Aunt Jo was with us, she'd blister your ears. You shouldn't be out in weather like this. Do you want to perish from an influenza?"

He chuckled. "No, I certainly don't."

He'd lived his life with seafaring men, so he'd spent scant time with women. The prior evening, Jo had mentioned that she'd fret over him riding in the dark, and now, Daisy was fretting about him being in the rain.

It was rather pleasant, having a female fuss over him. He hadn't ever wondered if he'd like that sort of treatment, and if he *had* pondered it, he'd have assumed he wouldn't like it. But he enjoyed it after all. It was very . . . soothing.

They tiptoed up the stairs, and when they reached the landing, Newman emerged from the shadows, and they both jumped.

"I've been watching for you, my lord," he said. "I'm sorry I didn't hear you arrive."

"I just got back."

"Will you need supper? Should I rouse the cook?"

"No, don't trouble her. I ate on the road. I am cold and wet though."

Daisy added, "He's dripping everywhere, Mr. Newman. We were praying you wouldn't find out, but since you've caught us, we can't hide it."

"It's all right, Miss Daisy," Newman told her. "We'll clean it up."

"Daisy was upset by the thunder," Peyton explained to Newman. "I'm putting her to bed, but I'm tired and chilly. Could you stoke the fire in my bedchamber and lay out some clothes? I'll be there shortly."

"Yes, I'll see to it immediately."

Peyton kept on, Daisy's small hand clutched in his much larger one. He was trying to recollect if he'd ever previously strolled hand in hand with a child. If he had, he couldn't remember it. Again, it was rather pleasant. It conjured visions of family gatherings, of being a husband and father.

What would it be like to have a house filled with children? They'd bring noise and chaos and ... *happiness* he supposed. Would that be a bad thing?

They entered Daisy's room, and he hadn't lit a candle, but there was a bit of illumination wafting in the window. She climbed in bed, pausing first to place her apple on the nightstand.

"Will you be scared if there's more thunder?" he asked.

"Not now that you're home."

"I wouldn't let anything happen to you."

"It's what I tell Aunt Jo, but she worries constantly."

"She worries?"

"Yes. If you'd arrived earlier, you would have cheered her up." Daisy wrinkled her nose. "We had a terrible day."

He stiffened, prepared to be incensed on her behalf. "How was it terrible? I hope no one here was awful to you."

"No, everyone here has been very kind."

"What was it then?"

"We were shopping, and we ran into my mother."

"Your ... mother? Maud Bates?"

"Yes, she's my mother. She doesn't want anyone to know, but she *is*—no matter how she pretends."

"I'm glad you don't have any illusions about her. You're being very mature about all of this."

"I had to be, didn't I?"

"Yes, you did."

"She was very mean to Aunt Jo." Daisy sighed. "I hate that she's so mean. Aunt Jo doesn't deserve it."

"No, she doesn't."

"Could I ask a favor of you?" Daisy peeked up at him. "Is it allowed?"

"You can always ask. I can't guarantee I'll grant your request, but you can ask."

"Could you get Aunt Jo's clothes from my mother?"

"Her clothes?"

"Yes. My mother kicked us out, so Jo had to leave her clothes there. She's been so vexed about it."

"I can imagine."

It was another sign of how distracted he'd been. He hadn't delved into the circumstances of Jo's departure from her sister's house. He understood it had been contentious, but he hadn't reflected on just how contentious.

"I wish *I* could get them for her," Daisy said, "but I can't figure out how I would."

"I'll talk to her. I'll find out what she needs and how I can assist her."

He must have supplied the correct answer, for she beamed with satisfaction. "I just knew you would. And could I ask a favor for myself?"

"Yes."

"I had to leave a jar of pennies there."

"Pennies?"

"They were gifts—from my father. It's not right that I can't have them."

"I agree, and I'll work on getting those too."

"Thank you."

"You're welcome. Now promise me you won't be wandering the halls. It's too cold. You might make yourself sick."

"You're the one who's cold and wet. I should be lecturing *you*."

"Yes, you probably should."

She hesitated, then inquired, "Would you tuck me in? Aunt Jo always does, and I like it."

"I'll drip all over the blankets."

"I don't care."

He neared and tugged the covers up to her chin.

She motioned to the door. "You don't have to tarry. I'm very tired, so I'll fall asleep pretty fast."

"Does your Aunt Jo wait until you doze off?"

"Yes, but we already did this once tonight."

"I think we can engage in the ritual one more time. There's no rule that says we can't."

There was a chair by the bed, and he pulled it closer and sat down. He tamped down a shiver, watching her as she yawned and rolled onto her back. The room grew quieter, her inhalations slowing, her eyelids drifting shut.

"You're nicer than my father," she murmured.

"Am I?"

"Yes. I like you way more."

He'd love to have peppered her with questions, and suddenly, he was incredibly curious about her life at Benton. What was her opinion of Neville? What about Barbara and Richard? How had she really been treated? How many nannies and governesses had she had besides Miss Watson? Had she been happy? Had she been lonely?

He wondered if she'd had any news about her half-siblings, Bobby and Jane. Miss Watson had traipsed off to Cornwall with them, hoping Jane's uncle would provide shelter. Bobby and Jane were Neville's children too, so Peyton had to pay more attention to their plight.

He decided to remain at home in the morning, to interrogate Daisy. He'd quiz Jo too, to ensure she had what she required, to learn what she envisioned for herself and Daisy. And of course, he had to ask about Bobby and Jane. If Jo hadn't received any information, then Peyton had to track down Miss Watson to determine if she'd found a viable conclusion for them.

Daisy was sleeping, and he tiptoed out and hurried to his own room. Newman had built a toasty fire, and he helped Peyton strip off his heavy, damp clothes.

Shortly, he was dry and warm, and he shooed Newman off to bed.

It had been a grueling day. The fight with Richard and Barbara had him more confused than ever about his return to the navy. He couldn't abide the bickering he'd been forced to endure because of them. But how could he sail away from England when they were at Benton? He could install a team of managers, but Barbara and Richard would never relinquish power if Peyton wasn't there to insist.

He was at a loss as to how it should all proceed. He'd given them a deadline to move out of the manor, but he was certain they wouldn't heed him. He'd likely show up in a month, and they'd be sitting in the dining room where he'd left them. He'd have to personally, physically evict them, then stand guard so they didn't slither back. The whole notion was exhausting to contemplate.

Should he speak to his commanding officer and request an extension of his furlough? Any such request would be granted, but did he want to do that? Did he want to loaf in England merely to guarantee that Richard and Barbara behaved as he'd bid them?

Even from the Dower House, Barbara and her brother would be a lurking presence to obstruct, complain, and hinder.

On top of it all, the trip to Benton had prevented him from calling on Amelia and Evan. At the moment, he was too weary to consider how awful that conversation would be. His quarrel with Barbara and Richard had been bad enough. He'd never previously squabbled over issues such as finances and children, and he didn't like it one bit.

Newman had set out a decanter of brandy, and Peyton plopped down on a chair and poured himself a glass. He sipped it as he studied the flames. He was feeling particularly morose, stress and aggravation taking their toll.

The walls seemed to close in, and the house was empty and quiet. Too quiet. Normally, he spent his evenings on his ship, surrounded by his crew. He was never alone there, not even in his cabin.

He was swamped by the most urgent need to talk to somebody, to tell somebody about his horrid journey to Benton. Josephine was just down the hall. She'd ordered him not to sneak in again, but she was a female. Why listen to her about anything that mattered?

He downed his brandy, refilled the glass, and downed that too. Daisy had mentioned Jo's day had been horrid as well. Was she also wishing she had someone to talk to? Might she be glad to talk to Peyton?

There was only one way to find out.

He marched directly to her bedchamber, and he didn't try to be furtive. He was that determined to be with her.

To his great relief, the silly girl hadn't locked her door, so he was saved the embarrassment of having to knock and be denied entrance. He walked in, and he'd figured she would be sound asleep, but while the blankets on her bed were folded back, she wasn't in it. There was light emanating from the dressing room, and he strolled over and peeked in. She was seated at the dressing table, attired in her nightgown and robe.

She saw him in the mirror, and she froze, her expression exasperated.

"Why are you creeping in, Lord Benton?" she asked. "What is your purpose?"

"Call me Peyton."

"No. I could have sworn we debated this last night. We agreed you wouldn't visit me."

"*We* didn't agree. You announced your edict, but I didn't consent to it."

She spun to face him. "You can't be in here."

"I already am, so your point is moot."

She stood and, crude oaf that he was, he stepped in. Suddenly, their bodies were crushed together.

"Move," she said, and she shoved him to no avail.

"No."

"You're being a bully."

"Yes, I admit it."

She was just so pretty, and merely from staring at her, he felt better. How did she do that? How did she soothe the beast that always raged just under the surface?

He ought to tamp down his fascination, but apparently, he couldn't. She simply had an effect on him that no other female had ever been able to generate. There was a road opening for them. Why not travel down it with her?

He dipped down and kissed her, his arm going around her waist to pull her even nearer. For the briefest instant, she tensed, then she kissed him back with all the fondness she could muster. They kept on for quite awhile, the sweetness of it being more than he could bear. He didn't want to ever desist which was ridiculous in the extreme.

"Where have you been?" she asked as he finally drew away. "I've been worried all day."

"I rode to Benton."

"Were you out in the dark again?"

"Yes."

"Then you must have been caught in the rain."

"I was."

She tsked with irritation. "What should I do with you?"

"I can think of a dozen things."

"Of course you can. You're a man, and from the hot gleam in your eye, it's clear that none of them are ideas you would dare describe to me."

"You could be right."

He was exhausted, the weather and the trip leaving him drained. He had to lie down before he fell down, but if he suggested it, they'd quarrel, so why voice a futile request?

He scooped her up and headed out to the bedchamber.

"Put me down!" she demanded, her scowl fierce.

"I'm worn out, and I have to lie down."

"Well, you're not lying down in here. We discussed this."

"No, Jo, *you* discussed it, and I had no comment. You didn't seek my opinion."

"That's because it would have been absurd."

"You've convinced yourself that we should avoid each other, but there's another perfectly viable path."

"What is it?" she sarcastically inquired. "I can't wait to hear."

"This is the perfect path."

He dropped her on the bed, and she squealed with affront and attempted to slither away, but he was too quick for her. He tumbled onto the mattress too and stretched out, and though she fussed and protested, he kept her in place until she recognized escape was impossible.

"Hold on, you little wildcat."

"No! You're so rude, and we're not doing this!"

"I told you I'm incredibly fatigued." He draped her across his chest so she was nestled close. "Stop complaining, and tell me about your day. Daisy claims it was horrid."

She popped up, frowning. "Daisy! When did you speak to her? She's supposed to be asleep."

"She was downstairs when I came in. The thunder woke her."

Jo stared at the door. "I should check on her. Let me up."

"She's fine, and you're not getting away from me, so don't try."

"How can you be certain she's fine?"

"I tucked her in myself."

"*You* tucked her in?"

"Yes. Is that so hard to believe?"

She chuckled. "I won't answer that."

"I like her."

"You should like her. She's your niece."

"Besides that, she's . . . a nice girl."

"Don't sound so surprised."

"I haven't spent much time around children," he said. "My life isn't one that's ever included them. I like having her here."

"Good."

He snuggled her down. A fire had been lit earlier, but it had mostly dwindled to ash, and the temperature was cooling. Despite his dry clothes, he was very chilled, and without meaning to, he shivered.

"You're so cold. How long were you out in the rain?" She scoffed with disgust. "No, no, don't tell me. I shudder to imagine, and any true statement would only make me angry."

"I wouldn't want you to be angry."

"I swear, Peyton Prescott, if you catch a lung infection, I won't nurse you."

"Ooh, you vixen! How could you be so cruel? You can't be serious. If I grow deathly ill, you have to remain by my bed every second."

"I won't agree to that. It would simply stroke your massive ego, and it doesn't need stroking."

She pulled the blankets over them, covering them with a heavy quilt. They dawdled for a bit, then she inquired, "Is that better? You're warmer already."

"Yes, I'm warming up very fast—with you right next to me. I guess you can't move or I'll be shivering again."

"You're a rat. You're using your personal discomfort—and my concerns about your health—as an excuse to coerce me."

"I might be." He grinned, shameless and unrepentant. "Daisy mentioned you saw your sister when you were out shopping."

She stiffened. "We bumped into her by accident."

"It must have been upsetting."

"It was, but I've had all day to calm down. I'm fine now."

"Is she missing you? Is she regretting that she tossed you out? Did she beg you to come home?"

He was on tenterhooks, nervous about her response. If she had somewhere to go, she'd leave him, and he wasn't prepared for that moment to arrive. In fact, he suspected he might manipulate her affairs so no opportunity for departure could arise.

"She didn't invite me back," she said, "and I can't predict what she's thinking. She's probably glad to be shed of me, but lamenting it too. Without me in the house, she only has the servants to yell at, and they can quit if she becomes too obnoxious. I could never *quit* being her sister. It's the disadvantage of being a relative."

"Daisy told me she left a jar of coins there."

"Yes. Your brother always slipped her a penny when he visited her. She kept all of them." Jo scowled with consternation. "But it's a pathetic pile—indicative of his lack of attention. I doubt there are a dozen coins in it."

"She'd like to have them."

"Of course she would. They're all she has from him."

"And what about you? She said your clothes are still there. Would you like me to retrieve them for you?"

She popped up again, and it was clear she yearned to say *yes, please*, but she didn't. Instead, she shook her head. "No, I don't need you fussing about it. I don't want to be a bother."

"You're not a bother."

"Not yet anyway."

Then and there, he decided he would learn where her sister lived, and he'd get Jo's things from her. He wouldn't inform Jo first. He'd simply show up in London with them. He could just picture how grateful she'd be.

"I'm worried about Maud," she admitted. "I shouldn't be—not after how she treated me—but I can't help it."

"Why are you worried?"

"She's marrying in September, but I don't like her fiancé."

"What's his name?"

"Thompson Townsend. Do you know the family? His oldest brother, Charles, is her lawyer."

He pondered, then nodded. "I do know them. Isn't there a hoard of Townsend brothers?"

"Yes, five of them."

"One of them went to school with me for a year or two, and if I remember correctly, they're a dodgy bunch. The parents had too many sons and not enough money to go around. They were always scrounging for funds."

"You've described them exactly. Maud—for all her flaws—is a matrimonial prize. She inherited her house and receives a small stipend from her maternal grandmother, and her dowry hasn't been stolen by anybody."

Peyton laughed. "Hopefully, it won't be."

"Charles introduced his brother to Maud, and Thompson proposed on the spot."

"Considering the fiscal condition of those boys, I can certainly understand why he would."

"He doesn't have her best interests at heart though," she said. "He seems to have a mistress of whom he's very fond."

"Why would you assume so?"

"When I initially came to London, I observed them brazenly kissing out on the street."

"My goodness. That is brazen."

"Then they drove by us today, and they were snuggled together in a carriage."

"Did your sister see them?"

"She pretended not to, but she's adept at ignoring what she doesn't wish to see."

"Like an unwanted, bastard daughter?"

"Yes, just like that," Jo said.

"Who was your fiancé again?"

"Holden Cartwright."

"If he hadn't jilted you, and you still had your dowry, would you like to marry?"

He suffered a peculiar rush a jealousy when she replied with, "Wouldn't every woman? What other option is there for a female?"

"Not all women share that view. I've spent my life around doxies in port towns. They're incredibly happy to carry on without husbands."

"How shockingly modern."

"Isn't it though?"

"But let's not talk about marriage or Mr. Cartwright or my being jilted. It's embarrassing and depressing."

"I'll agree that it's depressing, but why would you be embarrassed? It wasn't your fault he was a cad."

"When I recall that terrible episode, I'm reminded that I have no common sense. Why didn't I recognize him for the scoundrel he was?"

"Some men are simply criminals, and they prey on the unsuspecting."

"Well, he definitely knew how to prey on me, and I only had Maud to advise me. He tricked her into thinking he was wonderful, and she signed over my dowry without hesitating. Neither of us realized I should have had a ring on my finger first. We had no idea a man could be so unscrupulous."

He snorted with disgust. In his opinion, men were capable of any wicked conduct, but a female—especially one as young and naïve as Jo—wouldn't necessarily comprehend that fact.

He made a mental note to reflect on her vanished fiancé, Mr. Cartwright. How difficult would it be to track him down?

Peyton concurred with her assessment that her money would be gone, but he'd love to inflict a bit of physical punishment. An arrest would be satisfying too.

Could he arrange that conclusion for her? He'd certainly like to try.

"Why did you travel to Benton?" she asked.

"I had to scold Richard Slater for evicting Daisy."

She batted her lashes. "My hero! Thank you!"

"You're welcome. He and his sister need to leave Benton, but they won't depart without a fight. I'll probably have to bring an army with me to drag them away. They're that opposed to my implementing any changes."

"I can imagine. Benton has been their home for ages. They wouldn't deem it fair for you to force them out."

"Precisely. They believe I'm an ogre."

"You're not an ogre," she loyally stated. "I've been acquainted with some ogres. You're not one."

He sighed with contentment. She understood him so well which was refreshing and intriguing. Her insights seemed to bind them tightly, as if Fate had decided they should be connected.

"Is there any news from Miss Watson?" he asked.

"Not yet, but it hasn't been that long. I have her cousin's address, and I wrote to her. I'm waiting for an answer."

"Does Daisy miss Bobby and Jane?"

"Why would you have to inquire? Yes, she misses them. They're her siblings, and she grew up with them. She doesn't talk about their separation much—she's determined to never be a burden—but I can read between the lines."

"Perhaps—after we find out their circumstances—we could have them visit her."

She stared at him for an eternity, then she murmured, "Would you really invite them to London for a reunion?"

Would he?

He'd tossed out the remark without assessing the ramifications, but why shouldn't he proceed? He was rich, and he owned a very large town house. He could host a few guests, and after he rid himself of the Slaters once and for all, why couldn't he return the three children to Benton? Why not?

If Barbara left the estate, there was no reason to keep them away. They could live in the cottage where they'd been raised. What was to stop him from pursuing that ending?

It occurred to him that he was falling asleep, so his thoughts were muddled. It sounded as if he responded with, "Yes, we could have a reunion."

"Can I tell Daisy about it?"

Again, it sounded as if he mumbled, "Sure."

"I won't get her hopes up unless you're positive."

"I'm positive."

At least, he assumed he was, but in his weary condition, he wasn't clear on what he'd agreed to do.

After that, he drifted off, and he could feel her shaking him, frantically saying, "Peyton Prescott! Don't you dare doze off in here!" She went on and on, muttering comments such as, "Wake up, you idiot! Wake up!"

But he was dreaming of a beach in the Caribbean that he'd always judged to be the most beautiful spot in the world. He was loafing on the white sand. The sun was hot, a tropical breeze blowing. He stripped off his shirt, and as he waded into the balmy turquoise water, he grinned.

Life was very, very good.

CHAPTER
15

Jo WAS SEATED IN a chair by the hearth. The flames were out, and it was dark and cold. She was still dressed in her nightgown and robe, wool socks on her feet, and she'd wrapped herself in a blanket to ward off the chill.

Peyton was asleep on her bed.

She'd tried to wake him, to make him leave, but he was exhausted from his ride to Benton in the rain. She couldn't guess how long he'd been out, but she was starting to panic.

What if—once he roused—the servants were up and stoking the fires? What if he was observed sneaking out? Or what if a housemaid knocked on her door?

She didn't have a sitting room. Her bedroom opened directly into the hall, so there could be no hiding the reality that her bed wasn't empty. There was a man in it.

She wanted to be furious with him for placing her in such a predicament, but she couldn't muster any outrage. With each passing minute, she liked him more and more, and thus, was content to forgive him many sins. How could she not?

In light of her debacle with Mr. Cartwright, she knew not to be fond of any man, but Peyton was rich, handsome, and generous. It was skewing her view of their relationship.

Where she was concerned, he couldn't have honorable intentions. Marriage was the *only* honorable intention for a female of her station, but it wasn't a remedy he could offer or supply. So what was her plan?

If she'd had any sense, she'd pack her bag in the morning, pack Daisy's too, and they'd depart. Continued fraternization was insane, but if she left, she'd imperil Daisy, and she wouldn't endanger her niece merely because she couldn't force herself to behave as she ought.

He finally stirred, and he frowned up at the ceiling, perplexed about where he was. Then he saw her over in her chair.

"Aren't you freezing?" he asked.

"A bit."

"Come here."

"I probably shouldn't."

"Don't be ridiculous. It's lonely without you by my side."

He smiled and extended his hand to her. He had such a commanding personality, and she had no defense against it. They were secluded in the quiet house, and it seemed as if the rules of propriety had ceased to apply.

This type of decadent situation was how a girl got herself into trouble, so catastrophe beckoned. Though she'd been reared in a moral home, when he grinned at her, when he was so eager for her to join him, none of it mattered. She didn't care about any rules. She didn't care about propriety. She was anxious to make him happy, and she was terrified she might engage in any act he suggested.

She went over and clasped hold. He yanked hard, and she tumbled onto the mattress.

"What time is it?" he inquired.

"I have no idea, but morning has to be quickly approaching."

He glanced out the window where it was still storming. "Well, it's not morning yet. Let's pretend it will never arrive."

He positioned them so she was beneath him, and he was stretched out on top of her. He began kissing her in a frantic, desperate way, and she participated with incredible relish. Her breasts were pressed to his chest, and with her wearing just her nightgown, she seemed to be naked, as if they were touching skin to skin.

Down below, their loins were flexing in a thrilling rhythm her feminine anatomy definitely recognized. In his trousers, there was a firm rod that was evidence of his desire for her. Their housekeeper in Telford had explained it when Jo had been marching toward her wedding.

A man's private parts were different from a woman's, and those differences allowed them to mate and create a babe. She wasn't clear on the specifics, but on realizing how she'd tantalized him, she was inordinately delighted. It had her wishing she was a tad wanton, that past experience had taught her how to entice him.

He broke off the kiss and dipped under her chin to nibble down her neck, to her chest, to her bosom. He nuzzled at her breasts, stroking and massaging them, then he sucked a nipple into his mouth. The sensation was so shocking and so exciting that she arched up, not sure if she was trying to move away from him or move closer.

His hand was roaming up her thigh, gradually raising the hem of her nightgown, circling higher and higher. He caressed her between her legs, then slid his fingers into her woman's sheath.

From her prior conversation with her housekeeper, she had a vague perception that this kind of contact was common in a romantic encounter and to be permitted. But none of the housekeeper's comments had prepared her for how raucous and naughty it would be. It had to be a grave sin, and all of it was transpiring much too fast, but she was quite overwhelmed and couldn't slow it down.

He shifted his fingers in and out, in and out, as he nursed at her breast and, suddenly, the most delicious wave of exhilaration swept over her. She gasped with surprise as she soared to the heavens, as she reached a sort of peak. Then she tumbled down and landed safely in his arms.

He was hovered over her, smirking and looking very proud of himself. On her end, she was embarrassed and drained.

"Was that marital pleasure?" she managed to inquire.

"A bit of it."

"Am I ... I ... still a virgin?"

"Yes, Jo, you're chaste as the day is long."

"I'm not with child, am I?"

"No. There's more to it than that."

Her housekeeper had described the process, but still, Jo was confused by it. She was positive no babe could be planted by a man's fingers, but she was so unschooled in amour. And with good reason! She wasn't a doxy, so she wasn't free to flaunt herself so egregiously. The problem for her though was that she loved what they'd just done and she'd like to do it again—the sooner the better.

He rolled onto his side and rolled her too, so they were nose to nose.

"If we'd kept on," he asked, "are you aware of how it would have concluded?"

"I have a general understanding, but I'm not certain on all the details."

He studied her, and he was still smiling, still merry and cocky. "What will become of us, Jo? There's an amazing connection sparking. Do you feel it?"

"It would be silly to deny it."

"We should give in to it."

"What are you talking about?"

"I think—while you're living with me—we should engage in an affair."

"And I think *you* are mad for suggesting it."

"Why would you? We're so compatible, and we like each other so much. We'd both be very happy."

"You're a man, so you would believe that."

"We'll never be able to fight our attraction. It's too strong."

"Maybe you won't be able to, but *I* will."

"But, Jo, why would you want to fight it?"

She frowned at him, forcing herself to recall that he'd sailed the globe in the navy, and it was widely accepted that sailors had a distorted view of manners and morals. They mingled with foreigners and natives, and they trifled with loose slatterns who weren't bound by the restrictions placed on females in a civilized country like England.

He'd conveniently forgotten where he was while *she* had conveniently forgotten to watch herself around him. She was exhibiting such risqué conduct that he thought she'd be amenable to a passionate indiscretion.

"What exactly are you hoping to have occur?" she said.

"We'll enjoy a torrid fling. We'll dally and play and amuse ourselves, and when the time comes where we have to part, we'll move on with fond memories."

She scoffed with irritation. "What benefit would there be for me to participate? I'd be ruined and disgraced, and in the future, I could never wed."

"Don't worry about any of that."

"We might be found out too."

He scowled. "Who would find out?"

"Anyone might. How about Mr. Newman? How about the housemaids? They're not blind, you know."

"They're not allowed to have an opinion about how I behave."

"Well, they could definitely have an opinion about *me*."

"They wouldn't dare."

"I could wind up with child! There's been no mention of you putting a ring on my finger. What would I do then? What would *you* do?"

"In your eyes, everything is so complicated."

"It *is* complicated. For me anyway. I'd be destroyed, but you'd suffer no consequences at all."

She noticed he hadn't jumped to proclaim that, *yes,* he'd marry her if the worst happened, so she was deranged to trust him. There were rules and laws against debauchery, and a maiden couldn't blithely fornicate, couldn't casually walk down the salacious road he was so eager to travel.

He glanced outside, and the sky appeared to be growing lighter. Dawn was probably about to break.

"I should sneak out," he said, "while I still have a chance."

"If you're caught, I'll have to kill you."

He grinned. "I won't be caught."

He leaned in and kissed her, slowly, desperately, then he drew away and slid to the floor. He straightened his clothes while she was stretched out on the bed. She felt decadently wonderful, like a harem girl who'd been enter-taining the sultan.

"We're not finished discussing this," he said.

"Yes, we are."

"No, I intend to nag until I've convinced you."

"You'll never convince me."

"Ha! You don't think so?" He gestured to her prone form. "We're halfway there already. I just need to push a bit more, and you'll give me whatever I ask."

"You are very possibly the vainest person I have ever met."

"You're correct. I am."

He bent down, his palms on the mattress, and delivered a final kiss. She was putty in his hands and couldn't resist him. She didn't *want* to resist him.

"Get some sleep," he murmured. "I'll see you in a few hours."

"Will you stay home with us today? Please don't ride in the rain again."

"I will stay with you every second. I'm on a mission, remember? You have to be mine as fast as I can wear you down."

"You say that like a threat."

"No, I say it like a promise."

He laughed and strutted out. He didn't tiptoe, didn't peek to discover if the hall was empty. He simply sauntered away.

She flopped down, terrified over what they'd set in motion. Where would it lead? Where would it end?

To her great horror and shame, she yearned for it to lead in every wicked direction. Where had her common sense gone? Where had her morals and probity gone?

There were no answers to those questions. There was merely the frighten-ing realization that she was all alone in the world, and he'd offered her safety and security. She was making bad choices because of it, and she suspected he was right. She would disgrace herself if it would guarantee he continued to help her.

Like a foolish ninny, she was starting to hope she could remain by his side forever. A permanent situation was outrageous to consider, but why was she so keen to accept that conclusion? Why couldn't she have a fairytale ending?

He'd just become an earl, but he didn't care about that elevation. Plus, he'd turned thirty, and he needed to wed. Why couldn't he pick Jo? Why not? She'd always been so willing to oblige others, to never ask for more than she was given, but why couldn't she have Peyton Prescott?

The prospect—that she was counting on him, that she was envisioning a future—was alarming, but she ignored any of her reservations. She was ecstatic and excited and absolutely ready to learn what would happen next.

My, my but wasn't she in trouble?

Peyton sat on a sofa in the front parlor. He was sipping a brandy and staring at the fire in the grate. It was late in the evening, and he was trying to decide what sort of day it had been.

On the one hand, it had been the best day ever. The rain had fallen unabated, so he hadn't ventured out. Instead, he'd dawdled at home with Jo and Daisy. They'd played cards and read to each other and told stories. It had been incredibly domestic in a fashion he typically scorned and usually avoided.

On the other hand, it had been especially dull. He wasn't a fellow who tarried in parlors, playing games and drinking tea. He was a man of action and adventure, and he didn't like to be idle. So what was he thinking?

He was entirely too fixated on Jo, and he had to impose some distance between them, but he couldn't persuade himself to get moving. He recognized he had to change his behavior, but he kept devising reasons as to why he didn't have to begin just yet.

He hadn't initiated a single conversation about her and Daisy and their predicament, but if he pestered her over important topics, they'd have to proceed toward solutions, all of which would involve her leaving.

Obviously, he had to find her a place to live and figure out how she would support herself. Or should *he* offer to support her? He wasn't sure. He had no connection or duty to her. But didn't he have a duty to Daisy? After all, she was his niece. Shouldn't he support Daisy? Should he pay Jo to mind her?

That would be appropriate, wouldn't it?

Yet the Benton estate was in dreadful fiscal shape, so there wasn't a ton of money to toss around. The cheapest option would be to send them to Benton to the cottage where Daisy had grown up, but Peyton understood Barbara's position.

He'd always viewed himself as a better man than Neville, and he refused to torment Barbara. Even though he didn't like her very much, he would never deliberately hurt her.

"What to do? What to do?" he muttered to himself as Jo walked in.

She'd been upstairs putting Daisy to bed, a chore that made it seem as if they were married and Daisy was their daughter.

"Are you talking to yourself?" she asked.

"Yes."

"Isn't that the first step down the road to insanity?"

"Only if I start answering." She came over and sat by him on the sofa, and he inquired, "Would you like a glass of wine? Shall I pour you one?"

"No, I'm fine. Thank you."

"Is Daisy asleep?"

"Yes, but it took an eternity for her to nod off. She's nervous about the future, and she kept peppering me with questions."

"Was she happy at Benton?"

"Happy enough, I think."

They were quiet for a bit, both of them gazing into the dwindling flames.

"This was a good day," Jo ultimately said.

"It was," he agreed.

"It was kind of you to loaf with us, but weren't you horribly bored? You were like a caged tiger."

"Yes, I confess to being bored. I hate all this rain. I hope it will pass by soon."

"Why were you talking to yourself?"

"I'm confused about everything. You know that."

"My arrival with Daisy hasn't helped."

He scoffed. "You two are the least of my problems. Will you scold me if I list my complaints again?"

"No, go ahead, you poor, beleaguered aristocrat."

He counted his grievances on his fingers. "I want to return to the navy. I don't like having my in-laws at Benton, but I feel too guilty to kick them out. My brother was a spendthrift, so the finances are a disaster. I should stay in England and sort out the whole mess, but I can't bear to do that. I've always lived a very different life. I'm not a farmer, and I have no desire to be."

"If you're that desperate to escape, you could retain people to watch over the estate for you."

"*If* I can come up with the funds to pay them a salary. And Barbara and Richard would have to depart before I could hire a manager. I'd probably have to hire all new servants too. The ones working in the manor were brought from Barbara's family home when she and Neville were initially married."

"So they're loyal to her. Not you."

"Exactly, but how could I assemble an entire staff of strangers, then flee the country? Who would train them? Who would supervise them?"

"It sounds as if you need a wife and a countess. Perhaps you should be attending fancy parties and courting debutantes. There are dozens of girls who would love the chance to be installed at Benton as your bride."

He nearly choked on his brandy. "Could you picture me wed to a debutante?"

She laughed. "No, I couldn't picture it."

"I could never marry some idiotic child, then disappear for years at a time. She'd be on her own, trying to administer that huge monstrosity of a house without me. It would be a nightmare."

"Then maybe you need an heiress with a big, fat dowry. That would resolve many tricky issues. Are there any rich industrialists peddling their daughters right now?"

"Oh, gad. Your suggestions are terrifying."

He reached over and clasped her hand, linking their fingers as if they were adolescent sweethearts. With Daisy and various footmen constantly in the room all day, they'd had to pretend they weren't dying to touch each other, but he'd sent everyone to bed, so they were alone. They could misbehave if they chose.

She turned toward him, and he turned too, so they were snuggled close, their sides pressed together all the way down.

"Here's what I think," she said.

"I figured you'd have some brilliant ideas."

"First of all, I'll admit to having an ulterior motive."

"What is it?"

"I wish you would remain in England and that I could be part of your life. I've grown partial to your company, and I'd be sad if you left."

"You've grown partial? Ha! I'm rubbing off on you. I knew I would."

"Yes, you're irresistible. But..."

"Uh-oh. I never like sentences that start like that."

"Ever since I met you, you've waxed on about the navy and how much you miss it. It's clear you should go back at once."

He was surprised by her declaration, and her blasé attitude exasperated him. She'd be *sad* if he left?

It was such a paltry little word. If he sailed off into the sunset, she should be inconsolable, bereft, and barely able to continue on.

"You make it sound so easy," he said.

"It is. Find a manager who suits you, and don't worry about the Benton servants or your in-laws. Leave them at the estate for now. The property will always be there, and you won't always be young and fit. You'll eventually decide you're finished with having adventures. You'll be eager to settle down."

"I can't imagine that moment ever arriving."

"I can. It happens to every wayfaring man sooner or later."

He studied her, then snorted with amusement. "How old are you again?"

"Twenty."

"How did you get so smart?"

"I'm not. I just want you to be happy. Recently, you've been overwhelmed with problems and choices. So ... go to the navy; it's what you yearn for most of all. After watching you pace all day, your path seems obvious to me."

"I was pacing?"

"Yes."

"And here I thought I was so relaxed."

"You weren't."

They sat for a minute or two, pondering, then he murmured, "Thank you. I needed to hear that."

"You're welcome."

They smiled, and he pulled her onto his lap and kissed her. The embrace wasn't tepid or gentle. His tongue was in her mouth, his hands in her hair, her pert breasts crushed to his chest.

He was riveted by the mischief he'd instigated the prior night, but he wasn't sorry and didn't feel guilty.

He'd suggested they engage in an affair, and she'd refused—as he might have expected. His proposition had been immoral and wrong. She was living under his protection, and in addition, she was doing his family an enormous favor by helping Daisy. He should have been grateful, and she should have been safe from him, but he couldn't control himself.

She was penniless and desperate, and he didn't doubt he could coerce her into giving him what he craved. Was he that awful? Was he that brazen? He was afraid he might be. Perhaps he was more like his brother, Neville, than he cared to admit.

He kissed her forever, deeply, passionately, but when his busy fingers began to massage her breasts, she drew away.

"We're not carrying on like this in your parlor," she scolded.

"All right." He grinned. "Shall we retire to your room? We can—if you'd rather."

"No! I will head there by myself, and *you* will stay here until I am inside and have spun the key in the lock."

"What fun would that be?"

"Goodnight."

"Are you really going up without me?"

"Yes, I really am."

"You're cruel to torment me like this."

"You'll survive."

"It might not."

She chuckled. "You'll be home tomorrow, yes?"

"If it rains? Probably. But if it quits, I have to visit Evan and Amelia. Then I have meetings with my lawyers and bankers."

"How tediously boring."

"Yes, it will be."

"I'm glad you'll visit your friends though. You'll feel better once you've resolved your quarrel with them."

He shrugged. "If they'll let me resolve it."

"Goodnight," she said again.

She stood and flashed a look as old as Eve's, then she sauntered out, and he could barely keep from chasing after her like a berserker. He'd sweep her into his arms and take her to his bed. The notion was so thrilling it was difficult to remain seated.

He listened as she crossed the foyer, as she climbed the stairs. The place was very quiet, so he could even hear when she shut her door, when she spun the key as she'd vowed she would.

It dawned on him that he could find another key and bluster in—if he truly wanted to. Her trivial attempt to bar him would only last if he allowed it, but apparently, he wasn't prepared to press the issue.

He was ready to head to bed too. He downed his drink and walked out to the foyer, and movement in the corner stopped him in his tracks.

Newman was standing in the shadows, a silent sentinel guarding the house. Earlier, Peyton had told him there was no need to wait up, but evidently, he'd waited up anyway in case his assistance became necessary.

How long had he been there? How long had he been eavesdropping?

It was a servant's job to conceal his emotions and his opinions, but Peyton was behaving very badly toward Jo, and they both understood that he was. Newman's concern for Jo was obvious, but his disappointment with Peyton was obvious too, and he made no effort to hide his reproach.

Peyton didn't know Newman and assumed he was a Slater family retainer, brought in after they'd sold their property. He braced, figuring Newman would comment on Peyton's conduct. Frantically, he wondered about his reply. It would be the height of folly for Newman to admonish Peyton, and it was definitely a firing offense. But Peyton wasn't the sort of employer to terminate a man for speaking candidly.

Any criticism would be spot on, but no chastisement was voiced. Newman swallowed down every word he was dying to hurl, so no argument erupted.

Peyton nodded. "Goodnight, Newman."

"Goodnight, Lord Benton. Sleep well."

"I will."

Peyton went to the stairs and trudged up them. He felt petty and small and very much in the wrong, and he could feel Newman's eyes cutting into his back the whole way.

CHAPTER

16

NEWMAN STOOD IN THE corner of the dining room. It was after nine o'clock. Miss Bates and Daisy had had their breakfast, then headed off on a shopping excursion.

Miss Bates had heard about a church bazaar where parishioners were selling their old clothes at a fundraiser. Apparently, she pictured herself as a seamstress, and she enjoyed scrounging for items she could redesign.

He doubted Lord Benton would like their rummaging through other's clothes and bringing them home, but it had gotten them out of the house which was a benefit.

He didn't understand how she'd become so cordial with the Earl or how she'd ended up ensconced in a bedroom upstairs. Newman had presumed Lord Benton was about to engage himself to Amelia Boyle, but with Miss Bates barging in, Miss Boyle had vanished.

The evening Miss Bates had arrived during his birthday party, she'd definitely been in a bit of peril. The Earl had rescued her from her predicament, and Newman recognized how knightly conduct could bowl over a woman. And Lord Benton was a rich, handsome bachelor.

That sort of combination could cause an innocent girl to make many risky choices.

He'd been surprised to discover that she was Daisy's aunt, and everyone who worked for the Prescott family knew who *she* was. He wondered if the Countess was aware that Daisy had been invited to live at Benton House. Newman hadn't written to the estate about it, and he couldn't guess if any of the other servants had.

Did Lord Benton comprehend the hornet's nest he was stirring? Did he care?

Newman hadn't settled his opinion as to what Peyton Prescott's true character would turn out to be, but he didn't appear to be cruel or stupid. So what was he thinking with regard to Miss Bates?

She was only twenty, so she was ten years younger than he was, and she was very much alone in the world. Newman eavesdropped on her constantly, and there had been no mention of parents, relatives, or friends. In particular, there had been no mention of any male authority figures—a father, brother, or cousin—who might protect her when she desperately needed protection.

Newman had witnessed an incident between the Earl and Miss Bates that he shouldn't have witnessed, and the spectacle had left him incredibly disturbed. He'd been awake until dawn, fretting and pacing about the rising danger to Miss Bates. It wasn't any of his business, but it was totally his business too.

They had a dozen servants. He and the housekeeper were older, but the rest—the footmen and the maids—were around Miss Bates's age. Lord Benton couldn't carry on an affair with her. Not with so many young people hanging on their every word.

The Earl didn't seem to realize it, but he had no secrets from them. There were already whispers among the maids as to how he gazed at Miss Bates when he assumed they weren't watching. They cleaned Miss Bates's room every morning, so it was only a matter of time before evidence leaked out that couldn't be explained away.

How far down the road to perdition had the pair traveled?

The prior night, when the Earl's shenanigans had been unmasked, he'd looked terribly guilty. It was clear he grasped that his behavior was very, very wrong. Someone had to admit it. Someone had to point out the hazards. If Newman remained silent, and Miss Bates was harmed, he'd never forgive himself.

He'd never been especially brave, and he was probably about to be fired, but Lord Benton had to be yanked to his senses. Newman prayed that the sophisticated, experienced naval officer would listen to reason. If he didn't, if he flew into a rage, then Newman would be out the door very soon. He'd packed his bags—just in case.

After a tad more waiting, the Earl sauntered in. If he was discomfited by Newman being there too, he didn't show it. There were two footmen hovering as well. They helped him with his food and his tea, then they all dawdled, observing him, eager to be necessary.

Once he'd finished his meal, Newman took a deep breath and stepped forward.

"Lord Benton, I must confer privately with you on an important topic."

The Earl froze, then he asked, "Are you sure you want to talk about it? Should you?"

"I've considered incessantly, my lord, and I have to."

The footmen were agog with speculation, and he shooed them out and shut the door. Lord Benton leaned back and tossed his napkin on his plate. He gestured to the chair across.

"Sit, would you?" he said. "I'd hate to strain my neck staring up at you."

"I'll stand if you don't mind."

"I *do* mind, but suit yourself."

Newman didn't hesitate. He had to spit it out or he'd lose his courage.

"It's about Miss Bates."

Lord Benton simply raised a brow. "What about her?"

"Please don't pretend to be unaware of what this is concerning."

"All right, I won't pretend. Speak your piece."

"First off, I'd like to state that I have enjoyed working for your family. I've always been grateful for my job."

"Good to know. Now get on with it."

"I hope I can be frank without jeopardizing my position."

"We'll see I guess."

Newman felt as if he was running toward a cliff, as if he was about to jump over. "Miss Bates can't continue to reside here, Lord Benton. She must leave immediately. Today—if we can arrange another place for her that fast."

"This is my house, and I can invite whomever I like to stay in it with me. I don't believe her presence is any of your business."

"I'm sorry, my lord, but I'm making it my business. She has no relatives to guide her in her decisions. It is a recipe for disaster."

Lord Benton shrugged. "Maybe, maybe not."

"Will you deny having wicked intentions? You can't. I heard the two of you chatting last night. You are much too worldly for her, and *she* is much too naïve to be involved with you."

"Maybe," Lord Benton said again.

"You are on your own as well, Lord Benton. You have no parent or relative to urge caution either, so *I* am urging caution. *I* am begging you to remove her before calamity strikes."

"You're very bold, Newman."

"Not really. I just can't bear to watch what's happening. A man can't contemplate what you're contemplating unless he's prepared to wed."

"I realize that."

"Are you about to marry her, Lord Benton? The question has to be posed, *and* it has to be answered."

It was a pretty speech, a daring speech, and it seemed to have an effect. Lord Benton's cheeks flushed, and he glanced down at his plate.

"No, I'm not ready to wed."

"As that is your reply, I categorically insist that you find new lodging for her. At once."

Lord Benton scowled. "I like having her here. Daisy too. I don't want them to depart."

"Lord Benton, we have a full staff at Benton House. Most of your servants are young and impressionable. You cannot carry on like this in front of them.

We are all good Christians, and we can't be party to such immorality."

Lord Benton blew out a heavy breath. "I hadn't considered how the servants might view this."

"Well, you need to think about them," Newman stoically said.

"I will. Thank you for being candid with me. I appreciate it."

He stood and marched out without further comment.

Newman wasn't certain where they'd left it, wasn't certain if his arguments had been persuasive, but he hadn't been fired. He was so relieved that his knees gave out, and he staggered over to a chair and collapsed down which meant he was sitting on a *family* chair for the first time ever.

He tarried until the footmen peeked in and asked if they could clean up the breakfast mess. If they had an opinion about Newman's condition, they didn't voice it.

He walked out and headed to his office behind the kitchen. He pondered and fretted, wondering what was best, wondering what was worst, then he plopped down and wrote a letter to the Countess about Lord Benton's antics with Miss Bates.

The star-crossed pair was about to turn the kingdom upside down with their salacious amour, and the Countess hated a scandal. She'd endured too many of them.

Newman wasn't a Prescott servant. He was a Slater servant, and he'd been lucky enough to be hired by her after her father's bankruptcy. He'd never stopped being grateful.

He bluntly apprised her of the dire situation, and he requested guidance and assistance. He was greatly worried that his words to Lord Benton had had minimal impact and would make no difference.

Barbara Prescott would know what to do. She could discuss it with the Earl on an equal footing and wring out concessions Newman could never garner on his own.

He read the message over and over, anxious to be sure he'd conveyed the correct sentiment. Then he sanded the missive, sealed it, and dropped it in the post so it could go out with the afternoon's mail.

PEYTON KNOCKED ON THE door, and it was quickly answered by a housemaid.

"May I help you?" the girl asked.

"I am here to see Maud Bates. Is she available?"

"I'll have to check. Who may I tell her is calling?"

"Peyton Prescott, Lord Benton." He didn't wait to be admitted. He simply barged in. As he swept into the front parlor, he said, "After you announce me, don't claim she won't attend me. If she doesn't show herself, I'll search room to room until I locate her."

He wasn't usually so rude, and he never tossed around his newly-bestowed title as if people should bow down, but the current circumstance seemed to require it. He'd never met Maud Bates, but he was positive he wouldn't like her.

He couldn't deduce his plan. It was ridiculous to waste any energy on the horrid woman, but after he'd been scolded by Newman—his own butler!— he'd had to flee for a few hours.

He'd like to be angry with the man for his sincere remarks, but Newman's attitude was completely justified. Jo had to leave Benton House, and he should have been in the city, talking to a rental agent about vacant lodging.

Instead, he'd ridden to the country, hoping the wide-open spaces would calm his temper. He'd assumed he was traveling aimlessly, but when he'd found himself in Telford, it appeared he'd had a destination in mind after all.

Maud's residence wasn't overly grand, but it was a fine property nonetheless. Two stories high, constructed of red brick with black shutters, it looked solid and sturdy. There were plenty of windows with flowerboxes under them, but there didn't seem to be a gardener. It was the height of summer, but no plants bloomed in the boxes.

The parlor was obviously a woman's room. There were numerous decorative tables, and they were covered with doilies, figurines, and other ornaments. Embroidered pillows adorned the sofa. They hinted at dreary winter evenings spent stitching by the fire.

He tried to imagine Jo living in the house, but couldn't. Had she ever been happy? Or, more likely, had she been bored to tears?

The maid hustled off to find Maud, and Peyton brazenly made himself at home, but then, no butler had strolled in to offer refreshments.

There was a tray in the corner with a brandy decanter on it. He poured himself a glass, and he was sipping it when Maud hurried in.

"Lord Benton," she nervously said, "this is . . . ah . . . a surprise."

"Miss Bates, I presume?"

"Yes." A man entered behind her, and she gestured to him. "May I present my betrothed, Mr. Townsend? He's visiting from London."

"How nice," Peyton muttered, his surly tone indicating he couldn't care less.

It was apparent she was terrified over his arrival. There was only one reason she had a connection to him, and that reason was her daughter. Mr. Townsend wasn't aware of that fact though.

She had to be panicked that Peyton had come to confer about Daisy, that he was about to spill the beans and ruin her engagement. But Maud and her pathetic fiancé didn't matter to Peyton in the least.

"We were just sitting down to eat," Maud said. "Will you join us?"

"No."

"You're Neville's brother, aren't you?" Townsend asked. "You're the new earl? Peyton Prescott, isn't it?"

"Yes."

"I think you went to school with my brother, Freddie."

"I can't recall," Peyton lied. "He must not have been that memorable."

Peyton hadn't glanced at Townsend who recognized he was being snubbed. He bristled, but didn't comment as Peyton kept his focus on Jo's sister. He couldn't conceal his disdain. She was homely, not ugly exactly, but not pleasing in even the slightest way.

She was chubby, and her gown bulged at the seams, accentuating her excess weight, but it was her eyes that were depressing. She looked like a cold, hard person who would be difficult to tolerate.

"I'm here on your sister's behalf," he said.

"Jo sent you?" She forced a smile. "I didn't realize you were acquainted."

"We are." Maud stared, expecting Peyton to elaborate, but he didn't. "You kicked her out without her clothes, and I've volunteered to retrieve them."

Townsend frowned at Maud, at Peyton. "Wait a minute. Maud didn't *kick out* her sister. She's away, staying with relatives."

"Is that what she told you?" Peyton scoffed. "If that's the sort of candor the two of you practice, I predict you will have a very interesting marriage."

Townsend glared at Maud, but she was stoically silent. Clearly, a quarrel would erupt after Peyton left.

"I assume you still have her wardrobe?" he asked Maud, his furious demeanor warning her that she better have.

"Ah . . . yes . . . I have her clothes."

"And there was a jar she needed, with some coins in it. It was special to her. Do you have that as well?"

"Everything is in her room. We haven't touched a single item."

"Good. I want it all, and I've arranged for a woman from the village to stop by and pack it. Then it will be shipped to London."

"Oh."

She might have argued with him, and he sternly inquired, "Will there be a problem with you giving her her clothes, Miss Bates? I'm sure there's not. You tossed her out on the road with nothing."

"That's not true!" Maud huffed.

Peyton tsked with offense. "You may wallow in your fantasy, but I won't lower myself by debating it with you."

Townsend butted in again. "I'm confused by all of this, Benton, and obviously, I've been in the dark with regard to Josephine."

"This situation doesn't concern you, Townsend." Peyton was still glowering at Maud.

"No, no, of course it doesn't," the obsequious toad agreed, "but we're fond of Josephine. We wouldn't like her to be uncomfortable or imperiled. We're happy to let her have her clothes." He nudged his fiancée. "Aren't we, Maud?"

Maud's jaw was clenched so tightly it was a wonder she could speak. "Yes, we're very happy to allow it."

"Marvelous," Peyton said to her.

"Ah . . . where is Jo living?" Maud asked. "I've been worried about her."

"*You* were worried? Your comment will have me laughing all the way to town."

"I have been worried!" she claimed, but he ignored her protest.

"The woman I've hired will arrive shortly. Josephine's belongings should be sent tomorrow, and if anything is missing, I'll hold you responsible." He raised a brow. "And I'll be back to find out why."

He whipped away and departed. Luckily, they didn't follow him out. He mounted his horse and rode away, and he figured he'd be angry and aggrieved, but actually, he was feeling quite grand. He'd recovered Jo's clothes and Daisy's jar, and he was excited to learn how Jo would react when her garments appeared. No doubt she'd be incredibly grateful, and any gratitude would ultimately work to his benefit.

Did that make him an unredeemable cad? Could it be? With Jo's happiness on the line, the answer to that question was irrelevant.

BARBARA WALKED INTO THE foyer of Benton House. She hadn't visited in ages, and she took a hasty appraisal to ensure naught had changed.

She didn't like to come to London. People knew about her awful marriage, about her father and brother going bankrupt and their losing all they owned. For her, London was an unrelenting slog of pitying glances, snide insults, and rank gossip, which she avoided by hiding in the country.

Newman was standing in the corner, and they shared a private look where Barbara informed him she wouldn't give him away to Peyton. His letter about Peyton's reckless amour had been completely appropriate. Later on, she'd reward him.

She was disgusted by Peyton's conduct, but not surprised by it. He was Neville's brother after all. She and Richard had been tiptoeing around him, terrified they'd enrage him and be evicted, but he'd proved himself a milksop when he had to put his foot down and mean it.

He'd ordered Richard to leave Benton and Barbara to move to the Dower House, but he hadn't checked to guarantee they'd complied. He'd warned that investigators would carry out an audit, but they hadn't. He was furious that Richard had expelled the three bastards from the estate, but he hadn't located them and brought them back.

So far, his only concrete step had been to seize control of the bank accounts, but Barbara rarely accessed them anyway, so it had scarcely caused a ripple in the fabric of her existence.

It was clear Peyton was all pomp and bluster. He liked to complain and strut about, but when tough decisions were required, he didn't follow through. He was a soldier, but not a fighter, and in Barbara, he'd met his match. She was done placating him.

"It's lovely to see you again, Countess," Newman said.

"I realize you weren't expecting me. I hope you don't mind my showing up without any notice."

"We're always delighted to have you. Will you be staying with us for a bit?"

"No. I'll stay with my brother, Roger."

She hadn't notified Roger that she'd be spending the night, and it would be for just the *one* night. She was eager to return to the country so she didn't have any unpleasant encounters with old acquaintances.

She could have tarried at Benton House, but she and her brother-in-law were about to quarrel, and if Miss Bates was in residence, Barbara would never sleep under the same roof. She viewed herself as a modern female and definitely not a prude, but there were some behaviors a Christian woman couldn't abide.

"Is Lord Benton here?" she asked.

"Yes, he's in the library. Shall I announce you?"

"Don't bother. He and I will have a quick chat, then I'll be off."

Newman looked relieved to be out of it. She handed him her bonnet and shawl, and she swept by him and down the hall. Peyton was seated at the desk in the ostentatious room and buried in a large stack of correspondence. She didn't knock or request permission to enter. She simply strolled in.

On observing her, his expression was unreadable, so she couldn't deduce if he was irked, curious, or shocked to see her—or if he had no opinion about her arrival at all. She suspected it was the latter.

"Barbara, this is a surprise. What brings you to town?"

"Hello, Peyton." She shut the door and pulled up a chair. "I had to talk to you."

"If you'd travel all this way, the topic must be vital."

"It is. I had a letter from the servants."

"Oh, so they *are* spying on me."

"They're not spying," she insisted. "They're simply concerned."

"About what?"

She hesitated. She'd assumed she could blurt it out, but now that they were face to face, it seemed appallingly difficult.

"Well?" he asked when she couldn't begin. "What is it?"

"I'm told Josephine Bates is living with you, and you've grown quite *fond* of her."

For a moment, he froze, and a fierce tempest flashed in his eyes, but it was swiftly masked. "Yes, Miss Bates is living here."

"I'm certain you understand that the situation can't continue."

"No, I don't understand that."

"I shouldn't have to spell it out. It will embarrass both of us."

"I demand you explain," he said. "I'm on pins and needles waiting to hear."

"You are a bachelor, Peyton, and Miss Bates is a maiden, so it's very improper. Also, we employ many young people. They can't be party to such a depraved spectacle."

"Yes, I've had that dilemma pointed out to me. In my own defense, Miss Bates is experiencing a few personal problems. I'm merely offering her shelter until I can make other arrangements."

"I won't dignify that false comment with a reply. I have it on good authority that there's mischief occurring, so it's only a matter of time until it's a catastrophe. You've just inherited the title. Would you like to immediately become immersed in a very public scandal?"

"Not really."

"And how about the navy? Aren't there morality rules for sailors?"

"There are."

"You could jeopardize your career. Have you thought about the ramifications?"

"No, but I suppose I should."

"As to Miss Bates, she has no ancestry to indicate she's a suitable wife for you, yet if she winds up ruined, that is her sole option. So I must inquire: Is it your intent to marry her?"

"No, I'm not ready to wed. Not her or anyone."

"Then—as she is nearly a stranger to you—she can't have any interests that would coincide with yours. You must get her out of the house, Peyton, and it has to happen today—if you can manage it. If not today, then by tomorrow for sure."

A muscle ticked in his cheek. Outwardly, he appeared very calm, but she sensed rage bubbling just below the surface. Would he explode in fury? Would he hurl expletives and throw things? That's how his brother used to carry on, and she'd learned how to weather any such diatribe unscathed.

"You're very brave to address this," he said. "I hardly know you, *and* you're a female, so I'm stunned that you would lecture me."

She shrugged. "I realize you'd rather not have any in-laws. I realize you'd rather be a single man, floating free with no encumbrances. After all, that's how your life has played out until recently."

"It's been a fine life too," he snottily retorted.

"But you're part of a family now—whether you like it or not. I am your sister-in-law, and you are the trustee charged with my welfare and that of my daughters. Your brother set that condition in motion with his Last Will. You're irritated with that resolution, and so am I, but we're connected in a manner that can't be severed."

"Yes, we are."

"We are tightly linked, so I shall be allowed an opinion on controversial issues—especially in a quagmire like this that could end up destroying what's left of my reputation. I've constantly waded through shame and disgrace. It's all my father and your brother ever delivered to me. I won't sit idly by and twiddle my thumbs while you deliver more of the same."

"I wouldn't dream of it."

She stood. "I expect that Miss Bates will depart at once."

"I'll definitely think about it."

"You won't *think*, Peyton. You will act on my request right away. Please drop me a note as soon as she's gone so I can cease my fretting."

Head high, she whipped away and marched out, but as she reached the door, he called, "Barbara?"

She glanced back. "Yes?"

"Which servant wrote to you?"

"All of them wrote, Peyton. It was a joint letter to convey their collective concern."

He nodded. "On your way out, send Newman to me."

"Why do you need him?"

"I'll discuss it with him. Not you."

"It wasn't Newman who contacted me—if that's what you suppose."

"It's not what I suppose, and thank you for speaking so candidly. I'm impressed and astonished that you could be so bold."

"You'd be surprised by what I can manage."

"I doubt I would be. Goodbye."

She kept on to the foyer. Newman was still there, and in a normal tone, she said, "I'm off, Newman, but Lord Benton asked for you."

"I'll attend him immediately."

He assisted her with her shawl and bonnet, and she leaned in and whispered, "He guessed it was you who tattled. I insisted it wasn't, but he didn't believe me."

Newman sighed. "I appreciate the warning."

"If he fires you, come to Benton. I'll find you a spot there."

"I'd be very grateful."

She flashed a wan smile, then hurried out. She'd told her driver to wait, so her carriage was parked in front of the house. As she went toward it, another carriage pulled up behind.

A footman rushed over and assisted the occupants in climbing out. The first to descend was a very pretty girl with auburn hair and big blue eyes. She was fashionably attired in a fetching manner that Barbara—for all her being able to hire the finest dressmakers—could never attain.

She assumed she'd stumbled on the elusive Miss Bates who was causing so much trouble. She was chic and beautiful, and she exuded a youth and vulnerability that would drive a man wild. No wonder Peyton couldn't resist.

Barbara had no desire to fight with Miss Bates. It was Peyton's problem, and he should handle it, so she might have continued on without comment. But when the second passenger was lifted out, and Barbara realized her identity, her temper ignited.

"What are you doing here?" she demanded of Daisy Prescott.

She stormed over, looming at them so threateningly that Daisy shrunk back as if Barbara might strike her. She wouldn't, but honestly!

How much degradation would the Prescott men inflict on her?

"Hello, Countess." Daisy executed a perfect curtsy.

"Answer me!"

"Ah ... ah ... "

Miss Bates stepped between them. "May I help you?"

"I am Barbara Prescott, Countess of Benton."

Barbara was taller, broader, and fiercer, but Miss Bates was quite fierce herself. She wasn't intimidated, and she didn't yield any ground to Barbara.

"Why is this child in my home?" Barbara pointed a condemning finger at Daisy. "She is not welcome on Benton property any longer. Who permitted this?"

"I apologize, Countess, but Lord Benton invited us to stay."

"He invited *both* of you? He invited *her*?"

"Yes."

Barbara thought she would shatter into a thousand livid pieces.

In Newman's letter, he'd conveniently failed to mention that Miss Bates had brought Daisy with her. Perhaps—if Peyton fired him and he slinked to Benton searching for work—she wouldn't aid him after all.

She blustered forward, eager to unnerve Miss Bates. "My husband's bastard daughter is not wanted here. You are not wanted here either, Miss Bates. You have shamed yourself with the Earl."

"I have not!" Miss Bates huffed with offense. "How dare you accuse me of wanton conduct!"

"All of the servants are talking about you, so you can't deny it."

"I do deny it! I absolutely do!"

"It's why I am in London—to speak with the Earl about you. We are decent, respectable people, and you cannot be allowed to wallow in our midst."

Miss Bates acquitted herself with grace and style. Despite Barbara's horrid allegation, she simply nodded. "It's obvious you're upset."

"You don't know the half of it, you little tart."

"I hope—when you've calmed—you'll grasp how hideously you've insulted me."

"You've imposed on us egregiously," Barbara seethed. "You've flaunted your niece in my face! There are dire consequences, Miss Bates, when a woman of your low station interferes with a woman of mine. If you don't wish to suffer them, I suggest you depart as quickly as you're able."

"Thank you for sharing your opinion," Miss Bates coolly replied. She turned to her niece. "Let's go, Daisy."

Barbara saw red. "Listen to me, you . . . you . . ."

"No, Countess, I won't listen. I'm Lord Benton's guest, and if you're angry about the situation, you should discuss it with him. Not me."

They hurried off, and the footman ushered them inside and shut the door. He remained outside though, and he glanced anxiously at Barbara. The carriage drivers glanced at her too. They'd been privy to the pathetic quarrel, but were pretending they hadn't been.

Barbara probably shouldn't have lost her temper, but she didn't have to worry that any of them might inform Peyton. They were her servants, not his, and if she chose to chastise a trollop in her driveway, none of them would criticize her for it.

She walked to her vehicle and climbed in, but as she signaled to the driver and they rolled away, she was being pelted by the worst sense that they were watching her, that they were judging her.

Well, let them judge!

She was a countess which meant she was always in the right, and their views didn't matter to her in the slightest.

"You wanted me, my lord?"

"Yes. Come in, Newman." Peyton was still seated at the library desk, and without preamble, he announced, "I've decided to close down the town house."

Poor Newman looked as if he might faint. "You're . . . what?"

"I'm closing the house. I'd like to have it completed in five days. How about if we shoot for Saturday? Can we accomplish it by then?"

"Ah . . . yes, of course. If I may ask though, will this be a short hiatus? Or were you considering a lengthy period? This will be quite a shock to the staff, and they'll have questions about their jobs."

"I suppose they will have questions, and no, it won't be short. In fact, I'm thinking of selling."

"I see."

"You may have heard rumors that the estate is having fiscal difficulties."

"I have heard it."

"We need to begin cutting back, and this place seems like a good start. It's empty most of the time, and I can't convince myself that it's worth the expense."

"But . . . but . . . where will you stay when you're in London?"

"There's an officers' club that rents rooms to navy sailors who are between postings. It would be much more economical."

They stared, and finally, Newman said, "Is this because I admonished you about Miss Bates? Is it because the Countess did? Are you retaliating?"

"No."

He was, and he wasn't. Newman and Barbara were correct that he was risking a huge scandal, and perhaps his career too, but he was absurdly fascinated with Jo and couldn't behave himself.

His obsession was ridiculous, and he wasn't stupid. He recognized the dangers, but he was disgustingly keen to keep on anyway. Barbara and Newman were merely urging caution, and he accepted their warnings, but any reprimand was for naught.

Where Jo was concerned, there was no benefit to moral conduct. She could never be a casual friend. She could only be a wife or mistress, and since he wasn't about to wed her, the role of mistress was the sole one available. It would be cruel and wrong to dishonor her that way, but he wasn't about to let her go. He *couldn't* let her go.

Newman and Barbara had pointed out the obvious, but their comments had left Peyton more incensed than he'd ever been. He wanted to lash out. He wanted to make someone pay. It was a petulant, juvenile attitude, but he couldn't tamp it down.

If he couldn't live in the house with Jo, then he wouldn't live in it. He'd sell the accursed residence and never set foot in it again.

Newman's shoulders slumped, and he gave Peyton a chance to stop acting like an immature ass.

"Are you sure, Lord Benton?"

"Very sure."

"I guess I should tell the staff they'll have to find new positions. They'll be distressed."

"Yes, I imagine they will be. I'll offer two month's severance, and please draft letters of recommendation to those who deserve one. I'll sign them."

"I will do that."

"If any of you wish to head to Benton and throw yourselves on the Countess's mercy, feel free. She may have some openings, but I have no idea what they might be. If she agrees to hire any of you, you'll get no severance money from me."

"I understand."

A fraught silence festered, and Peyton said, "That will be all."

"I'm sorry, Lord Benton. I've offended you, and I shouldn't have interfered."

"You haven't offended me, Newman. You couldn't possibly have. Very little about this family or its holdings has ever mattered to me. I won't regret parting with this property for a single minute."

"Regardless of your opinion, my lord, it's a fine dwelling, and it's been a privilege to work in it."

"I'm glad you've thought so, and thank you for tending it." Noise erupted out in the foyer, and his mood perked up. "Now then, it sounds as if Miss Bates and Daisy have returned from their shopping excursion. If you'll excuse me?"

Newman hovered, anxious for the conversation to continue, anxious to plead his case or beg Peyton to change his mind, but Peyton simply glared at him.

There would be no changing his mind, so there was no reason to beg, and gradually, Newman realized there wasn't. He sighed and marched out.

CHAPTER

17

Jo was seated in the parlor of the small house Peyton had rented for her. It had been arranged so quickly that her head was spinning.

After the horrid afternoon when Barbara Prescott had traveled to London to scold Peyton, he'd engaged in a whirl of activity that ended with Jo and Daisy being whisked away and the town house closed. Mostly likely, it would be put up for sale.

He was still debating about the property, and she was nudging him to calm down, to ignore his fit of pique before he reached any final decision. He shouldn't sell merely because he was furious with his sister-in-law. That wasn't a viable path to making a good choice.

It had been easy for him to find her current accommodations. He'd simply visited a rental agency to inquire about furnished lodgings, then he'd visited an employment agency that offered servants for hire. In a few quick days, he'd found her new quarters and the servants required to be comfortable.

If he'd done it just for her, she'd have been aghast and liked to assume she wouldn't have let him, but he was supporting his niece too, and in Jo's view, Daisy's security was paramount.

He'd mentioned fiscal problems at the estate, so she wasn't sure he could afford to pay her bills or for how long he would continue. If he changed his mind about assisting them, she'd have to have other plans in place.

As the weeks rolled by, she would watch and listen for alternatives. She would brood and ponder and generate lists. If he ever asked them to depart, she had to be prepared. But she refused to worry incessantly about the future, and why worry over what she couldn't control? There was no need to court trouble.

It was late, and Daisy was in bed. Jo was sewing by the fire and wondering if Peyton would stop by. He'd rented a room at a club that catered to naval officers. He was happy to be in familiar company, and she suspected—any minute—he would announce he was returning to his career and his ship.

She couldn't bear the notion of his leaving England. What if he sailed away, and she never saw him again? How would she and Daisy get on without him? How would Jo survive the loss?

He was like a tempest, like a stormy gale that had swept in and cleared away everything that was bad and untenable. She'd been weighed down by her miserable situation, by her dreary life in the country with her sister. Now she was constantly merry, constantly peeking out the window in case he was riding up her street.

The clock on the mantle chimed eleven, and she forced herself to admit he wasn't coming. She packed her sewing away, tamped down the fire, and blew out the lamp. Then she climbed the stairs to her bedchamber and dressed for bed, taking down her hair and donning her nightgown and robe.

She grinned with satisfaction, being delighted to note they were *her* nightgown and robe.

Peyton had retrieved Jo's clothes from Maud. The morning she'd moved into her home, her first and biggest surprise had been the arrival of her wardrobe. Daisy's jar of coins had been sent too. He hadn't informed her of the gift, hadn't provided a hint of his intent. Who wouldn't love a man like that?

She was brushing her hair when the front door opened, then his footsteps were on the stairs. It sounded as if he was tiptoeing, but there was no need for stealth. Two of her servants lived in, but their room was behind the kitchen. They'd never hear him.

As he slipped inside, she couldn't conceal her elation. Apparently, they were far beyond the point when she would admonish him for showing up in the one spot he should never be.

"I'd given up on you," she said, and she was smiling, her fondness wafting out.

"I meant to join you for supper, but I ran into some old friends."

"If you'd blustered in without warning, I guess I'd have fed you."

"Did you miss me?"

"No."

He chuckled. "You liar. Tell me the truth."

"All right. I missed you every second. Is that better?"

"Yes."

He drew her into his arms, and he kissed her thoroughly, passionately. He'd been drinking. She could taste liquor on his tongue, and his clothes smelled of horses, tobacco, and fresh night air. They were exhilarating, masculine aromas that aroused and excited her.

He'd rescued her from peril, had bestowed so many presents, with her not asking for any of them or being expected to compensate him for his many kindnesses, but it seemed she *should* compensate him. When she owed him such a great debt, how could she think otherwise?

The embrace grew ardent and heated. He stretched out on her bed and brought her down with him, and it was so deliciously thrilling to lie down with him. She had to start erecting some boundaries, but it was never the appropriate time to mention it.

Eventually, he slowed and pulled away. There was a candle burning next to the bed. He snuffed it out, so the room was dark, a whiff of moonlight shining in the window.

He snuggled her to his side, and she rested a palm on his chest, his heart beating under her hand. She sensed that his thoughts were tormented, that he was bristling with personal issues he wasn't comfortable sharing, but she wouldn't ignore his low mood.

"You're upset. What happened this evening?"

"I enjoyed seeing my friends, but they're all preparing to ship out. I'm jealous."

It was the main problem that plagued him. He was anxious to return to the navy, but familial constraints were keeping him landlocked. She'd frequently voiced her opinion about it, so there was no reason to harangue again.

They were quiet, and she presumed he'd fallen asleep, but he hadn't.

"I went to visit Evan and Amelia," he said.

"How was it? Are they still angry?"

"They weren't there. Their house is shuttered."

"They left town?"

"Yes. I talked to their neighbor, but he claimed he had no idea where they were."

"You didn't believe him?"

"No. He was rude and curt and didn't invite me in."

"That must have been embarrassing."

"It was." After a bit, he admitted, "Evan gave him a letter for me."

"Was it bad?"

"Yes. He was positive I'd slink in sooner or later, that I'd want to justify my behavior and worm my way back into their good graces."

"Well, you *did* want to do that."

"He said I shouldn't pester them. They are moving on with their life, and I should move on with mine."

She sighed. "I'm sorry. I realize you were counting on a different ending."

"I've known him forever. He's like a brother to me. Amelia is like a sister. I'm stunned that they'd cut ties."

"It's early yet, Peyton. They need space to fume and recover. If all of you are as close as you assume, they'll get over it."

"What if they don't?"

"Then the three of you weren't as close as you imagined."

"Yes, I suppose." Very quietly, he added, "He's requested a transfer."

"Out of the navy?"

"No—to another ship. He was always my First Officer. Ever since we were boys, we sailed together, but he's finished with me. It's a hard blow."

He fell asleep then, and she dozed too. When she awoke, she wasn't sure how much time had passed. He wasn't in the bed, and she figured he'd sneaked out without a goodbye. But he was over by the window, leaned on the sill and gazing out at the stars.

He'd shed his coat, shirt, boots, and stockings, so he was attired just in his trousers. In the moonlight, his skin was a silvery color, so he appeared ghostly and ethereal, like the most solitary man in the world.

She braced herself on an elbow.

"Why are you out of bed?" she inquired. "Aren't you freezing?"

"Not really. I'm too agitated to feel the chill."

"Are you fretting about Evan and Amelia? Please don't. You can't fix it tonight anyway."

"They are vexing me, but it's everything else too. Are you weary of listening to me complain?"

"Yes, I'm very weary of it."

She lifted the quilt, coaxing him to her, but he didn't budge. He simply stared at her, his focus riveting and unnerving. He was particularly morose, and his demeanor frightened her.

Suddenly, she was terrified he was about to leave her. Or perhaps he couldn't support her and Daisy after all. Perhaps he was out of money or Barbara Prescott had renewed her nagging about his relationship with them.

Jo had no illusions. He was buried in controversies. They seemed small to her, but they were weighing him down. Was she a burden he would no longer carry?

"I need to ask you a question," he said.

His tone was so somber that her alarm soared. "What is it? Just tell me."

"Don't laugh, and don't answer right away. You have to think about it."

"Yes, I'll think about it. I promise."

A lengthy pause spiraled out. He looked miserable and dejected, and she was awash with anxiety. So when the question was posed, she was glad she was lying down. If she hadn't been, she might have fainted.

"Would you marry me?" he asked.

She cocked her head, not certain she'd heard him correctly. "Marry you? Is that what you said?"

"Yes. Would you?"

Her initial reaction was one of unbridled joy. She was astonished by his proposal, but despite her immediate surge of euphoria, she retained a modicum of common sense. Why would he wish to wed her? Why would he suggest it?

They'd never discussed the notion, and he'd never hinted that he might be interested in her being his wife. In fact, the few occasions matrimony had been raised, he'd stridently insisted he wasn't prepared to marry. It was at the root of his quarrel with Evan and Amelia Boyle.

If he wasn't ready to wed Miss Boyle, whom he'd known all his life, he definitely wasn't ready to wed Jo. She wasn't a suitable bride for him.

The biggest obstacle would be his family. They'd never accept her as his countess. If she mentioned that problem though, he'd swear he wasn't concerned about their opinions.

But she'd had a bleak and dismal view of the ramifications when two disparate people married. Her father had been lured into folly by his affection for his nanny. It had been such a bizarre choice that, all these years later, neighbors still snickered and gossiped.

A man and woman who were so dissimilar in their backgrounds and ancestry shouldn't wind up together. Society had strict, unwritten rules about such odd pairings because experience had proven them to be unfeasible. He couldn't have reflected on any of those issues.

As to herself, she had once nearly shackled herself to a cad who hadn't been serious in his intentions. She wouldn't put herself in such a humiliating position ever again. She didn't necessarily suppose Peyton Prescott would jilt her at the altar, but he could definitely develop second thoughts.

At the moment, he imagined they should wed, but what if they proceeded, and ultimately, he recognized how foolish he'd been? What if he started to rue and regret?

It would be a different sort of jilt, and she declined to ever arrive at a point where he was dissatisfied with her. She would never agree to a scenario where she would be devastated by his disregard.

"Why would you want to marry me?" she asked.

"I was pondering you all day. I can't stand to be separated from you for a single minute. We've grown so close, and I can't have anything happen that might split us apart."

"Nothing will split us apart," she declared, even though she didn't believe it. "You're overly distressed this evening. Your visit to Evan Boyle, along with you meeting your old sailing friends, has you exceedingly morose."

A ghost of a smile flitted across his lips. "You could be right."

"You're feeling sorry for yourself, and you're trying to cheer up."

"It would cheer me immensely if you were my bride."

"Would it?"

The query hung in the air between them. He wasn't a *cheery* fellow, and she could never be the cure for what ailed him.

"Are you refusing me?" he asked.

"Not refusing precisely. I'm simply struggling to figure out why you proposed in the first place."

"Could it be because I'd like you to be my wife? Is that so hard to fathom?"

"Yes, it's very hard to fathom."

He snorted with disgust. "What if I went back to the navy and left England? Would you miss me?"

"Of course."

"How much."

"With every fiber of my being," she honestly replied, and she patted the mattress again. "Lie down, would you? You're in an awful state, and I can't bear to see you so troubled."

"Will you soothe me into a better mood?"

"I'm hoping I can."

"If you'd agree to wed me, it would work wonders."

"For the moment, it might, but I'm betting you'd suffer doubts pretty fast."

He scowled. "You suppose I'd regret it?"

"Yes," she firmly insisted. "We wouldn't have to walk to the altar for you to question your decision. I'm sure you'd be aghast much sooner than that."

"You're a difficult woman, Jo Bates."

"So you keep telling me. Now come and lie down."

PEYTON HURRIED TO THE bed, both of them laughing as he slid next to her. His skin was icy, and she was warm and toasty. She drew the blankets over them, snuggling them in a tight cocoon.

He nuzzled at her nape, inhaling her lush scent that drove him wild. It urged him on, making him anxious to engage in behaviors that were dangerous and destructive and—once embarked upon—could never be reversed.

Why had he proposed? What had he been thinking?

He was irked by her rejection, but incredibly glad too. When the words had spewed from his mouth, he'd been stunned to hear them voiced aloud. He wasn't ready to marry, and with his recent elevation to a higher social plane, he had to be careful in picking a bride. He couldn't blithely select a beautiful, intriguing commoner who didn't have two pennies to rub together.

His eagerness was rooted in deeper issues. He was restless and bored, impatient to return to the navy, and he was missing Evan too. He hated that they'd parted on such bad terms. Every facet of his life seemed wrong and out of joint. How often would he bemoan that fact before he took steps to mend his dilemma?

Jo was his sole link to normalcy. He'd gotten her away from the prying eyes at the town house. He'd found her and Daisy a safe, quiet home where they could develop a routine. He was trying to remain outside the space they were creating for themselves. He only visited occasionally, and he forced himself to avoid them for long stretches, not wanting to be a nuisance, not wanting to overstay his welcome.

Yet when he was away from Jo, he thought about her constantly. She was like an addictive drug, and he couldn't stop obsessing. He'd convinced himself—if he didn't ponder her so relentlessly—his enthrallment would wane, but as he'd stood by the window a bit earlier, watching her sleep so peacefully, he'd been swamped by a perilous yearning.

He'd offered matrimony without any consideration. She'd declined, but he was very vain, and her rebuff had merely ignited his need to possess her in every wicked way possible. He was desperate to bind her so securely that she could never escape.

The impulse was so strong that it scared him. In his current glum condition, he might commit any terrible act.

"I can't believe you refused me," he said.

"One of us has to keep a level head. If I let you take the lead, there's no predicting where we'd end up."

"We're not in such a horrid spot though. Are we?"

"No. We're in a very, very good spot."

He gazed into her blue eyes, so overcome with emotion that he felt as if he was drowning. He began kissing her and kissing her, and each minute of the embrace dragged him further into his morass of affection.

He'd desired her from the moment they'd met. Perhaps if he pushed them to the ultimate conclusion, he'd be shed of her intoxicating appeal. Should he deflower her? Was that his plan? Had that been his plan all along?

If she wasn't interested in having him as her husband, he shouldn't be in her room, in her bed, but he wasn't about to walk away. She was being perfectly ridiculous, and he didn't have to listen to her. He *never* listened to women, so why start with her?

Besides, if they waltzed to iniquity, he might realize that marriage to her was a brilliant idea. She might realize it too.

Or maybe it was the lust talking. His anatomy had a deed in mind that could never resolve to her benefit, but in his present chaotic state, he was weary of all his mental wrangling and was keen for a more basic event to occur. He was an active, physical man, and sexual play was a vital physical activity. If a bout of fornication couldn't fix what was wrong, what could?

If there was a warning bell clanging out the message that he was on the verge of reprehensible conduct, he didn't have to pay attention to it.

She was wearing a nightgown and robe, but in his opinion, she had on entirely too many clothes. Swiftly, he divested her of her robe. The nightgown was white and virginal, with tiny straps over her shoulders and pretty flowers embroidered on the bodice.

Gradually, he tugged down the straps to bare her bosom, and he dipped down and feasted on her exquisite breasts. He continued forever, sucking, nibbling, moving from one to the other as he worked the hem of her night-gown up her legs. His busy fingers roamed up and up until he could slip them into her tight sheath and send her soaring to the heavens.

She cried out with joy, and he held her, preening as she reached her peak, as she tumbled down.

"How do you do that to me?" she asked when she could speak again.

"It's simple. You're a trollop at heart."

Her jaw dropped in protest. "I am not a trollop."

He chuckled. "I didn't say you were. You merely have the *heart* of one, but I don't deem that a negative trait in a female."

"You wouldn't."

He'd slyly wedged his torso between her shapely thighs, his body posi-tioned precisely where he needed it to be. He felt as if he was perched on a cliff, and he had two choices. He could run to the edge and jump over or he could retreat and forget about committing an irresponsible act.

Unfortunately for both of them, the cliff beckoned, and the safe route vanished in a fog of passion.

"I want you to give me something special," he said.

"What is it?"

"You know *what*."

"You want to . . . to . . ."

She didn't possess the appropriate terminology, and her lack of prurient edification underscored how awfully he was behaving. But he didn't, didn't, *didn't* care!

"It's marital conduct," she said, "and we're not married."

"We don't have to be married."

"If we're not husband and wife, it's a sin."

"Preachers claim it is, but I'm not a religious man."

"Is that your excuse? You're not religious, so *sin* is irrelevant?"

"Yes." He kissed her again and again, and he was melting her defenses. "Let me be with you like this, Jo."

"We shouldn't, Peyton."

"Probably not, but don't you see? This is the only path for us."

"You just proposed, and I refused you. My decision should have quelled any notion of proceeding."

"Nothing could shove us off this road. It's meant to be. Can't you feel it?"

"I feel a *certain* emotion," she churlishly replied, "but I don't suppose it's Fate harping at me to ruin myself."

"Please? It will make me so happy."

She frowned at him, then groaned with dismay. "You don't play fair, and you use my fondness against me. I can't ever stand up to you."

"You're allowed to make me happy. I'm much nicer when I am."

"That's debatable." She scoffed with annoyance. "You're exploiting my good nature and pressuring me into misdeeds I shouldn't attempt."

"Am I pressuring you, Jo? Really? Tell me you don't wish to be closer to me."

"I can't tell you that."

"Do you trust me?"

"No."

"Don't be ridiculous. Of course you trust me."

"I *trust* you in some ways, but not in all ways."

"Trust me in this. It will be wonderful. I swear it."

"What if you plant a babe in my belly? What then?"

At the question, he nearly raised a fist in triumph. If she was thinking about consequences, he was obviously succeeding in his quest to gain her acquiescence.

"I know how to avoid it," he said.

"Promise me you'll be careful. Promise you won't hurt me."

"Hurt you! I'd rather cut off my arm."

Their banter dwindled, and she seemed to be out of arguments. Or perhaps she was actually keen to continue, but was too morally inclined to admit it. She nodded or at least he persuaded himself that's what he saw.

And why wouldn't she be amenable? They were so besotted, and even though she'd stupidly rejected his proposal, her reticence didn't alter anything. It didn't tamp down the ardent desire that simmered below the surface.

He started in, driving her up and up the spiral of amour. He was nursing at her breasts, touching her between her legs. All the while, he was preparing himself, unbuttoning his trousers, tugging them down to his flanks, freeing his cock and centering it.

Another orgasm swept over her, and as she tensed, he clutched at her hips and raced to folly. There was no other choice. When he'd told her their relationship was meant to be, he truly believed it. Fate had tossed her into his path, and she was destined to be his.

He flexed with his hips, once, twice, and just that easily, he was fully impaled.

She exhaled a puff of breath and murmured, "Oh."

"My God, but you are so sweet."

"Am I . . . are we . . . will you . . . ? Is that it?"

"Almost. Are you all right?"

She scowled, taking stock. "Yes, I'm fine."

"Hold on while I finish, so you can learn how it ends."

He began to thrust, pushing in all the way, pulling out to the tip. He'd intended a long, slow fornication, but she was tight and wet, her virgin's blood urging him on, coaxing his seed from his loins much before he was ready.

He couldn't delay, and he plunged in deep and spilled himself against her womb. Though his brain was yelling at him to yank away, to conclude in a sane manner, he was so overwhelmed that he couldn't exercise any caution.

You're mine now! Mine!

The words riveted him, and he preened with satisfaction. He'd been reckless and negligent, but he wasn't sorry. In the morning, when he was more lucid, he would suffer no remorse. They had arrived precisely where they were supposed to be.

He flexed until the last drop was spent, then he collapsed onto her. He lay very still, feeling her tremble beneath him. After a bit, he drew away, their bodies separating. He rolled onto his side, and she rolled too so they were nose to nose.

"What did you think of that, Josephine Bates?" he asked.

"It was quite shocking, Commander Prescott."

"Yes, the first time definitely can be, but it gets better with repetition."

"Can we try it again in the future?"

"I imagine we will do it forever. I can't resist you, remember?"

He turned her away from him, so he could spoon himself to her back. They were quiet, but she wasn't asleep. He perceived that her mind was galloping at a very fast clip as she processed her new situation.

"Are you glad I agreed to this?" she eventually asked.

"I'm so glad, Jo. I can't tell you how much." He leaned in and kissed her hair, her shoulder.

"It won't change our relationship, will it?"

"No. Why would it? Don't be silly."

"I wouldn't want you to wake up and have a bad opinion of me for my deciding to participate."

"Me—have a bad opinion of you? You say the most bizarre things. You're my favorite person in the world. I could never have a negative view of you— no matter what."

"I like the sound of that."

"We're good together. In fact, we're perfect together."

"I like the sound of that too." After another lengthy pause, she inquired, "Might you have . . . ah . . . planted a babe?"

He froze, then relaxed. "No. It never happens from just one time. You have to do it over and over. It's not easy to create a child."

He couldn't guess why he'd told the horrid lie—or why she'd believed it.

The sailors on his ship were exact proof that a child could be sired from a single coupling. He couldn't count how often his men had headed home on furlough and come back wed. Babies took root when a man least expected it.

"What now?" she asked.

"Now we nap, then we'll go at it again. If you're not too sore?"

"I'm not sore."

He sensed she was smiling, and soon, her respiration evened out, and she dozed off. He snuggled with her, cataloguing every detail: how she smelled, how she fit in his arms, how her slender torso felt nestled to his own.

But when he started dozing too, he slid away and climbed to the floor.

He didn't dare be caught in her room. It was a small house, and he couldn't hide his presence as he might have in the much larger town house. Daisy couldn't find him on the premises when he shouldn't be there, and he had to worry about the servants too. He couldn't let them garner a hint of his intentions toward Jo. They might suspect misbehavior, but he'd never overtly confirm their worst fears.

He tugged on his clothes, not able to stop watching her, and he yearned to kiss her goodbye or perhaps whisper an endearment, but if she roused and looked at him, he'd never escape.

He tiptoed out, and as he reached the front door and stepped into the cold, evening air, he was already missing her, already calculating how quickly he could be with her once again.

CHAPTER

18

THERE WAS A KNOCK on the front door, and Jo glanced to the foyer, figuring a housemaid would appear, but she didn't hear any footsteps.

She wasn't a grand lady or a snob. She could open her own door, except that she was feeling poorly. It was mid-morning, and her tummy had been queasy ever since she'd first awakened. At the moment, she was too fatigued to speak with anyone.

When the knocker banged again, she laid down her sewing and answered it herself.

A young lady about her same age was standing there. She was slender and pretty, with dark hair and big blue eyes. She looked familiar, but Jo couldn't place her.

"May I help you?" Jo asked.

"Are you Miss Bates? You are, aren't you?"

"Yes, I'm Josephine Bates."

"I am Amelia Boyle."

Jo sucked in a sharp breath, and a thousand questions raced in her mind. How had Miss Boyle located her? Why would she have searched? What could she want? Jo fervidly hoped she didn't intend to quarrel about Peyton.

"Hello, Miss Boyle," Jo said. "I'm sorry, but I didn't recognize you."

"I wouldn't have expected you to. You only saw me the one time, and it was very quick."

There was an awkward pause where neither of them could think of what comment to offer next, and Miss Boyle broke the silence.

"May I come in?"

Jo yearned to deny her request, but that would be rude. She forced a smile and gestured inside. "Where have my manners gone? Yes, please come in."

Jo took Miss Boyle's shawl and bonnet and hung them on a hook, then she guided her into the parlor. Miss Boyle sat on the sofa, and Jo eased into the chair across.

"Would you like some tea, Miss Boyle?" she asked.

"No, I'm fine." There was another strained pause, then Miss Boyle said, "I imagine you're wondering why I'm here."

"Well . . . yes."

"I must admit that I'm wondering too."

Her remark relieved some of the tension, and Jo chuckled. "I'll confess to being mystified."

Daisy was upstairs, assessing her wardrobe. Jo had promised to add lace trim to some of her dresses, and she was picking out the ones she'd like to have altered.

She hollered down, "Jo, do we have a visitor?"

Jo walked to the foyer and peered up to the landing. "It's no one you know. I'll tell you all about it after I'm finished."

Daisy hovered, anxious to eavesdrop, and Jo stared at her until she grinned and returned to her room. Then Jo rejoined Miss Boyle.

"I apologize," Jo said. "That was my niece, Daisy. She's a handful."

"How old is she?"

"Nine."

"Are you . . . ah . . . raising her on your own?" Miss Boyle blushed furiously.

"It's probably none of my business. You needn't respond."

"It's all right to inquire. Yes, I'm raising her." Miss Boyle was perched on the edge of her seat, eager for further explanation, but Jo wasn't about to discuss Daisy's parentage. She simply said, "It's complicated. Her parents . . . couldn't manage it."

"You seem very young to have assumed so much responsibility."

"I didn't have much choice. There wasn't anyone else to step forward."

"She's an orphan?"

"No. She's just . . . mine now." Jo forced another smile. "Where were we? I believe you were about to tell me why you're here."

"Not really. As I mentioned, I have no idea why." Miss Boyle peeked around the parlor. "It's just that there have been some awful rumors about you."

Jo blanched. "About me?"

"Yes, and about Peyton. I've always been much too inquisitive, and I had to learn for myself if they were true."

Jo was incredibly dismayed. Rumors were circulating? Who was spreading them? What information was being disseminated?

She viewed herself as having a very isolated existence. Her street was quiet, and she hadn't met the neighbors, but while *she* might have been invisible, Peyton definitely wasn't. He was an earl and a naval officer, and he attracted attention wherever he went. And London—for all of it being a large city—was a very small place in certain circles.

"From how you're frowning," Jo said, "I'm terrified to ask, but what have people been saying?"

"Nothing good."

"I'm afraid you've listened to stories that are completely inaccurate."

"Are they? Is Peyton . . . ah . . . living with you?"

"No!" Jo firmly insisted.

"Gossip has it that he put the town house up for sale, and he rented this house—with you—instead."

"He rented it *for* me, Miss Boyle. Not for himself. Not for us. There is no *us*. When he's in town, he stays at his officer's club."

"I see." Apparently, Miss Boyle was made of very stern stuff. "May I be blunt, Miss Bates?"

"Yes, of course."

"I've been acquainted with Peyton all my life."

"Yes, he told me that you'd been friends. I know he hurt you and that he and your brother are fighting. I regret all of it."

"So do I." Miss Boyle's cheeks turned a deeper shade of crimson. "I thought he might marry me."

"Yes, he told me that too."

"And now, a few short weeks later, I find he's rented a house for you. Are you . . . is he . . . are the two of you . . ." She was unable to forge ahead with what would obviously be a ribald question. "Perhaps I can't be blunt after all. It's beyond me to interrogate you."

"Miss Boyle, let me ease your mind."

"Can you?"

"Well, about part of it. Daisy's father was Peyton's brother, Neville."

Miss Boyle scowled as she struggled to decipher Jo's meaning, then comprehension dawned.

"Oh!"

"He had an appalling reputation with the ladies, and he wasn't very faithful to his wedding vows."

"I'd never heard that about him."

"It wasn't the sort of detail the family would willingly divulge."

"No, I don't suppose so."

"He was an immoral wastrel who sired several children outside his marriage."

"Several!"

"Yes, so Daisy is my niece, but she is Peyton Prescott's niece too. She and I were having a spot of financial trouble, and he's been assisting us. If he hadn't intervened, I can't guess what would have happened."

"My goodness. I understand. Thank you for confiding in me." Miss Boyle fiddled with her skirt and, looking wretched, she asked, "Is Peyton fond of you?"

"Yes, I'd say he's fond."

"Will you wed him if he proposes?"

Jo scoffed as if it was the strangest notion ever. "We never would. I wouldn't be an appropriate bride for him, and it would never have occurred to him that I would be. We don't have that kind of bond."

It was such a horrendous lie that she should have been struck by lightning.

In most ways, she and Peyton were *not* carrying on like a married couple. He hadn't hauled over any clothes. He hadn't moved in. He simply pretended to be Daisy's detached, cordial uncle.

He visited once a day: to dine with them, to have tea, to bring Daisy a treat. Then, after everyone was asleep, he'd sneak back. Those were the hours when they behaved like newlyweds. Those were the hours when Jo was racing to perdition.

She wasn't precisely sure how she'd landed on such a reckless path, but she was careening down it so fast that she couldn't jump off. She was madly in love with him and was disgusted with herself for rejecting his proposal. She hoped he'd mention it again, but he hadn't, and she couldn't deduce how to raise the topic herself.

They'd staggered into their relationship in a backward fashion. They'd skipped directly to the marital parts—even though she didn't have a ring on her finger. They ought to come to their senses and walk away from the abyss. They ought to fear sin and damnation. Peyton didn't care about any preachers, but *she* definitely cared.

How long would she continue her wicked conduct? Would she ever muster the fortitude to call a halt?

The problem was that she didn't want to end it. She couldn't imagine him staying away, leaving her alone. The quiet intervals they spent in her small bedroom were undeniably precious.

She was a fool who had stupidly ruined herself—for him. To make him happy. To make him love her in return. Yet no words of amour had been exchanged, and she'd delivered the core benefit of marriage without his having to confer the main benefit of matrimony—that being their wedding.

What man wouldn't be delighted with such a sordid scenario?

But she couldn't reveal any of that to Miss Boyle. An admission would break her heart, and Jo would never do that. Usually, she was a dreadful liar, but she kept her expression calm, having resolved to spew every necessary deceit the meeting might require.

"My brother, Evan, was Peyton's best friend," Miss Boyle said.

"Yes, and I hate that they're fighting."

"My brother is very loyal to me."

Jo smiled a genuine smile. "You're lucky then."

"Yes, I am lucky. When Peyton tossed me over, Evan was livid on my behalf. He probably always will be."

"I hope not. I hope he'll get over it. Peyton misses him very much."

"Evan thought you and Peyton might be romantically involved, and it's been bothering me, Miss Bates, so I had to discover the truth."

"Your brother is wrong, Miss Boyle. Peyton is helping me during a difficult time."

"Can you swear it to me?"

"Yes, I swear, and I'm sorry you've been fretting."

Jo hadn't realized she had such a penchant for fabrication. The falsehoods were rolling off her tongue. How was that possible?

She was very ashamed, but she wouldn't utter a remark that might distress Miss Boyle more than she already had been. Normally, Jo would have believed that candor should be practiced, but not in this case. Never in this case.

"I should be going," Miss Boyle murmured.

She stood, and Jo accompanied her to the foyer, observing as she draped the shawl over her shoulders, as she tied the bow on her bonnet.

"I'm curious," Jo said. "How did you learn about this house?"

"It was servants' gossip. You know how they like to talk and spread stories."

Jo wondered which servants were discussing her. Were they ones from the town house who'd lost their jobs when it had been shuttered? Were they ones at the estate in the country who were faithful to Barbara Prescott? Peyton had to find out who was responsible and put a stop to it.

They couldn't have a scandal erupt or they'd have to abandon their relationship. Her neighbors wouldn't tolerate immoral shenanigans. Nor would her staff of servants. She'd have to move out of London, then Peyton wouldn't be able to pop in unannounced. He wouldn't be able to sneak up her stairs in the dark.

She couldn't bear to have their circumstances altered. She was anxious for their situation to remain as it was forever.

"Can I tell you a secret?" Miss Boyle asked.

"If you think you should."

"I was determined to *not* like you."

"I can certainly understand why you'd feel that way."

"But now that we've chatted, I like you very much."

"I'm glad. I like you too. Perhaps if your brother and Peyton ever mend their quarrel, we can be friends."

"I'd like that."

Miss Boyle reached out and squeezed Jo's hands, and Jo squeezed back. Then Miss Boyle opened the door and walked out. She'd arrived in a cab, and it was waiting on the street. She waved to Jo, then climbed in, and the vehicle lumbered away.

Jo watched until the cab rounded a corner and disappeared, then she came inside. Her tummy roiled, her nausea increasing, the stress of the encounter incredibly fatiguing.

Daisy was on the landing. "Is your visitor gone?"

"Yes, she was in a hurry. She had errands."

"She was pretty. Who was she?"

"No one." Jo wasn't inclined to explain. "She was no one at all."

"WE'VE SURVEYED ALL THE barns and the stables and the equipment and . . ."

Peyton was at Benton and seated at the desk in what had been Richard Slater's office. A clerk he'd hired in London, Arthur Cummings, was seated across from him. The man was droning on and on about inventory and account ledgers and crop rotation.

Peyton couldn't focus and was struggling vigorously to keep his eyes from glazing over.

He'd intended to have an appraisal accomplished much earlier, but incessant rain had left the roads too muddy to maneuver, so events in town with Jo had occupied his energy and time instead.

Arthur noticed Peyton wasn't really listening. He shut his portfolio. "It's obvious I've bored you to tears, Lord Benton. Shall we continue this conversation later?"

"Yes, we should. How much work has to be completed?"

"We should wrap it up tomorrow."

"And when will you finish writing your report?"

"A week, maybe less."

Peyton gazed out the window and stared at the park. It was the middle of the afternoon, and he'd like to jump on his horse and rush to London, but he couldn't flit off while the investigation was in progress.

Barbara and Richard were huffing and puffing, complaining and being generally discomfited by the assessment. Peyton was ignoring them. He'd warned Barbara that an evaluation would occur, but inclement weather had delayed it. Most likely, she'd assumed the men wouldn't show up, but they had, and she was incensed.

He hadn't grown up at Benton, so he was clueless as to what his ownership entailed. He had to find out and shouldn't have to justify his actions. He recognized that she was galled to have her authority usurped, but she exhausted him. Her position had totally changed, but she didn't feel she should have to make any concessions.

Previously, he'd ordered Richard to depart Benton and Barbara to move to the Dower House, but as he'd predicted, they hadn't heeded his edict. They were unwilling to cede any clout, unwilling to give him a voice in how they carried on.

How was he to view their recalcitrance? If he'd been on his ship, there would have been numerous options to gain their compliance—and penalties to impose if they'd declined to obey. But how could he be upset that they loved their home and wanted to stay in it?

Initially, he hadn't cared about Benton, but he was developing an interest. The more he visited, the more he enjoyed the place. There was a serene beauty that appealed to him.

Jo popped into his head, and he allowed a flight of fancy to take hold. What if they wed? What if she came to Benton as his countess?

Life at Benton would be very sweet if he could spend it with her. She'd chase away the ghosts and demons and would turn the property into a home where he could be content.

It dawned on him that he was contemplating marriage to her again, and he snorted with disgust. He was vain and proud, and he'd always be irked that she'd refused him, but he wasn't a glutton for punishment, so he wouldn't ever ask her again.

He realized he'd been woolgathering. How embarrassing! How long had he been in his trance? Arthur was frowning, clearly disconcerted by Peyton's mental lapses.

"Let's call it an afternoon," Peyton said.

"Very good, Lord Benton."

When Peyton had first arrived at Benton, he'd been aggravated by his new title, and he'd had everyone refer to him as Commander Prescott, but it was time to exhibit more power, time to remind others of his rank and his ability to command them.

Was he beginning to like the sound of *Lord Benton*? No, but people snapped to attention when he used it.

"I'll see you in the morning," he told Arthur.

"By nine o'clock or so, I'll be in the upstairs bedchambers with the other men."

"I'll track you down. In the interim, if you encounter any difficulties, please locate me. I'll get things squared away immediately."

Arthur nodded. He was young, only twenty, and a wounded soldier who'd had to resign from the army because of it. He'd witnessed several of Peyton's quarrels with Barbara and was aware of the tribulations Peyton was facing. Arthur wouldn't be prevented from completing his assignment.

He stood and left, and a terrible quiet settled in.

Peyton decided he'd benefit from a lengthy walk. He rose and hurried out too, hoping to escape the manor for a few hours, but as he marched down the hall toward the foyer, Barbara stepped out of the receiving parlor. He couldn't bear to chat, but he couldn't avoid her.

"There you are." She smiled slyly. "Could I talk to you for a minute?"

He tamped down a sigh. "Can it wait? I've been in the house all day, and I need some fresh air."

"I'm sorry, but no, it can't wait. I'm afraid you'll depart when I'm not looking, and I'll miss my chance."

"All right."

"I'll be brief."

She dashed into the parlor, and he followed her. She'd staged the room with an eye to his comfort. A fire burned in the grate, and two chairs were positioned in front of it. There was a table between the chairs with a brandy decanter and a glass on a tray.

She went to the chairs, and she gestured for him to join her. He sat as she poured him a brandy. Then she sat too.

"I won't dither," she said.

"Praise be."

She chuckled. "I have a proposal I wish to tender. It might shock you, but I'm tendering it anyway."

"I'm quite *un*shockable, Barbara. I doubt there's a topic you could raise that would astonish me."

Without preamble, she proclaimed, "You and I should marry."

He was so taken aback he was glad he was sitting down. If he hadn't been, his knees might have buckled.

"You and I? Marry?"

"Yes. It would solve so many problems."

"Well . . . ah . . . ah . . ."

He was sputtering, choking on his liquor. He couldn't formulate a coherent sentence, and she jumped into the awkward breach.

"It's obvious you don't care about Benton, and you're eager to return to the navy."

"I am."

"If you sail away, who would run the place? Who would ensure we kept things on an even keel?"

"It's been vexing me. I admit it."

"Would you bring in strangers who have no connection to Benton?"

"I wouldn't be too enthused about that."

"If you picked *me,* you wouldn't have to worry about the estate. You could resume your career, and while you were away, I could be your manager."

He thought that comment was categorically false—he'd worry constantly—but he didn't mention it. Instead, he mumbled, "That might work."

"We've had some fiscal issues, but they're your brother's fault. I swear! Without him squandering every penny, I'm convinced I can get us back to normal. Won't you let me try? Please?"

She paused, her gaze beseeching, and he noticed he was gaping. He'd insisted she couldn't shock him, but evidently, she could.

"Barbara, we don't even like each other."

"What does that have to do with it?" she absurdly replied.

"You've already had one horrid marriage, and you're young. You can wed again. Wouldn't you like to shoot for a better man the second time around?"

"You're not your brother."

"Thank God," he muttered.

"We could keep it all in the family. I understand you'd like to kick us out, but you wouldn't have to."

"It's not that I'd *like* to kick you out. It's just so complicated to have you remain."

"If I was your wife, the complications would vanish. We'd be a team. We'd be pursuing the same goals."

"We would?"

"Yes! We both want what's best for Benton, don't we? You could leave England, and you wouldn't have to wonder if strangers were performing their jobs correctly. *I* would be in charge, and the property would be here—in pristine condition—whenever you're able to visit."

"Wouldn't it seem ... ah ... disturbing to have me as your husband? The notion sounds positively incestuous to me."

"I could put aside any reservations. Could you?"

"I don't think so," he said. "Why would you attach yourself to another Prescott male? Aren't you afraid you'd be making a huge mistake?"

"Trust me. After my experience with Neville, no husband could surprise me in the least."

"Is that a compliment or an insult?"

"We'd get on fine, Peyton. I'm certain of it."

It was such a peculiar remark. Her dislike of him had always been blatantly clear. Why would that alter merely because they were married? And what about her brother, Richard? Would he stay and be a permanent thorn in Peyton's side?

He suffered a fleeting vision of Barbara and Richard in one corner of the room and Peyton in the other. With them, it would always be two against one, and the prospect was exhausting. How could she not see that?

She was practically rippling with excitement, and she was very brave to have broached the subject with him. In most families, her ploy would have been viewed as the perfect solution, but Peyton didn't feel himself to be a Prescott and never had.

It had been his parents' choice to send him away and cut ties, and it had skewed his perception of ordinary topics that others took for granted. He would never do what *most* families would do.

Barbara was the type of female who demanded power, who fought for what she craved. She was the type who could completely emasculate a man without his even realizing she was holding a very sharp knife.

He downed his brandy, poured himself another glass, and downed that too. He hated to upset her, but honestly! There wasn't any other option.

"I'm sorry, Barbara," he said, "but I could never wed you."

"Don't decide yet," she implored. "Promise me you'll consider it."

"I don't have to *consider*. I'm flattered by your suggestion, but I couldn't have you as my wife." He leaned over and patted her hand. "It's not in the cards."

She frowned. "Is there someone else? Are you about to become engaged? Don't tell me you are. You can't bring an interloper into my home."

"I have no engagement in the works—and won't have for many years."

Her shoulders slumped with defeat. "Why won't you ponder this? If you'd explain the root of your concerns, perhaps I can chase them away. You have to give me a chance to persuade you."

"You could never persuade me," he insisted, but gently.

"Is that your final answer? May I raise the issue in the future?"

"I won't ever change my mind."

He stood, and she glared up at him. Suddenly, she appeared much older than thirty, and he was disheartened by her fretting. Before he could talk himself out of it, he said, "We'll leave matters as they are for now. You don't have to move over to the Dower House."

"Thank you."

"I'll deliberate over the resolution I should implement, and I'll discuss any plans with you prior to my executing them."

"As you're contemplating, will you include my idea about marriage?"

"No, I won't. I can't."

He walked out, and though she called to him, he continued on. He left the manor and went out into the park, and he crossed to the woods so he could be swallowed up by the trees. He kept glancing over his shoulder, terrified she'd follow him outside.

She was like a dog at a bone. When she bit her teeth into a situation, she didn't release it until she got her way.

He wondered if he should create a trust account for her and hire a lawyer to manage it. The lawyer could deal with her, so Peyton wouldn't have to, but that seemed unworkable and wrong.

There was a reason his brother had bequeathed everything to Peyton. Obviously, Neville had felt Barbara required male guidance in her affairs. And what about her daughters, Nancy and Alice? Peyton was in charge of them too, but he'd barely ever spoken to either of them. Could he dump them on a lawyer?

He hadn't known Neville at all, but Neville had intended for Peyton to look after his daughters. He hadn't wanted Barbara to be in control of them. Was it simply Neville being spiteful? Or had Barbara's influence needed to be tamped down?

He was wandering down a trail, and he arrived at a pretty glen he enjoyed. There was a fallen log in the middle, and occasionally, when he sat quietly on it, a deer would meander by without noting his presence.

His mind awhirl, he plopped down, and after awhile, an acorn dropped on his head. He peeked up, expecting to find a squirrel, but instead, Barbara's younger daughter, Alice, was perched on a branch in the tree above him.

She scowled down at him, clearly irked that she'd given herself away.

"Hello, you," he said.

"Hello, Commander Prescott."

"You can call me Uncle Peyton if you like."

"I'll think about it," she churlishly grumbled.

"Why are you up there all by yourself?"

"I'm hiding. Why would you suppose?"

"I get that, but why?"

"I . . . just . . . figured I should hide."

"I understand perfectly." He indicated the spot next to him on the log. "Would you like to join me? I often come here. A deer might stroll by."

"I know that. I see them too."

She dithered forever, not happy he'd intruded, but in the end, she scooted down. She was only ten feet off the ground, but still, his pulse raced when she jumped the last few feet.

Her hands were scraped, her knees too. Her skirt was filthy, her cheeks smudged with dirt. How long had she been out in the woods by herself? Had anyone missed her? How about her mother? Didn't she have a governess? Shouldn't someone be watching over her?

He was such a pathetic guardian that he had no answers.

She was tough and brave, and she didn't appear to be afraid of him or anything else. With Neville's blond hair and blue eyes, she was very fetching, and she resembled Daisy exactly.

"How old are you these days?" he asked when she finally seated herself.

"Nine, but almost ten."

Daisy was nine too which was a potent sign that his brother had been a philandering dog.

"Ten is a good age," he told her. "When I was a boy, I liked being ten."

She shrugged. "I imagine it will be all right."

"I attended a military academy, and we used to go sailing all the time."

"You were permitted to sail as part of your lessons?"

"Yes."

"Boys are so lucky," she furiously muttered.

"I've always thought so," he agreed. "Should you be out in the woods by yourself like this?"

"Don't worry about it. If I'm missing, no one will notice or care."

"Where is your governess?"

"Uncle Richard fired her."

"Why?"

"He said she was lazy."

"Was she?" Peyton asked.

"Probably, but I liked her anyway. The people I like all leave sooner or later."

"That's a sad statement on your condition."

"Well, it's true," she sullenly replied. "Uncle Richard claims he'll hire a new one in the fall—when we have to start school. Do you believe he will?"

"I don't see why he wouldn't. You shouldn't grow up without an education. We don't want any dunces in the family."

"It doesn't matter if I'm a dunce. I hate studying. I wish I could be a sailor like you."

"It's a grand life. I admit it. I wish you could be a sailor too."

She frowned. "You won't tell Mother I was out here, will you? She gets so angry with me. She'd put her foot down, and then, I wouldn't be able to come back."

"No, I won't tell her. Mothers don't have to know everything."

"No, they don't!" she heartily concurred.

She was aggrieved and livid, as if she'd been unfairly accused or unjustly chastened.

"Why are you hiding?" he asked. She was mulishly silent, and he nudged her with his elbow. "You can confide in me. You seem upset. What happened?"

"Nancy thinks she's so smart, and I'm tired of it."

Nancy was her sister, older by two years. "Why are you tired of it? I won't stop pestering you until you spit it out."

She dithered again, struggling to determine what to share. "There were some children at Benton besides Nancy and me. They stayed in a cottage out past the lake."

"Yes, I'm aware of that."

Suddenly, he was very wary. She was referring to her half-siblings, her father's *other* children, Bobby, Jane, and Daisy. Was she aware of their actual relationship? Had they been friends? If so, had Barbara discovered a connection was formed? She definitely wouldn't have liked it!

"There were three of them," Alice added. "They left Benton a few weeks ago."

"Yes, they did."

"Nancy said Uncle Richard sold them to an orphanage. I told her she's a big, fat liar, but she swears Uncle Richard was talking to Mother about it."

"No, they're not in an orphanage. Daisy is with her Aunt Jo in London."

"You're sure?"

"Yes, and Bobby and Jane have gone to Jane's uncle in Cornwall. Their governess, Miss Watson, traveled with them to guarantee they arrived safely. They're fine too."

Peyton wasn't positive the information was accurate. Last he'd heard, Jo had corresponded with Miss Watson's cousin, but there had been no message from Miss Watson. Alice's questions reminded them that he had to check on Bobby and Jane. The second he was in London, he'd have a man ride to Cornwall.

"Are you certain Miss Watson is with them?" Alice asked. "Nancy said Uncle Richard fired her too. They quarreled, and he kicked her out on the road with just the clothes on her back."

"She wasn't fired. She quit so she could accompany Bobby and Jane. She didn't want them to make the journey on their own. Nancy is teasing you."

"She can be so spiteful sometimes."

"This might be one of those times."

Alice blew out a heavy breath. "I've been very worried."

"Were you friends with them?"

"Yes. We played together constantly. I miss them."

"Of course you would."

He was awash with unease. He should have expected all of them might meet. Benton was a small area and a scandal was difficult to conceal. He was dying to learn if she realized her link to them, but he wasn't about to dive into the issue.

If she hadn't been apprised, he wasn't about to explain about unfaithful husbands, broken marriage vows, and bastards.

"Can I tell you a secret?" Alice asked.

"Absolutely."

"I wasn't supposed to ever hear about it, but Bobby told me."

Peyton's spirits flagged. "Told you what?"

She leaned nearer and whispered, "They're my siblings. My father didn't like us, and he had a different family from ours—one that he liked better. He had other children."

Peyton sighed. "It wasn't that he didn't *like* you, Alice."

"My mother knows about it, and she's very angry."

"Yes, she is."

"Could they live here again someday? They were very scared about what occurred, and this was their home."

"Yes, it was."

"Why are adults so mean?"

Out of the mouth of babes . . .

"I have no idea, Alice. I've wondered about it myself."

"You won't make *us* leave Benton, will you, Uncle Peyton? Mother said you hate us and you'll eventually kick us out too."

"I don't hate you," he scoffed. "She shouldn't say things like that."

"If you force us to depart, where will we go?"

He stared out at the trees, feeling a heavy weight press down.

Each and every minute, his burdens seemed to crush him more completely. While he dickered over his decisions, he conveniently forgot that there were real people involved in any resolutions he chose.

If he evicted Alice's mother, where would they go? It was an urgent query that had no good answer. Alice and Nancy were the daughters of the Earl of Benton. Would Peyton send them to London to reside in a seedy apartment with Barbara's brother, Roger? Could he treat them so shabbily?

He didn't think so.

"You won't ever have to leave Benton," he said before he could come to his senses and shut up.

"Promise?"

"I promise. The only time it might happen is when you grow up and marry. Then you'd live with your husband at his estate, but until then, you'll remain right here."

She solemnly nodded. "Thank you. I've been fretting over it."

He stood. "Now then, let's return you to the manor so your mother doesn't have a fit. I've had all the excitement I can tolerate for one day. I don't want to throw her into a rage."

"Believe me, I don't want that either."

She stood too and slipped her tiny hand into his. They walked off together, and he couldn't help recollecting how he often walked the same way with Daisy.

He was an uncle. He had nieces. And . . . ? Apparently, he liked it.

CHAPTER

19

EVAN WAS STUFFING THE last of his clothes into a portmanteau when footsteps echoed out in the hall.

Officially, he was in Peyton's cabin, but they shared the sleeping space. They weren't supposed to, but he and Peyton had been close, so no one ever complained.

He glanced up, enraged to discover that Peyton had arrived too, just at the moment Evan had stopped by to retrieve his belongings. What were the odds? Why would he suddenly strut in? Wasn't he busy with his grand life? Why would he bother with his paltry ship?

Since the horrid afternoon when he'd finally spurned Amelia, Evan hadn't seen him again. Evan had mustered his mother and sister to shut up their house, then they'd traveled to Bath for an extended summer holiday.

But Evan's time wasn't his own. He wasn't a great lord like Peyton and couldn't dawdle in England forever. He had to get back to work. He'd requested a transfer away from Peyton, and it had been granted. He was preparing to join the crew on a different vessel.

"If it isn't Commander Prescott," Evan snidely said. "What are you doing here?"

"I miss my ship. What are *you* doing here?"

"I'm packing."

Peyton frowned. "I heard you put in for a transfer. How could you?"

"Believe me, it was an easy decision."

"We've always sailed together. Always. It's wrong for us to separate."

"Yes, well, all good things must come to an end."

He peered around to be positive he hadn't forgotten anything. Then he buckled the straps on his portmanteau. Peyton lurked in the doorway. Evan tried to ignore him, but it was impossible. Peyton was like an elephant, large, looming. He took up too much space in any room he occupied, and ship cabins were notoriously small.

He marched over to Evan and attempted to yank the bag away, but Evan held firm.

"Let go," Evan demanded as they engaged in a pathetic tug of war.

"No. You're acting like a lunatic. How long will this fit of pique continue?"

"I'm betting forever."

"You're being ridiculous." Peyton tsked with offense. "Can we discuss this?"

"No. We've said what we need to say."

"So . . . just like that? Twenty years of friendship are over?"

Peyton looked bewildered, but where personal relationships were concerned, he was usually clueless. Evan was the one who understood people and social situations. Evan had pulled Peyton through the world, tamping down his awkwardness, smoothing over his gaffes.

Evan was incensed on his sister's behalf and probably always would be, but Peyton could never comprehend that type of loyalty. He could never comprehend why Evan loved his sister so much.

He turned to depart, but Peyton blocked him in.

"Move!" Evan fumed.

"No. You can't leave. Not until we resolve this."

"It's resolved, Peyton. I've clearly explained my position, and I wish you'd accept it. I won't listen to you rationalizing your conduct."

"You closed your house and left London." Peyton's tone was accusing—as if Evan should have checked with him first.

"We *left* because we were certain you'd eventually skulk in and pretend all was fine, but it can't be fine ever again. How can I get you to recognize that fact?"

"I still haven't been able to talk to Amelia. She should tell me herself that she's cutting all ties."

Evan rolled his eyes. "Stop being an ass."

"I'm not being an ass. I'm trying to mend this."

"You can't. I warned you that there would be consequences if you tossed her over, but you refused to heed me."

"I can't figure out what's generating all this hostility."

"Of course you can't."

"I especially can't figure out why you'd change ships. We're partners. You can't want that to be over. And what about Amelia. She must hate all this upset."

Evan swallowed down a wave of fury, not sure why he was wasting his breath.

"How is Miss Bates?" he inquired.

"Miss Bates? Jo?" Peyton looked bewildered again. "Why would you ask about her?"

"It's all over town, you know."

"What is?"

"How your servants caught you crawling in and out of her bed, how Barbara made you kick her out to hide the scandal. Apparently, you couldn't bear to part from her, and you've rented her a little love nest."

Evan might have punched Peyton. He appeared that stunned. He staggered over to a chair and eased down.

"People are gossiping about me and Jo?"

"Yes. What did you think would happen? You're an earl now, an aristocrat. You're not invisible. How could you suppose people *wouldn't* gossip?"

"I merely rented lodging for her."

"Yes, Peyton, we're all aware of how generous you've been—seemingly for no reason at all."

"She's having personal difficulties. I'm simply being kind."

"You're a bachelor, Peyton. Will it ever dawn on you that your behavior is entirely inappropriate?"

"It is not," Peyton claimed, but his cheeks flushed bright red, and he glanced away.

"Amelia visited her," Evan said.

"Who? Jo?"

"Yes."

"When? I've been in the country. I haven't heard any news."

"Miss Bates was quite convincing as to the innocent nature of your association. Amelia was completely persuaded that there is no immorality occurring."

"There isn't," Peyton insisted.

"Nice try, Peyton, but I'm not as gullible as my sister. What if Miss Bates winds up with child? What then?"

"She won't," Peyton firmly stated, a tacit admission that dissipation was in progress.

Evan felt terrible for Miss Bates and was greatly worried about her, but it wasn't any of his business. That last afternoon, he'd begged her to be careful, yet she'd jumped from the frying pan into the fire.

At Barbara's urging, Peyton had shuttered the town house and sequestered Miss Bates in a spot where he presumed they could carry on unobserved. But in his social circle, London was a very small place. There could be no concealing an illicit affair.

"Goodbye," he said. "Don't pester me. Don't pester my sister. Just leave us alone."

"I won't say goodbye to you. I can't."

"Good luck with Miss Bates. I hope your amour brings you everything you deserve."

Peyton was still seated and not blocking the door. Evan lifted his portmanteau and stomped out.

Peyton entered Jo's residence and removed his hat and cape.

When he arrived during the day, he knocked and pretended he was a visitor. He'd knocked this time too, but it wasn't answered, so he'd used his key. Usually, Jo and Daisy were in the parlor, sewing or reading, but the room was empty.

Footsteps sounded on the stairs, and he peered up, expecting it would be Jo, but it was a servant, an older widow who did the cooking. She halted and gaped with astonishment.

"Lord Benton, my, my, but don't you look grand?"

"Thank you."

"Or—in light of your clothes—should I address you as Commander Prescott?"

He smiled. "I will reply to either."

"I love a man in uniform."

"I've been told it's the best way to bedazzle a female."

"You're correct. It is."

He was wearing the garments a naval officer was meant to wear: blue frock coat, white trousers, black boots. The items had been packed in a trunk for months, and he'd finally retrieved them.

"I'm sorry no one greeted you," she said as she descended to the foyer.

"I didn't want to bother all of you, so I let myself in. Is my niece at home?"

He always maintained the ruse that he'd come to see Daisy, but according to Evan, his ploy hadn't worked, and he'd been publically exposed as a cad.

"Miss Daisy was feeling housebound. I sent our footman to pick up some meat from the butcher, and she tagged along."

"How about Miss Bates? Is she here?"

"She's in bed . . . ah . . . resting."

He was unnerved by how the woman pronounced the word *resting*. Jo had more energy than anyone he'd ever met. She was never idle.

"Is she under the weather?"

"She was a tad nauseous, so I delivered some tea to settle her stomach."

"I need to confer with her at once. Is she sufficiently hale to attend me in the parlor?"

The woman stared at him for an eternity, studying his uniform, the shiny gold buttons, the epaulettes and medals pinned to the front. Her assessment was so meticulous that he could barely keep from fidgeting.

"May I speak freely, my lord?" she eventually said.

"Yes, always."

"It's just that I wouldn't like to anger you."

"I'm not a man who angers easily."

"I'm glad—for this might be disconcerting."

She leaned in and whispered her secret, and his initial instinct was to call her a liar, but he bit down any strident response. She was watching him carefully, and he was positive she'd thoroughly describe his reaction in the kitchen later on.

"Are you certain?" he inquired.

"Certain enough. I've birthed six children of my own."

His mind was awhirl with how the information had thrown a wrench into his plans. Or had it? Would he let it alter his course? Should he let it? Could he allow Fate and circumstance to ambush him? He didn't think so.

"I appreciate you confiding in me," he calmly said. "Now then, if you'll excuse me, I have to chat with Miss Bates. My own news is dire, and I can't wait until her condition improves."

Clearly, she'd like to retort with, *It's your house. Do what you bloody well want!*

Yet she was very composed. "She'd like that." He started up the stairs, and she asked, "If my worries turn out to be correct, Lord Benton, will it change things?"

"It's too soon to tell, ma'am. I'll keep you apprised."

"I've liked my job."

"Miss Bates has enjoyed having you. She constantly sings your praises."

He continued on to Jo's room. She was on her bed, a damp towel over her eyes.

"Daisy, is that you? How was your shopping?" She pulled the cloth away and peeked over. "Oh! It's you. What a fabulous surprise, and you're in your uniform! You're magnificent. If you claim you're off to be presented to the King, I will absolutely believe you."

She rose up on an elbow, and he said, "Don't get up."

He walked over and balanced a hip on the mattress. He clasped her slender hand in his, and a thousand unvoiced comments swirled between them. There was only one reason for him to have donned his uniform, and she recognized what it indicated.

Was she aware of her cook's suspicions? If they were true, where did it leave her? Where did it leave him?

She was the first to speak. She scrutinized his uniform, taking in the fine sewing, the fancy adornments. "You're going back to the navy?"

"Yes."

"When will you sail?"

"Thursday night."

She inhaled a sharp breath. "Three days."

"Yes. There was a posting to the Caribbean—if I could depart immediately."

"I've been convinced that you'll be happier this way, so I won't ask if you're sure."

"I am sure, but I'm not sure too. I'm very confused."

She flashed a sad smile. "It's been your state ever since I met you."

"I already feel better."

"Good." She scowled. "It seems very sudden."

"It is."

"Have I upset you somehow? Is that why? Are you angry with me?"

"No. I could never be angry with you."

"Then what happened?"

"I checked out my ship yesterday, and I talked with my crew."

"You've missed them."

"Yes."

"They spurred you to a decision."

"Not really. Evan was there."

"Well. That's . . . interesting."

"If I have to cite a motive for what prodded me, I suppose that's it."

"You quarreled?"

"No. We had . . . *words.*"

"Is he still livid?"

"Yes. He said Amelia visited you. You didn't tell me."

"I haven't seen you since she stopped by."

He hadn't sneaked in for several nights, having been determined to exercise some restraint, and it seemed silly now to have erected obstacles. With so little time remaining, why deny himself such a guilty pleasure?

"Was Amelia awful to you?" he asked. "I apologize if she was."

"No, no, she was very sweet."

"What did she want?"

"She's heard terrible rumors about us."

"Yes, Evan too. Apparently, they're spreading like wildfire."

"She was curious if they were true, and I lied and insisted they weren't."

"Why, Miss Bate," he sarcastically mocked, "*you* told a lie? I'm shocked."

"I am too. I've become a sluggard and a deceiver. When I die, I'm probably going straight to Hell."

"It's all right. I'll be there too, so you'll have a friend waiting when you arrive."

Their banter dwindled, and those unvoiced comments swirled again. He couldn't delve to the core of the matter, and he definitely needed to. He wouldn't have many more chances.

She rested a palm on the center of his chest and asked, "What is it, Peyton? What's wrong?"

"After I bumped into Evan, I was so distraught. I'm devastated to learn that people are gossiping about us. I thought we were being so discreet."

"These things have a way of leaking out. It's not easy to hide an illicit amour. It's why a sane person never engages in one."

"I can't abide that I've gotten you into trouble. I won't have your reputation destroyed because of me."

"You should worry more about your own. No one knows me from Adam, but you are quite a prominent fellow. You can't seduce an innocent maiden without paying a very steep price."

She'd offered the remark in a light and teasing manner, but it fell flat because that's precisely what he'd done. He'd seduced an innocent maiden. He'd understood it was sinful and wicked, but he'd done it anyway.

In his own defense, he'd never wanted anything as desperately as he'd wanted Josephine Bates. Even now, even after she was ruined and he was disgraced, he wasn't sorry. He'd do it all over again in a trice.

"Your cook informs me you've been sick," he said.

"I must have a touch of the flu. For the past week or two, I've been dizzy and nauseous. She had me lie down, and she brought me some tea. I'm much better."

So . . . she doesn't realize . . .

He studied her, thinking she was glowing, but then, she always glowed. He'd like to claim to be skeptical, but he wasn't. From the first night he'd deflowered her, he'd been too overwhelmed to be cautious. He'd dallied as if salacious conduct carried no consequences, as if he were a god who could control the future.

Wasn't it typical that this calamitous situation would crop up just when he couldn't bear to deal with it?

"You don't have the flu, Jo."

She scowled. "What is it then?"

"Your cook is afraid you might be increasing."

"Increasing . . . with what?" The naïveté of her query was blatant evidence of how despicably he'd treated her. Comprehension dawned swiftly. "Increasing . . . with a baby? Is that what you're telling me?"

"Yes. Your cook has had many children herself, so she recognizes all the symptoms."

She froze for an eternity, then she murmured, "No, no, no . . ."

She drew away from him and slid off the bed. She walked over to stand by the window, and she gaped at him as if she had no idea who he was or how he'd wandered into her bedroom.

"You said it took a long time for a babe to catch." Her tone was aghast and accusatory. "You said a woman had to participate in the marital act over and over. You said it could take years."

He shrugged. "I guess I was wrong."

She stared in horror toward the stairs. "The servants know?"

"Yes, so here's how we'll proceed."

He went over to her, but she held out a hand to ward him off. "I can't listen to this now. I need a few minutes to myself. Could you . . . ah . . . come back later?"

"No. We don't have a lot of days to arrange everything."

"Even with this dreadful news revealed, you're still planning to depart?"

"Yes. I have to. I've given my word."

She scoffed with derision. "I'm in trouble and facing the greatest threat I'll ever face, and you'll sail off into the sunset? You'll abandon me to manage on my own?"

He wouldn't squabble over his decision to return to the navy. His conversation with Evan had forced him to acknowledge the extent of his folly with Jo. He couldn't continue to shame her and shame himself.

He'd visited his superiors, had signed all the papers, had promised to assume his command on Thursday. An officer had fallen gravely ill, and they'd asked Peyton to step up and replace him. Jo's predicament couldn't alter that fact. He was a man who did his duty.

"I've given my word," he repeated.

"Break it."

"I can't. I won't."

It probably wouldn't be that hard to renege on his vow to the navy. With his title of earl, he would be granted leeway another sailor might not receive, but he didn't want to renege.

He'd been unhappy for months, twiddling his thumbs and questioning his options, and he'd finally seen the road he had to travel. He had to resume his old life, the one he loved and had missed so intensely.

He wasn't a farmer who could loaf in the country and watch his crops grow. He wasn't a dandy who could gad about town with nothing to do. He wasn't a Romeo who would shuck off his responsibilities merely to wallow in a pretty woman's bed.

As he'd ridden to Jo's house, he'd rehearsed the speech he'd use to explain himself. He'd been certain and prepared. He was *still* certain and prepared, but he had to ensure she was safe while he was away, and he didn't have much time to sort it out.

He wouldn't argue with her, wouldn't allow her to dither and decline to heed him. She couldn't be stubborn or unbendable.

"I'm going to propose again, Jo," he told her, "and I won't let you refuse."

"Oh, I'm so perplexed. This is all occurring too fast. It's bad enough that you're leaving. I can't cope with an added catastrophe dumped on top of that."

"You knew I would eventually depart, Jo. You thought I should."

"I never expected you to head out at once, without any warning."

"I don't have control over where or when I'm posted. I can't ignore a direct order."

He conveniently neglected to mention that he'd volunteered, that he'd practically begged for the mission. After his recent visit to Benton, he was anxious to escape and pretend he was the man he'd previously been: a man with no familial obligations to weigh him down.

"I understand you're in the navy," she said, "and you have to obey orders, but what if you never come back?"

"I'll come back. Don't worry."

"I will worry. I'll worry every day."

"I have nine lives, and I'm lucky. You needn't fret."

"I can't help it. What if your luck has run out? Where would I be then?"

They glared, on the verge of a quarrel, but he wouldn't fight with her.

"I won't debate this with you," he said.

"Well, you'll have to debate it. I don't want to marry you. Not like this. Not in such a huge rush that there's not a second to so much as stitch a string of lace on a gown."

"When I return, we'll have another wedding. We'll find a church and invite a hundred guests. We'll throw a big party and celebrate for a month, but not now. *Now* we have to accomplish it quickly so I can make arrangements for you."

"What are you imagining? Will Daisy and I remain in this rented lodging? You won't move us to Benton, will you?"

"No. It's probably best if you stay here."

"I suppose." Then she groaned with frustration. "I take that back. I have no idea if it's best. You're behaving like a lunatic, and you're pressuring me unmercifully when I can't bear to be pressured."

"How am I pressuring you?"

"We're not even sure I'm increasing!" she protested. "My tummy has been upset, and my cook—who I've only known for a matter of weeks—has announced that I'm about to have a child. You believed her, so you're ready to march to the altar."

"Jo, I can't loiter in England until we're positive. Nor can I ship out and act as if this isn't happening. There's no option but a swift wedding."

"But Peyton, think! I'll be your countess. I'll become *Lady* Benton. You don't want that. You've never wanted that. *I* don't want that."

"We'll figure it out later, Jo. I can't deal with it now. I have so many other chores to complete."

"I'm one more pesky detail?"

He scowled. "Don't make it sound as if I'm disrespecting you. I have to meet with my bankers and lawyers, and I have to ride to Benton to tell Barbara what's transpiring. *And* I have to marry you. By Thursday!"

"When would we hold the ceremony?"

"I thought Thursday morning. I sail Thursday night when the tide turns."

"You're deranged." She pushed him away. "Why can't we wait? Why can't we slow down? Once you're in England again, if you're still inclined to ask me, we could do it then."

His gaze dipped to her stomach. "We can't wait. It's impossible."

He was losing patience with her. He had a dozen important tasks dragging him away, and he couldn't continue to bicker. She was a female, so she would view issues in an emotional way. He was a male, and he had to keep them from any sentimental sparring.

He dropped to a knee and clasped her hand.

"Marry me, Jo. Just say yes. Let's don't argue about it."

"This is all wrong, Peyton. I don't want you to *have* to wed me. I want it to be because you're madly in love. I want it to be because you can't live without me."

It was on the tip of his tongue to respond with, *Of course I love you!*

But he'd never spoken the words to anyone, and he had no desire to wallow in a maudlin morass. Any strident declarations would seem frivolous and false.

"Jo, you may not want me to *have* to wed, but that horse has left the barn. We don't have a choice, and I don't mean to rush you, but I have to get going.

I can't leave until we've resolved this."

She stared down at him, her eyes beseeching. Finally, she murmured, "I accepted a proposal once in my life—from a man who didn't really care about me. I vowed I'd never put myself in such an untenable situation again."

"I'm not Holden Cartwright, Jo. Don't claim he and I have any traits in common."

"If circumstances have forced you into this, how can I be sure you'll follow through?"

"Give me some credit. You know me, don't you?"

"Sometimes, I assume I do, but usually, I don't have a clue of what sort of person you truly are."

"You know this: I would never do anything I didn't wish to do. If I wasn't eager to have you as my wife, I wouldn't have asked you."

"Swear one thing to me."

"If I can."

"Swear you will never regret this."

"I won't dignify that comment with a reply. Now stop complaining and answer me."

"I need *your* answer first. Swear you'll never suffer a minute of regret."

"Oh, Jo, I never will. I will always be glad."

She took a deep breath, and she looked miserable and dejected. Ultimately, she said, "Yes, Peyton, I will marry you."

She pulled him to his feet, and he bent down and stole a quick kiss.

"You'll never be sorry," he told her.

"I already am," she churlishly retorted.

He could only chuckle. "For a girl who's about to be a bride, and who will have a brave, dashing member of the Royal Navy as her husband, you're not very happy."

"I'll become happy. I promise. At the moment, I'm too overwhelmed."

"I'm an overwhelming fellow, so I completely understand." He kissed her again, then started for the door. "I'll try to join you for supper, but if I don't, please don't worry."

"All right. Will you make the wedding plans? Or should I?"

"I'll obtain the Special License, but if you could find a vicar and a chapel, that would help me immensely."

"There's a place where we can schedule a hasty service."

"I'll keep you posted on my whereabouts, but if I don't see you until Thursday, don't fret."

"I won't."

"If you have to contact me, send a message to my club. I'll be running around the city, but someone will track me down."

"I hope this ends as you're expecting."

"Why wouldn't it? Don't be such a pessimist."

"I'll attempt to be more optimistic, but I have to ask you a question. You've been so generous, so I'm embarrassed to raise it, but what about Daisy and me? Will you pay our rent and provide us with some money for expenses? If you don't, I can't imagine how we'll carry on."

"Yes. A lawyer will be in charge of your affairs. You won't have to concern yourself."

"I'll tell myself to trust you."

"Why wouldn't you trust me? Have I ever steered you wrong?"

"Not yet."

"You'll be fine, Jo. I guarantee it."

He froze, taking in the sight of her, filling his vision with her sweet beauty and poise. She was wearing the lavender dress he liked so much, the one that made her eyes appear more violet than blue.

Her distress washed over him, vividly reminding him that, from this point on, her safety and contentment were his responsibility. She was young and vulnerable, and she was about to be his forever. Fate had pushed that conclusion onto his shoulders, and he felt quite grand about it.

He had a thousand tasks to accomplish, the biggest hurdle being a trip to Benton. Initially, he'd thought to simply sail away without informing Barbara, but that was the coward's route. As she'd caustically mentioned, he was part of a family now, and she deserved to hear about his decision.

So...he couldn't dawdle in Jo's bedroom. He'd been in the navy for fourteen years, so he was an expert on packing and shipping out with scant notice, but in the past, he'd never had to furnish funds to a lawyer. He'd never had to arrange a speedy wedding and organize a wife's security.

He had to do all of that, and he had to do it in the next two days. He'd like to stay and bask in her sunny presence for a few more hours, but he couldn't.

He spun and left before he realized he couldn't bear to go.

Jo listened as Peyton bounded down the stairs and hurried out the door. Then she staggered to a chair and slid down.

She was alarmed and terrified and brimming with joy. Wasn't she?

She was about to be Mrs. Peyton Prescott. That's how she'd picture herself anyway. When the wider world learned of their folly, they'd view her as Lady Benton, as Lord Benton's countess, but she couldn't worry about that.

She didn't have the ancestry or training to be a countess, and she'd never yearned to be an aristocrat's bride. She didn't want to live at Benton with its winding halls and chilly, ostentatious salons. She didn't want to manage dozens of servants and supervise one of the kingdom's most splendid manors.

She liked the small, cozy house Peyton had rented for her. It suited her, and it was more than enough. She wished they could be normal people, an ordinary couple, but with Peyton as her husband, that prospect wasn't possible.

She should have refused him. None of his kin or acquaintances would ever accept the union. Everyone would agree—for the rest of his life—that he'd married *down*. He'd be the butt of jokes and horrid gossip, but he'd been in such a rush that he hadn't considered the ramifications.

A baby! Could it be?

She rubbed a hand over her abdomen, wondering if there was a child growing inside her. The notion was scary and thrilling, and she shook her head with dismay. She couldn't believe he'd actually wed her. Surely he'd come to his senses.

If naught else, Barbara Prescott would yank him to reality. She would never welcome Jo into the family, would never welcome Daisy, and who could blame her?

Jo needed a friend she could talk to, but she was on her own, floating free, and about to marry Peyton Prescott, even though she was certain it was a huge mistake.

Noise erupted down in the foyer, and it sounded as if Daisy and their footman had returned from the excursion to the butcher.

"Aunt Jo?" she called. "Are you home?"

She was always afraid that Jo might vanish when she wasn't looking, and Jo figured she was suffering lingering effects from Richard Slater threatening to lock her in an orphanage.

"Yes, Daisy," she called back, "I'm upstairs."

Daisy skipped up to Jo's room. Jo was so stunned that she was still seated. She didn't bother to stand, and she must have seemed stricken because Daisy was smiling when she entered, but it immediately altered to a frown.

"What's happened?" she asked.

"Sit with me for a minute." Jo patted her thigh. "I have some news."

Daisy hesitated. "Is it good or bad?"

"It's a little of both."

"I'm not leaving, am I?" Daisy's perpetual fear was always close to the surface. "I'm not being sent away?"

"Don't be silly. We'll never be separated. Your Uncle Peyton promised, remember?"

"Yes, but adults don't always tell the truth."

"You're correct, but he meant this. We'll always be together." Jo reached out to her. "Now come and sit."

Daisy trudged over, and Jo drew her onto her lap.

"Your uncle stopped by a bit ago," Jo said.

"Drat it! I missed him. I hate that."

"He told me two significant things."

"Will they upset me?"

"One of them is a tad upsetting, and it's sad, but it's happy too."

Daisy's frown deepened. "How can it be sad and happy at the same time?"

"Your uncle has decided to return to the navy, and he has to ship out right away."

"How soon?"

"On Thursday."

Daisy's jaw dropped. "It's in three days!"

"Yes."

"That's not happy. That's very sad."

"I'm deeming it *happy* because it's what your uncle has craved most of all, and he's very excited. He was only in England because your father died. His furlough was temporary. You know that."

"Yes, but I didn't think he'd go. I thought he might stay with us."

"Men have important events in their lives that don't include women."

"Yes, I suppose."

"If he hadn't done this, he'd have been miserable forever."

"How long will he be away?"

"He didn't provide many details, but I expect it will be several months."

"I see . . ."

"Here's the good news"—Jo forced some cheer into her tone—"and when you hear it, you have to smile."

"I will."

"Your uncle is very fond of me."

"That's not a secret."

"And . . . he's asked me to marry him."

Daisy gasped. "Really?"

"Yes."

"You'll be his wife!"

"Yes," Jo said again.

"If he's departing on Thursday, when is the wedding?"

"On Thursday morning, then he'll sail Thursday night."

"A wedding! In three days?"

"Yes. Will you help me get ready?"

"Of course I will." Daisy wrapped her arms around Jo and hugged her as tightly as she could. "This is the best ending ever, Aunt Jo. I've been praying for it."

"You have?"

"Yes, I've been praying—ever since I first saw you with him. It's meant to be."

"You never mentioned it."

"I was afraid to jinx it, and now, everything will be perfect."

Jo didn't think so at all, but she didn't dare admit it. She just nodded. "Yes, it will be perfect from now on."

CHAPTER

20

"Hello, Peyton. I'm surprised to see you in the country so soon."

"Hello, Barbara."

"On your last visit, you couldn't wait to depart. Are you intending a longer sojourn this time?"

"No—a shorter one."

Her hostility practically oozed out.

She was vain and proud and would never forgive him for rejecting her marriage proposal. She'd never forget it either. For the remainder of his life, she'd devise methods to remind him he'd spurned her, *and* she'd make him regret it.

He sighed with irritation. He truly thought she'd been extremely brave about it and considered telling her how impressed he'd been, but he doubted she'd like to hear any compliments from him. In his view, it would be better for both of them to pretend their prior conversation had never transpired.

"You're wearing your uniform," she said, stating the obvious. "Does this indicate you've decided to become Commander Prescott again?"

"Yes. I'm shipping out tomorrow."

"That was fast."

"My services were needed immediately. There was no reason to delay."

They were in the front parlor at Benton, and Barbara was sitting on a sofa. Her brother, Richard, stood behind her, a hulking, angry sentinel.

It was incredibly brash of Richard to show his sorry face. He hadn't vacated the property as Peyton had demanded, and Peyton had to deal with him once and for all, but it wouldn't be today. It probably wouldn't even be in the next year.

Peyton was eager to be out on the sea, and he wouldn't be slowed down by Richard. Perhaps, if he was lucky, Fate would solve the dilemma for him. Richard might die or glom onto an heiress and move away. Although it wasn't likely, he might quarrel with his sister and part company with her.

If Peyton's experience in the navy had taught him anything, it was that a strange event could occur when a person least expected it. His fingers would be crossed.

"Is that why you're here?" Barbara asked. "To notify us of your plans?"

"Yes, and to inform you that I've arranged for my attorney, Mr. Thumberton, to handle my business affairs while I'm away."

Barbara bristled. "What exactly do you mean?"

"I mean he'll have charge of the bank accounts, and he'll determine which bills are paid and which aren't. He has the report from the inventory I conducted, so he has an idea of the income and debts. You'll have to travel to town to speak with him about how much money you'll require, and you'll get a stipend."

"I'm to beg a stranger to keep me clothed and fed?" she snidely inquired.

Peyton shrugged. "It's up to you. If you'd rather not confer with him, you don't have to, but then, you won't receive a penny."

"Am I to have no say at all?"

"There's no time for me to debate the issue with you. You'll be able to state your case to Thumberton as to your expenses, but *he* will choose what to allow. He has complete discretion, so don't harangue at him. It won't help."

"What about me?" Richard whined. "Am I to provide my labors for free? Or am I to be compensated for my work?"

"No, Richard, you won't collect any further salary. You've been terminated from your position. For insubordination—remember? Thumberton will be hiring a manager to replace you."

"You bastard!" Richard spat.

"Now, now, let's don't bring my mother into it." Peyton realized what he'd said, then he chuckled. "Actually, I suppose you can denigrate her if you wish. Hasn't it always been the rumor that I'm a bastard and not a Prescott? Is that what galls you two the most? I've inherited everything, and I'm not even a relative."

At his mentioning the ancient gossip, they stiffened with affront, and Barbara huffed, "I won't dignify that comment with a response."

Peyton ignored her and focused on her brother. "Richard, I won't point out that you're still on the premises when you shouldn't be. I'd love to engage in a hard fight with both of you, but I can't dawdle. But please take a bit of advice from me: You should leave Benton. My new agent is about to arrive. Could you stand it?"

Richard was very snotty. "I'll try to bear up."

"Fine. Have it your way. As I said, I won't bicker." He shifted his gaze to Barbara. "If you'd like, there are funds for Nancy and Alice to attend school in September. We haven't discussed it, but they're nine and eleven, so they're certainly old enough. It might be good for them to get out of Benton and be around some other girls."

Barbara bristled again. "My daughters are much too young."

"It was just a suggestion, but I'd like you to contemplate it for the future. Once I'm back in England, I may insist on it."

"You're not sending them away," Richard seethed. "I won't permit it. Not when she doesn't want it to happen."

"Well, Richard, there's the problem for you *and* for her. Alice and Nancy may be her daughters, but they're *my* wards. My brother put me in charge, and I will have the final say about them—in every instance until they come of age."

Richard glared with an enormous amount of malice, and if a glower could slay a man, Peyton would be dead on the floor.

Peyton pretended not to note his venom though. He thought Alice would be delighted if she went away to school. He kept recalling how miserable she'd been that day out in the woods. She'd enjoy the chance to have an adventure.

"What if Alice and Nancy need important items?" Barbara asked. "You'll be on the other side of the globe. What if they grow out of their dresses or need lesson books?"

"Talk to Mr. Thumberton."

"We have to hire a governess. May I proceed with interviews?"

"Yes, but Mr. Thumberton will tell you how much you can spend." He stood, his patience exhausted. "Is there any other topic you'd like me to address?"

Richard scoffed. "There are a thousand subjects you haven't covered, but that's your style, isn't it? You're the most flippant ass I've ever met. You float through the world, never caring about anything."

"I care about *some* things," Peyton replied. "Just not Benton. Just not *you,* Richard. I'm trying to care about your sister and my nieces, but you're making it difficult. Every time you open your mouth, I'm less inclined to be generous."

"Prick," Richard muttered.

Peyton merely rolled his eyes. "While I'm away, Richard, do me a favor. Don't burn the place down. When I return, I'll expect it to be in pristine condition."

He spun and walked out. The butler was at the door, and he noticed it was Mr. Newman from the town house. He wondered if Barbara had let any of the other servants work at the estate, but he doubted she had. She wouldn't have had the money for wages.

Newman handed over his hat and cape, but from his caustic expression, his dislike of Peyton was undeniable. They probably didn't need to chat.

He donned his garments and strolled out. His horse was still saddled, and a footman was tending him in the driveway. Peyton bounded down the steps to the animal, and he practically leapt onto it. He was that excited to be away, but he paused to stare up at the manor.

It was a beautiful building, in a cold, drafty, haunted kind of way. There was no one peering out of any of the windows to wave as he departed. For a moment, he envisioned evicting the current occupants someday, then moving in with Jo and Daisy.

Could it become a happy spot if they joined him? Perhaps. Anywhere Jo lived might become a happy spot.

He pulled the horse around and urged it into a gallop, and he raced off down the lane. His conversation with Barbara was over, so he was finished with all his tasks but the wedding. It would be held the following morning.

Jo had arranged it. She'd found a chapel where the preacher conducted quick services, one after the next. Theirs was scheduled for eleven, so afterward, he could tarry with them for a few hours. Then he'd have to head to his ship.

He'd barely checked the vessel, but his crew was reliable, and they'd been preparing for weeks, waiting for him to declare himself ready to sail.

Jo had told him to spend the evening at his club, feeling it would be bad luck for him to see her before the ceremony, so he'd agreed to meet them at the church. But he thought he'd stop by anyway and persuade her to misbehave.

Just from thinking of the possibility, he grinned from ear to ear.

He felt awful that he wasn't able to give her a grander celebration, but he'd make it up to her in the future. He'd promised her a big wedding, with guests and gifts and suppers, and he meant for her to have it.

He loped along, and his merry disposition kept being interrupted by misgivings. Was he mad to marry her? Was he acting like a lunatic?

With how rapidly he'd decided, it certainly seemed as if he should be locked in an asylum. He wished Evan wasn't angry. He'd have liked to ask his friend's advice, although Evan would have counseled him to pick an aristocrat's daughter. Or he'd have insisted Peyton locate an heiress who could bring a fortune to the table.

Yet Peyton didn't want a bride like that.

Besides, Jo was very likely increasing with Peyton's child. It might be a son who would inherit Benton after Peyton, so of course, he had to proceed. He couldn't risk any delay and put that birthright in jeopardy.

As he realized he was fretting over Benton and continuing the family line, he laughed aloud. If his dastardly father hadn't been rolling in his grave before, he definitely was now. Peyton couldn't help gloating and being delighted with himself.

He hadn't slowed down for a single second, and with his mood so joyous, he was distracted and not being cautious, so he didn't precisely know what startled his horse. He was cantering across a rickety bridge, and the wood slats were damp and slick from all the recent rain.

Suddenly, the horse shied and reared up, and it happened so fast that Peyton couldn't keep his seat. The horse lost its balance and slammed into the railing, and the boards snapped off and collapsed. The animal screamed, Peyton shouted, and they plunged off the bridge and down to the stream below.

The descent took forever, and the ground approached with a sort of peculiar fascination—as if he were in a dream. He tried to kick free of the saddle, but his foot was caught in the stirrup, and he couldn't.

His last coherent memory was that he landed very hard, and after that, he remembered nothing at all.

Jo WARNED HERSELF TO buck up and stride forward bravely. Then she climbed the chapel steps. She would be fine, and she had to cease her worrying, but she was incredibly anxious. It had all played out much too swiftly for her liking, and what was the old adage? Marry in haste, repent at leisure.

Peyton's situation with the navy had altered in an instant, and it was the type of incident that would occur frequently. His life wasn't his own, and his commitment to the navy would always come first.

Mentally, she understood that fact, but emotionally, it was difficult to accept her new reality. She'd like to have an ordinary husband who worked in London all day and returned home for supper in the evening, but her illicit conduct had guaranteed that she'd fallen off the common path.

And what female wouldn't love to have a naval officer for her husband? Her years with him would never be dull, that was for sure.

Still though, she had jitters that couldn't be quelled. Her initial attempt at matrimony had ended so horribly, and she was about to participate in another wedding that would be speedy and slapdash, with no guests and no kin to sit in the pews.

At the prior disastrous occasion, Maud was the only one who'd been present. This time, Jo had Daisy which was a lot, but the church would seem very empty.

She felt very sorry for Peyton. He had many friends in the navy who should have been invited, but she didn't know any of them, and he'd been too busy to write a guest list. He'd told her they could have a large ceremony later on, when he wasn't in such a rush, and she intended to hold him to that promise.

Not for herself, but for him. He deserved to have a grand event.

Daisy stared up at the dull gray bricks. "Is this it?"

"Yes."

"Have you been here before?"

"Yes, once."

"Was the bride pretty?"

"Very pretty."

"How about the groom? Was he handsome and dashing?"

"He was quite handsome, but I wouldn't describe him as dashing."

She was talking about her own debacle with Mr. Cartwright.

When Peyton had asked her to arrange the service, she'd agreed that she would, but she wasn't very familiar with London. The current chapel was the only spot she'd ever heard of where a minister performed hurried ceremonies. She'd had no idea where else to inquire on such short notice.

Quick weddings with Special Licenses were the preacher's forte.

A more superstitious bride would have avoided the spot like the plague, but after careful consideration, she'd decided to thumb her nose at Holden Cartwright and the terrible past he'd dumped on her. She would march into the same chapel—happy and optimistic—and she wouldn't be afraid. She wouldn't fear she was courting bad luck.

Daisy glanced down the street. "Where is Uncle Peyton?"

"He's probably inside already."

"Shall I check?"

"Let's both check."

"No. If he's in there, he shouldn't see you before we start."

"It's not that fancy of a place. I think I can risk him catching a glimpse of me."

"No, Aunt Jo. You stay here."

Daisy skittered through the door, but Jo didn't follow her. In many ways, Daisy was more excited than Jo. Jo was *trying* to be excited, but she was too panicked. She kept being swamped by a dreadful sense of . . . of . . . *tragedy* which was absurd. Peyton had dealt with the necessary details. What could go wrong?

She suspected she was suffering so many qualms because she would be left on her own to manage Daisy and the house and the birth of her baby. It was all too much to contemplate, and she often waxed nostalgic for the quiet period when she'd lived with Maud in the country.

Her sister had been overbearing and spiteful, but the days had drifted by with no drama or problems. Now Jo had a niece to raise, a military husband to fret over, and a baby to welcome. It was thrilling and exhausting.

Daisy peeked out, and she was grinning.

"Is your uncle there?" Jo asked.

"I haven't looked, but may I have your reticule?"

"My reticule? Why?"

"I'll show you."

Jo handed it over, and Daisy went in. When she returned, she was holding a lavender bouquet that matched Jo's gown.

"We forgot that you should have flowers," Daisy said.

"Aren't they lovely? Where did you get them?"

"There's a boy selling them in the vestibule. It's why I needed money. Let me find Uncle Peyton. Don't come in until I tell you."

"I won't."

Daisy flitted inside again, and Jo took several deep breaths, determined to hide her anxiety. Once Peyton laid eyes on her, she wanted to seem poised and happy rather than frantic and bedraggled.

Daisy was gone forever, and Jo's concern mounted.

Peyton had ridden to Benton the previous morning. He'd begged to stop by the house after he was back, but she'd forbidden any visit. But she'd been certain he'd sneak in anyway. She'd tossed and turned all night, being positive she heard him creeping up the stairs, but he'd never arrived.

He hadn't joined them for breakfast either, hadn't sent a note. She wasn't worried precisely. They'd agreed to meet at the church, so there was no reason to be agitated, but she was awash with nerves.

Finally, Daisy emerged. Jo smiled, expecting he'd be standing behind Daisy, but he wasn't.

"Is he there?" Jo asked.

"No. There's a ceremony concluding, and there are a few people watching. He's not one of them."

"You're sure?"

"Yes, I'm sure."

Daisy slipped her hand into Jo's. They tarried together, peering down the busy street, but no matter how vigilantly they searched, he didn't appear.

The church doors opened, and the wedding couple burst out. She and Daisy scooted down the steps, observing as the couple's friends clapped and threw rice. All of them climbed into their carriage, and the vehicle rolled off. It grew ominously quiet.

Eventually, Jo said, "It's silly to dawdle outside. Shall we go in and sit down?"

"We probably should. You and Uncle Peyton are next."

They entered the chapel, and she was greeted by a woman who introduced herself as the vicar's wife. Fortunately, she wasn't the one who'd been there two years earlier, so she wouldn't gape at Jo and try to figure out where she'd seen her before.

"We're the Prescott party," Jo told her. "We're waiting for my fiancé. He should be here shortly."

"Have a seat in the rear pew," the woman said. "That way, he'll find you the moment he walks in. The vicar will be ready whenever you are."

Jo glanced toward the altar, and the vicar was still there. He closed his prayer book and tiptoed out a side door. Fortunately again, he was a different vicar too. There was luck all around, and she breathed a sigh of relief.

They slid into the pew. Daisy was grinning, whispering, chattering incessantly. Jo mostly ignored her, offering a remark when it was required. She didn't have a timepiece, but the minutes were passing much too rapidly, and her pulse accelerated.

She'd been in this predicament once prior, and it was a revoltingly awful spot to occupy. She supposed every bride secretly wondered if the groom would show up, but it wasn't like Peyton to be late. It wasn't like him to make her fret.

She noticed she was tapping her foot, the sound echoing, and she forced herself to stop. But then, she was fidgeting. Then she was trembling.

The vicar's wife bustled over. "It's almost eleven o'clock. Is your betrothed here?"

"Not yet."

"We have another service at eleven-thirty. If he doesn't come by a quarter past the hour, we'll have to reschedule."

"He's a sailor with the Royal Navy, ma'am, and he's shipping out this evening. We can't reschedule, so I hope you can accommodate us."

"I'll have to confer with my husband. In the interim, why don't you check the street again? Perhaps he's riding up even as we speak."

"Yes, perhaps he is."

The woman smiled a tight smile, and Jo rose and marched out, Daisy hot on her heels. They stared and stared, yearning, praying, but to no avail.

When Jo had been eighteen and Holden Cartwright had failed to appear, she'd been perplexed and devastated, but she wasn't devastated this time. She was very, very angry. How dare Peyton do this! How dare he shame her!

Daisy was blessedly silent, realizing the cheery event had gone terribly wrong. Ultimately, she asked, "Where is he, Aunt Jo?"

"I have no idea, Daisy."

"Something must have happened to him. Something bad. He must have gotten sick or had an accident."

"Nothing's happened," Jo staunchly insisted. "He's just been . . . delayed."

She started to pace, having to step out of the way again as the next group raced in for their hasty ceremony. The vicar's wife peeked out and asked, "Any news?"

"No," Jo said. "You can proceed with the other couple. We'll continue to watch for him."

"That might be best. In light of your fiancé's dilemma, the vicar is willing to fit you in, but he'll wrap up by three o'clock. He's not as young as he used to be, and he tires easily."

"Yes, yes,"—Jo was overly snappish—"I understand the situation."

How many brides had stood on the same sidewalk, having been jilted by their bridegrooms? Was she the only unlucky one? Or had there been many others in the past?

The whole place was a wedding factory where people could accomplish the matter in a hurry. By its very nature, it catered to a lower class of person, one who didn't plan in advance, one who had to make rushed decisions, one who—as Jo had done—got herself into a jam and had to quickly get herself out of it.

She and Daisy went into the chapel, and they waited through two more ceremonies, but that was all Jo could abide.

"Let's go home, Daisy," she said.

"But...but...what about the wedding? What about Uncle Peyton? What if he arrives, but we're not here?"

"He knows where we live. He knows how to locate us."

Jo motioned to the vicar's wife and whispered that they were leaving. She described Peyton and asked—should he design to show his face—that the woman tell him they'd departed. They trudged out, and Daisy was stoically morose.

As to Jo, she wasn't depressed or worried, wasn't concerned or moping. No, she was more incensed than she'd ever been, and she truly thought—if she'd owned a pistol—she'd have sought him out and shot him right in the middle of his cold, black heart.

She'd told him about Mr. Cartwright and the great disgrace he'd inflicted, yet Peyton had forced her into disgrace again!

She refused to accept that he was ill or had been in an accident. It was much more likely that he'd simply changed his mind. He'd probably spent the night drinking with his officer chums. He had to have confided that he was marrying a girl with no dowry, family, or ancestry, and they'd have laughed until dawn.

They'd have worked valiantly to dissuade him, and they must have finally succeeded.

Hadn't she been convinced he'd grow to regret his proposal? She'd assumed it would occur down the road after he remembered he could have picked someone richer and better.

The furious, aggrieved musings rocked her. What was his intent? Would he sail away later in the evening without a goodbye? Had he instituted the fiscal arrangements he'd promised? Would the rent be paid? Would an allowance be set up? What if he hadn't provided for her? What then?

She'd cast her lot with him, had persuaded herself to depend on him, so she'd become lazy and negligent. She'd stopped searching for employment and hadn't found a job. Instead, she'd let him take charge, and she'd stupidly abandoned all responsibility for her own security.

Look where her foolishness had left her! Hadn't she learned the hard way from Mr. Cartwright that a woman couldn't rely on a man? Hadn't she learned that a woman could only rely on herself?

"I'm sorry there wasn't a wedding," Daisy said. "I was so excited."

Jo snorted with disgust. "Believe me, so was I."

"Are you sad?"

"No," Jo calmly lied. "We'll reschedule it—the minute we discover what happened."

"Do you suppose Uncle Peyton is all right?" Daisy asked.

"I'm sure he is, and I'm positive he'll bluster in soon."

And if he doesn't?

The question was so terrifying she couldn't answer it. Discreetly, she tossed her bridal bouquet in the gutter and walked on without glancing back.

CHAPTER

21

"You're awake!"

Alice tiptoed over to the bed, but didn't lean on the mattress. The doctor had advised that Uncle Peyton would be in a great deal of pain for a long time, and she supposed the slightest movement might be unpleasant.

His broken leg was in a splint, his broken arm too. He had a huge bump on his head which seemed to worry the doctor more than the shattered bones. His skull was wrapped with a thick bandage, so he looked scary, like a monster in a fairytale.

"Where am I?" he inquired.

"You're in your bedchamber. At Benton Manor? Don't you remember? You ask me the same question whenever you open your eyes."

"Yes, I remember." He was silent for a bit, then he said, "I'm starving."

She grinned. "Then you must be feeling better. Would you like something to eat? The doctor insists we feed you broth, but I'll order whatever you'd like. You just have to promise not to tell."

"Maybe some eggs and toast? And some tea?"

The housemaids were watching over him, and the current woman peered in. On seeing Alice hovering, she frowned.

"Lady Alice, leave him be."

"He's awake, Peg. He's hungry."

"I'll get some broth."

"The Earl has requested eggs, toast, and a pot of tea. Fetch them at once."

"The doctor won't like it."

"I don't care. You can discuss the issue with him when he returns. In the meantime, we'll obey the Earl. Hurry to the kitchen for a tray."

Alice peeked at her uncle, and he winked, their alliance complete.

Peg hesitated, nearly argued, then stomped out.

"For a minute there," he said, "you sounded just like your mother. Your bossy tone was exactly right."

"I've listened to her often enough. It's not difficult to imitate her."

"When will the doctor be back?"

"Not until after supper."

She pointed to the medicinal jar on the nightstand. "Are you hurting? You can have some laudanum. You're due for more."

"Have I been taking a lot of it?"

"Yes. Would you like me to pour some in a glass?"

He wrinkled his nose. "I'll wait. It's made me groggy. I should clear my head."

"The doctor says you should sleep all you can. He says you'll heal quicker that way." There was a chair next to the bed, and she pulled it closer and sat down. "Do you recall what happened?"

He paused, pondered. "I had an accident? On my horse?"

"Yes." Her grin widened. "You *are* better. The first day or two you couldn't recollect a single thing."

"How is my horse? We had a terrible fall."

"He's fine," she fibbed. "The stable master is tending him."

"Good."

He shut his eyes, and she breathed an uneasy sigh. His horse had been so badly injured it couldn't be saved. Her Uncle Richard had fired the shot to put the animal out of its misery. They'd all agreed they wouldn't tell Uncle Peyton though. Not until he was more hale and could bear to hear the news.

He'd visited her mother on Wednesday, then he'd ridden for London so he could sail away on his ship. But he'd suffered his mishap on a bridge that was a few miles from Benton. He'd lain in the river bottom for hours, until a teamster had crossed the same bridge and noted the ruined railing.

He'd stopped his cart and peered down into the muck, and Uncle Peyton had been there unconscious.

The manor had been in an uproar ever since. The doctor insisted he'd mend eventually, but no one believed him.

Alice would never admit it, but she was delighted that he was trapped at Benton. She didn't like that an accident was the reason, but she was glad all the same. From the moment he'd been carried up to his bedchamber, she'd been his devoted nurse.

He woke again. "You've been here practically every time I've roused."

"I had to be certain you were receiving appropriate attention. I don't trust that stupid doctor, and it's not as if I'd let my mother be in charge of you. Her skills as a healer are a bit lacking."

He chuckled. "Thank you. I appreciate it."

"You're welcome."

"Aren't you weary of dawdling in this sickroom with me? Don't you have better things to do?"

"Not really."

"If you're bored, you can go out and play. I don't mind."

"I'm not bored, and I hate to play."

"Wonderful. I like having you as my companion."

"There are no children to play *with* anyway. Uncle Richard sent them all away."

He glanced out the window. It was gray and cloudy, and it seemed to have been raining all summer. "What day is it?"

"Monday."

He scowled. "Monday? You're positive?"

"Yes."

"When was my accident? Wednesday?"

"Yes."

"It's been six days."

"Yes," she said again.

"There are several people who must be missing me. I have to write some letters."

"Mother contacted the navy for you, so don't worry about that."

"That's a relief, but . . . ah . . . I have to write to someone else. Is there a desk in here?"

"Out in the sitting room."

"Can you bring me a piece of paper and a quill?"

"I'll be right back with them."

She was so thrilled to be useful, to provide him with what he couldn't retrieve himself. Since the day they'd chatted in the woods, she'd been totally obsessed with him.

It was difficult to live with her mother and Uncle Richard. They were so grouchy and unhappy. They'd filled her head with dreadful stories about Uncle Peyton, but after she'd talked to him—without her mother butting in—she'd learned that he was the best person ever.

She wished her mother and Uncle Richard would leave Benton, and her Uncle Peyton would stay instead. It was a horrid wish, and she'd probably go straight to Hell for thinking it, but she couldn't help it.

No one was ever kind to her. No one ever noticed her or listened to her. Her half-sister, Daisy, had been her only real friend. Their entire relationship had been a secret from the rest of the world, but it had been so special that they'd pretended to be twins. And why shouldn't they have? They were the same age, and they looked just alike.

Besides Daisy, her Uncle Peyton was the only one who'd ever seemed to like her. She didn't care how her mother denigrated him. Alice would love him forever, and she'd never stop!

She slid off the chair, and she hurried to the other room. She found a tray, and she grabbed the items he required, then she carried them into the bedchamber. She placed the tray on the mattress, and she had to fuss with everything so he could balance the paper. With all his splints, bandages, and casts, it was hard for him to maneuver.

He contemplated, reflecting on how to craft his message. Finally, he penned a short note, and she struggled not to read it, but she was so curious. She glimpsed a few words like *very sorry* and *accident* and *wedding*.

Was he getting married? Her mother hadn't mentioned it, but then, he didn't confide in her, and it drove her mother mad with fury.

If he married, and Alice wasn't invited to the wedding, she'd just die! He couldn't proceed without her being there! Who was his bride to be? Was she stunningly beautiful? Was she a princess? Was she a duke's daughter? Alice couldn't imagine what sort of female would be perfect enough to be his wife.

He finished the letter, folded and sanded it, and she had to assist him as he swiped on the wax and stuck the Benton seal into it. To her enormous aggravation, she never managed a clearer peek at the text.

"Can you put this into the post for me?" he asked.

"Yes, I'll take it down right away."

"It's very important that it be mailed as soon as possible. I have a . . . *friend* who will be fretting over my absence. She has to be apprised of what happened to me."

So it was a *she*. He must be betrothed. She was certain of it. She glanced at the name: Miss Josephine Bates. She wasn't a princess or duke's daughter after all, and Alice was terribly disappointed. A commoner could never be worthy of him.

"It will go out today," she told him. "I promise."

He smiled. "You're a good girl, Alice."

"I try to be."

The small exertion had depleted him. He drooped against the pillows as Peg came in with his breakfast. Cook had prepared precisely what Alice had ordered.

She set it on the nightstand, and she poured the tea and arranged the plate, cutting the toast into tiny pieces so he wouldn't have to press with the fork.

He'd closed his eyes, but he hadn't dozed off.

"Is that my food?"

"Yes."

"It smells delicious."

"My old nurse used to claim—if you're hungry—it's proof you're on the mend."

"Let's hope she was correct."

"May I help you to eat?" she asked. "Would that make it easier for you?"

"In a minute."

He dozed then. She and Peg observed him, both of them worried and anxious.

She remembered his letter, and she had to deliver it downstairs, but in case he awakened, she couldn't bear to be away from his side. She picked it up and motioned to Peg. They stepped into the other room.

"Can you take this down for me?" she inquired. "The Earl wrote it, and we can't miss the afternoon post."

"Yes, I'll take it down."

Peg left, and Alice returned to the bedchamber, dropped onto her chair, and resumed her vigil.

BARBARA WAS SEATED AT her desk in the library, catching up on correspondence, when Newman walked in. He hovered, content to wait until she gave him permission to speak.

He was still in the dog house over his hiding the fact that Daisy had been living with Peyton. He hadn't entirely wormed his way back into her good graces, but her other butler had resigned on the spur of the moment, so she'd offered the job to Newman. She'd reduced his pay substantially though, so she'd gotten even.

Eventually, she tossed down her pen and glared at him. "What is it?"

"The Earl is feeling better, and he wrote a letter that must be mailed at once. A maid brought it to me." He peered around to be sure they were alone. "I figured you might like to look at it prior to it being sent."

Barbara's initial impulse was to retort, *Why would I care about Peyton's mail?* But Newman's expression silenced the question.

"Let me see." She waved him over, and he slid it onto the desk. She studied the name on the front. "Josephine Bates. How . . . interesting."

"I thought so."

She pointed to the address. "Do you know this residence?"

"No. When the staff was moving out of the town house, there was a rumor circulating that he'd rented lodging for her, but we never learned if it was true."

She hesitated, wondering at the ramifications of snooping—but not wondering very long—before she flicked her thumb under the seal. She read the words over and over, and her fury spiked higher with each repetition.

"It appears, Newman, that the gossip about a love nest was accurate."

"He actually proceeded?"

"Yes, and apparently, he's planning to marry her."

"No!"

"Yes!"

Newman was typically very stoic, but this news was shocking by any standard. "Such a disparate match wouldn't be appropriate for the Earl of Benton."

"No, it wouldn't be," Barbara agreed.

"Miss Bates is very nice, but honestly!"

"My opinion exactly," Barbara said. "Daisy is there with her, so we're still supporting her with estate funds."

"I have no comment to share, my lady. You've rendered me speechless."

"There's naught *to* say really."

"No, I don't suppose there is."

They stared, a thousand complicit messages flitting between them. Then Barbara said, "That will be all, Newman. Thank you."

"As always, I am your most devoted servant."

The obsequious toad bowed out, and the instant he shut the door, she whirled in her chair and gazed out across the park.

From the day she'd wed Neville Prescott, her life had been a tedious slog of humiliation and disgrace. He was dead and buried, and he was still shaming her.

He'd bequeathed every farthing to his vain, imperious brother. She couldn't buy a dress or choose a supper menu without begging him first for a few pennies. Yet he was taking money—*her* money—and spending it on his paramour and Neville's bastard.

All the while, she, Alice, and Nancy were expected to restrain themselves and make do with less.

The gall of it! The ignominy!

And now, on top of every other mortification, he intended to wed Miss Bates. He would replace Barbara with a girl who was nothing and who had nothing. Would Barbara blithely allow it to occur? She didn't think she could.

At the moment, he was upstairs, and his broken leg would have him incapacitated for at least eight weeks. He'd need a cane after that, and he'd likely always limp. In fact, with his arm damaged too, his career in the navy was probably over.

He'd never sail the seas again, would never command a naval vessel. That sort of grueling existence required enormous physical stamina, and he'd squandered it when his horse plunged into that ravine under the bridge.

He'd have to remain in England and devise another way to keep busy. Wouldn't he move to Benton—with his new, common bride? But Miss Bates would never rule at Benton. She would never lord herself over Barbara and her daughters. She would never bring Daisy to Benton, and Daisy would never reside in the manor.

It would happen over Barbara's dead body.

She'd warned Miss Bates to be careful, but the foolish ninny hadn't listened. She hadn't assumed she *had* to listen. She'd been living under Peyton's protection, and she viewed it as a shield that would avert any bad consequences.

Well, Peyton would be bedridden for two months, and during such a lengthy period, a stupid dunce like Miss Bates could vanish. Daisy could vanish too. Why not? Who was there to prevent Barbara from orchestrating that very conclusion?

Although no one realized it, Richard was Daisy's guardian. When she was born, the role had been dumped on Neville, but he'd shucked off the responsibility to Richard quickly enough. Miss Bates and Peyton weren't in charge of Daisy and couldn't act on her behalf if Richard disagreed.

On the afternoon when Miss Bates had left with Daisy, Richard hadn't signed any paperwork regarding custody. Everything had wrapped up so swiftly that he'd forgotten. Richard was certainly in a position to determine if his ward should be wallowing in immoral conditions with a loose doxy.

If Barbara retaliated against Miss Bates and Daisy, would Peyton ever learn of it? Or might Barbara rid herself of them so completely that Peyton could never locate them? Was it worth the risk? She thought it absolutely was.

She walked over to the fire and pitched the letter onto the flames, watching it dwindle to ash. Then she went to her desk and began making plans.

"Josephine!"

Jo pulled up short, startled to hear herself summoned. Her sister, Maud, was the only female who'd ever beckoned her so rudely, and Jo glanced about, discovering Maud glowering from a carriage parked across the street.

Maud waved her over, and Jo vacillated forever, not inclined to chat. In light of Jo's foul temper, she didn't have the patience to be civil.

As she'd been doing every day since being jilted at the altar for the second time, she'd been tromping around the city to inquire about her purported fiancé. It had been over two weeks since Peyton had abandoned her. To her great surprise and dismay, he hadn't shown up—late and apologetic—to explain what had transpired. She'd received no letter. No messenger had arrived.

She'd passed by the town house, but it was shuttered, and there was a notice posted about it being for sale. She'd written to Benton, but her letter had been returned as undeliverable. A note had been penned on the back that he was out of the country with the navy—and he'd be away for months or perhaps years.

Her rent was due, the kitchen larder about empty, but she had no money. He was to have set up an allowance, with a lawyer to disperse the funds, but he'd provided no details about any of it.

She'd visited naval headquarters and had spoken to an officer who'd apprised her that Peyton's ship had definitely sailed on the Thursday evening when it was scheduled to. As far as the man was aware, Peyton had been on board as the captain. Even with his departure being verified by the military, she was stunned.

She was also worried and afraid and out of ideas. Who could help her?

Peyton's friend, Evan Boyle, had once told her to seek him out if she was in trouble, but she couldn't guess how to find him. She'd asked about him at the naval office, but they only supplied personal information to family members—and she wasn't one.

Gradually, she was being forced to accept that Peyton had fled and wasn't coming back, so she was hunting for a job, but she hadn't had any luck. Her safety and security were collapsing fast.

She couldn't bear to converse with Maud. Even in the best of circumstances, it was never pleasant and wouldn't end cordially.

"Josephine!" Maud called again. "I can't wait all day."

Jo took a deep breath, prayed for strength, then trudged over. Her house was around the corner, and she doubted the meeting was an accident. How had Maud tracked her down? Why would she have?

"What is it, Maud?" she asked as she approached the carriage.

"Climb in, Jo. I have to address a difficult matter, and I don't believe you'd like any of your neighbors to eavesdrop."

Maud pushed the door open, and Jo stood, debating. Finally, she hefted herself in and sat down.

"I won't dither," her sister said.

"I'm glad to hear it. I'm very busy."

"Yes, you're so very *busy.*" Maud cackled in a snide manner. "I'll get right to the point. I received an anonymous letter about you."

It was the last comment Jo expected, and she frowned. "About me?"

"Yes. Apparently, you've ruined yourself with Lord Benton."

"I have not!" Jo indignantly scoffed, even though she had.

"Don't pretend, Jo. The whole city has learned of your disgrace."

"What?"

"He's not an invisible man, and people always gossip about their betters."

"If they're gossiping about *me,* then it's obvious they have too much time on their hands."

"So you haven't shamed yourself? You deny it?"

"I won't discuss him with you."

"Yes, you will. I am about to marry, Josephine. I can't have a scandal arise, not now when my wedding is so close. My name can't be attached to this."

"Why would your name be attached?"

"Sins are never committed in a vacuum, Jo."

"I don't agree with that," Jo flippantly retorted. "You kept your scandal secret for an entire decade."

Jo's arrow hit its target. Maud's cheeks flushed, and she bristled.

"We're not talking about me," Maud firmly stated. "We're talking about *you* and your current predicament."

"I'm not in a *predicament,*" Jo insisted.

"Aren't you? You're consorting with a notorious cad who isn't your husband. He's been paying you for services rendered."

"That's not true!" Jo hotly responded.

"Isn't it?"

Jo was the worst liar, and she couldn't hold Maud's gaze, for of course, she was in the wrong. Peyton had showered her with many boons that should never have been tendered. She should have been tougher and stronger and refused them, but she hadn't, so what now?

"You will break off your relationship at once," Maud said.

"Is that an order, Maud? For if it is, I must admit that you're exhibiting an enormous amount of gall. When you threw me out of our home, you forfeited the right to lecture me on any topic."

Maud didn't swallow Jo's bait, but pressed ahead with her argument. "My anonymous pen pal claims the Earl promised to wed you."

"What if he did?" Jo mulishly inquired.

"Why would he propose to you, Jo? Have you asked yourself that question? You're a commoner, a nanny's daughter. He's an earl. Why would he pick you?"

Jo shrugged. "I already told you, Maud. I won't discuss him."

"He's gone back to the navy. It's what my letter said."

"Yes, I know."

"He toyed with you, you little fool! And you fell for it! Don't you understand what rich, powerful men are like? They trifle with girls like you for sport. They falsely offer love and marriage so you'll give them what they crave."

"It wasn't like that between us."

Maud ignored her protest. "Then—after you've surrendered what they desire—they abandon you. They move on to the perfect debutante, to the duke's daughter with the stellar bloodlines or the American heiress with the huge dowry. I am living proof of that hideous reality."

Jo sighed with frustration. Maud had always hated her, and Jo had worked to counter her animosity by being kind and tolerant, but it had never helped. Since Maud had kicked her out, she'd suffered one calamity after the next, and she wouldn't permit Maud to harangue.

"Will there be anything else, Maud?"

"He's left you in the lurch, Jo!"

"Maybe."

"What is your plan?"

"Daisy is still with me. May we come with you to the country?"

"Absolutely not, and why you've taken that urchin under your wing is beyond me. She'll be your ruin."

"At least I'm trying to do what's proper. It's more than I can say about some people." Jo's glare indicated she meant her sister.

"You're disgraced, Jo," Maud scolded, "with a reputation as a harlot. There's not a decent female in the kingdom who will open her door to you."

"I have my own door. I have my own home." Jo couldn't guess how much longer she'd have them, but for the moment, they were hers. "I won't be traipsing around London, begging for alms."

"You will cut all ties with Lord Benton immediately. I demand it."

"*You* demand it?"

"Yes. The gossip is all over town. Mr. Townsend hasn't mentioned it to me, but I can't risk that he might learn of your shame. Nor can others realize you and I are connected. These scandals have a way of scorching everyone who's too close to the flame."

"I'll keep any of the fire from burning you."

Maud scoffed. "You think you're so smart. You think your youth and beauty will guide you through this, but you should beware, Josephine! Your pretty face will only get you so far."

Her sister constantly managed to bring any quarrel around to the fact that Jo was younger and prettier. Once the typical insults began, there was no point in continuing.

"Will that be all, Maud?"

"No, that won't be all. You haven't given me your word that you'll break it off."

"He's left the country, Maud. You don't need to worry about it."

"Yes, but he'll return, Jo, and he'll crawl into your bed again. You have to disappear so he can never find you. If you don't, how will you ever be free of him?"

"Perhaps I don't wish to be free."

"Will you spend your life, waiting for him to slink back? Don't you want more for yourself than that?"

Actually, Jo had always wanted quite a bit more, but a better ending was always just out of reach. Was she cursed? Were the gods allied against her? Was Fate determined to see her fail? It certainly seemed like it.

"I appreciate your stopping by, Maud," she sarcastically said. "It's always such a *pleasure*."

Jo climbed out, and Maud leaned out the window and fumed, "Give me your word! You will cut ties and vanish. Mr. Townsend can't hear about this."

"Yes, Mr. Townsend is definitely my biggest concern."

"Nor can you tarry and allow Lord Benton to discover your whereabouts. You must hide."

"I will take your opinion under advisement. Now stay off my street."

Jo hurried away, depressed to admit the conversation had been as awful as she'd predicted it would be. She shouldn't have let Maud coerce her into chatting. When Jo was sure it would lead to a fight, why participate?

She rounded the corner, and her house was up ahead. There was a carriage parked in front, and as she neared, the horses trotted off. For a brief instant, she thought Daisy was in it and waving madly, but she was yanked out of sight.

It transpired so rapidly that Jo figured she had to be wrong. Daisy would be inside the house, eagerly watching for Jo. Cook had promised to keep her busy in the kitchen.

Jo went to the door, and she paused to steady her breathing and her expression. She wouldn't enter in an agitated state. After she'd calmed, she grabbed for the knob, but before she could turn it, her footman stepped out. He was wearing his coat and hat.

"Are you off to run some errands?" Jo asked him. "It's so late in the day. I hope Cook hasn't driven you out when supper is approaching."

"Well, I'm *going*, Miss Bates. I wouldn't call it *out* though."

It was a strange comment, and she scowled. "What do you mean?"

"I've enjoyed working here, Miss Bates. Tell Commander Prescott, would you? I doubt I'll see him again, and I'd like him to know I was grateful for my job."

"You're quitting? Why? Has someone upset you?"

He didn't clarify. He simply doffed his cap and continued on.

Jo walked into the foyer, and the cook and her maid were there. They were dressed to depart as well.

"What the devil?" Jo was frantic for an explanation. "You can't be leaving too."

"This is a dirty business, Miss Bates," Cook said, "and I'm very sorry."

"What are you talking about?"

"You were kind to me, Miss Bates," the maid added, "and I don't care what they say about you. They'll never make me believe it."

The two women rushed out, and as they dashed away, Jo almost fainted as Barbara Prescott emerged from the parlor.

"We were starting to think you'd never arrive, Miss Bates." The Countess smiled a tight smile and gestured into the room. "You must attend me at once."

"Why are you in my home?"

"It's not really *your* home, is it?"

"It's as much mine as anyone's."

"You're not in any position to be snide with me."

Richard Slater appeared behind his sister, and suddenly, Jo was very scared.

"Where is Daisy?" she asked.

They didn't reply, and she went to the stairs and yelled for Daisy over and over, but she received no response. She whipped around to face them, her gaze livid.

"Where is my niece?" she demanded of Mr. Slater.

"She's been sent away," Mr. Slater said.

"To where?"

"To a place where she won't be living in a den of iniquity."

Jo's heart skipped a beat. "I have no idea what you're implying."

"Are you aware, Miss Bates," the Countess said, "that my brother is Daisy's legal guardian?"

"He is not," Jo huffed. "He gave her to me. He couldn't wait to be shed of her. *I* am her guardian."

"Have you any documents to prove it?" the Countess inquired.

The query stopped Jo in her tracks. Of course she didn't have documents. When Jo had initially left Benton with Daisy, it had never occurred to her to have Mr. Slater sign an agreement. He'd insisted Daisy be removed from the property, and Jo had obliged him. He had incredible gall to show up and pretend to be in charge.

"Where is she?" Jo fumed.

"I told you, Miss Bates," Mr. Slater said, "she's been delivered to a spot where carnal sins are not being committed on a daily basis."

"How dare you take her!"

Jo marched toward him as if she might strike him, but in the end, she didn't. He was bigger and taller, and she'd never hit anyone in her life, *and* he was a brute. She suspected he'd hit her back.

They were interrupted by people tromping down the stairs. She peered up to discover a trio of Benton servants, and they were hauling down boxes and trunks.

"What are you doing?" she asked them, but they didn't acknowledge her, so she spun to Barbara Prescott. "What's happening?"

"As of today, Lord Benton will not be renting this house."

"This house—and his renting it—is none of your affair."

"That's where you're confused, Miss Bates. He's sailed for the Caribbean, and while he's away, he's put me in control of our finances. I doubt you'll be surprised to hear that I don't choose to support you."

Jo's pulse was racing. "Meaning what?"

"We've contacted the landlord and informed him that we're cancelling the lease." The Countess grinned malevolently. "We'll be locking the doors when we leave so we can drop off the key before we head to Benton."

"But ... but ... this is my home!"

"We've packed your belongings." The Countess pointed to the boxes and trunks that the servants had brought down. "We're not cruel, Miss Bates, so we've secured a room for you at a woman's boarding house. We won't throw you out on the street—despite your low tendencies. We've paid for a month's lodging, but after that, you'll be on your own."

"I won't go."

Mr. Slater chimed in with, "I'm afraid you'll have to. Weren't you listening? We're finished paying your rent. You're welcome to remain—if you can pay it yourself. Can you?"

She glared at him, ashamed that he knew she couldn't afford it.

The servants carried the trunks outside. A cab had pulled up, and they were loading her things into it. She couldn't accept what she was witnessing and felt as if she was in the middle of a peculiar dream and she couldn't wake up.

"As my sister mentioned, we've provided you with a month's lodging." Mr. Slater handed Jo an envelope. "And I'm furnishing you with ten pounds to ease your way. The Earl was fond of you, and he wouldn't want you imperiled."

"The *Earl* wouldn't?" Jo bit down a hysterical laugh.

If she'd been prouder, she'd have refused the money, but she snatched it away from him. Tears welled into her eyes and dripped down her cheeks. She swiped them away, hating to have them observe her raw emotion, but the past weeks had been so grueling. Who wouldn't weep?

"What happened to the Earl?" she asked the Countess.

"It annoys me to repeat myself, so concentrate, would you? He resumed his career in the navy and sailed to the Caribbean."

"Yes, but I can't understand why he flitted off. We had ... ah ... made some plans."

The Countess smirked. "*You* may have had plans, but as far as I'm aware, he had no plans at all with regard to you."

"You're wrong. We were going to marry. We had it all arranged."

When she spoke the words aloud, Jo felt like a complete dunce. Commander Peyton Prescott, Earl of Benton, was never going to marry her. Was she joking? Who was she anyway but the lowborn, common daughter of a nanny? Maud had just reminded her of that fact. Only a gullible fool would have leapt into such a fairytale.

The Slater siblings were much taller than she was, and they gazed down at her, their expressions exasperated and pitying.

"Did you really imagine he was sincere, Miss Bates?" Mr. Slater's tone was actually very kind. "Please don't tell me you were that silly."

"I *did* think he was sincere," Jo said. "Why wouldn't I have?"

The Countess tsked with irritation. "Then I'm sorry, Miss Bates, but Peyton has quite a reputation as a cad."

Mr. Slater added, "He's engaged in this sort of nonsense before. It's embarrassing to admit, but where young ladies are concerned, he's notorious. He's too much like his brother and can't curb his worst impulses."

Jo didn't want to believe him. The Peyton Prescott who'd befriended her had seemed funny and clever and generous. He'd helped her, he'd rescued her, and she was positive they were lying, but how could she verify it? He'd vanished, and the naval office had confirmed his departure.

What else was there to discover?

"Where is Daisy?" she asked Mr. Slater. "I'm so worried about her."

"She's in a safe place, Miss Bates. It's all you need to know."

"She'll be so frightened."

"Children adapt," he snottily replied. "She'll be fine."

"Now then, Miss Bates," his sister said, "let's get you into your cab. The driver has the directions to your boarding house."

"I won't leave!" Jo protested.

"Miss Bates, may I be frank?"

"No. I'm weary of listening to you."

The Countess ignored her. "Gossip has spread that a harlot resides here."

"Who spread it? You?"

The Countess ignored her again. "Rumor has it that you entertain gentlemen for money. Will you tarry and be identified as the female in question? What if the neighbors complain to the authorities? You'd be arrested. Are you willing to risk it?"

Jo felt trapped and terrified and very alone. She wondered if Maud was still parked around the corner. If she ran to her sister, would Maud aid her? She was sure not.

"I won't leave," Jo said again, but with much less conviction.

"It's not up to you, Miss Bates," Mr. Slater told her. "We can't have our name attached to this scandal, and with the Earl having left town, you have no protector and your character is destroyed."

The Countess walked out, and Mr. Slater followed her. As he passed Jo, he grabbed her arm and marched her out with him. She was so stunned she staggered after him, not objecting as he escorted her to the cab and lifted her in.

The Benton servants stood like a phalanx of guards, their scowls critical and condemning. Was the whole city tittering over her? Was the whole kingdom?

Jo collapsed onto the seat, and Mr. Slater signaled to the driver. He clicked the reins, and the horse took off with a surprised jolt that nearly pitched her to the floor. She steadied herself and managed a final glimpse of her home.

Barbara Prescott was locking the door, and Mr. Slater was holding a chain, ready to snap it shut and bar it even more securely so Jo could never sneak back inside.

CHAPTER

22

PEYTON'S CARRIAGE ROLLED TO a stop in front of Maud Bates's house outside Telford. It looked as if she was home. Smoke billowed from the chimney, the curtains were open, and the knocker was on the door.

He'd called on her earlier in the summer, but it was November now. Jo had mentioned that her sister was marrying Thompson Townsend in September, but she'd never specified the date. If Maud had been away on her honeymoon, he wouldn't have been surprised.

He doubted Jo would be living with her sister, but he was out of ideas and had to inquire.

Jo had vanished into thin air, and he couldn't blame her. She'd been jilted at the altar twice, and Peyton was responsible for the second humiliation. With his suffering his accident, he hadn't been in any condition to avert what occurred, but still, it had occurred.

As soon as he'd been able to muster a coherent thought, he'd written to apologize, but she hadn't replied, and he'd been irked by her silence. He'd been too incapacitated to travel to London, so he'd written a dozen more letters that weren't answered. Finally, he'd sent a footman to town to check on her.

The man had delivered the distressing news that she'd moved, and there were other tenants in her house. They had never heard of her and could shed no light on where she'd gone.

Peyton's health was better, not one-hundred percent, but better. Unfortunately, it appeared he would never regain his former physical stamina. The break to his leg had been too severe.

In the future, he'd never run races at a picnic or trek for miles to snoop out every inch of the Benton estate. He'd never stand on a ship's deck and brace himself against the roll of the waves. He'd always walk with a limp, and rainy weather would make him ache with rheumatism as if he were elderly and decrepit.

But . . . he continued to improve, and he was too vain and impatient to lounge around feeling sorry for himself. The minute he could, he'd started searching for Jo. He'd begun at the house he'd rented, discovering for himself that she'd truly left.

He'd talked to the neighbors and had been unsettled by their terrible gossip about her. They'd whispered that she'd been a doxy who'd illicitly entertained paramours until she'd been chased off by the authorities.

The landlord though had refuted the possibility of her being swept up on a morals charge, so it had probably been a vicious rumor. The man had simply received a note from her—with no notice or warning—apprising him that she was vacating the premises immediately. She'd provided no forwarding address.

Where might she be? He was such a conceited ass that he'd never probed for details about her personal life. He knew she had a sister and that was pretty much it. Were there cousins who might have offered her shelter? Were there friends?

He would interrogate Maud Bates, and if she wasn't cooperative, he couldn't guess what he'd do next.

He was so afraid that Jo might be imperiled. Daisy too. Although they hadn't been sure at the time of the wedding, it was likely she was increasing with his child. By now, she'd be several months along, so her condition would be visible to others which would bring on a host of problems.

He could accept that she was angry with him for jilting her, but he was angry with her too, for not trusting him, for not wondering why he'd failed to arrive. She had to have realized something bad prevented him. Why was her only reaction to flee? Why didn't she travel to Benton? Why didn't she write or send a messenger to inquire?

What was she thinking? With a baby on the way, she couldn't strut about town with no husband and no ring on her finger. If naught else, she needed to marry him to give her child a name—despite how furious she might be.

Arthur Cummings opened the carriage door and lowered the step. He was the young veteran who'd worked on the Benton inventory. Peyton had hired him to be his clerk and aide. It was mortifying to contend with reality, but Peyton wasn't completely hale and, on occasion, required assistance.

He climbed out, hating how Arthur had to stabilize him as he descended, that his balance wasn't as firm as it had been in the past. Arthur was marvelous about it though. He never let on that he was lending a hand with any task.

Peyton went to the door and knocked, and when he asked to speak to Maud, he was shown into the parlor. He was a bit surprised to be welcomed. During his prior trip, when he'd retrieved Jo's clothes, he'd been rude and abrupt. If Maud had claimed to be indisposed, he couldn't have complained about being snubbed.

Before too much time had passed, she marched in. In their previous meeting, she'd been aflutter with anxiety as to his purpose and whether he might reveal her secret to her betrothed. Now she was simply annoyed. He stood to greet her, but she didn't invite him to sit again. She didn't sit either.

"Thank you for seeing me, Miss Bates. Or is it Mrs. Townsend?"

"It's Mrs. Townsend."

"Congratulations on your marriage."

She didn't acknowledge his well wishes. Instead, she stunned him by snottily saying, "I'm amazed that you have the audacity to call on me, Lord Benton. I wouldn't have thought you'd have the nerve."

"Really? Why is that?"

She ignored his question. "How may I help you?"

"I'll come straight to the point."

"Please do."

"I'm looking for your sister. Is she here?"

"You're looking for Jo?" She appeared aghast.

"Yes. I had an address for her in London, but she's moved, and I can't locate her."

"You are trying to locate her?" She was repeating his comments as if she didn't comprehend English and it was difficult to decipher his words. "Have you no shame?"

He scowled. "What are you talking about?"

"As if you didn't know," she spat with a huge amount of venom.

"No, I don't *know,* ma'am, so perhaps you should enlighten me."

"I received an anonymous letter about you and your antics with her."

"An *anonymous* letter. Just out of the blue?"

"Yes, and I visited her in town because of it. I had a very stern discussion with her, and I warned her to hide where you could never find her. It didn't seem she would heed me, but if she's vanished, maybe she came to her senses after all."

He remembered her neighbors and the stories that had spread down her street. He remembered Evan fuming over lurid gossip. The capacity for Londoners to butt their noses into other people's business never ceased to astound him.

Who would have written to Maud about him? Who would have realized Jo had a sibling? Who would have investigated to discover her address?

The entire scenario was exhausting and ridiculous. It left him livid with rage.

If he'd been braver, he might have confessed the affair, declared his affection for Jo, and told her sister to sod off. But apparently, he was a coward, for he refused to fan the flames of innuendo. They didn't need to burn any hotter.

"I have no idea what you mean, Mrs. Townsend," he lied. "I was merely being kind to Josephine. She was in dire financial straits—because of you."

"Don't blame any of this on me, Lord Benton. If she's ruined, *I* am hardly the culpable party."

"She was never ruined. Not by me anyway. The extent of my involvement was to pay her rent—for her and *your* daughter."

At his mentioning Daisy, Mrs. Townsend blanched. "I can't imagine to whom you refer, Lord Benton. I have no daughter."

A muscle ticked in Peyton's cheek. He recognized that the world was a harsh place for a woman, that the birth of a child out of wedlock was never a truth anyone cared to divulge, but she'd pushed him beyond civility.

"Mrs. Townsend, I won't play games with you."

"I won't play them with you either, and I will have to ask you to leave."

"You can ask all you want, but I won't depart until I have a few answers from you. When did you last see Jo?"

"In August—in London."

"After you spoke to her, you never heard from her again? You've had no contact?"

"No, but I wouldn't have expected to. She made choices in her life that I cautioned her not to make. Josephine has always thought she was smarter than everyone else, but there are consequences for that sort of vanity."

The callous remark incensed him. "She offered shelter to your daughter when you specifically insisted she shouldn't, but once my brother-in-law kicked Daisy out of Benton, she might have ended up in an orphanage. Weren't you concerned about that? Are you concerned about her now?"

She gestured to the door. "You'll have to excuse me, Lord Benton, but I'm busy this morning, and should you stop by in the future, I will *always* be busy."

He didn't budge. "They don't have any money. What if they're in danger."

She sighed with exasperation. "Lord Benton, you are laboring under the mistaken impression that I have information about my sister. I don't."

"Has she any old friends? How about any relatives?"

"No."

"Where would she go then, Mrs. Townsend? If you can't admit to being worried, can you at least admit to being curious?"

"In my last conversation with her, I advised her to think about what she was doing with you, but Jo assumes she knows best. It's her greatest failing."

"She's a good person, a kind person!" he fumed. "You never understood that about her."

"Am I her nanny, Lord Benton? I don't believe I am. She made her bed, and she's definitely lying in it. If she's gotten herself in a jam, it's not my fault, and I don't feel guilty."

"She was protecting your daughter!" he furiously stated, his temper sparking.

"I keep telling you I have no daughter, and I've given you much more time than you deserve. Let me show you out."

She huffed away, and he followed her. He could have tarried and traded barbs, but it appeared she was clueless as to Jo's whereabouts, so further bickering was pointless.

But as he stepped into the foyer, she was frozen in her spot, an expression of horror on her face. Her husband was standing on the stairs, and from how he was glaring, he must have eavesdropped on their heated discussion.

Peyton broke the awkward moment. "Hello, Townsend."

"Benton." Townsend's nod was curt. "I didn't realize we had a visitor or I'd have come down."

"I'm not actually visiting. This was a quick stop for me. I'm looking for your wife's sister, Josephine. She seems to have vanished from her lodging in London, and she can't be located. I'm afraid she may be imperiled."

"If she's *imperiled*," Townsend snidely said, "aren't you the culprit?"

Peyton warned himself to ignore the stupid oaf, but he couldn't. "Careful, Townsend, or I might consider that comment an insult."

"Heaven forbid," Townsend muttered.

Mrs. Townsend shook herself out of her stupor, and she yanked the door open. "Lord Benton was just leaving."

"You're in quite a hurry to get rid of him, Maud." Townsend descended until he reached the foyer too. He turned to Peyton. "I couldn't help but overhear the two of you."

"I'm sorry we disturbed you," Peyton said. "I should have lowered my volume."

"I'm not disturbed," Townsend claimed. "I'm absolutely fascinated. What's this about Maud having a daughter?"

Mrs. Townsend peered frantically at Peyton, visually beseeching him to deny Daisy, but he couldn't abide her, and he detested how awful she'd been to Jo and Daisy both. He and Mrs. Townsend weren't allies, and he had no reason to conspire with her against her spouse.

He didn't like any of the Townsend boys—they were all wastrels and cads—but no husband should have such a hideous secret concealed from him.

"I don't know a lot, Townsend," Peyton said, "but here's what I can tell you. Your wife was seduced by my brother when she was sixteen."

Townsend sucked in a sharp breath. "They had a child together?"

"Yes, and her name is Daisy. She's nine this year."

"Isn't that . . . interesting?" Townsend shot such an angry glower at his wife that Peyton was surprised it didn't knock her over.

Maud emitted a mewling sound of distress, but Peyton continued talking to her husband.

"My brother had custody of her, and she resided at Benton, but after he died, my in-laws didn't feel they should have to keep supporting her. They pressured Mrs. Townsend to take her—or Daisy would have been sent to an orphanage."

"Nice family you have there," Townsend taunted.

"Your wife refused to aid her, but Josephine tried. It's why Mrs. Townsend kicked her out, so I've been assisting her."

"Really?" Townsend sneered. "Is that what they call a wild fling these days? You were *assisting* the innocent maid in question?"

Normally, Peyton wouldn't have tolerated such cheek. If he'd been healthy, he'd have beaten Townsend to a pulp, but he wasn't healthy, and Townsend wasn't worth a brawl.

"Daisy is Josephine's niece," he said, "but she's *my* niece too, and I'm very worried about her. I believe they're in jeopardy, and I'm desperate to find them so I can assess their situation. Mrs. Townsend insists she's had no contact with them, but if there's any news, I'd be very grateful if you'd drop me a note."

Peyton started out, and Townsend said, "You're limping, Benton. What happened to you?"

"I had an accident."

"It must have been a bad one."

"It was." Peyton halted next to Maud. "I guess I've butted in where I shouldn't, but you've been such a shrew about Daisy. I couldn't remain silent."

"Go, Lord Benton!" She wouldn't look at him and was staring outside in a sort of trance.

"Your husband deserved to know the truth."

"Have mercy! Please!"

"I intend to locate your sister—and your daughter—and when I do, I won't lie about Daisy's paternity. Nor will I pretend to be unaware of her mother's identity, so your husband would have learned about it sooner or later."

Peyton left, and behind him, Townsend called, "Thank you, Benton. I appreciate your candor. It will give me and my wife plenty to discuss over the supper table."

The door was slammed, blocking any other of his remarks.

Maud Bates Townsend was rude, unlikable, and cruel. He couldn't stand her, but still, he felt sorry for her. He wasn't celebrating how her scandal had been revealed to her spouse. He wasn't smug, wasn't about to gloat.

He wondered how her marriage would fare in the future. Townsend would view himself as being duped and deceived, and Peyton had to hope that Townsend wasn't a violent man, that he wouldn't react in a violent way.

He walked to his carriage, and Arthur dawdled, watching as he climbed in. The encounter had drained him, and he tarried, bewildered as to what his destination should be. Finally, Arthur peeked in and asked where they were going.

Peyton had no desire to trudge to Benton where he'd just spent so many weeks incapacitated. For the moment, he'd had about all of Barbara and Richard he could stomach.

He probably ought to schedule some meetings with the navy. So far, he'd delayed any decisions about his career. As he'd convalesced, he'd received a commiseration letter from his commanding officer, but under the words, there was a hint of exasperation.

After he'd failed to report for duty, his ship had sailed with a different captain. If Peyton went back to work, he'd have to wait in line for another assignment and vessel which was annoying and depressing, but it really didn't matter.

In his current reduced state, he *couldn't* return to work. When would he admit it—both to himself *and* the navy? His commander hadn't said as much, but it was clear that Peyton had exhausted everyone's patience. So . . .

Perhaps he should head to London and put the navy out of its misery. Perhaps it was time to retire. Plus, London was the last place Jo and Daisy had been. Why not proceed to town? What other choice was there?

"Where will you be?"

"In London."

"When will you be back?"

"Never?"

Mr. Townsend whirled on Maud so rapidly that she stumbled away, being terrified he might strike her.

"I don't want you to go to town," she said.

"I don't care."

They were in his bedchamber, and he was throwing clothes into a portmanteau. She was anxious to stop him, but didn't know how. They'd only been wed a few weeks, and all of them had been dreadful. She didn't like how he bossed her, how he was so imperious and dictatorial.

Before the ceremony, he'd been charming and courteous, but once it was over, he'd grown surly and vulgar. He didn't like the country, and he complained about every pesky detail. The house was too small and the furnishings outdated. The servants were lazy and disrespectful, and the meals Maud had the cook prepare were disgusting. She couldn't do anything right.

Mostly, she loathed the behaviors he forced her to perform in the bedchamber. During her affair with Neville Prescott, they'd been endurable, but her husband enjoyed conduct that was vile and revolting, and he wouldn't allow her to refuse to oblige him.

She'd been so proud to be a bride. She'd assumed it would render the perfect existence. Now, she ceaselessly found herself yearning for the tedious days when she and Jo had limped along together with no issues or problems.

She was quickly discovering that there were many facets to being a wife that she hadn't considered. Here was one occurring in full view! He could pack a bag and leave, and she couldn't prevent him.

"Lord Benton was lying," she claimed.

"Oh, Maud, shut up. You're embarrassing yourself."

"I don't have a daughter."

"You must think I'm an idiot—or a fool."

He peered at her so scathingly that she felt young and ridiculous, and her fury with Jo spiraled. Jo had pushed Daisy front and center where no one had ever wanted her to be.

Wasn't it bad enough that Neville Prescott had seduced Maud? It had been a month of temporary insanity when she was sixteen, and she'd paid a very steep price for her sin. Couldn't a woman move beyond a single, pathetic mistake? Was there no forgiveness in the world?

"You're my husband," she loyally stated, "and I hold you in the highest regard. I could never deem you an idiot or a fool."

"Neville Prescott, Maud? Seriously? He was a rutting dog. Everybody knew it."

"*I* didn't know," she quietly said.

"You've concealed a humiliating secret from me, and I had to learn about it from that prick, Peyton Prescott. In my book, it indicates you married me under false pretenses."

She glanced down at the floor. "I was afraid to tell you. I'm ashamed of what happened."

"As you should be. You seem like such a prude. Who could have guessed you're actually a harlot?"

He'd finished filling his portmanteau. He buckled the straps, yanked it off the bed, and marched out. She chased after him, following him down the stairs and outside. The carriage had been brought round, and it was parked in front of the house, their footman his driver. He was in the box, waiting for Mr. Townsend to arrive.

"Please don't let this matter," Maud begged. "It doesn't matter to *me*. It never has, and I've spent the last decade trying to forget it."

He tossed his bag on the seat. "You have a child, Maud. She's nine years old. That's a little hard to forget."

"You have to stay here with me. You can't depart."

"After this dire news, how could you presume I'd remain?"

"This doesn't have to change anything."

"You truly are a dunce, aren't you? It changes everything, and I'm glad it has. There's no reason to continue hiding my activities from you."

"What do you mean?"

"I *mean* that I married you for your money."

"Well, of course you did. From the start, you recognized I was quite an heiress."

"No, I married you so I'd have the funds to support Prudence."

"Who is Prudence?"

His smile was very smug. "Who would you suppose?"

Maud remembered Jo's warnings about his special *friend*, but Maud had been too alarmed by the possibility to believe her.

She couldn't bear to pose the question. "Are you planning to . . . to . . . betray me with another woman?"

"Yes, absolutely."

"I don't give you my permission."

"You're my wife, Maud. You have no rights." He snorted with disgust. "I swear, you are the stupidest female I've ever met."

"There's no need for insults."

"Yes, there is. You're a liar and a fornicator who wasn't in a pristine condition when we wed. I've been cheated, Mrs. Townsend. I've been duped. I will talk to my brother, Charles, about an annulment. Perhaps I'll sue you for damages. I'm certain I could collect a substantial amount due to your prior infidelity."

"You wouldn't dare," Maud huffed.

"Oh, but I would. I'd have your money, maybe your house too, but I wouldn't have to have *you*."

It was the most vicious comment ever uttered in her presence. If she hadn't been so stunned, she might have slapped him or at least verbally defended herself. But the footman was glaring down at her, his expression condemning, as if her husband deserved to be offended.

She was rooted to her spot—as if she'd been turned to stone. Mr. Townsend jumped into the carriage and slammed the door in her face, and she managed to ask, "What if I have to contact you? Where will you be?"

"Weren't you listening? I will be with Prudence."

"What if I need funds or other help? What then?"

"Write to Charles. He'll know where I am." He studied her derisively, then he studied the house, and he wrinkled up his nose as if Maud emitted a bad smell. "I can't figure out how Charles convinced me to wed you. I must have been mad."

"I was a good catch!" she hotly insisted. "You were lucky to get me!"

"Only in your deranged mind is that statement true."

He banged on the roof, and the footman clicked the reins. The horse raced off like a shot. In the blink of an eye, the vehicle disappeared down the road.

She stood forever, watching the dust settle. Then she went inside. To her quiet home. To her quiet life.

She staggered to the parlor and sat in the chair by the window. It was where Jo used to sit when she sewed. If Jo had still lived with Maud, her sister would have commiserated, would have sympathized over Maud's plight, but Jo was gone, and Maud was glad of it. She was glad! And she wouldn't pretend otherwise.

She dawdled, unmoving, unseeing. She yearned to visit friends, to tell them what had transpired or to seek their advice. But she didn't have any friends.

She just had her small staff of servants. She thought one of them might peek in to check on her, but no one came, and no one checked.

CHAPTER
23

Jo TRUDGED DOWN THE street, her mood at its lowest point. She couldn't remember ever being so tired or afraid. A cold blast of wind whipped past, and she tugged on her cloak, wishing she had one constructed from a thicker fabric.

Autumn had arrived with a vengeance, and winter would follow much too soon. Where would she be then? The likely answer to that question was scary.

It was getting harder to hide her predicament. So far, she'd been modifying her gowns so her belly wasn't obvious, but she was slender and willowy. She wouldn't be able to continue her furtive concealment.

She was still living at the women's boarding house Barbara Prescott had sent her to. It was clean and quiet, but the owner was a Christian female who demanded stellar moral conduct from her tenants. Jo wouldn't be allowed to remain once the truth was revealed.

Fortunately, she'd been hired as a seamstress at a dress shop. She worked twelve hours a day, six days a week, in dingy, cramped conditions. Her fingers and back ached, and she'd developed a constant headache from straining to see the needle and fabric.

As with her rented room, she wouldn't be permitted to keep her job after her shame was noted. What would she do then?

Luck had deserted her. Fate had abandoned her to her own devices. She didn't dare court trouble, for she was certain it would find her.

She halted at the officer's club where Lord Benton used to stay when he was in London. She often loitered outside until a footman would come out and chase her away. People thought she was a prostitute soliciting customers, and she'd be deluged with salacious offers, but she ignored them. A coarse comment couldn't affect her.

She didn't imagine she'd bump into Lord Benton. He'd sailed to the Caribbean and was out of the country, but she hoped she'd meet an acquaintance who might have an address for him.

She'd relentlessly debated if she should try to locate him. Yes, he'd tricked her. Yes, he'd pretended to be smitten so she'd ruin herself. Yes, he'd insisted he'd wed her to rectify the damage, but he hadn't been serious. She comprehended that now, but she had been left in the lurch, and she was very, very angry.

A man couldn't blithely fornicate with a woman, sire a bastard on her, then walk away. If Jo had had any money, she'd have hired a lawyer to confront him. There were laws to prevent a cad from acting as he'd acted. There were rules and obligations to prevent it.

Jo needed help—both to have a roof over her head, but also so she could quit working after the baby was born. London was enormously expensive, and currently, she didn't earn enough to support herself. How was she to support a child too?

Did Lord Benton expect her to starve in the gutter? Did he expect his child to starve?

She simply couldn't believe he'd want that, but when she'd been so blind, wasn't it time to admit she'd been wrong as to what sort of person he was deep down? She only had to look at her ridiculous debacle with Holden Cartwright to be reminded that she had no ability to judge a man's character.

Most of all, she was terrified about Daisy. Barbara and Richard Slater had removed Daisy from Jo's custody and control. Was Lord Benton aware of their perfidy? Had he sanctioned it? He'd seemed to be fond of Daisy, so why would he let Richard Slater take her?

Jo was a fool in many ways, but not with regard to Mr. Slater and his sister. They'd claimed Daisy had been delivered to a more decent setting, but Jo didn't trust them and was alarmed over what type of alternative they might have arranged.

Had Daisy been placed in an orphanage after all? There were hundreds of those facilities in London, and whenever Jo heard about one, she'd visit and inquire about Daisy, but it was futile to search in such a large sea of anonymous urchins. How could she ever find one little girl? Yet she would never stop hunting.

Since dawn, she'd toiled away at the dress shop, and she was exhausted. Supper was served at her boarding house at nine. If she didn't leave soon, she'd miss the meal which would mean she'd go to bed hungry. She had to hurry.

A group of sailors strolled by, and they whistled and hurled risqué remarks.

"Do any of you know Commander Peyton Prescott?" she calmly asked.

"Why, you brazen trollop? Is he your best customer?"

The query ignited ribald laughter, and they kept on into the building. They must have complained about her because, shortly, a footman emerged. He had a broom—as if he could sweep her away.

"We've told you not to loiter," he fumed. "You can't lurk on our stoop. Get off with you!"

He shook the broom menacingly, but she stood firm. "If you'd just provide the information I seek about Commander Prescott, I wouldn't tarry. I swear."

"We have no information, and even if we did, we wouldn't share it with the likes of you."

"He's inherited his family's title, so he's Lord Benton now. Surely there must be someone in your establishment who can assist me."

"How many times will you make me say it? We have no information!"

She stared at him with her most beseeching expression. It had no effect, but she hadn't supposed it would.

"Get!" he seethed. "If you dawdle again, we'll call for the law. If you spend a few months in jail for trespassing, I'm betting you won't be quite so cocky."

He aimed the broom at her ankles, and he whacked her shin.

"Ouch!" she protested.

She leapt away, but her feet tangled in her skirt, and she tripped and fell, landing on her hip and elbow. Her bonnet flew off, and her reticule slid away. She huddled on the dirty bricks, feeling small and pathetic and very, very incensed.

Why was life so difficult? Why was she being pummeled by misfortune? She'd always been kind and compassionate. Her sole moral lapse had been her amour with Peyton Prescott, but she'd loved him! She'd believed he would marry her!

Of course she'd been completely deluded, but nevertheless, she'd proceeded with pure motives.

Tears welled into her eyes, and the man scoffed.

"Don't think tears will generate any sympathy. Be gone!"

He swung the broom as if he'd strike her, and suddenly, another man rushed up and jerked it away, furiously saying, "That's enough!"

"She's a whore, sir," the footman explained. "She bothers our customers."

"I'm not a whore," Jo mulishly stated, simply wishing she could vanish. "I don't care how virulently you accuse me. I'm not."

The man froze and glared down at her. There was a peculiar charge in the air, and she glanced up to discover what had caused it. When he saw her face, he gasped.

"Miss Bates?" Evan Boyle said. "Is it really you?"

"Yes, Mr. Boyle. It is I, Josephine Bates."

He reached down and lifted her to her feet, and he scooped up her bonnet and reticule and put them in her hand.

"My goodness," he murmured, "are you all right?"

"Yes, I'm fine. A tad rattled but fine."

"It's dark and cold. Why are you out and all alone in this part of town?"

"I'm anxious to contact Lord Benton. I have been for weeks, and I can't figure out how. I . . . I . . ." She couldn't finish her sentence, and she started to cry in earnest. Eventually, she caught her breath and forced out the words, "I've been having the worst time, Mr. Boyle."

"You look positively bedraggled." He turned to the footman. "This is Lord Benton's most devoted friend. How dare you treat her so shabbily!"

The footman blanched. "She claimed to be, but we didn't . . . that is she seemed to be . . . well . . ."

Mr. Boyle silenced him with a glower, then whispered quick commands that had the footman jumping to obey, and Jo never ceased to be amazed at how easily a man could exert influence.

Mr. Boyle ushered her into the lobby of the officer's club, and he hustled her down a quiet hall. They entered a small room that appeared to be an office. There was a desk and filing cabinets. A fire burned in the grate. The footman was hovering, and Mr. Boyle ordered hot tea for her, then shooed him out.

He guided Jo to a chair, and she was shivering. He frowned and clasped her hands.

"Gad, your skin is like ice."

There was a coat hanging on a hook by the door, and he draped it over her shoulders, then he scooted her next to the fire.

The footman bustled in with a tray and set it down. He hovered again, no doubt hoping to eavesdrop, and Mr. Boyle shoved him out, then poured her a cup of tea. There was a decanter of brandy on the desk, and he added a dollop to the tea, then he offered it to her.

She was so cold she could barely grab the cup. He had to wrap her fingers around it and hold them in place. After a bit, he asked, "Better?"

"Yes, much better."

He stepped back and pulled up a chair. "I haven't seen you in months."

"Not since July—at Benton House."

"You've suffered numerous calamities since then."

"You have no idea, Mr. Boyle."

He tsked with offense. "What did Peyton do to you? Let it all out, then we'll decide how I can fix it."

Jo didn't have to ponder whether or not she should unburden herself. From the moment Lord Benton had jilted her at the altar, she'd been dying to confide in someone, but she'd also been desperate for advice and assistance.

She had no resources and scant experience out in the larger world.

She felt as if she was dangling from a rope and was gradually losing her grip. Any second, she would plummet to the ground, and it was a very long fall. Where would she be when she hit bottom?

She began talking, and he was a good listener. If he interrupted at all, it was to clarify a detail. She told him every embarrassing fact, even confessing about the babe in her belly. It was why Lord Benton had agreed to wed her, and it was the root of all her problems.

It was her shame and disgrace too, but she'd tumbled so far down society's ladder that it was silly to conceal the worst aspect of her predicament.

"I have to contact Lord Benton," she said as her tale of woe wound to an end. "How would I?"

"I'll take care of all of this for you. Don't fret over it."

"What about my niece, Daisy? I'm so afraid for her."

"With valid reason. Richard Slater is a cretin, and his sister is a shrew. I'll deal with that issue too."

"I'm so glad I ran into you, Mr. Boyle."

"So am I. I merely wish you'd located me sooner."

"I didn't know how to find you."

He patted her hand. "Everything will be all right."

"How will it?"

"For starters, you're coming home with me."

"Are you certain that's wise?" Jo asked.

She thought of his sister, Amelia, and how Amelia had assumed for years that Lord Benton would marry her. Why would she welcome Jo? Then again, when she'd visited Jo, they'd realized they might have been friends if Lord Benton and her brother hadn't been quarreling. Would she still feel that way?

"It's the best notion ever," he said. "If I didn't help you, and my sister and mother learned I didn't, they'd never forgive me."

"I would hate to cause any trouble."

"You couldn't possibly." He stood. "Now let's get out of here. Let's get you home."

PEYTON WASN'T SURE WHY he had his driver pass by the Boyle residence. He was positive they wouldn't allow him in the door. But he was very dejected, and he was eager to chat with people who might commiserate.

He'd just spoken to his superiors and announced his retirement. He'd been brief and concise. He'd succinctly explained why he couldn't continue to serve. He'd been completely detached—as if they'd been discussing the weather. He hadn't waxed nostalgic. He hadn't broken down and cried like a baby over all that had been relinquished.

He was no longer a sailor. He was no longer a member of the Royal Navy, and he couldn't wrap his mind around the sudden change. If he wasn't Commander Peyton Prescott, who was he? Would he finally have to become a farmer? Would he withdraw to Benton to watch the crops grow?

The prospect was so depressing that he wondered if he might curl into a ball and cry like a baby after all.

After he'd left the meeting, he'd felt totally isolated from all other human beings. He might have been the last man on Earth. Evan was the only person in the kingdom who would recognize what Peyton's career had meant to him. Evan was the only person who would comprehend the depth of Peyton's anguish.

The coach rattled to a halt, and as the dust settled, he recollected how much he abhorred having to utilize a coach. It was the most powerful indication of how the accident had altered his life. He'd always been a man in a hurry. When he'd traveled from one spot to the next, he'd ridden a horse and galloped as fast as he could.

He liked speed and alacrity and excitement, and he'd scoffed at tedious gentlemen who lumbered on in their heavy, pretentious vehicles.

He would eventually be able to ride a horse, but for now, his doctor had insisted he not, and Peyton hadn't argued. The idea was simply too painful to consider. So . . . he was rolling across the country—like an aging spinster.

He peeked out, seeing that the Boyle siblings were definitely home. The curtains were pulled back, and smoke billowed from the chimney. It was a brisk, windy November day, and they had a fire burning inside.

Arthur yanked on the door and lowered the step, then he reached up so Peyton could grab his hand to maintain his balance if he felt inclined.

"Wait for me," Peyton said as he descended. "If I'll be awhile, I'll send a servant out to apprise you. I'll have you brought into the kitchen for tea."

Arthur grinned. "I'm happy to wait, Commander Prescott. It's not as if I'm busy."

Arthur was aware that Peyton had resigned his commission, and Peyton said, "You probably don't need to refer to me as *Commander*."

"You'll always be Commander Prescott to me. It's like having blue eyes. They can't take them away from you."

"I suppose, but with me retiring, it doesn't seem proper."

"Would you like me to call you Lord Benton instead? Didn't you claim your title sounded too fussy?"

"Cheeky devil," Peyton muttered.

He stomped off—as much as he could stomp anyway—and he went through the gate and started up the walk. As he approached the door, Evan emerged and shut it again with a determined click, curtly informing Peyton that he wouldn't be invited in.

Evan's expression was grim. "What are you doing here, Peyton?"

"I wanted to see you."

"Then you must be going deaf. I told you to never pester us."

"Yes, but I was in the neighborhood, and I took a chance that you'd be home. May I come in?"

"No, you may not."

Peyton blew out a frustrated breath. "Now just a damned minute!"

"You're not welcome here, Peyton."

"Will you be angry forever? Is that your plan?"

"I haven't begun to be angry with you."

"When did you develop such a penchant for melodrama?"

"It flourished after I realized how much I despise you, so please don't dawdle."

Evan glared at Peyton in a condemning way, and Peyton was bewildered by the level of his hostility. It made no sense.

Evan wasn't the sort of man to hold a grudge. He might lose his temper, but he quickly shucked off any upset. Apparently, it was too early for Peyton to have visited. He had to give Evan more of an opportunity to calm down.

He sighed with regret and followed after Evan who was headed to the coach and disdainfully studying the Benton crest on the side. He would grasp how odd it was for Peyton to be traveling in a carriage, and he thought Evan might offer a snide remark about it that would provide a basis to chat, but he didn't.

He spun to Peyton, and he noticed Peyton was limping.

"Are you injured?" Evan inquired. "I'd ask what happened, but I don't really care."

"I had an accident." He paused so Evan could comment, but he didn't, so Peyton added, "On my horse. The animal fell off a bridge, and I broke my leg. My recuperation has been ghastly."

Again, Peyton expected Evan might display some sympathy or curiosity, but he simply said, "Don't call on us in the future—even if you're in the neighborhood. You shouldn't use it as an excuse."

Arthur opened the door and waited for Peyton to climb in, but Peyton couldn't depart.

He was so sad! He was mourning numerous difficult issues: Jo, Daisy, his naval career, his health, his change of circumstance. Evan was the only man he'd ever been close to, and he was anxious to confess his troubles, but from how Evan was glowering, it was clear he wasn't concerned over what might be vexing Peyton.

"I resigned my commission today." Peyton mentioned it even though it was obvious Evan wasn't interested. "That's why I stopped by I guess. I yearned to tell somebody who would understand. I'm feeling a little . . . forlorn."

Evan peeked down at his bad leg. "Was it because of your injury?"

"My arm too." Peyton forced a smile. "I'm a bit of a mess physically."

"I'm sure you'll be fine," Evan coldly replied. "You being an *earl* and all, the universe wouldn't dare to lay you low."

It was an awful statement, and Peyton bristled. If he'd been more hale, he'd have beaten Evan to a pulp. "What is your problem, Evan? Why are you being such a prick?"

"I enjoy being a prick to you. Besides, you deserve it."

Peyton might have punched him anyway, might have started a brawl he couldn't finish, but the door to the house opened, and to his stunned amazement, Jo appeared. He had to blink three times to be certain he wasn't hallucinating.

She was beautiful as ever, willowy and ethereal, like a ghost or a fairy. But the bulge in her tummy reminded him he had responsibilities to her that he hadn't handled.

"Lord Benton," she said, "why are you here? You're supposed to be in the Caribbean."

"Jo!" he murmured, and he stepped toward her, but Evan slammed a palm into his chest.

"Leave her alone," Evan seethed.

"I have to speak to her! I've been searching everywhere. Why is she in your home? Why didn't you notify me?" He turned to Jo. "Where have you been? Why are you with Evan?"

Evan shifted to block his view so he couldn't see her. He and Peyton tussled, shoving and scrapping as Peyton tried to skirt around him, but Evan refused to let him by.

Evan called to Jo. "Go inside, Jo. I'll deal with this."

"Please don't quarrel." Her tone was beseeching. "I don't want you two fighting."

"We're not fighting," Evan lied.

Amelia walked up behind Jo, and she cast a contemptuous frown at Peyton, then she pulled Jo in and shut the door. A dangerous silence descended, and Peyton whirled on Evan.

"Talk fast, Evan, and don't slow down until I decide I've heard enough."

"We don't owe you any explanations."

Peyton grabbed Evan's shirt and yanked him close so they were nose to nose. "You don't think so? Tell me why she's here or I swear to God, I will beat the living shit out of you."

It was a threat he probably couldn't carry out, but he'd be delighted to attempt it. At the moment, there was naught he'd like more than to deliver a sound thrashing.

"I found her hungry and wandering the streets," Evan spat.

"What? That's not possible."

"I figured you'd pretend not to know anything about it."

"I'm not pretending. I don't know."

"A likely story." Evan scoffed with derision. "I brought her home so we could take care of her."

"Thank you. I'm grateful."

Peyton spun as if he'd march to the house, but Evan seized him by his coat and jerked him to a halt.

"You're not going in there," Evan said.

"I have to speak to her," he repeated as he shook off Evan's tight grip. "Then she's leaving with me. I appreciate you helping her, but *I* will take care of her from this point on."

"You?" Evan laughed. "If you imagine she'd risk trusting you again, you're deluded."

"Your opinion has been noted, but I suggest you bugger off."

He tried to push by Evan again, but Evan wouldn't release his coat.

"Jo has no desire to meet with you," Evan claimed.

"She can tell me herself."

"It doesn't matter what she wants."

"If that's what you believe, then you don't know her very well. She can make her own decisions. She doesn't need an ass like you to make them for her."

"Maybe not in the past, but I have every right to command her now."

Peyton scowled. "What do you mean?"

"I *mean* that Jo and I are married."

"What?"

"She's my wife, so I have the authority to determine who talks to her and who doesn't, and I have determined that *you* will never talk to her."

Peyton felt as if the Earth had tipped off its axis, and he collapsed against the side of the carriage. He had to slap a palm onto the vehicle to steady himself.

"You married her?" he hissed. "Why? Why would you?"

"As if you can't guess, you prick."

"Tell me! Why would she agree?"

"She's in the family way!" Evan shouted the accusation. "She desperately needed a husband, and I was willing to volunteer."

"It should have been me! *I* should have been her husband. I proposed to her. I vowed to support and protect her forever."

"You! All you ever did was jilt her at the altar like the cad you are!"

"I didn't intend to jilt her. I didn't! I was hurt!"

"It's too late for you to rationalize your conduct. I wouldn't listen anyway."

"But . . . but . . . I love her!" Peyton declared. "I always have. And she loves me. She wouldn't have forsaken me like this."

"Really? If that's how you picture your relationship with her, then I can only assume your accident has left you deranged."

"She can't want this ending for herself. *I* don't want it. She's having my child!"

"No, she's my wife, so she's having *my* child." Evan tsked with disgust. "If you'd like to make yourself useful, you can find her niece for us."

"Who? Daisy? Why isn't she with Jo? Where is she? What happened to her?"

"Well, that's the thousand pound question, isn't it? You seem to be in the dark about many issues."

"I absolutely am."

"After you jilted my bride," Evan fumed, "Barbara and her brother barged into Jo's house. They evicted her on the spot."

"They did not," Peyton insisted. "Jo departed of her own accord. I visited the landlord. She wrote to him that she was vacating the premises."

Evan snorted with disdain. "You are such an idiot. She didn't blithely traipse off. She was tossed out on the street, and Richard attached a chain to the door so she couldn't sneak back in."

"You're not serious."

"Oh, but I am. Before they threw her out, they kidnapped Daisy, and they wouldn't reveal where they'd taken her." Evan stepped in. "If you'd like to redeem yourself in Josephine's eyes, *Lord* Benton, you can start by searching for her niece. She and I would like to have her returned to us."

"I will locate her, and please inform Jo that I'll begin looking for Daisy immediately."

"Don't refer to my bride by her Christian name," Evan said. "I don't wish to recall that you were once on familiar terms with her. If I ever have the misfortune to bump into you again, I will expect you to address her as Mrs. Boyle. Now go away and don't come back."

Evan marched off, his demeanor very regal, and Peyton watched, stunned and livid, as he went into the house and shut the door. The key spun in the lock. He continued to watch, hoping Jo might emerge or at least glance out the window.

For a fleeting instant, he considered rushing to the door, kicking it in, and forcing his way inside. But why would he? She was married. She was *Mrs. Evan Boyle.* There could be no changing that fact. Why would Peyton want to talk to her? What was the point?

Since the day he realized she'd vanished, he'd incessantly wondered why she hadn't sought him out. Hadn't she been worried about him? Hadn't she been frantic to discover why he'd missed the wedding?

Obviously, she hadn't cared enough to ponder or investigate. So . . . to hell with her. She could have Evan and good riddance!

If there was a tiny voice in his mind, clanging with the distressing awareness that he'd never see her again, that he wouldn't have the chance to be her husband, to rear their child, he didn't have to listen to it. She'd made her choice, and she'd chosen Evan.

Why be crushed? Why be devastated? Strident emotion was for fools.

"Let's get you in the coach, Commander," Arthur gently said as if Peyton was a decrepit imbecile. "There's no reason to linger, is there?"

Peyton stared at the house where he'd spent so many joyous hours as a boy. The happy family belonged to Jo now, and he would never be part of it again. He couldn't bear to reflect on all that had been lost: his career, his niece, his child, his best friends, and his beloved Jo Bates. She was Jo Boyle now, and he had to remember she was.

She would never be his.

A bubble of rage ignited deep in his breast, and it swiftly grew into a frightening inferno. He was eager to lash out, to make every person in the kingdom pay for what had been taken from him. He wouldn't stop until he'd extracted every ounce of available vengeance.

He'd start with Barbara and Richard. Why not? He'd ignored them and put up with them. He'd tried to be patient and understand their situation. Why had he? Look where his compassion had left him!

"You're correct, Arthur. There's no reason to linger."

Arthur stepped away, letting Peyton climb into the carriage on his own. As he settled himself on the seat, Arthur peeked in and asked, "Where to, Commander?"

"First, I have to travel to London. I have to hire a team of men who are willing to perform a difficult task. Are you acquainted with anyone who might like a few weeks of temporary work?"

"I have a ton of friends who are veterans like me. They need jobs, and any job will suffice."

"Are they tough and reliable?"

"Definitely."

"We'll round them up and head to Benton."

"What will we do when we arrive?"

"We have some relatives to evict."

Arthur raised a brow. "Are you sure you should?"

"Yes." Peyton pulled the door closed. "Tell the driver our destination and that I'd like to hurry. This episode won't be pleasant, and I'd like to finish it as quickly as possible."

CHAPTER
24

"He's gone."

Evan nodded to Jo, and she shuddered with relief.

"I'm surprised he didn't force his way inside," Amelia said.

"I was sure he would," Jo concurred.

"He suffered some sort of accident," Evan told them. "He wasn't sufficiently hale to engage in a quarrel."

At the news, Jo looked stricken. "What sort of accident?"

"I guess he broke his leg."

"Even though I'm furious with him, I hate to hear he was injured."

"He's not completely healed, so it was easy to push him around. Normally, he's not so obedient."

The two women were lurking in the corner, peeking out the window to watch as Peyton's carriage rolled away. The entire incident had been distressing, and Jo seemed to deflate. She staggered over to the sofa and plopped down.

"I feel awful," she said.

"Don't let him upset you," Amelia firmly insisted. "He's distressed you enough."

"He's the father of my child, and there's no ignoring that fact. I can't bicker with him."

"He deserves some bickering," Amelia fumed, "and a sound thrashing too. What do you suppose, Evan? Might you be interested in delivering one?"

"I'll wait until his condition improves. I'd want it to be a fair fight."

Jo tsked with exasperation. "I won't have you fighting. Not over me. We have to deal with him in a civil fashion, so he'll support my child."

"I can support your child," Evan reminded her. "You don't need him."

"I haven't agreed to wed you. You haven't convinced me it's a good idea."

Evan steadied his expression, determined Jo never discover the horrendous lie he'd spewed at Peyton. He'd declared that he and Jo were married, but it wasn't true. Evan had proposed, but for the moment, she'd declined, claiming she had to ponder for a bit.

He shouldn't have tricked his old friend, but he understood Peyton all too well. Peyton would never blithely permit Jo to slip through his fingers. It wasn't so much that he was fond of her, but he didn't like to lose and he was very vain. He always had to get his way.

Jo was anxious to move on with her life, and by deceiving Peyton, Evan had helped her accomplish her goal.

People would probably be astonished to learn that he'd proposed, but it wasn't such a wild notion. He'd been contemplating matrimony for years, but he hadn't met a female who was worth the bother.

Jo was worth it. His sister and mother adored her, and why wouldn't they? She was beautiful and sweet, educated and loyal. She was all a fellow sought in a bride. No, she didn't have a dowry, but she brought every other positive attribute to the table.

What sane man wouldn't pick her?

"I will convince you to marry me though—eventually." Evan glanced at her tummy. "It's not as if you can traipse around much longer without a husband."

"Yes, but you've already been much too kind to me. You don't have to sacrifice yourself."

He scoffed. "I've informed you over and over, Jo. It will hardly be a sacrifice."

"I'm having another man's child, Evan. I don't believe you've considered all the ramifications."

"It's not as if the child will be a stranger to us," Evan insisted. "Peyton practically grew up in this house."

"I don't deem that a compelling basis for you to wed me. It only makes the match sound more peculiar."

Evan turned to his sister. "Tell her it will be all right. Would you please?"

"I have told her, but she's dubious."

"With valid reason!" Jo added.

"You should remember, Jo," Amelia said, "that Evan is as vain and driven as Peyton. He never does anything he doesn't want to do. If he didn't *want* you to be his wife, he wouldn't have asked you."

Jo scowled. "I wish all of us had more time to reflect on our choices."

"Well, Evan has all the time in the world, but you don't have that luxury. You have to focus on how fast the clock is ticking."

"I've thought of naught else for months," Jo admitted, "and it's wrong to rope your brother into a quandary he didn't create and shouldn't have to fix."

"Don't worry about him," Amelia said. "He's a master at fixing quandaries."

"Yes, but maybe *I* should have to fix this on my own."

"How would you?"

"I could buy a cheap wedding ring and move to a village in the country. I could pretend to be a widow."

"I'm sure no female has ever used that ridiculous story before. How would you support yourself?"

"Lord Benton would support me."

Evan and Amelia laughed, and Evan said, "You can't rely on him. If you could, wouldn't you be his bride about now?"

"You're correct of course." Jo sighed. "This entire episode has exhausted me."

"I'm sorry," Evan murmured.

"It's not your fault. It's Lord Benton's fault."

"It certainly is."

"I need to rest for a bit."

Jo headed off, and they were frozen in place until her door closed.

Then Amelia whispered, "How did you force him to depart? What did you really say?"

"I told a little white lie." Evan paused, then shrugged. "Actually, it wasn't little *or* white. It was quite a whale of a falsehood."

"What was it?" his sister asked.

"I told him Jo and I are married."

"Evan! You didn't!"

"I couldn't figure out how else to persuade him to leave her alone. I claimed she was my wife, and I didn't want him talking to her."

"He believed you?"

"Yes."

"What if she never weds you, Evan? What if he finds out you deceived him?"

"I don't care if he finds out. He's not entitled to any honorable conduct with regard to her. He's behaved despicably."

"I know, but what if *she* discovers you tricked him? I like her so much, and I'm glad we're friends. I can't envision a better conclusion than to have her as my sister-in-law."

"I'm delighted to hear it."

"But this is a terrible secret to keep from her."

"Do you think she loved him?"

"Probably."

"Do you think she still does?"

"I can't guess, and I haven't asked her."

"Whatever her opinion," he said, "she was yanked to her senses quickly enough when he failed to attend his own wedding. Can you imagine how she must have felt?"

"No, I can't. What happened that day? Why would he treat her so shabbily?"

"It doesn't matter, but we've had a whole lifetime to learn what he's like. She had to learn in an instant. She can never trust him."

"I suppose," she grumbled.

"And *I* will wear her down. I want her to marry me. It's the perfect ending for both of us."

"Yes, it is, dear brother, and don't forget that you relish the chance to play the part of knight in shining armor."

"I admit it. I have a soft spot for damsels in distress, and Peyton's not the only one who always gets his way."

"No, he's not."

"She'll ultimately agree to have me," he predicted. "After all, it's not as if she can refuse to make up her mind. I was betting it will occur by Saturday."

"Why Saturday?"

"We've invited all the neighbors to supper, and it will be a festive occasion. Why not announce an engagement while we're merry and celebrating?"

"Why not indeed?"

"WHAT IS IT?" BARBARA demanded.

She was in her boudoir, and she whipped around to glare at her maid. The woman had run in as if the house was on fire.

"Lord Benton has arrived."

"Thank you for apprising me. Inform him that I'll be down shortly."

"You should come now, my lady."

"Why?"

"He has a dozen ruffians with him, and when I was eavesdropping, he ordered them to begin packing Master Richard's things first."

Barbara scowled. "Packing what *things*? His belongings?"

"Yes. Lord Benton sent them to his bedchamber, then he asked Mr. Newman for the names of all the servants who traveled to Benton with you from your father's property."

"Why would he have to know that?"

"He told Mr. Newman that we'll all be leaving with you."

"Leaving? The man's insane. I'm not going anywhere. Neither are any of you."

"Lord Benton said we're all going *now*—this morning."

"Help me finish with my clothes."

Barbara was alarmed and furious. Wasn't it enough that they'd nursed him back to health after he'd nearly killed himself? Wasn't it enough that they'd worked themselves to the bone for him—when none of them could abide him?

She dashed into her dressing room and grabbed her simplest gown. Her maid assisted with laces, buttons, and shoes, and in a quick minute, she was racing down the stairs.

The scene in the foyer was chaotic. Men were scurrying about, carrying in crates and trunks. They appeared tough and dangerous, like pugilists who fought in the boxing ring. The front door was open, and out in the drive, there were numerous wagons, the field horses hitched and ready to haul away heavy loads.

Peyton was standing in the middle of the mayhem, barking commands, giving directions, and acting very much like the pompous aristocrat he'd become upon his brother's death.

She hurried over and forced a calm expression onto her face, even though she was livid.

"Peyton, what's happening? You're creating an enormous amount of turmoil. Must you stir such a commotion?"

"Hello, Barbara," was his only comment.

"How about if we step into the library? Let's find a more private spot where we can talk."

"We don't need to talk."

He glowered at her so coldly that she staggered back. If he'd struck her, she wouldn't have been surprised. He looked that angry.

Her brother rushed up, and he gaped at the stacks of trunks and boxes.

"Peyton!" Richard snapped. "I heard you were blustering around like a mad hornet. What the devil are you about?"

Peyton didn't respond to Richard. Instead, he turned to the man next to him and said, "This is Mr. Slater. Escort him down to the wagons and be certain he stays there. He won't be allowed inside my house again."

"But . . . but . . . you can't be serious," Richard stammered.

Peyton still hadn't addressed him, and the man seized Richard and started out. Richard glanced at her over his shoulder, imploring, "Barbara! Stop this lunacy!"

"Peyton, please!" she tried.

"I won't go!" Richard insisted. "You can't make me!"

He was yanked through the door at a brisk pace, and though he attempted to wrestle away, the man simply tightened his grip. Richard continued to complain though, calling to Barbara, but his words rapidly faded.

Peyton gestured into the parlor. "Now we can chat."

"Yes, of course we should. Clearly, you're distraught, but I can't imagine why. What have we done? I wish—just once—you would behave like a rational human being."

He didn't reply, and she kicked herself for hurling an insult. Why would she? He'd merely grow more incensed.

They entered the parlor, and without preamble, he asked, "Where is Daisy?"

She hadn't expected the question, and she blanched before she could conceal her reaction.

"Daisy Prescott?" she innocently inquired. "Is that who you mean?"

"Yes, that's precisely who I mean."

"Why would I know where she is?"

"Are you sure that should be your answer?"

A perilous silence stretched out, and he waited, then waited some more for her to expound. How had he learned about the blasted girl? And so swiftly too! Was he a sorcerer? Would Barbara ever succeed in thwarting him? Her mind was racing to devise a suitable lie, but in the end, she figured it was best to deny and deny and deny.

"I haven't a clue where she is," Barbara firmly stated. She'd go to her grave pretending she didn't know.

"I will give you one chance to confess your treachery toward Josephine Bates. Depending on your candor, I will then decide how much compassion to show you."

He had the most aggravating knack for making her feel small and irrelevant, and she frowned, feigning confusion. "Josephine Bates? Why would you ask me about her?"

"One chance, Barbara. That's it. You were married to my brother, and I realize your life with him was horrid. I'm sorry for what you endured, so I'll let you tell me the truth. If you do, I will rein in my temper, and I won't punish you quite so severely."

A thousand possible avenues flitted in her head at lightning speed. What was safest? What was the most believable? Or should she admit her perfidy and beg for mercy? He'd never seemed very merciful though, so it probably wasn't a good plan.

"I have no information about Miss Bates or Neville's bastard daughter."

"Fine. Have it your way."

A young man poked his nose in. "May I interrupt, Commander Prescott?"

"Yes, Arthur. What is it?"

"I found out where they sent your niece."

"Marvelous."

Peyton waved him in, and Arthur slapped a document into his hand.

After perusing it, Peyton asked Arthur, "Where did you find this?"

"In the estate agent's office, in Mr. Slater's desk."

"Excellent work," Peyton said to him. "Now that I've discovered Daisy's whereabouts, I don't need to confer with my sister-in-law. Her brother is outside with the wagons. Escort her there too."

Arthur glared at her. "If you'll come with me, my lady?"

"I most certainly will not."

"Get her out of here," Peyton seethed, "before I grow angry."

Arthur stomped over and grabbed her arm, and he marched her out—just as Richard had been marched out. Arthur was a lean, thin fellow, and Barbara struggled with him, but she couldn't wrench free.

As they reached the door, she peered back at Peyton. "Can we discuss this?"

"No, and if Daisy has been harmed, there will be a price you'll have to pay."

"It was all Richard's idea."

"Really?"

"I warned him not to move against Miss Bates, but he's always been too loyal to me. He wouldn't listen."

"I've already unraveled what happened, Barbara. You were both there at her house. You both participated. You can't deflect the blame."

"When you were injured, we managed the finances for you, and we didn't understand the expenditure for the rent on that house. You'd ordered us to cut down on our spending, and we went to check. That's all. We were . . . were . . . trying to be fiscally responsible!"

"Shut up, Barbara. With every word you utter, you dig a deeper hole."

"Peyton!" She actually stamped her foot—like a toddler having a tantrum.

He shifted his gaze to Arthur. "Get her out to the wagons, then round up the Slater servants and get them out too. I won't give them a final opportunity to steal or break anything."

Alice took that moment to run in. Her sister, Nancy, was hot on her heels.

"Mother," Alice frantically asked, "what is it? What's wrong?"

"Your uncle is evicting us," Barbara furiously spat.

"Not all of you," Peyton said. "Alice, Nancy, come here." Alice complied, but Nancy dithered next to Barbara, and Peyton snapped, "Nancy! Come!"

He was very authoritative, and when he hurled a command, it was difficult to defy him. Nancy walked over and stood with Alice. Barbara gaped at the three of them, instantly recognizing that they'd formed a trio that didn't include her.

She'd never been an overly maternal person, but they belonged with her.

"You can't keep them!" Barbara raged. "I won't allow it. I'm their mother."

"And I'm their guardian," Peyton retorted, "so your opinion is irrelevant."

"You can't keep them," she repeated.

"It's not up to you, and they can't live with you. I don't believe they'd be safe."

"Not safe?" she huffed. "You're being ridiculous."

"I witnessed your capacity for malice in how you treated Daisy and Miss Bates. I can't risk that your temper might flare and you'd imperil your daughters."

"That's absurd!" Barbara fumed. "I would never imperil them."

"Well, this way," Peyton said, "I can guarantee that you never have the chance."

"Is Miss Bates Daisy's aunt?" Alice asked him. "Mother hates her. I heard her and Uncle Richard talking."

"I know your mother hates her," Peyton said.

"Is Daisy all right?"

"I *don't* know that, Alice, but I intend to find out." He focused on Barbara again. "Have you ever wondered what became of Miss Bates? Has her condition ever crossed your mind?"

"I did nothing to her! I told you it was Richard's scheming."

"Ever since my brother died, I've been confused as to why he put me in charge of Nancy and Alice. Your recent escapade has proved what you're really like, so it's all clear to me now. I won't leave my wards with you. I'd be too afraid you might harm them, and I wouldn't be present to stop you."

"I'm their *mother*," she stated again, as if he hadn't noticed the relationship.

"I'd like to stay with her," Nancy dared to say, but Alice mumbled, "I wouldn't."

Their uncle shook his head at Nancy. "I can't let you depart with her today. For the time being, you'll have to remain here with me. We'll check on her in a few weeks to assess her circumstances, then we'll discuss it."

"Where am I to go?" Barbara demanded. "Tell me that—if you can!"

"I don't care where you wind up, Barbara, so long as you are removed from my sight immediately." He nodded to the fiend, Arthur. "Get her out of my home."

Barbara was dragged away, but she managed a fleeting glimpse at her daughters. Nancy looked stunned, but Alice looked quite pleased.

"Alice! Nancy!" she called. "Come with me! Come at once!"

Then she was whisked into the foyer, and as their uncle rested a steadying hand on their shoulders, neither of them took a step to obey.

"You're a big fat liar."

"I am not."

Daisy sat on the floor in the common room at the workhouse. She stared at the girls surrounding her. There were some who were friendly, but they were grossly outnumbered by those who were older and tougher.

Most of them had grown up in the terrible facility, and it had made them cruel. They fought for every little scrap, acting like wild dogs with no trainer to teach them how to behave.

Daisy had learned to keep her head down and her mouth shut. It was dangerous to draw attention to herself. She was different from all of them. She'd been reared at Benton, had been schooled by Miss Watson and her other governesses. She was pretty and smart and educated, and they resented her for it.

She'd arrived with a bag of clothes, but every item she'd brought had been stolen. When she saw other girls strutting about in her dresses, her complaints had simply invited derision and punches.

Her arms and legs were covered with bruises and bite marks. She'd been hit and kicked and pinched, with the nastier bullies eager to ensure she knew her place. But she would never bow down to them.

"I *am* Lord Benton's daughter," she seethed, glaring at the most malevolent of the pack. "It doesn't matter what you say. It's true."

"Ooh-la-la, your ladyship. Aren't you special?"

"I was raised at Benton. I had my own cottage, with my siblings, Bobby and Jane. My father's other daughter, Alice, was my secret twin sister."

"You're so full of yourself, Daisy. You're not the daughter of some fancy lord. I'll bet you're a by-blow he sired at a brothel. If you're better than us, how'd you end up here?"

"My father died, and there was no one to protect me."

"Well, who hasn't had that happen? At least all of our parents were married. *We* are orphans. You're a bastard. It puts all of us above you—despite what you think."

Daisy was eating her noon meal, a bowl of oats and a slice of bread. They were fed twice a day, and she wouldn't eat again until they staggered off to bed.

One of her tormenters knocked the bowl away, splashing the oats on the floor. Then she stomped across it, grinding the gruel into the wooden slats to guarantee Daisy wouldn't bend down and lick at the remnants. To her great shame, she'd considered doing just that. She was that hungry, but she wouldn't give them the satisfaction of watching her grovel.

She closed her eyes and remembered her home at Benton. She pictured the dining table, and she was completing her school lessons with Bobby and Jane. Those had been the best times, before her father had passed away, before Mr. Slater had evicted them.

She wondered where her Aunt Jo might be. That last afternoon, when the Countess and Mr. Slater had sent Daisy away, Jo had been approaching on the sidewalk. Daisy had had a moment to frantically wave, to notify her that the Countess was waiting to accost her, but she doubted her warning had helped.

A woman as kind and nice as Jo could never win against such awful people.

Daisy would be kept at the workhouse until she was twelve—three more years!—then she'd have to leave and make her own way in the world. She couldn't guess how she would. She often fantasized about escaping, and she'd imagine herself rushing back to their house to be with Jo so she'd be safe again.

But it was a child's dream. Mr. Slater had told her they were sending Jo away too, so even if Daisy could locate their prior residence, Jo wouldn't be there. Where would Jo go instead? Daisy had no idea.

She fantasized too about traveling to Cornwall, finding her half-siblings and Miss Watson. They'd welcome her, but it was another child's dream. How would she get to Cornwall? She might as well plan a journey to the moon.

She thought she could find Benton though. It wasn't that far from London, and she could live in the woods. Alice would sneak her food and blankets, and she'd hide Daisy from Mr. Slater. Alice might know how to contact her Uncle Peyton too.

After he'd jilted her Aunt Jo, Daisy wasn't positive he'd offer any assistance, but she couldn't stop hoping that he might be worried about her. She couldn't believe he would approve of Mr. Slater's conduct.

The bell clanged to announce that their meal was over. Daisy pushed herself to her feet, as did all the other girls. She was still holding her slice of bread, and one of the worst bullies snatched it away.

Daisy was so angry she might have lunged to retrieve it, but the matron entered and barked at them to stand in line as was required. Tears flooded Daisy's eyes, and she swiped at them.

"Cry baby," the girl behind her muttered.

"You'll be sorry someday." Daisy was so furious she couldn't tamp down the words. "My Uncle Peyton will show up and take me away. I'll tell him how mean you've been."

"Who's your Uncle Peyton? Another fancy lord?"

The girl pinched Daisy very hard, and she squirmed and groaned in pain. All the others snickered, and the matron snapped, "Silence!"

They marched into the workroom and sat at long tables. They were stuffing mattresses with straw, and Daisy actually had a more important job. Jo had taught her to sew, so she had a skill, and she'd been assigned to stitch the fabric closed at the end. It was a cleaner task than what was allocated to the others, and they loathed her for it. She was new and should have had to wrestle with the straw which left cuts and welts on the skin.

She picked up her needle and began to sew. The hours dragged by, and occasionally, her speed would lag. The matron tracked all of them, and she'd notice immediately. She'd clomp over and pull Daisy's hair or pinch her again so she'd move at a faster pace.

Initially, she didn't realize anything had changed. Whispers and elbow nudges furtively skittered around the table.

When Daisy finally glanced up, she froze in her seat. Her Uncle Peyton seemed to be on the other side of the room, but she was certain she had to be hallucinating.

He looked very dashing: blue frock coat, tan trousers, knee-high black boots that had been polished to a shine. His cravat was the finest Belgian lace, and it was perfectly tied in a complex knot.

Alice seemed to be with him. She, too, looked very grand, attired as she was in a red wool cloak, a matching bonnet with a jaunty feather.

"There she is, Uncle Peyton!" Alice gestured to Daisy.

The other girls watched, stunned and agape, as her uncle and Alice rushed toward her. Alice reached Daisy first and flew into her so hard that Daisy was surprised they didn't fall over.

"Where have you been?" Alice asked. "I've been so worried!"

Then her uncle was there too, and he scooped her into his arms and hugged her so tightly she couldn't breathe.

"You scamp!" His affection was very clear. "We have been searching everywhere for you."

"We didn't know you were missing," Alice told her. "We thought you were with your Aunt Jo."

"I'm so sorry, Daisy," her uncle admitted. "I would have come sooner, but I had an accident, and while I was recuperating, I had no idea you were in trouble."

"It's all right," Daisy murmured. "You're here now."

"My mother and my Uncle Richard did this to you," Alice said, "but Uncle Peyton made them pay for being so awful."

"How?"

"He kicked them out of Benton, so we don't have to see their terrible faces ever again."

"Where is Aunt Jo?" Daisy inquired. "Is she with you?"

Her uncle frowned. "No, she's not with us, but let's go. We should hurry out of here or they might lock the door and refuse to allow any of us to depart."

"Where are we going?" Daisy asked him.

"To Benton."

"Can I live in my cottage again? Can I have Bobby, Jane, and Miss Watson live there with me?"

"We'll talk about that," her uncle said, "but for now, you'll live in the manor with Alice and me."

Daisy was astonished. "In the manor?"

"Yes," Alice confirmed. "You'll be with both of us. Nancy will be there too, but we don't have to be friends with her—unless you want to."

"Let's go," her uncle repeated.

"I can just . . . leave?" Daisy couldn't believe it.

"Yes. There's no one to stop us."

Daisy studied the ringleader who'd instituted so much of the torture she'd endured. "Uncle Peyton, would you tell all of them who you are—and who *I* am? I've tried to explain it, but they call me a liar."

She peered up at him, her gaze beseeching, and in an instant, he understood all that she'd suffered. He didn't disappoint her. He pulled himself up to his full height, his haughty expression settling on each girl in turn.

"I am Commander Peyton Prescott, a ship's captain in the Royal Navy who has sailed the globe over and over. I am also Earl of Benton, and I am Daisy's uncle. Her father was my brother, Neville. He was Lord Benton before me."

Alice added, "She and I have the same father, so she is *my* sister."

Her uncle stared down at Daisy. "Is there anything else you'd like them to know?"

"I think that's plenty."

Daisy cast a contemptuous smirk down the table, then she slipped her hand into her uncle's. Alice clasped hold of the other, and the three of them walked out together.

CHAPTER

25

"DID YOU LOVE PEYTON?"

Jo scowled at Amelia. "Did I *love* Peyton? Yes, I suppose I did."

"How much would you guess? Madly? Passionately? You couldn't live without him?"

"If I admit any of that, you'll decide I'm the biggest fool ever."

"Tell me though," Amelia pressed. "I want to understand the depth of your affection."

"Why? Are you a glutton for punishment? Don't make me confide sentiment that will hurt your feelings. I haven't forgotten your history with him. I butted in and wrecked your future."

"You didn't wreck anything. Peyton was never going to wed me, but I was too stupid to realize it. Your arrival simply forced him—and me—to recognize that fact."

"Yes, but you assumed you'd be his bride, and I prevented that from occurring."

"No, you didn't. He was like a second brother to me. If you asked me the same question I just asked you—did I love him—I'd laugh."

"Must we discuss him?"

"Yes. I insist on hearing your opinion. Were you in love with him? For I'm certain he was in love with you."

"You really believe that?"

"Yes. That night at Benton House, I saw how he looked at you. He definitely never looked at *me* that way."

They were huddled in a corner at the Boyle's home, having a quiet conversation away from their guests.

The residence was filled with people, and a very fine party was in progress. A supper buffet was laid out in the dining room. The furniture and rugs had been removed from the front parlor, and dancing was about to start. A trio of musicians was tuning their instruments and about to strike the chords to announce the first set.

It was such a happy scene, and Jo was joyful at being included. The Boyle siblings and their mother, Lydia, were kind and generous. They'd opened their hearts to her, and she could never repay them.

They were liked and respected by all, and Jo was lucky they'd taken her under their wing. If they hadn't, she shuddered to imagine what might have happened.

"All right, Amelia, I confess. I was madly in love with Peyton Prescott. I was completely and ridiculously bowled over by him. Is that sufficient information to satisfy your curiosity?"

"Would you say he felt the same about you?"

"If you'd pestered me about it before my wedding, I'd have said *yes*, but after he jilted me, I had to accept that I might have been a tad confused about the state of his attachment."

"Aren't you interested in how he's kept himself busy the past few months? Last summer, that navy official told you he'd sailed to the Caribbean, but obviously, he hadn't. And he broke his leg in that accident."

"I hate to think of him being injured. He's always seemed so dashing and fit to me. He can't like being incapacitated."

"No, he wouldn't like that at all." Amelia peeked down at Jo's stomach.

"What if you have a boy? Have you considered that?"

"What do you mean?"

"If you marry Evan, and you have a girl, it probably won't matter very much, but if it's a son, he should grow up to be the next Earl of Benton."

Jo wrinkled her nose. "Let's not talk about that. I have enough on my plate without worrying about the succession of the Benton heir."

Amelia chuckled. "But have you thought about it?"

"Yes, I've thought about everything."

Evan was across the room, chatting with some friends. He was such a wonderful man, and Jo was stunned by how he'd leapt to rescue her. He'd offered to wed her, to save her from scandal and disgrace. His actions went far beyond what was required or expected, and she was so grateful to him, but she felt terribly guilty too.

It wasn't fair for her to have dumped all her troubles on his sturdy shoulders. Could she rope him into marriage? Could she be that selfish? Yet if she didn't proceed, what was her plan?

She tried to never ponder Lord Benton—what was the point?—but a vision of him flashed in her mind. She remembered him in the driveway when he'd stopped by a few days earlier.

For a fleeting moment, she'd assumed he'd arrived specifically to find her. Clearly, he hadn't realized she was present, but after he'd seen her, she'd been positive he'd storm in to fetch her away, and she was crushed that he'd cared so little.

He and Evan had exchanged insults, and they'd been so awful that Evan wouldn't repeat them. What had Lord Benton said about her? Had he laughed at her condition? Had he called her a doxy with loose morals? Had he blamed her for being gullible and easy?

She'd loved him so desperately. He'd been her life and her world. Since he'd vanished, she'd been grieving and imperiled and anxious to make sense of what had transpired.

But he hadn't been concerned in the slightest. He hadn't been searching, hadn't been frantic, and when he'd finally bumped into her, when he'd discovered she was staying with Evan and Amelia, he hadn't bothered to come inside. He'd been that disinterested.

Why hadn't he pushed his way into the house and demanded they speak? Were there no questions he needed to have answered? Apparently not, and his lack of regard was a wound she would always carry deep in her heart.

"What is your opinion of my brother?" Amelia asked.

"He's marvelous, and I'm lucky he wants me."

"What about you though? Do you want him?"

Jo allowed one last vision of Lord Benton to settle in. She allowed herself to recollect how she'd worshipped him, how urgently she'd yearned to have him for her own. Then she recollected how—when he'd stumbled on her at Evan's home—he hadn't come inside.

She was several months down the road toward having a baby. How long would she continue to dither?

Evan Boyle was willing to provide a refuge from scandal and shame. Would she refuse that protection? Who wouldn't want Evan as a husband, Amelia as a sister, Lydia as the mother Jo had never had? Who wouldn't want that?

"I would like to wed your brother, Amelia." She smiled even though she was a bit queasy and unnerved. "I'd like it very much."

Amelia smiled too. "Are you sure?"

"Yes, I'm very sure."

"Could you ever picture yourself falling in love with him?"

Could she? Jo figured it would develop in time. They were friends. They were compatible. They enjoyed and respected one another. What couple needed more than that? After all, the hot, searing sort of attraction she'd shared with Lord Benton only left a person singed to ashes when it burned out.

"I'm certain I'll grow to love him," Jo cautiously stated.

"And Peyton? Are you truly over him?"

Jo managed to spit out the huge lie. "Yes, I'm over him."

Amelia was dubious, but in the end, she accepted Jo's assertion. "You'll never regret being Evan's wife."

"I'm positive I won't."

"Shall we go over and tell him your decision?" Amelia asked. "Or would you like to tell him when the two of you are alone?"

"You'll be my sister," Jo said. "Let's tell him together."

AMELIA EXITED HER CARRIAGE and climbed the steps at Benton Manor. She was probably on a fool's errand and was butting in where she didn't belong, but she'd proceed anyway.

When she reached the door, no one whipped it open to greet her which was odd for such a grand residence. She waited a suitable interval, knocked, then peeked into the empty foyer. The house was particularly quiet, as if all the servants had been sucked off into the sky.

She tiptoed in, and before too much time had passed, a young man came down the hall. He wasn't wearing Benton livery, and he didn't appear to be a servant.

"Oh, hello." He seemed astonished to see her. "I didn't realize we had a visitor."

"Where is everyone? The place is absolutely deserted."

"We had an upheaval recently. Most of the servants departed."

"It must have been quite an upheaval."

"It was," he agreed, but he supplied no further information.

"I'm Miss Amelia Boyle. I'm an old friend of Lord Benton's."

"It's a pleasure to meet you, Miss Boyle. I am Arthur Cummings. I am his . . . ah . . . well, I guess I'm his clerk?"

"You don't know?"

"I carry out any task he requires."

"Then we'll say you're his clerk. By any chance, is he at home?"

"He is. Have a seat in the parlor, and I'll fetch him." He frowned. "I don't have a footman to deliver any refreshments."

"I don't need any."

"It may take me many minutes to locate him."

"Don't worry about me, Mr. Cummings. I can entertain myself."

She shooed him out, then went into the parlor and sat on a sofa.

Previously, she'd never been to Benton. She hadn't been acquainted with Neville Prescott, and after Peyton had inherited, there hadn't been an opportunity to be invited. She studied every detail, so she could reflect later on.

An eternity dragged by, and finally, she heard him marching down the hall. She stood and braced herself. She hadn't seen him since his birthday party. What would his opinion be of her showing up unannounced? More importantly, would he be able to explain his actions toward Jo? Amelia was dying to find out.

She didn't believe people ever truly changed. They didn't suddenly become cold and unfeeling. He could be oblivious and detached, but he was never deliberately cruel, so what had produced his dreadful behavior? She had to unravel the mystery, and she hoped he wouldn't disappoint her.

"Amelia!" He entered the room, and he was grinning. "This is such a surprise."

"Hello, Peyton."

He walked over and clasped her hands, and he actually leaned down and kissed her on the cheek. In all the years she'd known him, he'd never done such an intimate thing.

"Will you sit?" he asked.

"No, thank you."

"I'd offer you refreshments, but I'm not sure I could track down a servant to order them."

"Your man, Mr. Cummings, mentioned that you'd suffered a disruption. May I inquire as to what happened? Or should I mind my own business?"

"I had a quarrel with my in-laws, Barbara and Richard."

"Barbara was Neville's wife?"

"Yes, and Richard is her brother. I kicked them out, and I sent all their servants with them. Barbara had brought them from her father's house when she initially wed my brother. They spied on me and annoyed me, and I decided to rid myself of all of them in one fell swoop."

"My goodness! That must have caused an enormous ruckus."

"Yes, it will involve enormous effort and energy to recover. I have some men here with me, but they're all retired soldiers. They're proficient at managing the horses and the cattle, but they're not very adept at cooking or polishing the furniture. I have to hire new people, but I can't seem to get it accomplished."

"You need to marry," she proclaimed without thinking. "A wife would deal with all of that for you."

"Well . . . ah . . . ah . . ."

They both blushed ten shades of red, and she hurriedly insisted, "I wasn't suggesting you marry *me*. I'm not interested."

"I'm sorry for everything that occurred between us. I wish I could go back in time so I could—"

She couldn't bear to discuss their history, and she cut him off. "Since you're not wed yet, you should retain an employment agency. They could drum up some excellent candidates for you. Once you have a basic crew in place, they can help you to gradually add others."

He assessed her, his regret clear, and he nodded, accepting that she wouldn't confer about the past. She didn't want any apologies and wouldn't listen to any.

"I will hire an employment agency," he said. "That's a terrific idea."

She glanced at his leg. "You're limping. Evan told me you'd injured yourself. Is it bad?"

"It *was* bad. It's better now. I was riding to London, and my horse was startled when we were crossing a bridge. We burst through the railing and plunged into the stream below."

Her jaw dropped in shock. "No!"

"The worst part was that we had to put the animal down. He was too hurt to save which was a crushing blow." He forced a laugh. "I survived though."

It was her turn to say, "I'm sorry."

"I'm fine though. Fine." He waved away any concern and gestured to the sofa. "Won't you sit? Please?"

"No."

He scrutinized her, years of remorse bubbling to the surface, then he shrugged. "All right."

"If anyone learns about my visit, I'll get into so much trouble."

"I certainly hope not."

"I'm only here to ask you a question." She whispered a quick prayer for strength, then, out of the blue, she inquired, "Did you love Jo Bates?"

She thought he might equivocate or deny any relationship, but he firmly asserted, "Yes, I loved her. I still love her. With her being another man's bride,

I probably shouldn't admit it, but it's the truth."

"Then why would you jilt her?"

"I didn't mean to. I had my accident the day before the ceremony. It's why I was racing to London, and I was so excited I wasn't paying attention."

"I see . . ." she murmured.

She'd assumed there would be a valid reason, but Evan—in his usual brusque manner—hadn't pressed Peyton to explain. Men could be such idiots!

"For several days," he said, "I was in and out of consciousness. After I was lucid, I wrote to Jo—over and over—to tell her what had happened, but she never replied. Eventually, I sent a footman to check on her, but she'd vacated the premises without a word and hadn't left a forwarding address. I figured she was furious and had given up on me."

"She didn't vacate that house of her own free will."

"I realize that Barbara and Richard were the culprits. When I heard about it from Evan, I traveled directly here and evicted them as punishment."

"You didn't!"

He chuckled. "I did."

"If you could still marry Jo, if that was still an option, would you?"

"I'd marry her in an instant. The first time I saw her I was doomed." In light of his history with Amelia, he recognized how appalling the comment would sound, and he blanched. "I shouldn't have confessed that to you, but I suppose we should be honest with each other."

"Yes, we should be honest."

Her conscience was ringing a strident warning bell. Her next sentence was on the tip of her tongue, and once voiced aloud, it would shatter the peace of her world. She would betray her splendid, devoted brother, would prove herself fickle and disloyal, and she'd do it all for Peyton who didn't deserve any consideration.

But she wanted Evan to pick a girl who adored him, a girl who thought he walked on water. She wanted him to stare at a girl the way Peyton stared at Jo. Evan didn't think it mattered, but Amelia believed it mattered very, very much.

Jo would wed him to save herself from shame and disgrace, to show him she was grateful, and Amelia didn't doubt that Jo would try her whole life to repay him for his many kindnesses. But Jo would never love him. They would have a cordial, tepid marriage, but it would never be more than that.

And despite what both of them imagined, after she birthed her baby, the child would be like a huge boulder in the middle of their existence that would constantly remind them of Peyton. Amelia was convinced it would eat away at any chance they might have had to be happy.

"Evan claimed he and Jo are husband and wife," Amelia said, "but it was a cruel lie."

Peyton frowned. "What part was the lie?"

"He and Jo aren't married. Not yet anyway."

He looked so surprised she might have punched him.

He gaped with astonishment. "Not married?"

"No. He just told you that because he was anxious for you to leave her alone."

"It definitely worked. It never occurred to me that it wasn't true."

"So . . . they're not shackled *yet,* but they will be soon. Unless you'd like to do something about it?"

"When is the ceremony?"

"Saturday at eleven. They've obtained a Special License so they can hold it immediately."

"Where will it be?"

"In our church—the one our family has always attended."

"I know it well," he mused.

She eased away from him, needing to exit the room so she could take a deep breath before she fainted. "Now then, I've said what I came to say, and I should be going."

"Are you sure you won't stay for supper? Or could you spend the night? I have plenty of empty bedchambers."

"No, I should get home. Jo and Evan will be worried about where I've been all day, and I would hate to have to explain."

She started out, and she was trembling. The entire meeting had been much more difficult than she'd expected it would be. Maddeningly, he hadn't furnished the tiniest hint of his opinion.

Would he visit Jo? Would he stop the wedding? Would he ride into the church like a berserker and make off with her during the recitation of the vows?

Amelia had tried her best. If he didn't intervene, then she'd have to accept his decision. She'd never mention their conversation to a single soul, and she'd welcome Jo as her sister-in-law. She would never regret her brother's choice of bride.

But . . . Jo belonged with Peyton.

Amelia reached the foyer, and at the last second, she glanced back. "In case you were wondering, Peyton, Jo still loves you. I think she always will."

"How can you be certain?"

"I asked her."

"Then why is she marrying your brother?"

"You know *why*—because she's having a baby—but it would be insane for her to bind herself to Evan, and you're the only one who can prevent it."

She whipped away and kept on. He didn't call out to her, didn't follow her out which was a relief.

She rushed down the steps and climbed into the carriage. In a quick minute, she was headed to London. She stared blindly outside, debating whether she'd done the right thing or the wrong thing.

Who could guess? Time would ultimately provide the answer.

CHAPTER

26

"THIS IS MY THIRD attempt to get to the end of my wedding," Jo said.

She was seated in a carriage with Evan and Amelia. They'd just pulled up in front of the church.

"I thought you'd done it once previous," Evan said.

"No, twice. On the first occasion, I was eighteen."

"But you're not a widow. What happened to your husband? Or your fiancé? Or ... or ...? Gad, I can't figure out what to call him."

"I was jilted at the altar."

"No!" the Boyle siblings gasped in unison.

"Yes."

"You have the worst matrimonial luck ever," Evan pointed out.

"I know. Not only did he jilt me, but my sister, Maud, handed over my dowry right before the ceremony." Jo blushed. "He absconded with it."

They were stunned, and Amelia said, "That's the most hideous story I've ever heard. Was he caught? Was he arrested?"

"No. We didn't have the funds to mount a search and had we located him, I'm certain the money would have been spent."

"You'd have received some satisfaction from having him jailed though."

"Yes, I definitely would have liked that." Jo grinned. "It's why I insisted we all ride to the church together. I realize it's customary for the bride and groom to remain apart before the service, but I'm not taking any chances with Evan."

"Are you scared that I'll disappear when you're not looking?" he asked.

"Yes," Jo firmly stated, and they all laughed.

Evan peeked out the curtain at the building. "It's a little late for me to sneak away."

"Well, Fate has proved that any bad conclusion is possible for me," Jo said, "so I intend to keep you in my sight until your leg-shackle is tightly attached."

"What is that old adage?" Amelia asked. "Third time's a charm?"

"I hope so," Jo replied.

"I hope so too," Evan concurred, "but could I please request that we not mention your failed weddings or Peyton today? It's *my* wedding, and it's Jo's wedding, and I'd rather not waste my breath talking about the idiots who didn't want her."

"I agree," Jo said. "I won't mention them again."

Evan climbed out, and he helped Jo and Amelia out too. Mrs. Boyle had left earlier to arrange some flowers and candles, so she was already inside.

It would be a small gathering, with just a few neighbors and servants invited to attend. Evan had finally been assigned to a new ship, and he was leaving England in a fortnight. They had many tasks on their plate, and they couldn't fritter away effort or money on a huge event.

They started in, and Evan entered ahead of them. Jo was walking with Amelia, and Amelia paused and gazed down the road—as if she was watching for someone.

"Are you expecting a special guest?" Jo asked.

"Ah . . . no, no one special."

Jo stepped toward the door, but Amelia continued to tarry. She was frowning, as if in dismay or consternation. Then she forced a smile. "Are you sure about this, Jo?"

"Very sure, Amelia. You constantly pose that question. Why? Are you afraid I'm not sincere about your brother?"

"I'm not doubting your sincerity."

"Yes, you are, and you have to stop." Jo clasped Amelia's hands in her own. "I'll be a good wife to Evan. I swear it. I'll always try to make him happy."

"I know you will. I'm just ... worried I guess."

"About what?"

"This all transpired so fast, and a few weeks ago, you were in love with Peyton. I'd hate to have you regret this."

"I will never regret marrying Evan," Jo staunchly declared. "Yes, I assumed I loved Lord Benton, but my affection wasn't reciprocated, and I can't wallow in the past. With my baby on the way, I have to move forward."

"Is this the best path though?"

"Yes. I'm saving myself from disgrace, Amelia. Evan is saving me, and I'll be eternally grateful. I plan to show him—each and every second—how thankful I am."

"I think gratitude is a paltry reason for a marriage."

"You're wrong, Amelia. It's a grand and wonderful reason, and remember Evan's request? We're not talking about Lord Benton today. Now let's join your brother, so I can speak my vows and become your sister."

Amelia's shoulders drooped. "I'm not as much of a romantic as I thought. I can't wait for this wedding to be over."

"Neither can I."

They went inside, and Evan was up by the altar, standing with the vicar and his mother. On seeing Evan, Amelia chuckled. "I'm delighted to report that Evan is still here. He didn't tiptoe out the back to escape your marital noose."

"There will be no reprieve for him. His bachelor days are over."

Amelia didn't look thrilled about that fact, and Jo would have liked to pry into her friend's odd mood. From the morning Evan had initially suggested they marry, Amelia had seemed fine with the idea, and it was Amelia's comments more than Evan's that had persuaded her. Yet Amelia was suffering many qualms which was hilarious.

Jo was the person who should have been awash with jitters. She'd been in this spot twice prior, and it was a precarious place—in her experience anyway. It wasn't easy to finish the service and walk out of the church with a husband.

"Are you ready?" Jo asked Amelia, as if Amelia—rather than Jo—was the bride.

"I'm as ready as I'll ever be."

They linked arms and marched down the aisle. There was no organ blaring, no choir singing. Their guests were scattered, so the seats were mostly empty, and their strides echoed off the ceiling. It was a lonely sound, and it would have been nice to have had some relatives to invite. They would have winked their encouragement from the pews.

Amelia laid Jo's hand in Evan's—as if she was giving Jo away—and they all smiled.

"I wish my father were still alive," Evan said, "so he could have joined us. He'd have liked you, Jo."

"I'm flattered that you think so."

Evan drew her to his side, and he entwined their fingers. She was trembling, and he noticed. "Are you frightened?"

"No."

But she was. He'd never previously touched her in an intimate way, and so far in their abbreviated courtship, she'd been able to pretend that nothing extraordinary was occurring. She'd been able to conveniently ignore that—once the wedding was over—she would have to engage in the martial act with him.

Could she do it? She'd have no choice really.

"Shall we start?" the vicar inquired.

Evan and Jo stepped closer to the altar. The vicar gazed out at the tiny crowd and offered introductory remarks. He'd barely begun when the doors were flung open so widely that a rush of cold autumn wind blew in. The abrupt chill in the air had her shivering as if it were delivering an ill omen.

"Aunt Jo! Have we arrived in time to stop you?"

Jo froze, then whipped around to observe Daisy running to her. In Daisy's excitement, she'd completely disregarded the notion that she was in a church.

"Daisy? Where did you come from?"

"Aunt Jo! You won't believe what happened to me!"

Daisy hurled herself into Jo so hard that they almost fell down. Jo collapsed to her knees and hugged her niece as tightly as she could. She whispered endearments as she stroked her hands over Daisy's body to ensure she was unharmed.

Evan had notified Lord Benton about Daisy being missing, and he'd ordered Lord Benton to search for her. He'd promised he would, and she'd accepted that promise, figuring he could force his in-laws to provide information Jo could never have retrieved. Apparently, he'd quickly located her. It was the greatest gift Jo could have received.

Suddenly, everyone's mood changed. She glanced up to find Evan glaring, his mother frowning, and Amelia biting down a grin. They were peering down the aisle, and Jo peered down too.

Of course Lord Benton had brought Daisy to the church—she wouldn't have come by herself—and he was swaggering toward Jo.

"Hello, Jo. Fancy meeting you here." He nodded to his old friends. "Evan. Amelia."

"Get out of my sight, Peyton," Evan said. "Your presence at this ceremony is neither wanted nor necessary."

The two men huffed and puffed and stuck out their chests—as if they might brawl. Jo released Daisy and stood, positioning herself between them.

She was irked to note that her pulse was racing, but with elation. She was so glad to see him! Her strident reaction was bewildering and appalling. Had she no pride? No sense?

He'd ruined her and broken her heart. He'd vanished just when she'd needed him the most. He'd proposed, then hadn't bothered to show up for the wedding. He hadn't contacted her later, hadn't tried to explain. He'd let his in-laws kidnap Daisy, then move against Jo without consequence.

Why would she be delighted to see him? What was wrong with her?

"Why are you here, Lord Benton?" she fumed. "Evan is correct. You weren't invited, and you're not welcome."

He didn't respond to her question, saying instead, "I have to tell you, Jo, I'm surprised to stumble on you in the middle of your wedding."

"Why would you be? When you visited Evan the other day, he was very clear about our plans."

"No, he wasn't clear. In fact, he told me a bald-faced lie."

"What lie?"

"He told me you were *already* married."

Jo scowled. "What?"

"I had been hunting for you everywhere, and I had no idea you were staying with him. Once I realized you were there, I intended to march in, offer my apologies, then take you home with me."

"You were not," she scoffed.

"He forestalled me by claiming you were his wife, and he wouldn't allow me to talk to you. I insisted you'd want to, but he declared—since he was your husband—it was his decision and not yours."

Jo turned to Evan. "Is that true, Evan?"

Evan dithered and seethed, then admitted, "Yes. I couldn't bear to have him upset you. Hasn't he done enough?"

Lord Benton's gaze dipped to her bulging tummy that was bigger and harder to hide. "I agree, Evan. I've done plenty."

"Yes, you have." Evan's tone was lethal. "I'm remedying the damage you inflicted. After how you hurt her, you don't get to interfere in this."

"I'm sorry," Lord Benton said, "but I'm afraid I have to interfere."

"Why would you?" Evan snorted with disgust. "You don't care about her. If you're interested in this at all, it's because someone else might wind up with her and your ego can't stand it."

"You're right. My ego definitely can't stand it."

"So get out—before I throw you out."

"I can't oblige you." Lord Benton spun to the guests and brazenly announced, "She's in the family way, and she's having my child."

There were many gasps, and Mrs. Boyle sighed and plopped down in the front pew. Amelia scooted next to her, looking as if she'd like to become invisible.

"Lord Benton!" Jo scolded. "Honestly! Be silent!"

Daisy chirped up with, "Are you having a baby, Aunt Jo? That's the greatest news ever!"

"Hush!" Jo warned. "We'll discuss it later."

"So you see, ladies and gentlemen"—Lord Benton was still addressing the guests—"I can't let her marry Evan."

"Lord Benton!" Jo was begging. "Please! You're embarrassing me."

"I won't deny my perfidy, Jo." He glanced up at the vicar. "Have you arrived at the part in the vows that asks if anyone objects to the match?"

"No."

"Then you don't have to continue reading because *I* object."

The vicar frowned, gaped, glared, then muttered, "This is highly unusual."

Evan butted in. "Keep going, sir. He can't be permitted to meddle, and I'd like to finish this."

The vicar shook his head. "When there's been an objection, Mr. Boyle, I can't keep going." He started flipping through his prayer book as if seeking instructions.

"Oh, for pity's sake," Evan grumbled, then he glowered at Lord Benton and demanded, "How did you find out about this?"

"Does it matter?"

"Yes, it matters." Evan pondered the situation, struggling to deduce who might have tattled, then he peered over at Amelia. "You told him! It was you, wasn't it?"

"Ah . . . maybe."

"Is that where you went the other day?" Evan furiously inquired. "You traveled to Benton specifically to ruin this for me? Why would you?"

Amelia was never one to be cowed or chastised, and she rose to her feet. "It was wrong for you to tell that lie. I decided he should know."

"What about me, Amelia?" Jo asked. "Did you think *I* deserved to know it?"

Amelia shrugged. "I couldn't figure out what was best, so I notified Peyton and left it up to him."

"And I'm glad of it," Lord Benton said, "for I'm informing all of you that the wedding of Josephine Bates to Evan Boyle will happen over my dead body."

"Lord Benton!" Jo scolded again. "You're not helping."

"I'm not here to help."

"Then why are you here?"

"Can't you guess?"

"I have no idea."

Jo was flummoxed by his arrival. Evan appeared stricken and Amelia incensed. They were two of the closest, most devoted siblings in the world, and Jo had brought discord and dissension into their home. She felt horrid, and she gazed up at the vicar.

"Vicar, is there a place where Lord Benton and I could speak privately?"

"Yes, yes, that's a good plan," the vicar said. "There's obviously a problem, and you should resolve it—if you can."

He gestured to a door off the side of the altar, and Jo turned to Lord Benton. "Come with me."

"I'd be delighted."

He was smug and annoying, and Evan pleaded with Jo. "Don't go off with him, Jo. You're aware of how cunning he can be. He'll confuse and confound you with his nonsense."

"He can't confuse me," Jo said. "My thought processes are very, very clear."

Evan clasped hold of her hands, and his expression was beseeching. "Don't trust him, Jo. Don't believe a word he utters."

"It will be all right, Evan. Don't worry."

She drew away, and she motioned for Lord Benton to follow her, then she huffed off. She didn't have to peek back to see if he'd tagged along. She perceived his presence like a large, hungry predator intent on devouring her.

"May I come too, Aunt Jo?" Daisy asked.

"No. You stay where you are."

Jo stomped into a room that must have been where the vicar donned his robes. It was small and packed with cupboards and dressers. Lord Benton blustered in behind her, and instantly, he took up all the space. He took up all the air in the sky too, so she could barely breathe.

He pulled the door shut, and he leaned against a cupboard. He looked handsome and magnificent and very, very confident.

"Since the moment I met you," she said, "I have suffered naught but catastrophe, and you have an enormous amount of gall to slink in and wreck this for me."

"It needed to be wrecked."

"Evidently, you have an issue to raise, but I have a few comments to offer too. You begin, then I shall reply, then I demand that you walk out of this church and out of my life and leave me alone."

"You don't mean that," he scoffed.

"I absolutely do. Now start talking. I'll give you about five minutes, then I will be done listening."

He grinned. "You grow more beautiful by the day."

"Don't flatter me. It won't work."

"You seem a tad angry, Josephine."

"There is no term in the English language that can describe how furious I am."

"Why are you so upset?"

"Why!" She feared the top of her head might blow off. "During our abbreviated relationship, I explained my past to you. I explained about my prior trip to the altar. You knew how much it would hurt me if you failed to arrive for our wedding, yet you failed anyway."

"Haven't you been curious as to why I didn't show up?"

"No. When you initially proposed, I insisted you'd have regrets in the future, but instead, you had them immediately. You simply didn't bother to share any of them with me. Then your hideous in-laws kidnapped my niece and tossed me out on the streets."

"Yes, Evan told me about it, and I was livid."

"Really? They told *me* that you didn't mind me being evicted. They said you had flitted off to the navy, and you'd furnished them with total authority to behave however they liked."

"I never said anything of the sort." He gestured to his person. "You know me, Jo. Can you truly tell me that you assumed—deep down—that I would treat you that way?"

"I *don't* know you, Lord Benton. That's the problem. I thought I did, but circumstances have forced me to admit that I was completely deluded."

He smirked. "I got even with Barbara and Richard for you."

"Short of cold-blooded murder, there's no act you could have implemented that would have delivered a sufficient penalty."

"Well, I threw them out of Benton—with no notice and just the clothes on their backs."

"You . . . what?"

"I deemed it a fitting punishment. They'd done pretty much the same to you, so I did it to them."

His remarks stopped her in her tracks. On occasion, he could be so exasperatingly wonderful. His bursts of generous conduct made it difficult to hate him, and she warned herself to buck up, to not be drawn in.

"Thank you. I appreciate it." She didn't sound grateful though. She sounded surly, but she couldn't help it. "And you found Daisy. Where had they sent her?"

"To a workhouse!"

"No." Jo's knees gave out, and she had to balance herself on a cupboard.

"She's fine though, Jo. Don't fret about it. She's tough and resilient, and she's home with me. She's very friendly with Neville's daughter, Alice, and she and Alice are together at Benton. They're thick as thieves and very happy."

"Good," Jo murmured, "I'm glad to hear it."

"Why don't you ask me why I missed our wedding?"

She wanted to be apprised, and at the same time, she didn't. He had the canniest knack for wearing her down, for convincing her to forget herself. Evan had advised her to be careful with Lord Benton, and he'd been right to worry. In her dealings with him, she'd always been an idiot. He could dangle any lie, and she'd swallow it whole.

He was determined to explain what had happened, and she doubted he'd desist until he got it off his chest. So it was probably best for him to spit it out, then she could hurl some furious invectives of her own.

"Tell me your story, Lord Benton. Let's see how much of it you can persuade me to believe."

"I'm betting you'll believe all of it."

"If I were a betting *man,* I'd take you up on it, but since I'm not, I will listen with a jaundiced ear."

"How about this? The day before the ceremony, I traveled to Benton."

"Yes, I remember."

"On the trip back to London, I was so excited to be marrying you that I was distracted. When I was crossing a bridge, my horse startled, and we fell off."

She scowled. "Fell off . . . what? The bridge?"

"Yes, it's why I'm limping. For hours, I was injured down below in the streambed, until a teamster passed by and noted the broken railing."

"Why didn't you send me a message?"

"I was in and out of consciousness for most of a week. The minute I was coherent enough to write, I penned a letter. In fact, I wrote numerous times."

Jo shook her head. "I didn't receive any letters from you."

"Not one?"

"No."

He pondered, then a fierce heat flashed in his eyes. "It's just occurred to me that I have yet another reason to loathe Barbara."

"What do you mean?"

"It's highly likely that none of my letters were ever sent."

"Oh."

"My niece, Alice, carted them downstairs and put them in the mail for me, but I never investigated whether they actually made it into the post. This provides additional grounds to extract some retribution from Barbara."

"I'd like to pretend I'm a Christian woman who abhors vengeance, but I guess I'm not that noble."

"Barbara deserves whatever justice I can mete out."

"I agree."

They stared, and Jo's mind was racing. Had his vanishing been as simple and as devastating as that? Could all of her misery have been caused by miscommunication arranged by Barbara Prescott? Lord Benton had been hurt and unable to contact her. Then he'd written, but the letters hadn't been mailed. If that was the truth, where did it leave her? Where did it leave *them*?

Evan was dawdling with their guests. Jo couldn't hide in the small room forever, but suddenly, it seemed as if she and Lord Benton had a lifetime of issues to discuss.

"You visited Evan last week," she said, "but you didn't come inside. Why not? You didn't even attempt to speak with me."

"Haven't you been paying attention, Jo? I didn't come *in* because Evan told me you were his wife, and he wouldn't let me talk to you. Since I believed him, what would have been the point?"

She nodded slowly, her confusion profound. What was she to think? How should she proceed?

He interrupted her tortured musings. "Now *I* get to ask a few questions of my own, and you'd better have some viable answers."

"I'll answer if I can," she mulishly retorted.

"Why didn't you try to find me? When I missed the wedding, why didn't you travel to Benton? Why didn't you write?"

"I wrote immediately, and the letter bounced back as undeliverable. A note had been jotted on it that you'd returned to the navy and had left the country."

"I didn't," he huffed.

"I see that, but I went to naval headquarters to be sure. I met with an official who informed me that your ship had sailed on that Thursday night and—as far as he was aware—you were on it."

"I can't imagine why anyone would have claimed that."

"It's what he said!"

"You thought I'd fled England without a goodbye."

"Yes, and then, the Countess and Mr. Slater showed up. I won't bore you with the details of what happened to me after that, but it was scary and awful."

"I'm sorry for what you endured, and as I mentioned, Barbara and Richard are paying dearly."

A knock sounded on the door. It was the vicar. "Lord Benton, will you come out? Everyone is waiting, and Mr. Boyle is upset."

"Go away, Vicar," Lord Benton called.

"How much longer will you be? What should I tell the others?"

"We will stay in here until we're finished."

Jo assumed the preacher would spin the knob and enter, but he didn't. He moved away, and it grew very quiet.

"Do you know what I think, Jo?" Lord Benton asked.

"What?"

"I think the stars have been aligned against us. Our relatives have been aligned against us. The whole world has been aligned against us."

"I suppose you could view it that way."

"But do you know what else?"

"What?"

"The entire universe can join forces, but we could never be kept apart."

Before she had any notion of what he intended, he dropped to a knee and clasped hold of her hand.

She started to tremble. "What are you doing, Lord Benton? We've already been down this road. We shouldn't walk it again."

"Hush, Jo."

"I can't be silent. This ending was never our destiny."

"Hush!" he repeated. "Listen to me."

"I can't. Not when you're behaving like a lunatic."

"You deem it crazy for me to want you, but you're wrong."

"Then talk fast. My patience is about exhausted."

Out of the blue, he announced, "I love you, Josephine Bates."

"No you don't. You're being ridiculous."

"I'm not. I love you, and if you refuse to have me, my life won't have been worth living."

"You're not serious."

"Oh, but I am, and I desperately, urgently need you to be mine."

Her trembling increased. She'd spent months recovering from their failed amour. She'd tamped down her feelings, had adjusted her attitude. She'd allowed Evan to rescue her. She'd ordered herself to forget about Peyton Prescott. She'd ordered herself to look to the future, not the past.

And here he was again, on bended knee and begging her to wed. It was all too much.

"Please, Peyton. I can't deal with this."

"When can you deal with it, Jo? Will you stroll out into the church and marry Evan? Is that your choice? Don't pretend it is, for I will never believe you."

"He's been very kind, and I'm grateful. I can't spurn him. Not after how he's helped me."

"Do you love him, Jo?"

The query rattled her, for of course, she didn't love Evan Boyle. In reality, she barely knew him. What she *did* know was grand and wonderful, but they hadn't enjoyed an acquaintance sufficient for strong sentiment to develop.

An excruciating interval played out, and she couldn't bear to reply. Nor could she bear to lie about Evan. She had only ever loved one man—and it wasn't him.

"Tell me the truth, Jo," he pressed. "Do you love Evan?"

She groaned with dismay. "No, I don't."

"You love me, Jo. It's always been me. Just say so."

"No, I can't. I won't."

"Say you love me, Jo. Say you never stopped."

"Get up, Peyton. Please!"

She grabbed his arm and tried to pull him to his feet, but he wouldn't obey.

"Answer me, Jo."

"Fine, Peyton! I love you, and I've never stopped."

"That's all I needed to hear," he arrogantly stated.

The words had been ripped from her soul, and she staggered away, worried she might simply collapse to the floor. He'd received the admission he craved, and he finally stood.

"You're having my child," he reminded her. "Could you actually suppose I'd permit another man to raise it? Even one I like as much as Evan? You'd have to be mad to imagine I would."

"I realize that."

"It's not happening, Jo. The child is mine, and *you* are mine. You have to accept it."

She yanked her gaze from his. When she looked at him, she was always overwhelmed. She couldn't think straight. She couldn't make good decisions.

While she was distracted, he dipped in and stole a quick kiss.

"Oh!" was all she could manage as a response.

"Here's what we'll do."

"No, Peyton, it's not up to you."

"Yes, it is." He reached into his coat and withdrew a piece of paper. "I applied for a Special License. It confirms that you and I can wed today."

She glared at him. "You and I? Marry—today? You were awfully confident about me."

"Why wouldn't I be? You never could resist me. We'll walk out to the altar, and we'll have the vicar wed *us* instead of you and Evan."

"You're deranged. I won't hurt Evan like that."

"He'll get over it, Jo."

"How would he?"

"Well, maybe he *won't* get over it," he said instead. "He's been angry with me for ages, but his opinion is irrelevant."

"It's not irrelevant to me."

"I won't let you go, Josephine. Haven't you been listening?" He laid a palm on her tummy where the bulge of their baby was visible. "Wed me, Jo. Keep me by your side forever."

"I'm so confused," she moaned.

"I love you, Josephine Bates. I love you so much that I can't breathe with wanting you. Say you'll have me."

Jo stared down at her feet.

Could she do it? Could she bind herself to him?

He'd deserted her at the altar, and afterward, she'd believed herself jilted by a cad, but he wasn't a cad. He was kind and generous and amazing. He was the man of her dreams, and though it was disgraceful and tragic, she couldn't follow through with her promise to Evan. Not with Peyton having come for her. Not with Peyton pleading with her to pick him.

She couldn't marry Evan—because she could never be the wife he deserved. But could she cry off at the last second? It was the same humiliation she'd suffered twice. Could she act that despicably? In light of how he'd assisted her, would she be damned? Would she be cursed?

"Say, yes, Jo," Peyton urged. "Tell me you'll have me."

"I can't," she wailed. "This all seems so wrong."

"It's not wrong. It's very, very right."

He dipped in and kissed her again, and it wasn't quick or sweet. It was determined and resolute. He was claiming her. He was putting his mark on her. She was his and could never belong to anyone else.

For the briefest moment, she stood like a statue and refused to participate, but she only hesitated for an instant. He was correct that she couldn't resist him. Where he was concerned, she never could arrive at the sane choice, the rational choice. She leapt into the fray with a wild abandon.

Someone knocked on the door again, and they ignored it, then it opened and Amelia cleared her throat.

"Pardon me, but I need to interrupt."

Peyton growled with frustration and drew away. "We're busy, Amelia. What is it?"

"Evan left."

"No!" Jo gasped.

"He said—when you didn't return immediately—he figured it was over." Amelia smiled at Jo. "He said to tell you congratulations and that this is probably for the best. And to not be sad or feel guilty."

"Did he really say all that?" Jo asked. "Or are you maybe fibbing a bit so I'll appear less horrid than I am?"

Daisy popped up behind Amelia. "Yes, Aunt Jo, he really said it. And he said too, if Uncle Peyton is ever mean to you, that you should find him, and he'll force Uncle Peyton to behave."

Peyton snorted. "It sounds to me as if he's stepped aside, Jo."

"Yes, he has," Amelia said.

"He'll never forgive me," Jo muttered.

"I'm betting he will," Amelia predicted. "He's not stupid, Jo. He realized it was over the minute Peyton blustered into the church. *I* realized it was over too. It's why I went to Benton to fetch Peyton—so he'd stop you."

"You didn't want me to marry Evan after all?" Jo inquired.

"I *wanted* both of you to be happy. Now you will be."

"Marry me, Jo," Peyton said.

"She hasn't agreed?" Daisy asked. "You've been in here all this time. What have you been doing?"

"I had to wear her down," Peyton explained, "so we've just been talking."

"The talking has to be finished," Daisy insisted. "Jo, the vicar is growing impatient, and Uncle Peyton brought the Special License. We have to hold the ceremony, so we can all go home to Benton."

"To Benton . . ." Jo murmured. She glanced up at Peyton. "Are you sure, Peyton? Are you *truly*, undeniably certain?"

"Yes, Jo. You. Me. Daisy. Let's be a family. At Benton."

Jo peered over at Amelia and Daisy. "Are you two sure?"

"For pity's sake, Jo," Amelia scolded, "cease your dithering. You whole life is waiting."

"Yes, I suppose it is."

Peyton raised a cocky brow. "Did I hear a *yes* in there somewhere?"

"Yes, Peyton," Jo said, "you heard it. Let's get married. Let's be a family."

Amelia and Daisy whooped with joy, and they rushed over and hugged Jo as tightly as they could.

"I knew I could convince you," Peyton said, looking very smug.

Jo didn't argue the point.

THE END

Don't Miss the Second Novel in
Cheryl Holt's "*JILTED BRIDES*" trilogy!

Jilted by a Scoundrel

The story of Miss Winifred Watson
and Lord John Dunn

Available now!

CHAPTER

1

Summer, 1815, an island off the Cornwall coast . . .

"WHAT DO YOU THINK of it?"

Winnie Watson forced a smile and stared down at her two charges, Jane and Bobby Prescott. Jane was eleven, and Bobby was twelve.

"It's scary," Jane said as Bobby enthusiastically said, "It's tremendous!"

They gaped at the open gates of Dunworthy Castle. It was a *real* castle, with drawbridge, stone walls, turrets, and battlements. It looked like an edifice out of a medieval legend. They might have fallen back through time, and if an armored knight suddenly rode out on his war horse, she wouldn't have been surprised.

"Do you suppose my uncle is here?" Jane inquired.

"There's only one way to find out," Winnie responded. "Let's go in and ask."

In the town on the mainland, they'd been told it was market day at the castle. It was also "Justice Day," where local citizens could appear before a magistrate, voice grievances about their neighbors, then have their cases arbitrated to a conclusion that probably didn't satisfy anyone.

There were people rushing in and out, many hauling carts of supplies, so the place was bustling with activity. A teamster with a heavy wagon lumbered up behind them, and they jumped off the trail so he didn't drive over them.

Winnie had grown up outside London, and she'd been reared in the upper classes. She'd attended the most expensive boarding schools and had rubbed elbows with the daughters of dukes and earls. She'd never previously been to Cornwall, and so far, she wasn't impressed. Everyone they'd encountered had been surly and unhelpful. They'd glowered and frowned, had whispered gruffly and pointed in amazement, as if they'd never observed a woman traveling alone with children before.

And perhaps they hadn't. Perhaps none of their personal horizons had ever delivered them a greater distance than the next village. Clearly, strangers were rare and not particularly welcome.

Dunworthy Castle was built on an island a few hundred yards off the coast. It boasted a small harbor, with a village—simply named Dunn—nestled around it. The castle was perched on a promontory that was surrounded by cliffs. It was windswept and desolate, and it fascinated her in an odd manner.

If she'd been partial to barren, inhospitable country—which she'd never been—she might have been enthralled, but she wasn't. She thrived on the culture and society found in the city, and she enjoyed interesting, sophisticated people.

She was dawdling, and Bobby impertinently asked, "Are we going in? Or do you plan to stand here all afternoon?"

"We're going in," Winnie replied, "and don't be smart."

"Sorry," Bobby mumbled.

"I realize we're nervous, but there's no need to be. We'll have this situation resolved in a quick minute."

She herded them through the tall entrance and into the inner courtyard, halting first to steal an anxious glance at the shore. It was low tide, so there was a visible path in the sand that they'd crossed to walk out to the island. But they'd been warned—if they weren't invited to stay at the castle—they shouldn't tarry. The tide would roll in, and they'd be trapped until it rolled out again.

There were no hotels or coaching inns on the island, so unless they were offered lodging, they wouldn't have shelter. In light of their recent spate of bad luck, that sort of calamity would be typical and completely expected. The past five months had been a long slog of mishaps that had ultimately found Bobby and Jane evicted from their home and Winnie—their governess—fired from her job.

They were running on a wing and a prayer, and if they couldn't garner assistance at Dunworthy, she couldn't imagine what they'd do. She hadn't voiced her reservations to Jane and Bobby though. On their journey to Cornwall, she'd pretended to be confident that they would achieve an acceptable result, but her optimism simply proved that she was a tad deranged.

As a governess, she was meant to be an expert on all topics, especially one as elemental as geography, but she didn't know much about the ocean. She tried to recall how often the tide changed. Was it every six hours? Every twelve? She had no idea, but if it was a shorter period, they had to hurry and be about their business.

She yanked her gaze from the frothing sea water, not eager to contemplate how violently it might swallow up the sand and leave them stranded. It was like a scene out of a grim fairytale, where an innocent maiden was lured into danger by a wicked witch.

She fought off a shiver of dread and followed after the children.

They wandered through the busy courtyard where vendors had set up booths and were selling food and other merchandise. They stopped an officious-looking man and inquired as to the whereabouts of Mr. John Dunn. He was Jane's uncle who they were hoping to locate. They were directed into the main hall of the castle.

They entered into a huge room that was probably very much as it had been during the Middle Ages. There were rows of tables and benches for communal dining, as if the serfs still shared all their meals.

A large fireplace was built into the wall, and even though it was the first week of July, it was cool and cloudy outside. Massive logs burned in the grate, so the space was toasty. It was filled with people, and their packed presence increased the temperature. The smell of unwashed bodies was a bit overwhelming.

Up in the front, there was a dais where the family could eat and stare down at their servants as if they were royalty. As far as Winnie was aware, the Dunns had no noble blood, yet their castle gave every sign of their carrying on like ancient lords.

There was a hearing in progress, and a man on the dais was listening as two fishermen complained about pilfering each other's catch. A woman sat next to him, and occasionally, he'd lean over and they'd confer about the testimony.

He was very imposing, very commanding, and he had the air of a soldier, as if he'd spent his life barking orders and having them obeyed. His powerful personality wafted out across the assembled crowd, and it was obvious his elevated position was recognized by all.

He had black hair—worn longer than was proper—and very blue eyes. She thought he was the most handsome man she'd ever seen, but his stellar looks annoyed her. Since her failed engagement three years earlier to Holden Cartwright, who'd been dapper and charming and very good looking too, she'd developed a potent loathing for men.

Her low opinion had initially been stirred by her despicable father who'd passed away and left her in dire financial straits. Then she'd added Holden to the list, having suffered the humiliation of being jilted at the altar by him when she was just seventeen.

But her recent experiences with the Prescott family—Jane's and Bobby's relatives—had her convinced that males of the human species were beyond redemption. She'd cursed all of them to perdition.

Jane and Bobby, who were half-siblings, had been sired by Neville Prescott, the Earl of Benton. He'd been an amoral cad who hadn't been able to marry either of their mothers because he'd already been married.

They'd grown up at his Benton estate, and Winnie had been hired to work as their governess, but he'd had the gall to die and leave them unprotected. His brother, Peyton Prescott—the new earl—had decreed he would no longer support Neville's illicit offspring.

Winnie had been terminated, and Jane and Bobby had been kicked out. Bobby had no kin to take him in, but Jane had her uncle, John Dunn, at Dunworthy. Winnie had written him several letters as to the possibility of

Jane and Bobby coming to live with him, but she'd never received a reply.

After they'd been tossed out on the road, she'd decided to travel to Cornwall with them. She could hardly have let them go alone. She intended to throw herself on John Dunn's mercy and plead for his assistance, but if he refused to provide it, she had no alternate plan.

A man at the rear of the room appeared to be a guard of sorts. He noticed them and interrogated them as to their purpose. When Winnie whispered that she needed to speak with Mr. Dunn, the fellow gestured to the dais, indicating that Jane's uncle was the man holding court.

He asked her name, then had them sit on a bench in the back. He explained that they'd be called up when it was their *turn*. She couldn't imagine addressing the situation with so many people eavesdropping, but she was weary and hungry and in an awful mood. For once, she did as she was bid.

They watched the proceedings, as one case after another was brought before Mr. Dunn. They involved common village quarrels: stolen items, rustled cattle, physical fights, unpaid debts. There was even a stabbing and an adulterous affair.

She and Bobby observed it with a high degree of interest. Jane fell asleep though, her head drooping onto Winnie's shoulder.

Mr. Dunn was smart and brusque and an excellent judge of truth and character. He doled out penalties and sentences like an angry god, and no one argued with any of his edicts. He possessed complete and undisputed authority.

The drone of voices had lulled her into a stupor, so she was startled when the bailiff suddenly announced, "Miss Winifred Watson."

At first, she didn't move, then Bobby nudged her with his elbow. She eased Jane off her shoulder, and the girl woke up and rubbed her eyes.

"Shall we come up with you?" Bobby murmured.

"No. Wait here. Let me talk to him by myself. Take care of Jane for me."

"I always will," Bobby said, and he meant it.

He was a brave, loyal boy, and at twelve, he was perched on the edge of manhood. During their trip to Cornwall, he'd repeatedly told Jane he would shield and defend her, and Winnie thought it was sweet that he was so devoted. It made her wish he was her son or that she might have a son just like him someday.

She stood, and she ran a hand across her skirt and patted the same hand across her hair. She'd have liked an opportunity to wash and change clothes before they'd met with Mr. Dunn, but beggars couldn't be choosers. They'd been granted an audience, and it was obvious he viewed himself as being very important. He wouldn't brook any nonsense or tolerate any delay.

She walked to the front, hating how everyone was focused on her. She didn't like to be the center of attention, and she most especially didn't want to have others listening as she and Mr. Dunn conversed.

They had delicate matters to discuss, and they weren't the type that should be publicly debated.

"Hello, Mr. Dunn," she said.

The woman next to him snottily snapped, "It's *Lord John* to you."

Mr. Dunn looked to be thirty or so, and the woman was about his same age. She was voluptuously chubby, with black hair and cold, black eyes, and there was malice in her gaze that was unsettling.

Was she Mr. Dunn's wife? Could she be Jane's aunt? It was a disturbing possibility. Furtively, Winnie scrutinized their hands, but neither of them was wearing a wedding ring, so she couldn't guess at their relationship.

The woman's attitude was terribly rude. Winnie hadn't yet uttered a word as to her quest, and the suspicions as to her motives had already blossomed. They were probably fueled by a general contempt for strangers, and the notion was exhausting.

"Hello, Lord John," she said. "I'm Miss Watson."

"Yes, yes, you're Miss Watson" he grouchily replied, "and you're the last person on my list. State your case so we can wrap this up. I'm tired and eager to open a cask of ale."

The spectators mumbled with excitement, so it was likely the custom to end the legal day with a protracted bout of drinking.

Wonderful! She's arrived just as the occupants—Jane's unmet kin—would soon be addled with liquor.

Mr. Dunn was glaring at her as if he'd engaged in all the testimony he could abide for one afternoon, and it occurred to her that she'd better explain herself quickly or he'd boot her out before she could spit out the reason for her lengthy journey.

"I've traveled from Benton to speak with you," she told him.

He simply gaped at her, the name of *Benton* not registering, which was distressing and depressing.

"All right," he said. "You've traveled from Benton. I'm not familiar with the spot. Where is it located?"

"It's a property outside London. It's *Lord* Benton's family seat."

"I don't know him, and I've never heard of him."

People snickered, and she squared her shoulders. She might be only twenty, but she was Sir Walford Watson's daughter. He'd been quite an imposing character, and she'd inherited his more impressive traits. She couldn't be bullied, and she was never afraid or cowed.

A paltry veteran—if that's what Mr. Dunn was—could never intimidate her. Nor could a fake lord in a crumbling, decrepit castle.

"I must raise a very difficult subject," she said, "but I shouldn't reveal it in this crowded forum. Is there somewhere we could confer privately?"

"No. Get on with it please."

"I'm sure you won't like me address it this way."

"And *I* am sure I'm about to call it a day. Tell me why you've come, or I'll adjourn the proceedings."

From how he was studying her, as if she was insignificant and annoying, it was clear he was serious. He would be delighted to put her in her place, but he never could.

After her recent bouts of enmity at Benton, where she'd constantly battled with the estate agent, Mr. Slater, she was irked and drained. A man couldn't insult or aggravate her without consequence.

"I've brought your niece, Jane Prescott, to stay with you," she bluntly proclaimed. "She has nowhere to go, and I beg you to provide shelter to her."

Winnie intended to beg for herself and Bobby too, but she didn't suppose she ought to mention that fact in her opening salvo.

Her announcement flummoxed everyone. Mr. Dunn glanced at the woman beside him. "Melvina, do I have a niece named Jane Prescott?"

"No," the woman—Melvina—curtly responded.

He turned to Winnie. "I have no idea what you mean or *who* you mean. Will that be all?"

Winnie took a deep breath. She'd warned him about the delicate conversation she planned to have, but he was too vain and imperious to listen. Well, a pox on his head!

She could be just as vain and imperious.

"Jane is your sister Rebecca's daughter," she said. "Her father was Neville Prescott, the prior Lord Benton, and he seduced Rebecca when she was sixteen and away at boarding school. She died in childbirth, and Jane has been living at Benton ever since, but the Prescott family's circumstances have changed." Since Neville Prescott was now deceased, that was a massive understatement! "She's been evicted by them, and she's requesting sanctuary from you."

Her speech had sucked the air out of the room. It had grown so quiet she could have heard a pin drop. Spectators were scowling, nervously peeking at each other and not certain what to think. Up on the dais, Mr. Dunn—the haughty Lord John—was glowering at Winnie as if she were a bug he'd like to squash under his boot.

"You have some gall, Miss Watson," he ultimately seethed, his tone threatening.

"So I've always been told, Mr. Dunn."

Melvina practically shouted, "It's *Lord* John to you, you little harpy."

Mr. Dunn raised a hand to silence her. She bristled, but shut up as he'd demanded.

"Miss Watson," he said to Winnie, "in a few short sentences, you have denigrated my dead sister, thoroughly besmirched her reputation, and ruin our beloved memory of her that we hold so dear."

"I'm sorry if you find the truth to be painful, sir," Winnie replied. "In my own defense, I warned you that we should discuss this privately."

"Yes, you did, and that's enough from you. Thank you for coming."

He waved her off as if she would slither away with the dilemma unresolved. She huffed with offense. "You haven't answered me."

"What was your question again?"

"Jane needs shelter and support. Will she receive them from you?"

"No."

Winnie valiantly stood her ground. "Her half-brother, Bobby Prescott, has traveled with her, and I am here too."

"I see that," he caustically retorted.

"I am their guardian." It was a white lie. She had no official role with regard to either child, but she wasn't about to admit it. "I ask for shelter and assistance for Bobby and myself as well."

"I don't choose to extend it."

"Why not?"

Apparently, her query was too insolent to abide, and the audience groused and grumbled. Had no one ever argued with Mr. Dunn's edicts? Was no one ever permitted to disagree with his grand self?

"Why *not*?" he spat back at her. "Let me count the reasons. I don't know you. I don't believe you. I have no basis to trust you. And my sister, Rebecca, died of the influenza."

"No, she didn't. I regret that the details of her demise were concealed from you, but I'm telling them to you now."

"I won't allow you to spew any further falsehoods about her."

"They're not falsehoods."

Winnie gestured for Jane and Bobby to join her. They hesitated, then Bobby—the braver of the pair—took Jane's arm, and they approached.

With their Prescott blond hair and very-blue eyes, they were golden and striking: thin, lithe, fetching, and regal in their bearing. No matter what one thought of their disgusting, unscrupulous father, Neville Prescott, he'd been a very handsome man, and he'd produced very handsome children.

Winnie pointed to them. "This is your niece, Jane, and this is her half-brother, Bobby."

Mr. Dunn stared at them for an eternity, as did every person in the room. They were assessed so curiously they might have had three legs or purple skin. Winnie wanted to cluck her tongue and call them all idiots, but she forced herself to remain silent while they endured the odious appraisal.

Finally, Mr. Dunn relaxed in his chair. "My sister, Rebecca, had black hair and black eyes. All of the Dunns have black hair and black eyes."

"You don't. Your eyes are very blue."

The instant she commented she wished she hadn't. She hated to have him presume she'd paid sufficient attention to notice the color of his eyes.

"You're very perceptive, Miss Watson," he said.

"Aren't I just?"

"I'm told they're a throwback to some old pirate kin."

"I'm not surprised. I'm positive there are many nefarious characters in your family tree."

"You'd suppose correctly." He studied Jane again. "This girl doesn't resemble my sister in even the smallest way."

"Jane resembles her father, Lord Benton," Winnie insisted. "They both do. It's *his* powerful aristocratic blood that's defined their features."

"Why was I never contacted about this situation?" he inquired. "If you're being truthful, why didn't you write or send a messenger?"

"I wrote you several letters. The Benton estate agent, Mr. Slater, wrote too. You can't tell me you never received any of them."

"I *can* tell you that, Miss Watson, because I've never heard of you in my life, and I've definitely never corresponded with anyone named Slater."

"Then perhaps you should investigate the person who serves as your postal carrier. It appears he's not very competent at delivering your mail."

He narrowed his gaze, looking derisive and bored. "You have a very smart mouth, Miss Watson."

"I've always been told that too, Lord John."

"I like my women—"

She cut him off. "Your *women?*"

"Yes, *my* women. Everyone and everything on this accursed island belongs to me, and I like to surround myself with females who are meek and pleasant."

"Then I'm sure you and I would never be cordial."

"I'm sure we wouldn't," he agreed. "I couldn't imagine having you underfoot. You'd exhaust me with your superior attitude and fancy manners."

"I'd try to control myself," she sarcastically muttered.

He snorted out a laugh that sounded odd and unusual—as if his voice was rusty and he was never amused by any topic. He pondered for another eternity, scrutinizing Jane, then Winnie and Bobby. Just when she decided he might exhibit a shred of decency, Melvina leaned in and whispered furiously in his ear.

Suddenly, he said to Winnie, "No."

"No . . . what?"

"No, you may not tarry at Dunworthy. Not you or the two children you've dragged through my door."

"May I ask why?"

"No, you may not."

"Well, I'm asking anyway. We've journeyed across England to meet with you, and I'm begging you to have mercy on us. If you can't muster any mercy, then at the very least, I demand simple courtesy. Allow us to stay until we can make other plans."

A muscle ticked in his cheek, his patience clearly at an end. "As I previously mentioned, Miss Watson, I don't believe your story about my sister, and as the three of you are strangers to me—"

"Jane is not a stranger! She's your niece!"

He ignored her paltry complaint. "I don't care to have more mouths to feed, and at the moment, I'm fresh out of mercy. You'll have to seek it elsewhere."

Winnie was more incensed than she'd ever been. "Why are you such a fiend? Are you always this awful? Or have we merely caught you on a bad day?"

"I'm always this awful." He addressed the crowd in general. "Who let them into the castle? All of you know I don't appreciate outsiders wandering in unannounced. We have to be cautious, and this one"—he pointed scornfully at Winnie—"couldn't keep a secret to save her life. She's a risk we cannot assume."

The spectators nodded their concurrence, and he gestured to the man in the back who'd initially greeted them. "Escort them out, would you? And spread the word that they shouldn't be permitted onto the island again. If they show up, there will have to be consequences for whoever disobeyed my edict."

"I'll tell people what you've ordered, Lord John," the man said. "If you'll come with me, Miss Watson?"

Winnie didn't move, and for a horrifying instant, she worried she might burst into tears.

Why couldn't anything ever go right? She'd always been a good person, a kind person, a loyal person. She'd taken charge of Jane and Bobby when no one in the world had volunteered to help them—no one but her.

She was twenty years old and all alone, without friends or family or money or a job. It had been a mad scheme to head to Dunworthy without having a clue as to whether their arrival would be welcome, but she'd been afraid and desperate and out of ideas.

For pity's sake, Mr. Slater at Benton had evicted them! What other option had there been but to travel to Dunworthy where Jane had an uncle?

Throughout their reckless trek, she'd convinced herself that Mr. Dunn would aid them, but how could she have been so stupid? When she was so intelligent and so highly educated, why did she constantly make such idiotic choices? Why did she pick exactly the wrong path? Would she spend her life in peril and out of luck?

She opened her mouth to give Mr. Dunn a thorough dressing down, but Bobby prevented her. He stepped in front of Winnie and Jane, as if he could shield them from Mr. Dunn's wrath.

"Don't beg him, Miss Watson," Bobby heatedly stated, and his livid gaze was locked on Mr. Dunn. "I won't have you plead on our behalf, and even if you could change this tyrant's mind, I'd never let you and Jane stay here with him. We'll figure out a different conclusion, for I am sure *any* place in the kingdom would be better than this one."

He was a striking, courageous, and wonderful boy, possessed of his aristocratic father's best traits and none of his bad ones. His anger and righteous indignation had carried around the room, and his comments had shamed them. Even Mr. Dunn seemed embarrassed.

Bobby whipped away from the dais, and he pushed Winnie and Jane toward the door.

Jane was usually polite and quiet, but not always. She peeked over her shoulder at her uncle, imperiously saying, "I was hoping I'd like you. But I don't. I could never like anyone who was rude to Miss Watson."

Their insults caustically hurled, they marched out, people's eyes slicing into them as they passed, but Winnie didn't lower herself to look at any of them.

Who would treat a dog in the ditch as they'd been treated? She was a young woman on her own, with two children to protect, but they hadn't been offered so much as a bite of food or a drink of water.

Bobby was correct to demand they depart. Even if Mr. Dunn had leapt off the dais and implored her to remain, she wouldn't have. She was Sir Walford Watson's beloved daughter, and Jane and Bobby were Lord Benton's children. How dare the occupants of Dunworthy disparage them?

What was so special about any of them anyway? They were simply a bunch of illiterate, rural peasants, and she let her snobbish, city attitude flare into a hot inferno. If a single dolt had been brave enough to speak to her, she'd have ignited him with her vociferous response.

They tromped out of the hall, across the courtyard, and out the gate. They'd been inside for ages, waiting to address Mr. Dunn, so she'd forgotten the earlier admonition about the tide.

Evidently, it didn't change every twelve hours. Clearly, it swept in much quicker than that.

They were on the promontory where the castle was located, so it was easy to see that the island was surrounded by ocean and cut off from the mainland by surging, turbulent seas. The path on the sand had vanished.

How long would it continue like this? How long would it be before they could return to the dry ground of England?

They gaped, disconcerted and dismayed, and ultimately, Jane said, "What now, Miss Watson?"

"I have no idea."

Bobby assessed the water that prevented their escape, and he snorted with disgust. "This is just typical, isn't it?"

"I was thinking the very same," Winnie said.

"What else can go wrong?" They were silent for a minute, then Bobby muttered, "I'm not sorry for what I said in there."

"Neither am I," Jane added.

"You stood up for yourselves," Winnie told them, "and I'm proud of both of you."

Bobby bristled with annoyance. "What will they do to us when they discover we couldn't leave? Might they simply toss us into the waves to drown?"

"I wouldn't be surprised," Jane fumed. "They were so awful. I couldn't imagine living here with them."

Bobby pointed down the hill to Dunn village, where fishermen's cottages lined the shore, but it contained no lodging for visitors. "Shall we walk down to it? We might get lucky and encounter a charitable Christian who will help us."

Winnie was dubious. "I suppose anything is possible. There might be *one* kind, generous inhabitant on this accursed rock."

"Let's find out," Bobby said.

He took off, leading the way, and Winnie and Jane followed him.

What choice did they have?

ABOUT THE AUTHOR

CHERYL HOLT IS A *New York Times*, *USA Today*, and Amazon "Top 100" bestselling author who has published fifty-two novels.

She's also a lawyer and mom, and at age forty, with two babies at home, she started a new career as a commercial fiction writer. She'd hoped to be a suspense novelist, but couldn't sell any of her manuscripts, so she ended up taking a detour into romance where she was stunned to discover that she has a knack for writing some of the world's greatest love stories.

Her books have been released to wide acclaim, and she has won or been nominated for many national awards. She is considered to be one of the masters of the romance genre. For many years, she was hailed as "The Queen of Erotic Romance", and she's also revered as "The International Queen of Villains." She is particularly proud to have been named "Best Storyteller of the Year" by the trade magazine Romantic Times BOOK Reviews.

She lives and writes in Hollywood, California, and she loves to hear from fans. Visit her website at www.cherylholt.com.